Kate Fortune's Journal

Can you believe I'll be [...]
few days? Eighty! [...]
that my plane crash[...]
was forced to hide fr[...] family
until all the plots against the Fortunes were
unearthed. How I hated seeing them suffer,
thinking I was dead. I guess I've just been too
busy making up for lost time over the last
eight years to notice the days pass. It's been
such a joy to see all my children so happy now
that they've discovered life's greatest gifts —
love and family. And who would have thought
that I'd get a second chance at love with my
dear friend, Sterling? Maybe it's because he
still makes me feel like a June bride that I'm
not feeling my age.

Well, whatever it is, the surprise at this
birthday celebration is going to be on my
family. The last gifts I gave my children
brought such joy that I've decided to do it
again. The recipients this time are my great-
nephews — Chase, Ryder and Hunter. I can
hardly wait to see what the next year holds!

About the Authors

FORTUNE'S *Children*

Lisa Jackson is a bestselling author who has written over forty love stories during the past fifteen years. Lisa contributed to the original Fortune's Children twelve-book continuity series with *The Millionaire and the Cowgirl,* and is looking forward to the launch of her next miniseries for Silhouette Special Edition, **Bachelors and Babies.** The writer lives between the Cascade Mountains and the rugged Oregon coast and also writes mainstream romantic suspense novels.

Barbara Boswell is a bestselling author who has written over twenty category romances. She is also the author of a single title about the Fortune family, coming to Silhouette Books in March '99, and contributed to the original Fortune's Children continuity series with *Stand-In Bride.* Ms. Boswell loves writing about families. "I particularly enjoy writing about how my characters' family relationships affect them," she says. When this Pennsylvania author isn't writing for Silhouette and reading, she's spending time with her *own* family or writing popular single-title romances.

Linda Turner is an award-winning author of over thirty category romances for Silhouette Books, including her contributions to the twelve-book Fortune's Children miniseries, *The Wolf and the Dove. Christmas Lone-Star Style,* the final book in her popular four-book miniseries, **The Lone Star Social Club,** is available this month in Silhouette Intimate Moments. Linda began reading romances in high school and began writing them one night when she had nothing to read. The Texas resident travels every chance she gets, scouting out locales for her books.

A FORTUNE'S CHILDREN CHRISTMAS

LISA JACKSON
BARBARA BOSWELL
LINDA TURNER

Silhouette Books

Published by Silhouette Books
America's Publisher of Contemporary Romance

Special thanks and acknowledgment to
Lisa Jackson, Barbara Boswell and Linda Turner
for their contribution to the Fortune's Children series.

 SILHOUETTE BOOKS

ISBN 0-373-48368-6

A FORTUNE'S CHILDREN CHRISTMAS

Copyright © 1998 by Harlequin Books S.A.

ANGEL BABY
Copyright © 1998 by Harlequin Books S.A.

A HOME FOR CHRISTMAS
Copyright © 1998 by Harlequin Books S.A.

THE CHRISTMAS CHILD
Copyright © 1998 by Harlequin Books S.A.

CONTENTS

Fortune Family Tree

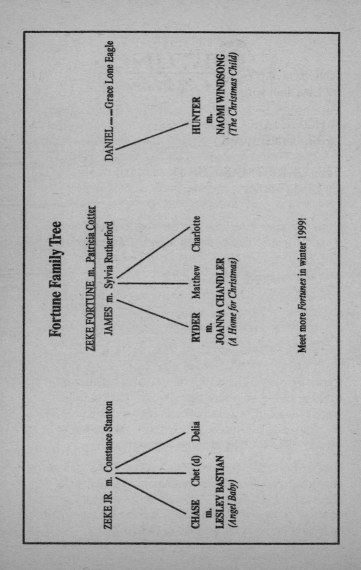

ZEKE FORTUNE m. Patricia Cotter

JAMES m. Sylvia Rutherford

DANIEL ___ Grace Lone Eagle

RYDER   Matthew   Charlotte
m.
JOANNA CHANDLER
(*A Home for Christmas*)

HUNTER
m.
NAOMI WINDSONG
(*The Christmas Child*)

ZEKE JR. m. Constance Stanton

CHASE   Chet (d)   Delia
m.
LESLEY BASTIAN
(*Angel Baby*)

Meet more *Fortunes* in winter 1999!

F☉RTUNE'S
Children

*Meet the Fortunes—three generations of a family with
a legacy of wealth, influence and power. As they come
together to celebrate the joys of the holiday season, three
Fortune cousins are given exactly one year to fulfill the
family traditions. And in the process, these bachelors
receive a Christmas gift more precious than mere riches
from three very special women.*

Kate Fortune: When the Fortune clan gathers for their
powerful matriarch's eightieth birthday, she surprises
them all by giving three of her great-nephews the
challenge of a lifetime.

Chase Fortune: The reclusive rancher. His fortitude and
expertise save a pregnant widow and her unborn child's
life on Christmas Eve. But can he put aside the pain of
his past to begin a new life with Lesley and her infant
daughter?

Ryder Fortune: The compassionate CEO. This hardworking executive has no time for romance, until his
virginal assistant wreaks havoc in his carefully ordered
life. And soon this thoroughly tempted tycoon has an
entirely different type of merger on his mind!

Hunter Fortune: The tenacious tracker. When a single
mom desperate to find the daughter her ex-husband
abducted enlists Hunter's help, he discovers that he's
better at finding lost souls than searching his own. Will
he follow his heart on the path to true love?

The Fortune family weddings continue
in Silhouette Books with the exciting new miniseries

Fortune's Children: The Brides

Coming Soon

January 1999
The Honor Bound Groom
by Jennifer Greene (Silhouette Desire #1190)

February 1999
Society Bride
by Elizabeth Bevarly (Silhouette Desire #1196)

March 1999
A FORTUNE'S CHILDREN WEDDING:
The Hoodwinked Bride
by Barbara Boswell (Silhouette Single Title)

And look for more
Fortune's Children: The Brides
stories by Leanne Banks, Susan Crosby and
Merline Lovelace, coming to Silhouette Desire
in Spring 1999.

ANGEL BABY
Lisa Jackson

Prologue

December
Minneapolis, Minnesota

"**I**'m dreaming of a white Christmas..."

The soloist's voice was hardly audible over the clinking of champagne glasses, chatter of conversation and bubbling laughter that permeated the celebration at the Fortune Corporation headquarters.

Chase Fortune watched the festivities with a jaundiced eye. He was as out of place as a range mustang at Churchill Downs, but there was nothing he could do about it now.

He took a swallow from his stemmed glass of champagne and wished he was anywhere but at his great-aunt-Kate's eightieth birthday bash in the middle of the heartland.

A twenty-foot Christmas tree decorated with twinkling lights and festive red ribbons stood in the center of the room, while an ice sculpture in the shape of an angel, complete with harp, wings and halo, was beginning to melt near the door. Liveried attendants checked engraved invitations against the guest list.

What a joke.

Chase yanked at the collar of his too-tight tuxedo,

then drained his glass. Relatives that had skimmed in and out of his life over the years filled the cavernous room. Dressed in holiday finery and bearing expensive gifts that were to be donated to charitable causes, they were here to pay tribute to Kate Fortune, the gutsy, elegant matriarch of his family.

What he wouldn't do for a cold bottle of beer, his dusty cowboy boots and a crowded, smoky tavern where you could watch a basketball game on the television mounted over the bar, grumble about the price of beef or hear the likes of Garth Brooks or Waylon Jennings from hidden speakers.

Instead he was here in the city, watching rain drizzle down the large windows, feeling his estranged sister, Delia's, cold shoulder as she, dressed in shimmering red silk, made a point of avoiding him. Not that he really gave a damn.

The singer, a tall, willowy woman with dark hair, a skin-tight gold dress and a Santa cap stuck jauntily on her head caught the guest's attention.

"Happy Birthday to you…" The crowd joined in and Kate Fortune, who'd been helped onto the slightly raised stage, smiled, her blue eyes sparkling youthfully despite the years that had propelled her into the category of elderly. Compact and aristocratic she laughed as the song was over, gave a short speech and began shaking hands and hugging her children, grandchildren and whatever other stragglers her huge family entailed.

Chase was in the last category. While the rest of the Fortune herd joined together, he was like the maverick calf, rough around the edges, wild at heart and not about to conform to whatever the rest of the Fortunes thought best. He had no use for the cosmetics company, stock options, business conglomerates or mergers.

So why the hell did you come here, if you didn't care?

Leaving his empty glass on a silver tray, he shouldered open French doors leading to a covered veranda. The air was clean and fresh, rain washed and ice-cold. Traffic rushed by on the street two stories below, tires spraying water from puddles, engines thrumming. The lights of the city glowed brightly, lending a festive air to the night, and on the street corners, bells were being rung by volunteers asking for donations.

"I thought I saw you duck out here."

Surprised, he turned and found that his great-aunt, a fur stole draped over her shoulders, had slipped onto the verandah. "I figured it might be a tad too crowded for you in there." She cocked her head to the closed glass doors where the party was in full swing.

"A little, yeah." He offered her a smile. "Happy birthday, Kate."

She chuckled. "At my age each one is special, believe me." Her eyebrows lifted as if at a private joke. "Who knows? This could be my last."

He didn't believe it for a minute. With her enthusiasm for life and energy, she'd probably outlive all her children and grandchildren. "I doubt it."

"Do you?" She walked to the edge of the verandah and looked up at the skyscrapers. Misting rain touched her face and she blinked.

"How'd you manage to break away?"

"Oh, some privileges come with age," she said,

turning to face him. "Besides I told Sterling and Jake that I wasn't to be disturbed. I think they can handle it." Sterling Foster was Kate's husband and attorney, the one man who had known she'd survived a plane crash eight years ago when she'd been the target of a failed murder attempt. Jake was her oldest son. "I wanted a few minutes alone with you, anyway," she said earnestly, "because I have a proposition for you."

"Sounds dangerous," he teased.

"Maybe." She chuckled again. "You have your father's sense of humor."

"I didn't know he had one." Chase wasn't going to fall into the trap of thinking he was anything like his old man. At one time Zeke Fortune had held the world in his hand—loving wife, adoring children, money in the bank and the best damned ranch in Western Montana. He'd managed, by a mixture of circumstance, poor timing, bad luck and even worse judgment to lose it all. If there was one thing Chase wasn't going to be, it was a loser in life. He'd lost enough already. More than anyone could possibly guess.

"Oh, Zeke had a colorful sense of humor." She sighed sadly. "Life robbed him of it. Don't let it do the same to you, Chase."

He didn't like thinking of the old man or of his own private hell. "You mentioned a proposition."

"Mmm." She placed both hands on the brick railing and didn't seem to mind that gusts of wind plucked at her hair. "It's a simple deal really. You know that some years ago I was supposed to have died and, while everyone thought I was situated comfortably on the other side of the pearly gates, I bequeathed to my heirs their part of the family fortune.''

Chase nodded. ''I remember.''

''It turned out well, I think,'' she mused. ''In one instance, if you remember, I left my grandson Kyle a sizable ranch in Wyoming. Of course there was a catch to his inheritance—he had to stay on the ranch six months before it was his. He was a city boy at the time, and I think he silently cursed me for making him give up his ways, but it worked.''

Chase recalled all too vividly and, truth to tell, he'd been envious when he'd heard that his playboy of a relative had inherited the vast spread. But he'd been dealing with his own problems at the time. Unwilling to show any emotion, he shoved his hands into his pockets. ''What's this got to do with me?''

''I have a similar bargain for you.''

The muscles in the back of his neck tightened, just as they always did when he sensed trouble. ''What kind of bargain?'' he asked, and heard the suspicious edge to his tone.

''Don't look at me like that. It's nothing sinister, trust me. I have a new ranch in Western Montana, one that unfortunately is in need of some serious help in order that it stay afloat.'' She rubbed her hands together, the fingers of one massaging the knuckles of the other. ''I'm not in the position to do it myself, obviously, and you're the most likely person in this family to turn it around as it's your line of work and, as luck would have it, in your neck of the woods.''

Chase didn't believe in luck, but he wasn't about to voice his opinion tonight.

"So, Chase, the deal is this—You'll have one year to turn the place around, get it out of the red ink that it's been mired in and show a profit. If you can do it by Christmastime next year, the ranch and everything that's a part of it will be yours. If not, well, you'll just have to give it up."

He couldn't believe his ears, but Kate, damn her, stared at him with all the intensity of a true Fortune. A mite of a woman, she was hard as nails and tough as tanned leather. And she had him. Oh, how she had him. "You're serious?"

"Dead serious."

His eyes narrowed skeptically, but he saw there wasn't a hint of deception in her—just grit. Pure, Minnesotan grit.

"I ended up with the spread as payment for an old debt. Now you, Chase, have a chance to make it yours. What do you say?"

He started to speak but the French doors opened and a woman with blond hair in a French braid, bright blue eyes and a serious expression poked her head outside. She pinned Kate with an intense gaze. "Sorry to disturb you, Ms. Fortune, but there are a couple of reporters who want to speak with you."

Kate touched her fingers to her hair. "In a second, Kelly. You've met my great-nephew Chase? Kelly Sinclair, my social secretary and Girl Friday."

"Glad to meet you," Kelly said with a half smile.

"Same here."

Kate bundled her fur more tightly over her shoulders. "I'll be there directly. Just give me a few more minutes."

"I'll handle them." Kelly winked before slipping through the doors again.

Kate turned to Chase. Despite the lines around her eyes and mouth, she was a striking, straightforward woman. She elevated an eyebrow. "Duty calls, I'm afraid." She tilted her head to the side, studying him as if she were trying to determine what he was made of. A horn blasted from the street below, and the distinctive notes of "Silver Bells" seeped through the windowpanes. "So, Chase, what do you say? Have we got a deal?"

He didn't think twice. All his life he'd hoped to own his own place, and this, if she was sincere, was the chance of a lifetime. And it had come at a perfect time for him, at a crossroads in his life. "Yes, ma'am," he said in an exaggerated drawl. "I don't think I'm fool enough to pass this up." It wouldn't take him long to pull up stakes and move. Nothing was tying him down.

"Good." She seemed relieved. "Sterling has the contract with him. I thought we should make it official."

"Thanks." He offered her his hand.

"Don't thank me just yet, Chase." She placed chilled beringed fingers in his palm. Her easy smile fell away. "There is something you should know."

Brace yourself. You knew this sounded too good to

*be true and it is. Now, she's about to let you know
what the catch is.* "What's that?"

She dropped his hand and walked to the door. Pausing, as if to add a little drama to an already-tense night, she looked over her shoulder. "The ranch is the old Waterman place in Larkspur."

Chase's gut clenched. He held his empty glass in a grip that caused his knuckles to show white.

"It's adjacent to—"

"Dad's place." Dozens of old, faded memories resurfaced—hot summer days bucking hay, the old tractor billowing black smoke in the clear blue sky; his mother's insistence of prayers before each meal and starched shirts on Sundays; his twin brother, Chet, laughing as he swung out on the rope swing before dropping into the icy depths of the old swimming hole, and a grizzled, crippled dog named Beau. His mouth turned to sand as he recalled all too vividly how it had all changed: everything he'd trusted, everyone he'd loved had disappeared from his life, including his wife and child.

"Chase?" Kate's smile was gone, her face sober as rain fell on the city below. "If this is too much for you—"

His head snapped up and his gaze drilled into hers. "I'll do it," he said without another moment's thought. So what if he had to deal with a truckload of painful memories and face the bald fact that everyone he'd trusted in his life had run out on him?

He'd wanted his own place for years, an opportunity to prove that he was better than his old man, that he,

Chase Fortune, could make good on his own. He didn't have to rely on his last name to get him by. Kate's offer was the chance of a lifetime. Besides, what did he have to lose? Nothing. Not a damned thing.

He opened the door and escorted her inside. "Just show me where to sign."

One

"This storm is the worst to hit this part of the country in twenty years, and that's goin' some because we've had our share of bad ones. Power lines are down and roads are closed from Helena west, so stay home by the fire this Christmas Eve, pour yourself a cup of holiday cheer and keep listening to—" The DJ's voice was lost over the crackle of static and a few faint notes of a country Christmas classic. Chase snapped the transistor radio off in disgust.

Merry Christmas, he thought sarcastically as he pulled on his gloves and down jacket. The cabin was warm and seemed, for the most part, to be weatherproof. On one end of the small cottage, a wood stove threw out heat from the kitchen, while a fire crackled hungrily in the river-rock fireplace in the living area. Aside from the cracks in the log walls and a few missing shingles in the roof, his new home in the foothills of the Bitterroot Mountains was cozy enough. Kerosene lanterns burned on the mantel and he'd draped the antlers mounted over the door with pine bows and mistletoe, his one concession to the season.

His dog, an old hound of no particular breed, whose once-black muzzle had grayed, lifted his head. "Let's go, Rambo," Chase ordered as he snagged his gloves from the screen in front of the fire. "We'd better feed the stock while we still can."

With a thump of his tail and a soft woof, the dog climbed to his arthritic legs.

On the back porch Chase laced up heavy boots, plopped his hat onto his head, grabbed his shovel and headed to the barn. *His* barn if he could somehow turn a profit on this miserable Montana ranch in the next year. Rambo led the way as snow continued to fall relentlessly. Icy pellets driven by the wind stung Chase's cheeks and drifted against the buildings. Chase was worried. Most of his best stock was penned in the barns and fields close to the house, but part of his herd was still unaccounted for, lost in the twenty thousand acres that climbed the surrounding hills and abutted the ranch where he'd grown up so long ago. Squinting, he glanced to the north, thinking he might see the neighboring ranch house through the heavy curtain of the blizzard. No way. He couldn't see ten feet in front of him, much less a quarter of a mile.

He plowed through the knee-deep snow to the barn. Icicles dangled from the eaves, and the old door mounted on rollers was nearly frozen shut.

Inside, the cattle were restless, but Chase, with the aid of a battery-powered lantern, made short work of filling the mangers with hay and grain, then filling the water trough. Thankfully the pipes had been wrapped, and he'd let the water trickle relentlessly, flowing enough to keep the ice at bay.

He trudged from the barn to the outdoor shelter—a huge roof on poles that provided some protection for part of his herd—then with Rambo on his heels, broke a path to the stables where the few horses were housed and the odors of grain, dust and horses greeted him. The horses shifted and snorted, their ears flicking in his direction, liquid eyes watching him curiously while he tossed hay into their mangers.

As he scooped the last can of grain from the oat barrel, Rambo trotted to the door and gave off a soft woof. His old ears pricked up and he started whining and scratching at the door.

"What the devil's got into you?" Chase, pulling on his gloves, opened the door and stared into the coming night. He couldn't see anything other than the continual snow. "It's nothing—" But there was something that wasn't right, something out of place—the muted, steady blare of an automobile horn. Squinting, he stared through the blizzard, but saw nothing. Still the horn blasted.

"Great," he growled. Just what he needed. His truck was four-wheel-drive, but the tires were bald, the transmission about shot and he doubted if he could make much headway in snow this deep. But a horse could. He turned, walked into the stables and saddled the largest gelding on the ranch. Part draft animal, the buckskin was strong and sure, not as quick as the quarter horses, but steady. "Come on, Ulysses," Chase said, snagging a bridle from its nail on the wall, "it looks like you and I have work to do." He flung a blanket and saddle over the beast's broad back, then led Ulysses outside where the wind lashed. "You stay," he ordered Rambo, but the dog ignored him and as Ulysses forged through the frigid powder, the old hound was at his heels, half jumping to keep up. All in all, it was a disaster.

Still the horn blasted, sounding louder as Ulysses plunged along the lane to the main road. Chase knew where they were by the position of trees that lined the drive of this broken-down ranch. Kate Fortune hadn't been kidding. It would take a miracle for him to turn the place around in a year.

Ulysses snorted as the shape of a dark rig appeared in the otherwise white landscape. What kind of idiot had decided to go out Sunday driving in this mess, Chase wondered as he recognized the shape of a sports utility vehicle that had slid off the road and tipped into the ditch, mired deep to its axle.

Snow covered the windows. He climbed off the horse and pounded on the car with a gloved fist. The horn stopped.

"Is someone there?" A woman's voice. It figured.

"Yeah." He yanked on the passenger door and it opened with a groan. The interior light flashed on, and he was staring at a woman of considerable bulk crammed behind the steering wheel.

"Thank God," she said, green eyes bright and grateful, cheeks rosy and lips thin with concern. "I was afraid, I mean...oh-h." Closing her eyes, she grabbed hold of the steering wheel so hard her knuckles showed white, and despite the subfreezing temperature, sweat trickled down the side of her face. She let out her breath in a long stream. "Thank goodness Sarah is with me."

"Sarah?" Chase peered into the dark interior. As far as he could tell this woman was alone. There was a sack of groceries and an overnight bag but no other person. "Who's Sarah and where is she?"

"Here. At least she was."

"You're the only one in the Jeep."

"But she was here. I think, no, I'm sure she's my guardian angel."

"Oh, right," he said sarcastically. The woman was obviously pulling his leg. Or hallucinating big-time.

"She brought you to me."

Was she serious? No way. Unless she was a bona-fide nutcase. "Only if she laid on the horn."

"No—" the woman shook her head and even in the darkness, the strands showed a fiery red "—that was me." Finely arched dark brows pulled together in confusion. "At least I thought so…" She was definitely disoriented.

"Don't worry about it. Let's get you out of here."

"But Sarah was here. With me." The woman worried her lower lip as if concerned about her own state of mind. "I mean, I think so…oh, maybe not…"

"You'd better get out of there—"

She started breathing hard. Panting. As if she were about to— For the love of Pete, she was pregnant! And from the looks of it, about to deliver. His heart shut down, and memories as vivid as if they'd been yesterday flashed in painful technicolor through his mind. Emily, his wife, had once been the love of his life. His jaw grew so hard it ached.

"Wait…just wait a minute.…"

Chase was jarred back to the present. Again the woman gripped the wheel, and Chase thought that if there was a damned guardian angel this would be as good a time as any for her to appear. The contractions were way too close together. "I'm sorry," she finally said as the labor pain subsided. She wiped a shaking hand over her lips and tried to look brave. "I was on my way to the hospital, the baby's decided to come a few weeks early, and the storm got worse and a deer bounded onto the road. I slammed on my brakes and then...I don't remember—"

"It doesn't matter. I'll get you out of here and back to the house." He stared directly into her frightened eyes. "We'll do what we have to do then."

"But—"

"Look, lady, we don't have much time, and if you haven't noticed, we're in the middle of the worst blizzard in years. I've brought more than my share of calves and lambs into this world, believe me, and so let's get a move on." There wasn't any time to argue. He helped her crawl across the passenger seat and saw her wince as she tried to stand.

She sucked in her breath.

"Trouble with your leg?"

"My ankle. I must've twisted it. Oh, Lord."

"Let me help you onto Ulysses."

"I don't know if I can ride—" As if she understood there was no other way back to the house, she cut off the rest of her words, set her jaw and with Chase's help climbed into the saddle.

"We'd better hurry," she said, and he wondered how long she could straddle Ulysses's broad back while in the middle of labor. Hunching his shoulders against the snow, he grabbed her suitcase, took the reins and walked ahead, plowing through the trail that the big horse had made.

The woman cried out twice, clinging to the saddle horn in a death grip, her face turning as pale as the surrounding fields. Chase paused each time, waiting as the contraction passed and wondering what in the world he was going to do with her. He didn't have much time to think, and when the ranch house came into view, he felt a mixture of relief and apprehension.

"Come on," he said, helping her off the gelding and carrying her through the back door. He didn't bother to take off his boots or shake the snow from his jacket, but hauled her, protesting loudly, into his bedroom.

"I couldn't possibly—"

"Looks like you don't have much choice."

"But this is your room."

"Now it's yours." Without ceremony he placed her on the old four-poster he'd brought with him, the very bed he'd shared with Emily so many years ago, the bed where they'd conceived their own child, the last bed she'd slept in before— "I'll be right back," he promised, his voice gruff with emotion as he forced his thoughts of his wife far into the back of his mind where they belonged. "I've got to get the horse to the stables. Rambo will keep you company." He pointed a gloved finger at the shivering, wet dog. "Stay," he commanded and strode through doorway leaving Lesley alone in a strange bedroom, with an ancient hound, waiting for a man she didn't know to help deliver her baby.

"This is unbelievable," Lesley muttered under her

breath. The last thing she wanted, the very last, was to be dependent upon a man. Any man. Especially one she didn't know, and yet she had no choice.

Count your blessings, a voice inside her head reminded her. *A few days ago no one lived here and if this would have happened then, what would have happened to you? To the baby?* She touched her rounded abdomen and sighed. This wasn't the way a woman was supposed to bring her first child into the world. A contraction began to grip her again and she closed her eyes, her fingers curling in the wool blanket that was the cover for the stranger's bed. Pain shot through her and she bit down hard, then remembered her breathing exercises and began to focus on a spot on the far wall, a black-and-white portrait of a family of five mounted over a bare dresser. The contraction eased and she went limp.

Who was the guy who'd found her? A member of the extensive Fortune family, she guessed as it was rumored around the coffee shops, churches and taverns of downtown Larkspur that Kate Fortune, matriarch of a vast, complicated and very wealthy family had ended up with the old Waterman place as payoff for some kind of debt. Speculation was that she would sell it and turn a tidy profit, but Lesley wasn't so sure. The tall man who had rescued her had all the arrogance and "can-do" attitude that were rumored to be Fortune family traits. She couldn't imagine where the rugged, taciturn cowboy fit into the world-wide conglomerate, where the children and grandchildren of Kate and her late husband, Ben, were anything from reed-thin models to pilots, authors to lawyers, chemists to ranchers. And there was something more to him, as well—a haunted look that he tried to hide.

Another contraction was beginning to squeeze her in its painful grip, and for the next few seconds she closed her eyes and breathed in shallow gasps, unable to think about the Fortune family or her new neighbor.

Life just wasn't getting any easier, Chase decided. He gave the gelding an extra ration of oats and listened as the wind ripped through the thin walls of the stables. The seventy-year-old siding was giving way, knotholes and gaps between the boards allowing the frigid air to seep inside.

Who was the woman who was lying in his bed? Where was her husband, the father of the baby about to enter the world? The last thing he needed in his life right now was another complication. The pregnant woman was that and so much more. He latched the door behind him and jogged through the snow to the back porch, where he kicked off his boots and hung his hat on a peg.

Inside, he took off his jacket and tossed it over the back of a chair that was near the fire, then he checked on the woman. She was settled into the bed, her coat and scarf on the floor, her red-brown hair damp and feathered around her head like a cloud on his pillow. His gut clenched for a minute. It had been a long time since there had been a female tucked under his blankets; no one since Emily. Her suitcase, now open to display folded clothes for a woman and infant, lay open on the bureau.

An old ache tore at his heart when he thought of

his own son, born healthy, or so they'd been told, only to die before his first birthday.

"Hi," the woman said weakly, and some of the ice around his heart cracked a bit. She looked so pale and drawn.

"How're ya doin'?" he asked.

"Compared to what?" Her smile was weak, her eyes wary as he approached the bed.

At least she had a sense of humor. "I'm Chase Fortune."

"I figured you were connected to Kate one way or another." She smoothed the blanket over her stomach.

"Her grandnephew."

"I'm Lesley Bastian."

Bastian, he thought. She was somehow related to the man who'd bought his father's place.

"I live next door. To the north."

The muscles in the back of his neck tightened. So she still lived in the old ranch house he'd called home when he was a kid. Well, that was great, just damned near perfect. He shifted from one foot to the other. Was she Aaron Bastian's daughter? His much younger sister? Or...he felt a chill as cold as all of December invade his soul. She couldn't be married to him. Aaron Bastian was much too old for her. Or was he?

"I can't call anyone to tell them you're here," he said. "The phone lines are down, and the electricity's out."

She nodded, then sucked in her breath. "I know."

"You picked a helluva time to deliver."

"I didn't pick anything."

"Does your husband have any idea where you are?"

"I don't have a husband. Oh…oh, dear God…" She pierced him with those wide green eyes. "I think this is it. I can't be sure…I, oh…this is my first." She moaned, and Chase took hold of her hand. Her fingers were tiny and white against his, but she squeezed his hand hard enough that he thought she might crush his fingers.

When the contraction eased, he straightened and ignored the rush of emotion that ate at him. "Hang in here for a few minutes, okay? I'll get some towels, warm water, antiseptic and a few other things. I'll be right back."

She didn't argue and already looked spent.

Chase walked briskly to the bathroom and heard her moan again. The contractions were coming closer together. He rolled up his shirtsleeves and washed his hands in hot water. As he toweled off he caught a glimpse of himself in the steamy mirror. Hard gray eyes stared back at him from a face that was just beginning to show a few creases from too many hours in the sun and too many nights lying awake worrying. He started filling a plastic bucket with water. "You can do this," he told his reflection. He didn't have time to second-guess himself.

A new baby was on its way.

Two

Twenty minutes later, the baby, a red-faced girl with a shock of black hair, gave out a lusty cry of protest as she entered the world.

Chase, choked with emotions he didn't want to face, remembered the hospital room where his son had been born and a team of doctors had assured him that the little boy was fine. They'd lied. They'd all lied.

But he couldn't think about all that right now, and he did his best holding Lesley's small, slippery infant, tied off the cord, then handed the little girl to her mother.

"She's beautiful," he said, surprised and disgusted at the lump in his throat.

"That she is." Lesley's voice was hoarse and her eyes shone with tears. She held the baby to her breast, stroking the wet hair. "That she is."

Chase looked away for a second, and he clenched his hands so that they wouldn't shake. Inside, his heart was racing, his head pounding, the old wounds fresh. He couldn't stand to see Lesley holding her child in his bed, her back propped up by his pillows, the sight, sounds and smells of birth filling the small room. She was humming softly, the pain that had been so intense only minutes before seeming to have vanished. He edged his way out of his bedroom and told himself he was just giving mother and baby time to bond or whatever they called it these days. It wasn't because the scene reminded him of the hospital bed where Emily held their child for the first time.

"Get over it, Fortune," he warned himself. In the bathroom he washed his hands, arms and face and gave himself a swift mental kick. Forget Emily and Ryan. They're gone. End of story.

He passed by the open bedroom door as he walked to the kitchen. It was small, just a corner of a larger room, but he didn't need much. He planned on living the rest of his life alone. Here. On these miserable acres. If he could turn this ranch around within the year.

But now he had to fix his unexpected company something to eat—Christmas Eve dinner. The irony of it caused his lips to curve into a bitter smile. He hadn't shared Christmas with anyone for years. He'd decided the entire holiday season was vastly overrated.

Tonight he'd planned to eat one of those frozen meat pies that he would cook on the woodstove, and he hadn't bothered buying a Christmas goose, turkey or even a ham. All he had was a frozen chicken that was thawing in his cooler. It would have to do. He stuck the bird into a pan with some potatoes, onions and carrots. A dash of salt and pepper, and he shoved the concoction into the oven of the woodstove. He had biscuits he'd baked yesterday morning that he could warm on top.

"It'll be a damned feast," he muttered to Rambo, who had stationed himself on the braided rug under the table and stared up at Chase hoping for a scrap.

"Later." He donned hat, jacket, gloves and boots again, then carried in more firewood and stoked the fire. Satisfied that there was enough oak for the night, he checked on the stock one last time, trying to see through the storm and hoping that the last of the strays had made it back to the barn. But his count was off. Between twenty and thirty head of cattle were still unaccounted for. "Great," he muttered as he walked back to the house. What a lousy way to start off his year of trying to pull these rocky acres into the black.

By the time he returned to the cabin, the aroma of roasting poultry mingled with the scents of burning wood and kerosene. He turned on the radio again, listened to a depressing weather report and, as a static-laden version of "O Come All Ye Faithful" filled the room with music, strode into the bedroom. Lesley was awake and had somehow managed, with the aid of sponge, towels and the bucket of warm water he'd left at the bed, to clean herself and the baby. Now the little girl was dressed in a white sleeper that was trimmed in red and green and looked a couple of sizes too large.

"Merry Christmas," Lesley's smile was infectious. He wondered if she was the prettiest woman he'd ever met with her silver-green eyes and teeth that over-lapped just slightly.

"Merry Christmas," he said gruffly.

"I'd like you to meet Angela."

For a second he thought she was hallucinating again, but she cocked her head to indicate the sleeping baby.

"Angela? That's what you named her?"

"Actually Angela Noel Chastina Bastian." Lesley blushed a little. "Angela because of the angel..."

"I remember."

"And Noel because it's Christmas."

"I figured as much."

"And Chastina after you, because if you hadn't come along when you did, I don't know what I would have done."

"No reason to think about it," he said, dismissing the dangerous emotions that seemed to settle in the small room. He silently cautioned himself to be careful. This was, after all, a dramatic night, and whether they'd chosen to or not, he and Lesley had already handled the heady, exhilarating experience of Angela's birth. "Maybe you should have named her after her father."

Lesley's smile disappeared slowly. Her face clouded and she looked away. "Aaron wouldn't have appreciated the gesture."

His gut clenched. So she was, or had been married to Aaron Bastian. The thought made him sick. But hadn't she said she didn't have a husband? Were they divorced? Had she ended up with the ranch?

Clearing her throat, she shifted the sleeping baby, who was snuggled against her breast. "Something smells good."

"Does it?"

"Mmm." When she turned back to him, her eyes held that special sparkle again, a lively brilliance that he was beginning to find fascinating.

"We can only hope."

"Tell me about yourself," she suggested. She

tossed a lock of springy curls from her face, and he found the act sexy, though he didn't know why. Didn't want to think about it. "All I know is that you're one of Kate's great-nephews. That's a pretty long list."

He settled into the old rocker, propped his stockinged heel on the edge of the bed and warned himself to be careful. This woman, whether she knew it or not, was touching emotions he'd thought were long dead. For a second he considered telling her that he'd once lived on the spread that she now owned, that her ex-husband had bought the place for a song when Chase's father had nearly run it to the ground, but she probably knew more than her share of what had happened. Besides, it was all ancient history. Water under the bridge. "The reason I'm here," he said, "is because of a deal with Kate. To coin an overused phrase, she handed me an offer I couldn't refuse." He explained about Kate's bargain, and Lesley listened while absently rubbing her daughter's tiny back. His gut clenched, but he continued to tell her about the birthday bash where Kate approached him.

"One year isn't much time to turn things around." Her forehead creased with lines of concern.

"I wasn't doin' much of anything else. I've been a foreman for three ranches, one in Wyoming, another in Texas and the last in Western Washington. Now I'm working for myself." He didn't add that owning his own place had been his lifelong dream, that ever since Zeke had lost the ranch next door, Chase had been determined to find another place, to stake his claim and make a home. Nor did he bring up that his dreams had died with the death of his son. "Now, maybe I should have a look at that ankle of yours."

"It's fine," she protested, but he moved his foot out of the way and raised the blankets at the foot of the bed. "Really, Chase, you don't have to—"

"Shh." He shot Lesley a look that was both tender and tough, a glance that warned her to be still, and though it rankled her a bit—just who did he think he was bullying her around?—she was touched at his concern. His callused fingers gently probed the skin around her foot and the back of her leg, carefully examining—the act nearly sensual. But that was foolish. She barely knew the man. He was just being cautious.

He rotated her foot. A shaft of white-hot pain shot up her leg.

"Ouch."

"That hurts?"

"Big-time."

His eyebrows drew together and he rubbed the stubble on his chin thoughtfully. "Looks like you either sprained it or broke it."

"No—"

"You'll probably need X-rays."

Lesley's heart sank. "It'll be fine," she said, refusing to doubt her own words. She had to be healthy. She was a single woman with a baby to take care of. She couldn't be laid up. Wouldn't.

"I'll bring you a couple of aspirin." He glanced at her for a second and her heart did a stupid little glitch. He was handsome in a rugged, harsh-featured sort of way. Tall, lean, with wide shoulders and slim hips, he wore faded, battle-scarred jeans, a pullover sweater and an expression that wavered between tender concern and irritated worry. His eyes were a steely gray and guarded secrets at which she could only guess. Lesley figured him to be a loner, a man who didn't like too many intrusions in his life, a man who had his own extremely private demons to deal with.

He sauntered into the bathroom in stockinged feet and returned with a glass of water and bottle of over-the-counter pain relievers.

"I've got coffee warming on the stove...or...hot water if you want something else. I might have a tea bag or two, I'm not sure."

"I'm fine," she said around a yawn, and was surprised when he threw the covers back again and propped her foot with a pillow.

"Needs to be elevated, and I'll get a bag of snow to help with the swelling."

"You don't have to go to any trouble."

"Sure I do," he said firmly, and left quickly only to return with an insulated rubber sack that felt ice-cold to her as he placed it upon her ankle. She sucked in her breath then let it out slowly. "It'll help," he assured her.

"If I don't die of frostbite first," she muttered, surprised at her cranky tone. It had been a long, hard day, and despite Chase Fortune's best efforts, she didn't like being told what to do. She ached all over.

One side of his mouth lifted in a manner she found disdainfully irritating as well as damnably sexy. "I'll wake you for dinner."

Dinner. It sounded and smelled like heaven, but she couldn't just lie in the man's bed, eat his food and expect him to take care of her and her newborn daughter. He was a neighbor, a stranger, a man she didn't know and shouldn't trust, one with his own set of problems. Besides which, she couldn't impose upon him, couldn't let herself become beholden to him in any way. And what the devil was she thinking, deciding that his smile was sexy? It must be the postpartum elation she was feeling, the exhilaration of holding her hours-old daughter close and knowing that the baby was healthy and safe.

"Listen, Chase. I have to thank you for everything you've done for me and Angela. I really don't know how I'm ever going to repay you, but I can't impose on you any longer. Really. I have to go home and—"

"No!"

He said it so sharply she jumped.

"I mean you can't be serious," he said, and all hint of a smile left his face. "You gave birth less than six hours ago and, if you haven't noticed, there's a blizzard raging. Your vehicle's disabled. You've either sprained or broken your ankle. You don't know how healthy your baby is. And, assuming you could get over to your place, which you can't, there's no electricity or telephone service, so you wouldn't be able to heat the house or communicate with anyone if you have a problem."

"Are you done lecturing me?" she demanded, even though she knew he was right.

"For the moment." His harsh expression softened a bit. "Until you come up with some other lamed-brained idea. Now, just take it easy. It looks like you and I are going to have to wait out this storm. Together.'' He slid a glance at the sleeping baby. ''Just the three of us.'' His slate-colored eyes told her that he wasn't any happier with the situation than she. ''Yell if you need anything.'' He turned on his heel and left, but his dog gave off a weary sigh and curled up near the bed, sad eyes on the light spilling through the open doorway as if he intended to guard the place.

Just the three of us. The words had an odd ring to them. For the past six months Lesley had told herself she was alone and that's the way she wanted things— a single woman making her way in a man's world. She had been certain that even after the baby was born, she wouldn't want another man in her life. No way. No how. One marriage was enough, thank you very much.

She felt her eyelids grown heavy and gave in to the sleep that might ease the throbbing in her ankle and the lingering pain deep inside from the birth. She wouldn't impose on Chase Fortune too much, she thought, drifting off, but for now, she didn't have any say in the matter. The best thing to do was trust in him, accept his hospitality and eventually, when she was up and on her feet again, find a way to repay him.

When she awoke, there was music coming from the living room. Over the sounds of pots rattling, the fire crackling and Angela's soft breathing, Lesley heard the fragmented strains of a Christmas carol.

''The first Noel, the angels did say...''

''Merry Christmas,'' she whispered to her baby and let slumber overtake her as thoughts of her new child, guardian angels and a very tough-looking rancher filled her head.

* * *

"Waaaa!"

The cry started out as a whimper, but quickly rose to a lusty full-blown wail.

Chase was just pulling the chicken out of the oven, and he heard Lesley's voice, muted and soft from sleep, as she talked to the infant who had one helluva set of lungs.

Within seconds the noise quieted, and Chase suspected that Lesley was feeding her daughter. Rather than interrupt, he cut up the chicken, placed the hot vegetables and meat on a platter and poured the gravy, if you could call it that, over the meat and potatoes.

By the time he carried a tray into the bedroom, Lesley was buttoning up her nightgown, but Chase caught a glimpse of one perfectly rounded breast. A dark, wet nipple peeked at him. He looked away quickly, but not before she met his gaze with her own, and for a heart-stopping second, he was lost.

"How's—how's she doing?" Chase asked as he set the tray on the nightstand near the bed.

"Fine, I think." Lesley's finely arched eyebrows drew together. "Near as I can tell. She eats well and sleeps all right and...has a decent voice on her."

"I noticed," he said drily. "I'll be right back." He walked into the living room and wondered why he felt so compelled to wait on her hand and foot. She didn't seem the kind of woman who expected that kind of treatment, but, for the first time since Emily's death, he felt a need to protect and help her and her tiny daughter. He consoled himself with the thought that this was only for a few days, until she was able to take care of herself and her baby and the storm had passed. Then she was on her own. He dug in the small closet where he'd seen an old TV tray, compliments of the previous owners. Quickly washing it off with a rag, he returned to the bedroom with the tray and a lantern.

Next he opened his bottom dresser drawer, dumped the jeans onto the top of the bureau and lined the empty drawer with a blanket. "I'm fresh out of bassinets and cribs," he explained, gently lifting Angela from her mother's arms and placing her in the drawer near the bed. The baby's body was warm, and she made happy little gurgling noises, but Chase told himself to stay detached. This little lump of flesh wasn't his kid and after a few days, wouldn't be his responsibility. Satisfied that Angela was content and comfortable, he straightened and motioned to Lesley. "Now, you, lady, have some dinner."

Lesley glanced down at the makeshift cradle. "Will she be all right there?"

"Unless you crawl out of the bed and step on her, and I don't think you'll be doin' much of that with that ankle of yours."

"I know, but—"

"If you need to use the bathroom, call me. I'll take you."

She blushed scarlet. "No, I couldn't. I mean I'll get there by myself." He sent her a disbelieving look, but didn't argue. He set her tray across her lap, then got a second for himself and watched as she ate heartily.

"So where's Angela's father?" Chase asked as he dunked a biscuit in a pocket of lumpy gravy.

Lesley cleared her throat. "Aaron died six months ago."

"I'm sorry."

"Me, too." She replaced her fork. "He was older than me by twenty years and...well, he had a heart attack one day." Her eyes clouded with what Chase supposed was grief, but there was something more to the story, as well, something she didn't want to confide. The corners of her mouth turned down a bit, and the slight dusting of freckles over her nose seemed more pronounced. She pushed around her vegetables with her fork, and he decided he didn't need to pry. She'd been through enough for one day. "When he died, everyone thought I should sell the ranch, move into town, but I wanted to try and make it on my own. With my daughter, of course."

"To prove a point?" he guessed.

"Maybe." She didn't elaborate, and he held his silence.

It had been years since he'd shared Christmas Eve with anyone. Even with all his relatives he'd chosen to spend the holidays alone since Ryan's death, ignoring the traditions of Thanksgiving and Christmas in favor of quiet solitude. On those holidays he'd usually spent time riding through snow-crusted hills, eyeing the scenery, telling himself that there was a God, that his son and wife were in heaven, that he could get by on his own, that he didn't need anyone. Now he wasn't so sure.

Within a few short hours Lesley Bastian and that mite of a daughter of hers had started turning his mind around. As he chewed on a tough bite of chicken and watched golden shadows from the kerosene lantern play over the smooth contours of her face, he had the distinct impression that the widow next door was about to change the course of his life forever, and he wasn't certain it was for the better.

Three

If you know what's good for you, you'll stay in that bed until I can drive you to a hospital so a doctor can look at your ankle.

Chase's words still echoed through the empty cabin as Lesley struggled to her feet. The baby was sleeping in her makeshift bed, Chase was outside, and Lesley wasn't going to let him boss her around. He'd been wonderful in his gruff way. For the past few days he'd waited on her hand and foot, taking care of both his place and hers, but she couldn't stand being idle a minute longer. She needed to get on with her life, and the thought of some man, any man, Chase Fortune included, telling her what to do, made her see red. This was as good a time as any to test her ability to stand.

Gingerly she placed her feet on the floor and pushed herself upright. Pain screamed up her ankle and leg. "Darn." Light-headed, she dropped back down on the bed for a second, then decided she wasn't going to let the sprain get the better of her. She tried again. The pain hit her hard, then dulled. It wasn't so bad this time. Gritting her teeth, she balanced on her good foot, then, using a cane Chase had found in the attic, hobbled into the living room, where a fire crackled brightly.

She and Angela were alone. Chase was out looking for the missing livestock.

Leaning against the counter, she took a good hard look at the place. The house was decorated sparsely with an eclectic array of used furniture that somehow jelled together to give an authentic mountain-cabin feel to the place. The couch had once been deep forest green and was now worn and lumpy. A sleeping bag was thrown over one overstuffed arm and had sufficed as Chase's bed. An old leather chair sat near the fire, and a drop-leaf table separated the living area from the kitchen. Four chairs surrounded the oval table, none of which matched another.

She'd asked enough questions to learn that most of the furniture had come with the place, and she supposed he was a man who traveled light, didn't collect a lot of possessions or dust, and was used to moving from one place to another.

In the kitchen she poured coffee from a thermos and stared through the frost-covered windows to the barn, where snow was piled high on the roof and icicles dangled, sparkling in the pale winter sun.

Livestock, black Angus and white-faced Hereford cattle, chewed their cuds under a pole structure or milled in the snow that had been trampled.

She was sipping from her cup when the house seemed to shudder. The motor of the refrigerator began to hum. Lamps were suddenly lit.

Electricity! Finally. She snapped on the television set and saw the familiar characters of a soap opera. "Good." Lesley's spirits lifted instantly. "Back to the twentieth century!" She hitched her way across the

room to the wall phone and nearly shouted out loud
when she held the receiver to her ear and heard an
honest-to-goodness dial tone for the first time in half
a week.

Her heart hammered, and she couldn't wipe the
smile off her face. There were so many people to call
to tell them about Angela.

First on the list were her parents. She dialed their
home in Seattle and waited impatiently, her fingers
tapping anxiously on the counter.

One ring. Two. Three.

''Come on. Be home.''

''Hello?''

At the sound of her mother's voice, tears filled Lesley's eyes. ''Hi, Grandma,'' she said.

There was a stunned silence and then her mother
shrieked. ''Lesley? You had the baby? Frank! Frank!
Get on the extension, it's Lesley! She had the baby!
Where are you? What happened? Oh, my God, we
were so worried!''

There was a click and she heard her father's voice.
''Les?''

''Hi, Daddy.'' Tears of relief spilled down her
cheeks. ''Mom's right. You're a grandpa now. Angela
Noel Chastina Bastian was born on Christmas Eve and
she's beautiful.''

''Well, I'll be—'' her father whispered.

Her mother began to sniff, and Lesley couldn't help
but giggle through her tears. They were all a bunch of
romantic softies deep at heart. ''As I said, we were so
worried,'' her mom repeated. ''We couldn't get hold
of you, not even through the police and…and the tele-

vision reports said the storm there was the worst ever." Her voice cracked. "There were pictures of stranded cars and frozen cattle and, oh, I just thank God that you and the baby are safe."

"Me, too."

"Are you at home?"

"No. At the neighbor's. If it hadn't been for Chase coming along..." She couldn't imagine what would have happened. Quickly she recounted the past few days, leaving out only those parts that would upset her parents and lingering on the birth and Angela. "I was lucky I guess."

"Very," her mother agreed, then promised to visit as soon as the weather allowed.

"She'll be there if she has to walk through another blizzard," her father said, chuckling. They'd been waiting to become grandparents for years, but Lesley's sister, Janie, wasn't interested in becoming a mother. A lawyer, married to another attorney in the same firm, Janie lived in San Francisco and enjoyed an urban professional life uncluttered by children.

"So this Chase fellow, he's still helping you out?" her father asked.

"I'm still at his house, but I think I can go home today or tomorrow. If not, you can reach me here," Lesley added, rattling off the telephone number. They talked a few more minutes about the holidays and relatives and Angela's future before hanging up, then Lesley called her sister and left a message on Janie's answering machine.

She'd hung up and was hobbling back to the bedroom when the phone jangled. Thinking her mother had decided to call back, she hiked her way back to the kitchen and snagged the receiver on the fourth ring just as Chase appeared on the back porch.

"Hello?" she said, smiling, as she watched Chase shake the snow from his jacket and hat.

"Oh...hello," a woman said. She sounded young and a little put off, as if she hadn't been expecting to hear Lesley's voice. Foolishly, Lesley's heart sank. "This is Kelly Sinclair. I'm trying to reach Chase Fortune."

"He's right here," Lesley replied, surprised at the knot of disappointment in her stomach. Chase shouldered open the door and gave the room a quick once-over. "The power's on."

"Finally." She held the telephone toward him and forced a smile she didn't feel. "It's Kelly."

His eyebrows elevated. "Who?"

"Kelly Sinclair."

"Oh. Good." His demeanor changed instantly. The hardworking, abrupt cowboy switched into an even-tempered man. He took the receiver and grinned. "Merry Christmas—well, it's a little late, but we've been snowed under. Suppose you heard."

Angela started to cry, and rather than eavesdrop on Chase's private conversation, Lesley started for the bedroom.

"Hey, wait. I'll help you," he said, but Lesley's spine stiffened. She wasn't going to depend upon him.

"I'm okay," she said over her shoulder as the baby's cries got louder.

"You're sure...what?" he said into the telephone

again. "Oh, no. Just the neighbor. Yeah, we had a little trouble here over the holidays."

Just the neighbor. Lesley's teeth clenched so hard her jaw ached. She gripped the cane even harder. Of course she was *just* his neighbor. What more did she expect? Sure they'd been trapped together for four days and in that time she'd seen through Chase's hard facade to the gentler man behind his brooding eyes and harsh expression. Though he'd avoided holding Angela, he'd been concerned for her well-being. He'd made sure that Lesley was recovering and she'd noticed that he'd slipped his old dog scraps from the table and watched him absently rub his ears. His concern for his newly acquired herd seemed to run deeper than a simple worry about profit and loss. Deep inside, Chase Fortune probably had a heart of pure gold; he just did a darned good job of hiding it.

Angela, red-faced, tiny fists clenched near her head, was screaming at the top of her lungs. "Shh. It's all right, I'm here," Lesley insisted, picking up her daughter, dropping onto the bed and immediately unbuttoning her nightgown. As the baby suckled hungrily, she closed her eyes and couldn't help overhear part of Chase's conversation.

"...as well as can be expected...yeah, that was an obstacle I hadn't counted on, but we're okay." A deep, rumbling chuckle. "I know, I know. The situation is only temporary, trust me.... Yeah, I know. I've got more than my share of work cut out for me. I don't have time for any distractions." There was a familiar tone to his voice, an intimate teasing quality that twisted Lesley's heart. Whoever Kelly Sinclair was, she was obviously very important in Chase's life.

"I think we've overstayed our welcome," Lesley whispered softly to her daughter, and dismissed the foolish pang of pain that seared her heart. "We should think about going home." It was time to give him his life back and get on with her own.

"I'll keep in touch," Chase promised Kate, who had finally had her secretary call to see how he was doing. He'd chatted with Kelly a few minutes before his great-aunt had actually picked up and in that time he'd mentioned the fact that he'd helped deliver a baby.

"See that you do keep in touch," Kate said with a deep chuckle. "I've got a stake in this, you know."

"Oh, I know." He squinted out the window to the snow-crusted fields and the tiny herd of strays he'd managed to drive back to the barn.

"And keep your eye on that widow with her newborn."

He hesitated.

"They're still staying with you, aren't they?"

"For a while."

Kate sighed. "Thank God you found Lesley when you did. Sometimes I think we all have guardian angels with us."

He didn't reply. What could he say? That Lesley had been so confused she'd thought an actual angel had been in the car with her?

"I know it must be hard for you," Kate ventured

to say, and Chase tensed. "What with it being the holidays and all."

"It's all right."

"You're sure?" He knew what she was asking, but he didn't answer. Couldn't. His son hadn't survived to see his first Christmas, and his wife...well, Emily had blamed herself and taken her own life on New Year's Eve. She'd mixed vodka and an entire bottle of sleeping pills. The results had been deadly.

"I'll be fine, Kate," he assured her.

"I know you will, Chase. Just remember no man is an island."

"No?"

"Have a good holiday."

"You, too." He hung up with the unsettling feeling that there was more to the old woman's bargain than first appeared. And she was wrong. A man could be an island. Self-contained. Self-reliant. Chase had told himself years ago that he didn't need anyone, not even his own family, to make it on his own. Meeting Lesley Bastian hadn't changed that.

He added a couple of chunks of oak to the woodstove, then checked on Lesley. She was lying on the bed, her eyes closed, the baby nuzzling at her breast. Something tightened in his chest, and he averted his eyes; he still hadn't gotten used to seeing her so uncovered, but it was fascinating and sensual in a domestic, earthy way that caused heat to climb up the back of his neck and an answering response between his legs.

It was beginning to seem right—her sleeping in his

bed, the tiny baby swaddled and sleeping either with her or in the make-shift bassinet.

At the turn of his thoughts he stiffened. What was he thinking? Just seconds ago he'd been on the right track, and now as he glanced at the sleeping woman and child he doubted himself.

"Angela and I are leaving in the morning," she said, surprising him. He thought she was asleep and didn't realize that she knew he was in the room.

"You can barely walk."

"I'll manage." Her eyes opened fully, and he was struck by the intensity of her gaze—green irises shot with silver—that didn't flinch. "I've imposed too much already."

"There's another storm on its way."

"This time we'll all be ready."

"I couldn't leave you over there all alone," he insisted.

"I don't think you're going to have much choice."

"Don't I?" he demanded. "How're you gonna get over there? There's no damned taxi service out here."

"How about your truck? I heard you start it this morning, and I can only think that you have chains. The radio announcer said that most of the roads are clear, so I think I should call a tow company for my rig and have you drive me and Angela home."

"I don't know if I'd feel right about it." He rubbed the back of his neck in agitation. He couldn't keep her here forever, not that he wanted that, but the thought of her and that baby alone in an empty house in sub-freezing weather bothered him.

It bothered him a lot.

"It's time, Chase," she said firmly, and he realized he couldn't change her mind. "You have your life— I have mine. I appreciate everything you've done for Angela and me, but I have to start taking care of my daughter and myself."

"You'd be taking one helluva risk."

"Mine to take."

"Lesley, think about it."

"I have," she said firmly.

There was no use arguing with her. The best he could do was bargain. Folding his arms over his chest, he stood at the foot of the bed and stared down at her. "If you insist on doing this—"

"I do. Absolutely." Her pointed chin thrust forward in determination.

"Okay, then I'll go over to your place, make sure the power's on, the furnace hasn't frozen and you've got running water. Then, in the morning, when the house is warm enough for Angela, I'll take you over."

"But—" Lesley started to argue, then threw up one hand. "Oh, sure. Fine," she said, obviously having trouble giving an inch. She was testy today, probably suffering from a bad case of cabin fever. "There's a key hidden behind a wreath by the back door."

"Then I'll go over now and take a look around." He whistled to Rambo and was out the door to the screened-in porch. If the woman wanted to be stubborn, so be it, Chase thought. She was right: he couldn't keep her at his place against her will. He buttoned his jacket, stepped into his boots and crammed a hat onto his head. The path he'd made to the barns, stables and garage was holding, as there hadn't been any new snow in the past couple of days. He hazarded a glance toward the sky and frowned at the dark, big-bellied clouds rolling slowly across the heavens. What would happen to her if another storm hit and she was stranded without power? What about the kid?

''Her problem,'' he told himself, but knew he was lying. Anything that happened to Lesley Bastian and her newborn daughter was going to affect him. There was just no way around it.

His boots crunched in the snow as he walked to the truck that he'd had the foresight to chain up this morning. Opening the passenger door he waited for Rambo to hop inside, then climbed behind the wheel.

The engine protested, refusing to catch on the first try, but after grinding a bit, the old motor finally fired and he rammed the transmission into first gear. Chains digging into the snow, the pickup shot forward. Carefully Chase drove down his lane, then onto the county road and past Lesley's disabled vehicle. Within minutes he was turning into the driveway that he hadn't used for nearly twenty years. The house was only a hundred feet off the main road, but the snow was deep, and the truck slid a couple of times before he was able to park near the old garage. It was an ancient building with a sagging roof where, years before, Chase had watched his father wipe the oil from his hands onto a greasy rag after working on the engines of the various farm equipment that seemed forever in need of repair.

Now he climbed out of his pickup and broke a path through the garden gate. Old hinges creaked in protest, the slats dug deep into the piled snow, but he managed to get through. Across a short yard, where he, Chet and Delia had built forts as kids, and up the back steps he trudged, stomping the snow from his boots on the back porch. The key was hidden just as she'd said. He let himself into the cold, silent kitchen and was thrown nearly twenty years back in time.

The furniture had changed, of course, and the walls had been painted a pale gold. Gone was his mother's strawberry-print wallpaper and faux-brick linoleum. Hardwood had been installed to match the cabinets, but the room configuration was the same, a different table and chairs where his parents' dinette set had once been. His boots rang hollowly as he walked down a short hallway and up the staircase to the bedroom he'd shared with Chet. Instead of twin beds with plaid comforters he saw a desk, small computer, printer and other office equipment. One wall had been shelved and was filled with books, but the old pine tree that had grown outside the house still spread its branches near the dormer window.

His sister Delia's room had been converted into a nursery, complete with crib and changing table. In the third bedroom, which had once been occupied by his parents, was a queen-size bed, antique dresser with an oval mirror and tiny bassinet.

He hurried back downstairs. Memory after painful memory flashed, like short movie clips, through his brain: his mother hanging laundry in the hot Montana sun; his father promising to make good, that he didn't need the Fortune family to bail him out; his brother waving wildly, acting like a clown as the tractor chugged up a deceptive hill. *Don't think about it,* he reminded himself as he strode through the living room and saw a gouge in the windowsill that he'd made with the heel of a boot when his argument with his twin brother had erupted into a wrestling match.

Damn it, Chet, why did you have to die?

One fist closed in frustration. It had been so long ago, and yet it seemed like yesterday. Since then so many more had left him.

"Get a grip," he told himself. He wasn't going to let old memories drag him back to times best left forgotten. He made his way to the pantry and a closet that hid a panel of circuit breakers, making sure they were all working, then relit the pilot light in the furnace.

Within seconds the unit was stoking up, sending heat through the ducts, and Chase locked up then followed a trail he'd made in previous days to the barn where her horses were stabled. Each day he'd tried to take them outside for a short period, allowing them to work off some energy by trudging or galloping through the snow-covered paddock, and today he did the same, watching as the round-bellied broodmares snorted and tossed their heads, blinking in the sunlight that sparkled against the ice and snow. They snorted loudly, the warm breath from their lungs visible in the crisp air.

How many winters had Chase trekked through the ice and snow to help his father feed the stock? How many times had he taken a hammer to the ice that had formed over the water troughs, or sawed through heavy twine with his dull jackknife after kicking heavy bales from the hay loft?

Scowling at his nostalgic thoughts, he let the horses exercise for a while, then penned them up in the barn again. One look at the sky convinced him that they were in for more snow. "God help us," he muttered, and decided that if another storm dumped even a few more inches onto the already-overburdened land, Lesley and that kid of hers would have to stay put.

He thought about telling her that he'd once lived here, that her husband had bought out his father, but decided to hold his tongue. He was a firm believer in letting sleeping dogs lie.

"But I told you I was leaving." Lesley couldn't believe her ears that evening. "We had a deal." She sat at the table, candles burning brightly as Angela slept in the next room. She and Chase were eating leftovers in the form of chicken tetrazzini which she'd altered a bit because of his sparse stock of spices and cheese.

"I intend to honor it."

"When you decide to."

"When it's safe."

"For the love of Mike!"

He glared at her as if she were a silly two-year-old. "No one's holding you prisoner, Lesley. But you've got to think of Angela." He sat across from her, his plate nearly clean, his face all angles and planes in the flickering light from the fire and candles.

"I do. All the time!" Who was he to boss her

around? "She needs to be home, and so do I. It's just time, Chase. I can't impose on you any longer."

"What you can't do is anything so foolish." As if hearing his sharp tone, he added, "Just be patient. As soon as the weather changes I'll take you home."

"You *can't* keep me here against my will!" She was on her feet in a minute, and her bad ankle seared with pain. She felt her face drain of color and she bit her tongue from crying out, but it didn't matter. Chase was at her side, and before she could say a word had swept her off her feet.

"Put me down."

"I intend to." Without much fuss he carried her to the couch and dropped her gently onto the lumpy pillows where he'd slept ever since she'd arrived. "Just take it easy."

"I can't," she admitted, still steaming. "It's against my nature."

"Then think of this as a vacation."

She snorted, and he chuckled.

"Make that a dream vacation."

"Right." She couldn't hide the sarcasm in her use of the word.

"When's the last time you were pampered?"

Shifting on the couch so that she could watch him clear the table, she shot him a look she hoped looked scathing. "There's a difference between being pampered and being held hostage."

"I'll remember that," he said drily, and the fact that he wouldn't rise to the bait only frustrated her further.

"I could call the police."

"Go right ahead," he invited, obviously amused at

her bluff. He crossed the room and sat on the battle-scarred coffee table directly in front of the couch. Resting his elbows on his knees, he stared hard and deep into her eyes. "I'm just trying to reason with you. You're laid up. Your infant isn't a week old, your Jeep is still out of commission, you live miles from town, and I'm the nearest neighbor you've got. It just doesn't make any sense for you to go back and end up stranded."

She wanted to squirm away from his stare, but she was caught, trapped like a doe in headlights. Besides, though she was loath to admit it, he had a point—well, more than one—but it riled her nonetheless. "I could call Ray."

The corners of his mouth pulled down a bit. "Who's Ray?"

"Ray Mellon is a—was a friend of Aaron's. He offered to help out when the baby came, but then Angela decided to come early, and Ray was in Phoenix visiting relatives. He's due back tomorrow."

A muscle worked in his jaw, and the intensity of his gaze caused her blood to heat unexpectedly. "Then let's talk about this when he gets back."

"Fine. I'll go along with you, Fortune," she said, bristling. "But we've got to have some kind of agreement…a deal…another one, one that you'll honor, so that we get along and you quit trying to tell me what to do."

"You want a truce?"

"I think it would be a good idea, yes."

His gaze shifted to her lips, and her breath was suddenly lost, caught between her throat and lungs. For a second she was certain he was going to kiss her. He leaned forward so close that she could feel his heat, see the pores of his skin beneath his whiskers. She licked her lips. "Deal."

She glanced up to his eyes and was mesmerized in their shadowy depths. Blue-gray. Erotic. Promising forbidden pleasures.

For a second no one said a word, and she was conscious of the thudding of her heart.

He looked away first and said something unintelligible under his breath. "I, uh, I'd better bring in some more firewood." Rolling to his feet, he strode to the back porch. As the door slammed behind him, Lesley flung herself back on the couch and slowly let out her breath. Being that close to Chase was treacherous, and they'd just agreed she was cooped up here at least for a while.

"Great," she grumbled. What was she going to do? Being stuck in close proximity to a man who could stop her heart with one swift look was just plain crazy. And yet, secretly, a part of her was excited at the prospect. If she looked deep in her heart a part of her wanted to stay for a few more days. As much as she hated to admit it, she was getting used to Chase, this cabin and being together.

"Stop it," she warned herself. Those kinds of thoughts had to be tossed aside. Just because Chase Fortune was sexy as all get-out, tough as nails one minute and gentle the next, was no reason to fantasize about him.

He just wasn't the kind of man any sane woman would fall in love with.

At that thought she froze. She wasn't falling in love! Never again. Not with Chase Fortune or anyone else for that matter.

But as she shot a glance to the window of the back porch and saw him swinging the ax, his profile in stark relief against the white backdrop of snow-laden fields and trees, she knew she was in trouble.

Big trouble.

Four

"Happy New Year." Lesley tapped the edge of her wineglass of Chardonnay to Chase's. "It's not champagne, but it'll have to do."

"Thanks." He offered her a fleeting smile but not much more. Seated on the floor in the living room, his back propped against the couch, one leg bent, the other stretched out halfway across the room, he stared at the fire.

Refusing to be put off by his bad mood, Leslie tucked her knees to her chest and glanced at Angela sleeping soundly in her drawer-crib near the couch. Rambo had taken his usual spot under the table, and the ever present fire crackled merrily in the grate. "Here's to next year, may it be filled with joy and prosperity."

"Amen." He tapped the rim of his glass to hers again and shifted so that he was staring at her. His eyes were troubled, his body tense, but he cracked half a grin. "I'm all for the prosperity part."

"Me, too." She met his gaze briefly, then looked away. The room suddenly seemed too close, creating an intimacy that caused her throat to go dry. She took a sip. The Chardonnay was cool as it slid down her throat, but still she felt uneasy.

"So tell me about your husband," he suggested,

bringing up a subject that they'd both avoided. She swallowed hard. "What happened?"

Her good mood vanished, and she twisted the stem of her wineglass nervously. "He had a heart attack while boating. Couldn't get to a hospital in time." *Because his mistress didn't know CPR.* Quickly she took another swallow. She didn't like to think about Aaron.

"No, I mean, what happened to the marriage?" His voice was low and familiar, and for a second Lesley wanted to tell him everything about her complicated life. She hesitated, and he edged a little closer, so that his leg was only inches from her, his shoulder brushing hers as they were both propped against the couch. "You haven't said as much, but I get the feeling that you weren't happy."

"Oh. Well." There was no reason to lie, she supposed. Chase deserved the truth. After all, he had saved her life. "It wasn't a marriage made in heaven, if that's what you mean."

He waited, and she drew in a long, ragged breath. How could she explain how youthful exuberance had slowly eroded to apathy, that she'd believed Aaron when he'd said the twenty-year difference in their ages wouldn't matter. "He, uh, was quite a bit older and had been married before. No kids." She twisted the wedding band she still wore on her right hand. "He'd been divorced a few years when we got married, and I thought, no, I *believed* that I loved him and he loved me and nothing else mattered. That was foolish, of course." She shot Chase a glance and felt her cheeks wash with hot color. "Naive on my part. Eventually we lost sight of each other, and he found someone else. The trouble was, I was pregnant.''

Chase's eyes narrowed, his lips compressed and every muscle in his body seemed coiled, as if he was ready for a fight, but he didn't say a word, just watched her through shadowed eyes.

''We decided to try again, to piece the marriage together, because we were going to be parents. I thought that a baby would change everything.'' She rolled her eyes at her own naiveté. ''I guess I just wanted to think we could do it. We went to a few sessions of marriage counseling. Aaron told the counselor that it was over with the other woman, and I wanted desperately to believe him.'' She laughed softly, but the sound was without any hint of mirth. ''To make a long story short, it was never the same between us. Then, one day he went fishing. Supposedly alone. That's when he died.'' Her throat grew thick, and she stared at the fire, remembering the pain, feeling the heartache of betrayal all over again. ''That was a lie, of course. He was with the same woman that he'd supposedly stopped seeing.'' Lesley lifted a shoulder. She wasn't going to dwell on Aaron and his infidelity. ''And that, as they say, was that. So now it's just Angela and me.'' And it was fine. The way it should be. She didn't need a man in her life. Certainly not one who cheated on her.

''Did you love him?''

The question jolted her, though she'd asked it of herself a thousand times. ''Aaron?'' She thought for a moment. ''In the beginning I thought I did. Now—'' she shook her head at the complexity that had become her life; once, everything had been so clear "—I'm not so sure."

"Doesn't matter, I suppose," he said. "I think love's highly overrated."

"Do you?"

"Mmm."

"Sounds like the philosophy of someone who's been burned."

"We've all been burned. It's part of living." He took a long sip from his wine, then, without glancing in her direction, said, "I think tomorrow, if you're feeling up to it, you can go home."

"Thank you, oh, master," she teased, but the joke fell flat.

He didn't so much as crack a smile. All day long his mood had eroded, and now, near midnight, he scowled darkly, wrestling with his inner demons.

"What is it with you?" she finally asked.

"What do you mean?"

"You haven't been yourself today."

"Sure I have."

"Oh, come on, Chase." She wasn't about to play word games. "Something's eating at you, and I don't think it's a great, all-encompassing sadness because Angela and I are leaving." She shook her head, her hair brushing the back of her sweater. "Nope. There's something else."

Twirling the stem of his glass between the flat of each hand, he thought for a moment. "New Year's Eve isn't my favorite time of year."

"But it's a time for new beginnings."

"Fine." He rolled to his feet as if to dismiss the

subject, but she was having none of it. Not when they'd been getting so close. "I don't think the holidays are that big a deal."

"What is it with you?" she asked.

He hesitated. "Let's just say I've got some bad memories all tied up with tinsel and red ribbon, okay?"

Lesley wasn't about to be put off. This man had seen her naked, delivered her baby, cared for her and Angela for over a week, taken the time to tend to her stock and house. The least she could do was lend a sympathetic ear.

"What happened?" she asked as he walked to the kitchen.

"I don't want to talk about it."

"Why not?"

He reached for his jacket, which was hung on a peg by the back door. "It's private."

She'd pulled herself to her feet and gritted her teeth against a twinge of pain in her ankle. Anger propelling her, she hitched her way to the kitchen. "And having a baby and talking to guardian angels isn't?"

"Leave it alone, Lesley."

"Don't put me off, Chase. If there's anything I can do—"

"There's nothing, okay? End of subject." Angrily he shoved his arms through the sleeves of his jacket and reached for his hat. "I'm gonna check on the calves. I'll be back in a while."

"It's nearly midnight."

He didn't listen, just yanked open the back door and strode into the night. "You're running from something, Fortune,'' she said under her breath, and decided to wait for him.

She fiddled around the kitchen, cleaning up, then folded clothes at the table. Nearly forty-five minutes passed and she was starting to get worried, when she heard him stomp up the steps to the back porch. A few minutes later he opened the door, and cold air rushed into the room, causing the fire to flare and the candles to flicker.

''I thought you'd be in bed.''

''I didn't think our discussion was over.''

''Sure it was.'' He hung his coat on the peg, and she noticed that his skin was flushed with cold, the pupils of his eyes wide.

''Because you say so.''

''It does take two.''

She saw red. ''You know what your problem is?''

''I have a feeling you're about to tell me.''

She elevated her chin to glare at him. ''You're always the cynic.''

''Maybe I have a reason to be.''

''Do you?'' She didn't believe it for a minute. ''Why would anyone with the last name of Fortune be cynical? You can't really believe you ever got a raw deal in life.'' The words were out before she could call them back. ''I mean—''

''You mean that just because my last name is Fortune, everything in my life had to have been perfect.'' His gaze cut like a laser.

''Well, I—''

''Sometimes things aren't what they seem.''

"No," she said, wounded deep inside. "I suppose they aren't."

He didn't answer. Just snapped off the lights in the kitchen. Angela began to fuss, and Chase carried the baby in her bed into the bedroom. He said a gruff good-night to Lesley, and she tried to push aside their argument. She'd dug too deep, it seemed. Chase was a private man, and he wasn't going to share any of his secrets with her.

Chase was up before dawn. He hadn't slept much, and his thoughts, damn them, had been all tangled up in Lesley and Angela. The thought of them leaving today bothered him, and as he rode the fence line, searching for the last five strays he hadn't located, he experienced a jab of loneliness he hadn't expected.

"Get over it," he told himself. Ulysses snorted and tossed his head; the day was bright and clear. He should have been ecstatic to be rid of his widowed neighbor and her daughter. But he wasn't. For the first time since Emily's death he felt a ray of hope, a warmth in his heart. "Idiot," he growled, and pulled on the reins, urging Ulysses up a short ridge to a copse of pine. He sensed that something wasn't right. His chest tightened. Ulysses balked, then half reared. Chase's stomach lurched. He'd found the strays. All five of them. Dead.

Happy New Year.

After helplessly surveying the scene, he climbed back in the saddle. Clucking his tongue, he turned Ulysses back toward the ranch house. This was the hard part of ranching, one he never quite reconciled himself with. A nagging sense of guilt chased him down the ridge and back to the barn. He should have been able to save those animals.

Lesley was waiting for him. Bacon was sizzling in a frying pan, hash brown potatoes warming on a side dish, biscuits steaming from a pan. She moved around the kitchen without much difficulty. She hummed as she worked, only looking up when he opened the door.

"Perfect timing," she said with a smile, as if their argument the night before had been forgotten. "Wash up and sit yourself down. I figured that since this was my last morning here, the least I could do was fix you— What happened?" Her smile disappeared.

"I found the strays."

"Oh." She shook her head. "They weren't okay?"

"Dead. All of them." He tossed his gloves over the screen by the fire and unzipped his jacket.

"I'm sorry."

"It's not your fault."

"I know, but—" Her throat felt thick, and impulsively she threw her arms around him. There was so much to him she didn't understand, so much she wanted to learn. His arms wrapped around her, and he dragged her close, burying his face in the crook of her neck, not kissing her, but clinging to her. He smelled of horses and snow and leather. His body was warm and hard, and she sighed against him. "Sometimes it's not easy."

"Sometimes it's damned hard," he replied, and, clearing his throat, let his arms fall to his sides. "You didn't have to do all this,'' he said, eyeing the breakfast.

"I wanted to. You know, Chase Fortune, I owe you a lot, and there's something I want to talk to you about.''

"Shoot.''

She cleared her throat and forked the bacon onto a plate covered with a paper towel. As he watched, she deftly cracked three eggs and dropped them into the hot pan. "It's about the water on my place.''

"Is there a problem?''

She flipped the eggs, then reached into the cupboard. "There could be.'' Handing him a chipped plate, she said, "Dish up. While it's all still hot.''

"Go on. What about your water?'' He pronged several slices of bacon and a pile of hash browns.

"I've got a well on my place, but it usually dries up around August, so I use the spring in the late summer and early fall. The spring fills a pond, and I'm able to pump enough water from it for the horses and myself.''

"Is it enough?''

"It's never been a problem before, but—'' Her shoulders stiffened a little as she added, "The spring starts here, on this place, then flows into my land. I have a lease for water rights that the previous owners signed with Aaron ten years ago. But it runs out in June. Aaron claimed that he had a verbal agreement to extend it for another ten years with the previous owner, but I've searched through all my papers and I can't find anything in writing. So…I'd like to renegotiate with you. Otherwise I'll have to drill another well, and the truth of the matter is that I can't afford it this year, or probably next.''

''We'll work something out,'' he said, picking up a couple of hot biscuits and dropping them onto his plate.

''Good. I'll call my attorney when I get settled at home again.''

''You don't have to call a lawyer.'' He settled into a chair at the scarred table and noticed that she'd set out place mats, silverware and a tiny vase with a sprig of holly in it. She filled her plate and sat across from him. A whiff of her perfume floated over the scents of bacon grease and burning wood. He was getting used to being around her, listening to her talk to herself, watching the play of firelight burnishing her hair. He slathered a biscuit with butter and tried not to noticed that her sweater hugged breasts that were probably larger than usual due to the fact that she was breast-feeding. Though she was still a little plump in her mid-section, her figure was beginning to return. She was sexy and earthy and had started to fill a dark void in his soul. A void he'd decided to live with five years before.

He couldn't get involved with her. At least not now, he thought as he crunched on crispy bacon.

He had too much to do in the next year in order to make good on his end of the bargain with Kate. He couldn't be distracted with Lesley and her baby. He'd been on that road before, and it had only led to pain.

He glanced at little Angela sleeping soundly in her makeshift bed and felt a pang of protectiveness, but he swept that ridiculous emotion away with a steel-bristled broom of determination. For the next year all he could do was concentrate on getting this miserable scrap of land out of the red and solidly into the black. No one, not even Lesley Bastian, could derail him.

Five

"We're home." The words sounded hollow as Lesley, carrying Angela in her infant seat, stepped into her empty house. As if sensing a change she didn't much like, the baby squirmed and let out an irritated cry. "Shh, sweetheart. It's okay."

But the old farmhouse felt like a tomb. It was warm enough, the lights bright, but it seemed vacant inside, without that special glow that makes a house a home.

Stop it, Lesley. You're imagining things. Fool that you are, you just don't want to leave Chase Fortune, that's all. Get over it. Setting her jaw, she walked across the kitchen and tried to ignore the fact that she experienced no sense of homecoming, no relief at being home again.

Chase carrying groceries and Rambo were right behind her. "Stay," Chase commanded the old hound as he was bounding through the door.

"No, it's all right. He can come in." Lesley had become fond of the dog and didn't want him left freezing on the back porch.

"He's wet."

"Aren't we all?" she asked, lifting her eyebrows as she stared pointedly at the snow melting on the shoulders of Chase's jacket.

Rambo, as if understanding that he was the center

of the conversation, cocked his head, then, tail tucked between his legs, slunk into the house and took up residence under the table.

Chase muttered something under his breath about "spoiled mutts who don't know their place," as he set a sack of groceries they'd picked up at the local market on the table by the window. He shifted Lesley's suitcase from one hand to the other. "Where do you want your bag?"

"Just leave it anywhere. I'll take it upstairs later."

"I'll do the honors." He didn't say anything else, but she knew he was thinking of her ankle, and it touched her in a way that surprised her. For a rawhide-tough cowboy with a stubborn streak that would give any mule a run for his money, Chase had a kinder side, as well, one she only caught glimpses of.

She tucked Angela's blanket more tightly around her and set the carrier on the counter where the baby could watch Lesley as she turned on the coffeemaker and put away the groceries.

The coffee was just beginning to drizzle through the machine when Rambo let out a low woof.

Chase's boots rang on the hallway upstairs.

A truck's engine roared down the drive. Lesley peered out the window and recognized Ray Mellon's Dodge plowing down the lane. Snow was piled on the roof of the cab and inside the bed of the truck.

"We've got company," Lesley said, winking at her baby. Aside from Chase, Ray was the first neighbor she'd seen since Angela's birth. "You'd better be on your best behavior," she whispered to the baby as Ray cut the engine and hopped down from the pickup.

Wearing a parka, wool cap and insulated pants, he hiked through the snow and stepped onto the back porch. He brushed the snow from his clothes and started to knock, but Lesley threw open the door.

"Lesley, gal!" A wide grin split his face.

"I wondered if you'd made it back from sun country."

"Just yesterday. The airports were a mess, let me tell you." He stepped into the kitchen and shook his head. "Look at you!" Giving in to impulse, he grabbed her around the waist, picked her up and twirled her off her feet. "My God, girl, I was worried sick about you and don't tell me, this—" he cocked his head to the counter where Angela, peering through wide eyes, was focusing on the ceiling "—must be your new little girl."

"Meet Angela," Lesley said as he set her on her feet. Her heart was racing, and she felt her cheeks flush.

"She's gorgeous. The spittin' image of her mother."

Laughing, Lesley caught a movement from the corner of her eye and spied Chase, his expression guarded, standing in the archway between the kitchen and dining room. "Chase, meet Ray. Ray Mellon, remember, I told you about him? He's back from Phoenix. Ray, this is Chase Fortune, my new neighbor and the man who probably saved my life and Angela's."

Chase extended his hand, and Ray, after yanking off one of his gloves, grasped Chase's palm firmly. "Glad to meet you," Ray said. "You're related to Kate?"

"Her great-nephew." Chase sized the guy up as he dropped his hand. About five feet ten inches of wiry muscle, with brown hair beginning to turn silver at the temples and eyes that didn't linger on any spot too long.

"So you're ranchin' the old Waterman place?"

"Trying."

Ray sucked in his breath and shook his head. "Good luck. I don't know what there is about that place, but it seems to be a son of a bi—" he glanced at Lesley and caught himself "—a lot of trouble to keep afloat. Anyway, I want to thank you for showin' up and takin' care of Lesley and her little one." He wrapped a friendly arm around Lesley's waist. "She's special, this one."

"Ray!" Lesley shifted out of his embrace.

"Well, you are." He winked broadly at Chase. "I always said that when Aaron got tired of her, I'd take her anyday."

"Did you?" Chase said, his back muscles coiling. He didn't like the guy for a minute.

"I think I would have a little say in that," Lesley protested, and then, as if to change the subject, added, "The coffee's almost done. Would you like a cup?"

"Nah, I can't stay. Just thought I'd see if you were home so I could take a gander at the little one." He touched a finger to Angela's cheek, and Chase had to physically restrain himself. "She's a beaut, that she is. As I said, just like her ma." He rained a too-friendly smile in Lesley's direction, and for a second Chase thought he was actually going to plant a kiss on her cheek. "I'll give you a call later. Let me know

if there's anything, and I mean it, *any*thing you need."
Chuckling, Ray let himself out the back door.

Lesley, blushing a deep scarlet, let out her breath.
"Wow."

Chase managed a calm expression, though his teeth
were clenched so tightly his jaw ached. As far as he
was concerned Ray Mellon, friend or not, was full of
hot air and not much else.

Pouring two cups of coffee, Lesley half apologized.
"Ray's well-meaning, believe me. A heart of gold,
even though he comes on a little strong."

The understatement of the year in Chase's estima-
tion, but he tried to convince himself that it didn't
matter. Ray Mellon could dance stark naked on the
top of the barn for all Chase cared. So the guy was
Lesley's friend? So what? She was entitled. He took
a couple of swigs of coffee, decided it was time to
take off, then set his cup on the counter. "I'll check
on your horses before I leave."

"You don't have to go out and—"

"I want to. Okay?"

She didn't argue. "I…I don't know what to say."

"You don't have to say anything."

She bit her lip, then, as if on a whim, she stood on
tiptoe and kissed him full on the lips. Warm, feather
soft and filled with gratitude, the kiss struck a chord
in Chase he'd thought was long dead. "Thank you,
Chase Fortune," she said huskily as she turned away
and picked up her daughter. Her green eyes seemed to
shine a little brighter this morning, as if she were fighting tears. "I wasn't kidding when I said that you saved
my life and Angela's."

"It wasn't that big a—"

"It was." She placed a hand on his forearm and squeezed. "It was a very big deal. I doubt if I'll ever be able to repay you, and that bothers me. It bothers me a lot." She swallowed hard, and her gaze locked with his. For a second he was lost in the wonder of this bit of a woman with, it seemed, a heart as big as the state of Montana. She bit the corner of her lip in a nervous gesture he found fascinating, and it was all he could do to step away. He had the overpowering urge to sweep her off her feet, kiss her until they were both weak with desire, then carry her up the stairs to her bedroom and make love until they couldn't move a muscle.

As if she understood his thoughts, she blushed, and he gave himself a hard mental shake. He was walking on thin ice here. Thin and damned dangerous. He stuffed his hands into the pockets of his jacket. "I'm just glad it all worked out."

"Me, too." Her eyes held his for a second longer, and his gut grew taut. Hell, she was beautiful.

And off-limits. Way off. As were all women.

"I'll see you later." He whistled to Rambo and opened the door. A gust of cold air shot through the house as the dog scrambled to his feet and dashed outside. With one final look at Lesley cradling her baby close, Chase shut the door firmly behind him. It was a simple gesture and yet it took all his grit and determination to walk off the porch and leave mother and daughter to fend for themselves. He reminded himself that Lesley Bastian wasn't his. Not his wife nor his mistress nor even his damned girlfriend. She was only his neighbor, a woman who'd gotten herself into a little trouble that he'd helped ease. Nothing more. That's the way it was and, curse it to hell, that's the way it had to be.

But he found his cabin empty when he returned home. Empty and cold, though a fire burned brightly in the fireplace. He spied the sprig of holly in the tiny pitcher she'd used as a vase, and he picked it up, twirling it between his callused fingers. The cabin smelled of whatever perfume she used, soap and baby powder, and his bed, crisply made, the sheets clean, looked sterile and frigid.

She and that kid of hers had been in his life little more than a week, and he missed them. More than he'd ever thought possible. His thoughts took a dark turn to Emily and Ryan, but he found them farther from him than they had been; the pain had dulled with time, and, he suspected, Lesley.

He did his chores by rote, called Kate and reported in, ate sparingly and, much later, when the moon was high, he showered and told himself he wouldn't call Lesley, didn't need to know how she was doing; yet he stared out the window to the darkness beyond. Moonlight cast a silver glow on the snow that blanketed the ground and clung to the branches of the trees. Far in the distance golden patches of warm light shone through the narrow windows of the old farmhouse where he'd grown up, the farmhouse Lesley and Angela now occupied. In his mind's eye he saw her stand on her tiptoes, tilt her head and, with her eyes wide open, kiss him as she had this afternoon. He'd thought of little else since then.

Loneliness, an emotion he'd forced himself to keep under tight rein, pierced deep into his soul. He'd lost everyone close to him one way or another. His twin, Chet, a reckless youth, had made the mistake of driving the old tractor up a ridge a little too fast. The front wheels had hit a rock and bounced, flipping the rig over and pinning Chet beneath it.

Chase had seen it all, had run to the top of the hill crying and screaming, knowing that his brother was already dead. Chet's lifeless body had been in his nightmares ever since, and the tragedy had torn the family apart. His father gave up whatever ambition he'd once claimed, his mother had gotten sick and died of cancer, a disease unrelated to her son's death, or so they were told. Chase had never believed it: Constance Fortune's will to live, to fight, had been robbed of her when her boy died. That left Delia, always self-absorbed, to turn inward. Delia went through life these days unconnected to her family.

And what about you?

He didn't want to look too closely into the mirror of his own soul, didn't need to face his inner demons. He didn't believe in dwelling on pain, nor discussing it with any Tom, Dick or Harry. Nor would he talk to a psychiatrist or counselor of any sort. Nope. He believed in healing himself, and the best way he could cope with all the pain of the past was to ignore it, to bury himself in his work, to find another purpose in his life.

He'd tried marriage and it had only added to his

pain. He gritted his teeth as he thought of Emily. Sweet, sad Emily. And Ryan. His only son. A boy who hadn't lived long enough to see his first birthday.

The old ache burned through him.

Angry at the turn of his thoughts, he shoved another length of oak into the fire and sat at the kitchen table where he'd been going over the books. He punched figures into a calculator and scratched notes to himself as he pored over the accounting records and tax returns for the previous decade.

The Waterman place had been going downhill for years, it seemed, but Chase discovered ways to cut corners, to sell at higher prices, to reduce his overhead while upping his production of grain and cattle. It looked possible to make good on his bargain with Kate, even though a year was a short turn-around time. He spent hours huddled over the books until, sometime after one o'clock, Rambo whined to go outside.

Rubbing the back of his neck, Chase opened the door. Rambo wandered across the snow-covered backyard, disappeared around the corner, then in less than a minute reappeared, nose to the ground, as if he could scare up a rabbit or pheasant at this late hour. "Give it up, boy," Chase advised. Cold air slapped his face and ripped through his sweatshirt, but it helped clear his head of the numbers he'd been crunching.

With a disappointed snort, Rambo scrambled into the warmth of the house again. Chase shut the door and walked to the table. Despite all his efforts to find an answer, there was one dilemma that wasn't about to go away—no matter how he tackled it. Walking to the table, he looked over his projected profit-and-loss

statement for the dozenth time. It just wasn't possible.
"Hell." He wadded up the paper in frustration, because no matter how he adjusted the figures, when it
came to productivity, he had a problem. A serious one.
If he really wanted to ensure that the ranch would
become profitable in the next year, that he would be
able to fulfill his part of the deal with Kate and end
up owning these barren acres, he couldn't sell water
rights to anyone. Including Lesley Bastian.

Six

"**I** don't get it. I just don't get it." Jeff Nelson leaned back in his chair and tossed his hair from his eyes. At seventeen he was more interested in girls and basketball than algebra.

"You're doing fine. Just keep working at it," Lesley said as she corrected his homework. Jeff was one of seven students she tutored in high-school-level math. It brought in a little extra money, and she wouldn't have to think about a second job. She could stay at home with Angela.

"Algebra's impossible." He scooped up his book and stretched as he got out of his chair. At six foot four, he was still growing.

"Don't get discouraged."

He snorted. "I'm *way* past discouraged," he said, then flashed her his killer smile. As they walked out of the den, Lesley peeked in on Angela, who was sleeping soundly, her thumb tucked between her tiny lips.

"I'll see you on Tuesday," Lesley said once they were down in the kitchen, and she marked her calendar, noticing that today was Valentine's Day. Her first Valentine's Day alone in a long time. Not that it mattered, she supposed. As Jeff ambled out the back door she remembered last Valentine's Day and the single rose Aaron had bought from a roadside vendor. She'd been touched, until she'd found his credit card bills a month after he'd died and seen a bill for an expensive bouquet that went through on the fourteenth of February.

"Live and learn," she told herself as she wiped some crumbs from the table and wondered what Chase was doing. She'd seen more of him than she'd expected in the past month. He seemed to feel that she was somehow his responsibility, which was ridiculous.

But, if she was honest with herself, she'd have to admit that she didn't mind the attention. Not one little bit. Just as long as he didn't push her around too much.

He made sure her livestock was cared for, that her Jeep, after it had been pulled from the ditch and repaired, was safe, and that she made it to her doctor's appointments on time.

However, he kept his distance and didn't get closer to her, avoided touching her, and he smiled rarely. He'd come in for coffee a couple of times, but whenever she'd asked him to come to dinner or join her for an outing, he had quickly declined.

"Oh, well, nothing ventured, nothing gained," she told herself as she picked up the receiver and dialed his number. The phone rang eight times and no one answered, which wasn't much of a surprise as the man was out of the house more than he was inside and he had some antiquated aversion to answering machines. "Get into the nineties, Fortune, before they're gone!" she reprimanded as if he could hear her, then hung up. She could just give up, she supposed, but that wasn't her nature.

Angela started making noises upstairs, and Lesley decided it was time for some exercise. She raced up the stairs and found her daughter lying on her back in her crib, small arms flailing, face beginning to turn red as she started to cry. "No reason to fuss," Lesley said, feeling her breasts let-down and milk begin to flow. "I'm right here."

After feeding, changing and dressing the baby in a snug snowsuit, Lesley strapped Angela into her front pack and, with a card she'd picked up at the store—one with a funny message rather than the kind with a hearts and flowers message of undying love—she hiked the distance between the two ranches. It was cold as the dickens outside; the wind blew hard and snow still covered the ground; but the pale winter sun lingered in the Montana-blue sky and Lesley felt light-hearted as she walked up Chase's lane.

She hadn't been back to the small cabin since her short, emotional stay with him over the Christmas holidays, and she felt ridiculously as if she were coming home. "Idiot," she muttered under her breath, and sensed Angela stirring against her. "You know, don't you, that your mother's a bona fide fool?"

Rambo, lying on the front porch, barked a greeting and stood slowly, his tail whipping behind him. "I missed you, too, boy," she said as the front door opened and Chase in jeans and a flannel shirt stood behind the torn mesh of the screen door. He didn't smile, and she had the uneasy sensation that she was interrupting him.

Suddenly she was tongue-tied. "Hi," she managed, wishing she hadn't been so darned impulsive. What was she doing here? What possible excuse could she come up with? None. She had to go through with her plan.

"Come in." He held the door for her. "Is something wrong?"

"No. Uh, I just wanted some exercise." Good Lord, she sounded like a moron. "I came over here because...because it's Valentine's Day and I bought a card for you and...I'm rambling aren't I?" She unstrapped the baby, and Chase took her pack in his big hands. As she unzipped her jacket, he retrieved Angela from the pack. "I sound like a complete and utter ninny."

"Not at all." But he couldn't quite swallow his sudden smile, and his eyes, a second before so serious, lit with amusement. "She's growing," he observed as if to change the awkward conversation.

"All the time."

His expression was gentle as he looked at the baby. "Don't you think it's too cold to take her outside?"

"If I did, I wouldn't have taken the risk," she replied. Chase's concern for Angela touched her even if he was a little pushy about it.

"They're fragile."

"Of course they are. Believe me, I'm careful with her."

He nodded curtly. "I know you are." She sensed he wanted to say something else, but bit his tongue.

While he was paying attention to Angela, Lesley left the card on the table where she and he had shared so many meals. The drop leaf was covered with receipts, a general ledger book and calculator. "I thought I could repay you a little for all you've done for me," she said. "I was hoping you might come to dinner."

His head snapped up. "Tonight?"

"If it's not a problem."

He hesitated, and Lesley's heart plummeted as she realized he was trying to come up with an excuse, *any* excuse to decline. Oh, this was a stupid, impetuous idea. She should have asked him over any other night, but not tonight. Not on the night that was set aside each year for lovers.

The phone rang before the silence had become too awkward, and balancing the baby, he plucked the receiver from its cradle and barked a cold, "Hello." He managed a brief, soulless smile at Lesley while still holding Angela. "Oh, hi." His shoulders relaxed. "Pretty good. Just tryin' to turn this place around. Nothin' much to report." He laughed then, and the sound was rich and deep, reminding Lesley of the few times he'd relaxed during their week together. "Yeah, same to you. Happy Valentine's Day. Don't worry. I'm fine, Kate…Lesley? She's here right now." He looked at her, and their gazes locked. "The baby's doing great. Thanks, I will." He hung up and walked to the woodstove where an enamel pot was sitting. "That was my great-aunt Kate," he said, pouring two cups of coffee. "Checking up on me, her investment and you."

Still holding Angela in one arm, he handed one of the full cups to Lesley.

"I've never met her. Why would she even ask about me?"

"Maybe she's just nosy." Chuckling, he picked up his cup and thought for a minute. "I'm just kidding. She's interested in everything that goes on here, and I told her about you and the baby." He frowned a little, as if that particular thought bothered him, and Lesley took a long sip from her cup. The house was about the same as when she'd left, except that over the mantel there was a picture of a pretty blond woman holding a baby. As if drawn to the photo, Lesley walked to the fireplace. "Who's this?" she asked. The woman's hair was blowing in her face as she sat on a boulder, but she was smiling brightly and squinting into the sun.

He hesitated. "That was Emily. My wife."

The words settled like doom in the cabin. "Your wife?" she said weakly, then gave herself a swift mental kick. Of course he'd been with other women. Why would it surprise her that he'd been married?

"She's holding my son."

"I, um, I didn't know that—"

"They're both gone now," he said, as if he needed to clear the air. "They died a few years back."

Her heart was suddenly heavy. Tears sprang to her eyes. "Oh, Chase, I'm so sorry," she said, turning and seeing a glimpse of his anguish, a flash of tragic sorrow in his eyes, before his jaw was set again and that rigid wall of disinterest was firmly back in place.

"I am, too," he admitted, his voice thicker than usual.

"Why didn't you tell me?"

"No reason to dwell on it," he said, and before she

could ask what happened, she realized the subject was closed and the cabin seemed colder somehow.

"I didn't even know you'd been married."

"As I said, I don't think about it. It's the past. Over and done."

"But it still hurts," she said automatically, then wished she'd held her tongue as his expression shifted and he was once again the taciturn, unapproachable cowboy she'd first met weeks ago.

"Oh. Well." She took a long sip from her cup and made excuses to leave. If Chase wanted to shut her out, to pretend that the pain of his past didn't exist, so be it. For the first time since the days right after Angela's birth she felt out of place in the cabin that had once seemed so cozy.

"What time's dinner?" he asked, as she slid her arms through her jacket. So he was planning to come. She was surprised, but tried not to show it.

"Whatever works for you. Seven?"

"Fine. I'll be there. You want a lift home?"

She shook her head and yanked on her gloves. "The whole point of coming over here was to stretch some seldom-used muscles. I'll see you later." She placed Angela inside her front pack and felt a ridiculous bit of lightheartedness as she made her way back to her place.

It was silly, really. Chase was her neighbor, a man who had helped her during a difficult time in her life. Nothing more. That's the way he wanted it and the way she wanted it. But she hummed to herself as she cooked, and she paid special attention to cleaning the house.

"Grow up," she told herself angrily, but the smile that toyed at the corners of her mouth wouldn't disappear.

Chase kicked himself up one side and down the other as he drove the short distance to Lesley's house. What was he doing accepting her invitation to dinner, feeling tense and excited and suddenly concerned about how close he'd shaved? He couldn't get involved with her. Wouldn't.

And yet he couldn't stop himself. He'd jumped at the chance to be alone with her and Angela again, read the funny card she'd left for him half a dozen times. He felt foolish arriving with a bottle of wine, like a schoolboy with a corsage for his prom date, but he hauled it with him nonetheless.

She greeted him at the door, and he was stunned. He'd never seen her dressed up before. In a black skirt, white silk blouse and some kind of suede vest, she was more than striking. Her hair was pinned back, a touch of lipstick glistening on her lips, and a smile as warm as South Florida causing a dimple to crease one cheek. "I thought you might back out," she teased.

"Why would I do that?" He handed her the bottle of wine and she lifted an already-arched brow.

"Just a feeling I got. That you'd rather avoid me."

He walked into her house and shoved his hands into the pockets of his jacket. "Sometimes I think it would be wiser."

"Why's that?"

"It keeps life less complicated."

"And that's what you want? No complications?"

"Let's just say I've had more than my share."

Her smile faded slightly. "I'll let you in on a secret, Chase. We all have. Come inside and take a load off. I'll try to keep things uncomplicated for you." He knew she was needling him, but he let it pass as he walked into the kitchen where he'd grown up. The house smelled of baked ham, scalloped potatoes and lemon in the form of a meringue pie that she cut after he'd devoured two helpings of the main course. True to her word, she kept the conversation light, and if she flirted with him at all, it was at a shallow level that didn't delve too deep. Several times he thought about bringing up the problem with granting her water rights, but the perfect moment never seemed to arise, and he didn't want to spoil the mood of comradery they'd found.

He even let a few of his old barriers break down and couldn't resist the baby. She'd grown over the past month and a half, her eyes more focused, her tiny body filling out. Chase and Lesley played with Angela until she nodded off, and then they were completely alone.

That's when the trouble began.

He knew he should leave, that being with her any longer was begging for a kind of trouble he didn't want, but as they sat on the couch in the living room, the panes of the windows misting, candles flickering on the mantel, he couldn't find the words to say goodbye.

She was tense beside him, her leg close to his, her shoulder brushing his own. The room was too intimate, way too close. He yanked at the neck of his sweater. Couldn't breathe.

"I'm glad you came," she said.

"I'm glad you invited me." Oh, hell, he sounded so stiff and formal.

"I wish, I mean, I'd like—" She turned and stared deep into his eyes. "I don't want you," she said. "I...I don't want this, but—"

So there it was.

"But—I do."

His mouth was dry as he stared into eyes that glimmered like a forest in the rain. "I know."

She licked her lips, and he was undone.

His groin throbbed. His heart raced, and he saw her pupils widen as he slowly lowered his head. "This is a mistake," he whispered.

"A big one." An enticing flush crept up her neck, and he couldn't resist the temptation to wrap his arms around her and kiss her. Her lips parted willingly, her body molded to his, and if he felt any bit of resistance in her it quickly disappeared.

Don't do this, Fortune. Stop now, while you still can, a nagging voice inside his head insisted. But the kiss deepened and she let out a soft moan. His tongue slipped between her lips, his pulse raced and fire danced through his blood. One of his hands tangled in her hair, and her head lolled backward, exposing more of her throat. Deep inside, he began to burn, the heat between his legs becoming an ache. He slipped her vest off her shoulders and parted her blouse with fingers that felt clumsy with the small buttons.

Her breasts were full and spilled over the top of her bra. He kissed each rounded mound, then lowered a lacy strap, exposing her nipple, dark and dusky, hard as a button. With a groan he lowered his head and suckled, his lips teasing, his tongue lapping and the taste of milk filling his mouth.

Her fingers slid through his hair and held him close, her breath, in short pants, hot against his scalp.

Though he knew he was making a mistake, fording a river he wouldn't ever be able to cross again, he slipped her blouse and bra off her body, tossed his own sweater onto the growing heap of discarded clothes on the floor and kissed her everywhere. He half expected her to resist him, to tell him that she couldn't continue with the madness of lovemaking, but she arched against him and as he eased her skirt over her hips, she quivered with desire. "Chase," she said, but it wasn't a protest.

God, help me, he thought as she helped peel his jeans down his legs and he was naked as she, his body lying muscle to muscle over hers. Warm and willing, she stared up at him as he gently nudged her knees apart with his own.

"Lesley," he whispered, "sweet, sweet Lesley. I—"

"Shh, Chase. This is good," she said as if she could read the protests forming in his mind. Her eyes shined a vibrant green, her lush body was rosy with passion, her arms wrapped around his torso.

His erection throbbed and he knew that she was the only woman on earth who could assuage the ache deep in his body, the only one who could soothe the anguish in his soul. Staring deep into her eyes, he thrust into the welcoming warmth of her body.

She gave out a lusty cry, and he withdrew only to plunge forward again.

"Please," she whispered, tossing her head, her hair a fiery mass on the couch cushions. "Oh, please—"

He didn't stop. Sinew and muscle and bone seemed centered in that one spot between his legs. Sweat dotted his forehead and ran down his back. His brain thundered, his body strained as he held back, making love to her slowly until he saw the widening of her pupils. He felt the shift of her body beneath his, heard her breath catch, and he lost control. With a primal roar he let go, spilling himself inside her, feeling the release as he fell against her, flattening her breasts and kissing her as he'd never kissed another woman in all of his life.

Seven

"So, you've been seein' a lot of Chase Fortune, eh?" Ray Mellon had stopped by and was leaning over the top rail of the fence that separated the barnyard from the garden, where Lesley was planting a row of corn. The May sun was warm, the earth smelling fresh and wet, as winter had disappeared a month ago.

"We're neighbors," she said, wiping the mud from her gardening gloves before sticking them into the pocket of her apron, where she kept her unopened packages of seeds. "And he's been good enough to come over and help me out once in a while."

"I heard," Ray drawled, and Lesley bristled. She didn't like the idea of being the subject of gossip in Larkspur. "I guess it makes sense. You need a man around here to help out with some of the chores, and Chase, well, we know that he's connected to the place." He reached into his breast pocket for a pack of cigarettes and slid a glance at her from under the wide brim of his cowboy hat.

"I'm not so sure I *need* a man," she said as he lit up and waved his match out with the help of a cool spring breeze that raced across the land.

"Maybe that was a bad choice of words, but Chase

would certainly be the likely candidate as he's so familiar with your spread.''

"Familiar?'' she repeated, her eyes straying to a movement in the paddock near the barn. A sorrel foal with a crooked blaze and three white stockings was kicking up his heels, long, spindly legs flashing in the afternoon sunlight.

"Yeah, bein' as he lived here.''

"Wait a minute.'' Her attention was suddenly riveted on Ray. "He didn't live here. I thought he ranched in Wyoming and Western Washington and—''

"He did. But he was raised here.'' Ray's eyebrows drew together thoughtfully, and he took a long pull on his filter tip. "His folks owned this place.''

"Zeke Fortune was his father,'' she said, wondering why she'd never made the connection. She knew Chase was related somehow to Zeke, of course, but there were so many branches of the Fortune clan that she had never put two and two together and Aaron never spoke much about Zeke Fortune.

"You didn't know?''

"He never mentioned it,'' she said, stung. Why? Yes, Chase was a guarded man, a man who valued his own privacy, but they'd become so close, and this was not just any little topic he'd avoided.

"Well, I can't say as I blame him. A lot of bad memories here for him.'' Ray pointed a finger toward the north field where the grass was growing long and green as it climbed up a ridge. "That spot up there is where the tractor that killed Chase's twin brother overturned, pinning poor Chet beneath it.''

Lesley's stomach turned over. She thought she might be sick. "I had no idea." Her heart twisted painfully.

Shaking his head, Ray smoked for a few minutes. "That was the beginning of the end for Zeke's family," he thought aloud. "Once Chet died, the rest of the family fell apart at the seams."

Lesley felt as cold inside as all of winter. Only on a few occasions did Chase mention his family, and whenever he did, it was in broader terms that included his great-aunt and various cousins.

"Well, I'd best be gettin' along. I just wanted to see how you and that baby of yours were doin'."

"We're okay," she said automatically. "Angela's down for her nap right now, but she's growing like a weed."

"They all do." Stomping out his cigarette with the toe of his worn boot, he eyed the small herd of horses grazing near the barn. "Let me know if you ever want to sell any of your stock. I just might be interested." His gaze narrowed thoughtfully on her bay broodmare. "Matter of fact, I could use three or four."

"I'm not interested in selling," she said, refusing to give in just yet. Sure she had bills and a mortgage that didn't seem to quit, but her horses were the reason she stayed here. She planned to sell off a few, of course, maybe later in the summer, but not yet, not when she was feeling the pinch of desperation tug at her wallet.

"Fair enough. When you are, just give me a jingle."

Lesley watched him climb into his old truck and

leave, but she wasn't thinking about the plume of blue exhaust that followed Ray's pickup or his offer of buying some of her horses.

Absently she pulled on her gloves and dropped dried corn into the freshly turned earth. She worked by rote, not having to concentrate, her thoughts instead turned toward Chase.

They'd been lovers for three months, and though she felt lighthearted whenever she was around him, she'd suspected that something was bothering Chase. Something important. He hadn't said a word, been more than attentive, but beneath his smile, he was guarded. Lesley had told herself she was being sensitive, that he was just working hard to turn his ranch around, that he seemed distant because of his worry about his bargain with Kate, but deep inside she felt it was something more, something deeper, something to do with her.

She'd convinced herself she was imagining things, but now she wasn't so sure. She looked around her ranch and saw it through new eyes. Aaron hadn't bought the life insurance he'd promised, and Lesley had been making payments to the bank on the mortgage rather than keeping up with repairs. The farmhouse needed a fresh coat of paint and new gutters, the barn could be reroofed in the next couple of years, and each time she did a wash, she crossed her fingers that the old washer and dryer wouldn't give out on her. Despite its problems, however, these weary acres were home. Her home. Angela's home.

Never once had she thought that it might have been Chase's. Why hadn't he confided in her, she wondered as she added fertilizer to her fresh row of corn, then turned dirt over the exposed kernels. Well, he was due over tonight, and she'd find out why he was being so secretive. She'd just started for the house when she heard Angela's whimper. "I'm coming, I'm coming," she called, running up the back steps and unlacing her boots. She had a half hour before her next student arrived, and in that time she would be able to feed and change the baby. Later, after she'd finished tutoring for the day, she'd talk to Chase. He was scheduled to come over this evening, anyway. Good. It was time to have it out with him.

Chase punched out the numbers of his great-aunt's office and waited while the line connected. He hated calling Kate, but decided he had no option. He expected to hear Kelly Sinclair's cheery voice on the other end of the line, but was connected directly to Kate.

"Don't tell me you've been demoted," he joked.

"Chase!" She chuckled. "No such luck, I'm afraid."

"Didn't think so."

"I was wondering when I'd hear from you. As for answering the phone, well, Kelly's had to take a couple of weeks off." She hesitated, as if she wanted to say something more but didn't.

"Even Kate Fortune's secretary deserves a vacation."

"Yes, well, it's not that. It's not your concern. You called me with what I assume is a report on the ranch."

He launched into a quick report about the old Waterman place, about projected hay yield, wheat crop and cattle. Most of the calves had been born, he'd only lost a couple of heifers, the wheat was in, and he'd begun mending weak spots in the fence line while inoculating and tagging the herd. He mentioned that he'd been seeing Lesley and her baby, as well, but didn't add that he'd begun to suspect that Kate was pulling his strings—that she'd not only inherited the Waterman place as payment for a bad debt, but also that she'd chosen it specifically to put him in close proximity with his old home. Anything else relied too heavily on coincidence, and Chase wasn't one to believe in providence in a situation such as this.

Finally he got to the problem at hand.

"There's just no way around it, Kate," Chase admitted. "I can't divert any water to Lesley Bastian or anyone else without charging them." In frustration he raked his fingers through his hair with one hand while holding on to the receiver with another.

"And Lesley needs the water in order to keep her ranch afloat?" Kate surmised aloud.

"So she claims."

"Do you think she'd lie?"

"No!" he said vehemently, surprised at the strength of his convictions. Lesley was nothing if not honest. Brutally honest at times.

"How's that little girl of hers?"

Chase's gut clenched, and he felt an unlikely sense of protection toward the infant. "Growing. Smiling. Holding her head up and looking around."

"Sounds like you see a lot of her."

"Sometimes," he admitted. The truth of the matter was that Lesley and her daughter intrigued him more than he'd ever thought possible. More than he wanted to admit. He was getting too close to them, too tangled up in emotions that were dangerous, but he couldn't help himself. He knew the pain that came with love, the torture of losing a child, and he had no intention of risking his heart again. But his intentions seemed to crumble each and every time he looked at mother and daughter. "That's what makes this situation more difficult," he admitted warily. "Because Lesley and her baby are good friends."

"Mmm." Kate seemed to understand all too well what Chase was going through, as if, despite his being vague, she could see into the conflict raging in his soul. "Well then, I guess it's something you'll have to work out." Any hope he'd had of getting some sound advice from his aunt was instantly quelled. And, he supposed, she was right to keep her opinions to herself. This was his personal dilemma, part of figuring out how to turn his ranch around, as well as deal with his neighbors and friends. The trouble was Lesley Bastian was more than a neighbor. More than a friend. A lot more.

Lesley lifted Angela onto her shoulder and, humming under her breath, gently rubbed the baby's back. Within seconds Angela's little body stiffened, her head bobbed and she let out a burp. "Feel better?" Lesley said to the squirming little body. It was amazing how close she felt to this little lump of flesh who couldn't talk, couldn't walk, couldn't do much more than watch her with round eyes that were curious and bright and offer a smile that was a reflection of Lesley's own grin.

She set the baby in a mechanical swing that gently rocked, then finished peeling potatoes, her thoughts centered on Chase. He'd been a godsend, more of a guardian angel than the one she'd seen or imagined while in the throes of labor. Whenever he came over, he fed the horses and checked on the buildings as well as expressed more than a little concern about the baby. He'd shored up a broken step, replaced several shattered windowpanes in the barn, exchanged worn-out washers in the faucets with new ones, sawed down a dead tree that was threatening to fall on the back porch and offered advice about the baby. In return she cooked for him, and after they ate and Angela had gone to bed, they watched television, listened to music, talked and made love.

But Chase never spent the night.

There was always a reason he'd left before dawn, throwing on his clothes in the darkness and stopping to look in on Angela before he crept down the stairs. Lesley had accepted whatever excuse he'd given her; now, in light of what Ray had said, she wondered if his explanations had been simple platitudes that never really touched the heart of the matter.

She heard his truck pull into the drive and watched as he parked, climbed out of the cab and, with a quick look at the house, walk to the barn. Rambo ran ahead, nose to the ground, flushing a robin from a bush near the garage. ''I think it's time for a showdown,'' Lesley said to Angela as she found the baby's snowsuit. While Angela gurgled, kicked and smiled, Lesley bundled her up and placed her in the front pack.

Outside, the wind was racing across the land, smelling fresh and wet, tangling in Lesley's hair as she pushed through the gate and walked across the gravel-strewn parking area to the barn. The door gave way and the scents of warm horseflesh and aging leather greeted her. The light was dim, but she saw Chase, pitchfork in hand, tossing forkfuls of hay into the manger. Broodmares and foals peered at him with wide, liquid eyes.

He glanced at her and noticed the backpack. "Kind of cold out here for the baby, isn't it?"

"She's fine."

"Little things are tender." He slit the strings on another bale.

"Since when did you get to be such an expert?" she asked, and she noticed his eyes darken.

"I've brought a lot of calves and foals into the world."

"I know, I know, just like you helped with Angela's birth, and, trust me, I appreciate the advice, but she's fine."

"Whatever you say." He didn't seem convinced, but she let it go. Walking along the length of stalls, she patted one velvet-soft nose after another and watched as the horse's ears flicked with the changes in the conversation. As if they felt the tension in the air, they were restless, tails switching, hooves shifting in the straw.

"Why didn't you tell me you used to live here?" she asked.

He was shaking hay into one manger, but stopped, every muscle in his body coiling. For a second he seemed about to disagree with her, to deny that he'd ever set foot on these acres before meeting her, but instead he thrust his pitchfork into a bale and leaned his hips against the slats of a stall door. Dust motes swirled, and one of the horses let out a nervous whinny.

"I've been meaning to tell you."

"Have you? When?"

His mouth tightened at the corners and his gray eyes, usually so warm, turned frigid. "Whenever the time was right. It just never seemed to be."

"Zeke Fortune was your father."

"Yep. Zeke, Jr."

She let out her breath and glanced to the ceiling where the last rays of sunlight were burning through the circular window in the hayloft. "Some people around here think Aaron took advantage of him. Aaron didn't seem to think so."

"Dad was desperate to sell."

"Why?"

"The gossip mill hasn't given you the rest of the story?"

"I don't listen to gossip."

He inclined his head and proceeded to tell her about Chet's death and how it had affected his parents. "When the bank threatened to foreclose on the ranch,

Dad sold out to the highest bidder, which wasn't all that high.''

"Aaron," she said numbly.

"Bingo."

"I...I didn't know." All the starch left her and she felt suddenly sad and somehow responsible for Chase's pain as well as that of his family.

"Now you do."

Tears of shame burned behind her eyes, and her soul wrenched at the pain this man had borne. "You should have told me."

"Why?"

The question hung between them, seeming to echo against the dusty rafters and bounce against the walls of her heart. "I don't know," she admitted, feeling Angela snuggled against her. "But I think—I think I should have known."

He stepped closer, and she smelled his own particular scent, that of leather and a musky aftershave. "Would it have made a difference?"

"In how I feel about you?"

"In anything."

"I don't know," she admitted, and wished he would fold her into the safety and security of his arms.

"Well, don't worry about it," he said, standing close enough to touch. "There's something else I should have told you."

She braced herself. His tone convinced her that it wasn't good news. "What is it?" she asked, and noticed a tic beneath the corner of one of his eyes. "It's about the water rights, Lesley.'' Her heart sank, and she couldn't believe her ears. "If I want to make sure the place is profitable, I can't allow any of the water from the spring to be diverted. Not even for you.''

Eight

"So, I think, under the circumstances, it would be best if we...if we—" Lesley's voice broke, and she felt like an utter fool as she stared into Chase's eyes. They'd come to an impasse over the water rights.

"Better if we didn't see each other anymore," Chase finished for her. He was seated in the cab of his truck, ready to make tracks, the engine idling. Their usual routine had fallen apart after last week's announcement that he couldn't provide her with the water she needed. The tension between them had been unbearable, the strain and worry keeping Lesley awake at night. It was more than a simple issue of water, really: Lesley had begun to depend upon him and their relationship had become tense because of it.

"Yes," she said, dying inside. She was holding Angela who, as if sensing the drama unfolding around her, had begun to fuss.

Rambo, seated in the truck beside Chase, let out a low, unhappy whine.

"What ever you want, Lesley."

It's not what I want. What I want is you, Chase Fortune. Can't you see that? But I need to know that you want me, too. "Good." She forced a smile and prayed that the tears stinging her eyes weren't visible. "But we can still be—"

"Neighbors," he said, cutting her off.

"Right. Neighbors." She blushed. Of course they couldn't be friends. Not now. Not ever. They'd shared too much.

He reached out the open window as if to pat Angela's head, and then with a tightening of his jaw, withdrew his hand before the tips of his fingers twined in the soft, dark curls. As if he'd thought better of the intimate gesture. Lesley's heart cracked, and she realized as he rammed the truck into gear and stepped on the gas, how much she loved him and how foolish it was.

"I told you I'd buy the whole lot," Ray Mellon offered. Lesley stood with one arm folded over the top rail of her fence as she watched the foals frolic, racing from one end of the paddock to the other only to wheel and dash back, tails aloft, nostrils flared, eyes bright and wild.

"I know." The summer sun was warm against her back, a bit of a breeze toying with the wisps of hair that had escaped her ponytail. Angela was balanced on her one hip and showing interest in her earring.

Lesley had worked her fingers to the bone these past few months. The rewards of her labor—a garden that promised full bounty, students who were managing to graduate, a baby who was lively, healthy and bright, and a ranch that was running on a shoestring—should have given her some peace of mind, a reason to pat herself on the back, but she couldn't. Because August was looming on the horizon, and already there were signs of depleting water.

"So Fortune won't grant you water rights?" Ray asked, as if reading her mind.

"There's a problem," she admitted, and wished she'd never set eyes on Chase Fortune. Since the day she'd broken off her love affair with him, she'd seen much less of him. He had still dropped by, still somehow figured it was his duty to look in on her and Angela time and again, but their conversations were always stilted, and the joy she felt at seeing him was tempered by the realization that he was self-centered and single-minded and could never be more than an acquaintance who had once been her lover. The hard part was the way he stared at Angela when he thought Lesley wasn't looking. Her heart broke into a billion pieces when she recognized his pain, felt his anguish.

"Well, maybe we could work something out," Ray offered, bringing her crashing back to the present. "You know, Lesley, I always felt you and me, we had something special. I don't hang around just because you're Aaron's widow."

"I, um, appreciate that," she said, but cringed inside. She thought of Ray as a friend. Nothing more.

"And keep in mind that I'd buy your herd in an instant, especially that sturdy little sorrel mare." His eyes narrowed a bit. "She's a feisty one, she is, the way I like all my women." With a laugh that ended in a cough he slapped the top rail of the fence. "I'll see ya, honey," he said, and touched the top of Angela's head, though his eyes never left Lesley's face. "Think about what I've said. I'm serious. I think you're as pretty as anything I've ever seen and—" his eyes shifted away for a second before he looked at her again; when he did she saw a flicker of lust in his gaze and her insides withered "—I could use a good woman."

"I don't think I have to think about it, Ray," she said hastily. She wasn't interested in any man—any man but Chase. "I'll sell you the mare and maybe a couple of other horses, but that's it." She met his gaze directly, just so that he wouldn't get the wrong idea. "Angela and I are doing fine. Just fine. With or without Chase Fortune's damned water." That was a lie, of course, but she pasted on a brave smile.

Ray's mouth twisted into an odd, knowing frown. "You don't have to make excuses, Lesley. Aaron and me, we go back a lot of years. I know how much money this place makes or should I say, doesn't make. I thought maybe you and me, well, we could work things out between us, become sort of a team, but—" he lifted a tired shoulder "—if that ain't the case, then I might be interested in buying you out. I know how much the mortgage is, and I'd give you enough above that so as you'd have yourself a tidy little profit. You could rent the house back from me or buy a place in town."

Lesley was stunned at his offer. "I—I'm not interested in selling."

"I know, honey, I know," he said, and reached into his shirt pocket for his cigarettes. "But there are times in a man's life—well, a woman's, too, I suppose— where he has to do something he doesn't like much." His gaze fell onto Angela's dark crown. "Sometimes we have to think about what's best for those who depend on us."

Lesley felt a lump clog her throat.

"When Aaron died, I told myself I'd look after you, and even though it didn't turn out quite the way I thought, I'll make good on my offer." His smile was benign. "Maybe it's time you faced the fact that this place is too much for you."

Never, she thought foolishly, her pride wounded as he lit his cigarette and headed to his truck. Though his offer seemed to come from his heart, she couldn't just give up her home, Angela's home. Or could she? Wouldn't financial security be worth something? A house in town, paid for, with no worries about water rights, the fluctuating price of oats, harsh weather or complicated foaling. She could get a teaching job, have a steady income, and even if she wasn't home all day, she'd have security and summer vacations at home with Angela. She bit her lip and considered Ray's offer. Though she felt an ocean of relief when he climbed into his truck and rolled out the drive, she couldn't dismiss his opinion.

She didn't really trust Ray, especially when he'd hinted that she and he could get together. She shuddered at the thought. He was the kind of man who thought he was doing a woman a favor by raining attention her way. Some women ate it up, Lesley supposed, but not she. She wasn't that desperate. At least not yet. She'd tutor more kids, take in a boarder, rent out part of her land, do just about *anything* rather than become some man's paid trinket.

Or she could sell the ranch. Her gaze swept the outbuildings and rolling acres, the small yard and garden, the sagging fences and sturdy horses, to finally land on the pump house that was absolutely useless when the water table lowered in late summer. This place had once been Chase's home, his safe little corner of the world, until everything he'd trusted fell apart. He'd had to give it up once, she supposed she could, as well, though she'd come to love it here. She'd grown up moving from town to town until she settled here with Aaron. Despite her loveless marriage, she loved the land.

She held on to her baby more firmly, and Angela cooed softly. Lesley had to think of her child first. Before anything else. This wouldn't beat her down. She wouldn't let it. Stiffening her spine, she looked to the horizon and noticed the way the fields sloped ever upward into the forested foothills of the mountains.

Maybe she should sell out.

Maybe she had no choice.

"There's more than one way to skin a cat," Kate said as she sat behind her large, neat-as-a-proverbial-pin desk. "I know it's a hideous old expression but it's true, Chase."

He was seated in a chair in her office, one booted foot resting on his opposing knee. He'd come to Minnesota at his great-aunt's request and left her a printed update on his ranch's profitability.

"You don't like my idea."

"No matter how noble it is for you to give Lesley and her child your interest in the Waterman place, to sign over water rights, I think it's premature. Don't you want a place of your own?"

He glowered at his great-aunt. She knew what his

own ranch meant to him. "Of course I do. But some things are more important than owning a scrap of land."

Instead of being furious with him for throwing in the towel on the operation, Kate smiled, almost smugly, as if she'd *expected* his visit. "This is sudden, isn't it?"

"Yes. But it has to be done."

"Well, we have a deal, Chase, and you have nearly six more months to make it work. I think, if you explore all the angles here, you'll come up with a better solution."

He eyed the elderly woman, whose mind was as quick as that of a woman—or a man for that matter— half her age. "You know what I think, Kate," he drawled, watching her attention sharpen on him. "I think you deliberately set me up on the place because it was next to Dad's old ranch," he said, watching her reaction. "Next to Lesley Bastian."

Her eyes twinkled mischievously. "You're giving me far too much credit for being clever."

"Don't think so." He rubbed his jaw. "I got a call from my cousin Kyle the other day."

She sighed and glanced out the window. "I didn't know you were close."

"Not really, but he'd heard about me ranching the spread in Montana and told me about the deal you set him up with years ago. Sounds kind of familiar."

"There are similarities, yes."

Chase had made his point. Kyle, the playboy, had been offered the ranch in Clear Springs, Wyoming, if he stayed there for six months. What he hadn't counted on was that his neighbor was none other than his old girlfriend, a woman who had borne his daughter out of wedlock.

"Kyle settled down. Did better than I expected."

"And now you're playing with my life and, if the rumor's true, a couple of my other cousins."

"Don't forget, Chase, you wanted your life played with," she reminded him, and ignored his dig about the other deals she'd offered his cousins.

"You're not God, you know."

She chuckled. "Of course not. No one is. I prefer to think of myself as a kind of…well, for lack of a better word, a guardian angel."

"What?" he asked, thunderstruck at her particular choice of words.

"Well, that's a little lofty, perhaps, but you get my drift. I believe everyone makes their own decisions, no matter what he's given or offered in life. Others, like me, are there to help."

Chase wasn't certain of the details of Kate's other ventures, only that she was involved in some deals with Ryder and Hunter, his first cousins, and had set them up in similar situations as this bargain she and he had agreed upon. Not that it mattered.

Kate trained her attention on Chase. "I think you'll be able to handle anything that comes along, even the problems you're having with Lesley Bastian." She winked at her great-nephew. "Just search your heart."

"That's your advice?" he asked, clucking his tongue at the cliché. "'Search your heart'?"

"It's always worked for me."

Chase wasn't so sure that his heart could be trusted where his wallet, or more precisely, the ranch was con-

cerned, but he left Kate and the high-rises of Minneapolis to return to his new home in the foothills of the
Bitterroot Mountains. If nothing else, flying away from
the bustle and congestion of the city convinced him
that he belonged in Montana.

With Lesley. You belong with Lesley, a voice nagged
him, as the nose of the airplane broke through the
clouds and the jet cruised toward the setting sun. *You
belong with her because you love her. It's that simple,
Chase. As Kate advised, all you have to do is 'search
your heart.' You can't keep running from the past forever. Emily and Ryan are gone. Lesley and Angela are
alive.*

He ordered a drink from the waitress and told himself he was being foolish. Kate's advice was far from
simple. Or was it? As the jet banked slowly, the germ
of an idea began to take hold in his mind. It was an
idea he'd discarded long ago, but it was an answer,
and the only one that made any sense.

For the first time in a week he smiled, and a sense
of peace invaded his soul. Yep. As soon as he touched
down on Montana soil, he'd start the wheels in motion
to change the direction of his life. Forever.

Kate eyed the clock. Nearly 10:00 p.m. and she was
still at the office. If Sterling had a clue, he'd read her
the riot act. A woman her age was supposed to eat
tasteless low-sodium food, play bridge once a week,
have her hair styled every Friday morning and be in
bed by nine each evening. And she certainly wasn't

supposed to meddle, or as she preferred to think of it—playing guardian angel to her grown children, grandchildren, nieces or nephews.

"Phooey," she said, stretching from her chair and walking smartly to the bar. She poured herself a glass of chilled Riesling, smiled as the wine slid down her throat and decided that Chase needed a little help. Though she'd promised herself she would never take this next step, she decided she had no other choice and crossed the room again. Outside the window the lights of Minneapolis were bright against the backdrop of the night, the city alive with a pulse all its own. Oh, how she loved it here; almost as much as she loved her family. If her work was her inspiration, her family was her purpose. Always.

She touched the keyboard of her computer, found her address book within the files and reached for the telephone receiver when she unearthed Lesley Bastian's number. Yes, she decided, punching out the numbers, it was time to meddle a bit. Not much. Just a tiny little smidgen.

Far away in Montana, the phone on the other end of the line began to ring.

"So that's it," the woman who identified herself as Kate Fortune said. "I hope you understand."

Lesley was left speechless. She hung up, her mind spinning out of control, her heart filled with despair as she thought of Chase and all he'd gone through during his life. She'd known, via Ray Mellon, about Chase losing the ranch, his twin brother, and mother. Chase himself had once alluded to the fact that he was estranged from his father and sister, Delia, and he'd explained that his wife and son had died. What she didn't understand was that Chase suffered from guilt over their deaths.

Chase Fortune had become a lonely, bitter man. No wonder it was so hard for him to open up, to share his heart.

Well, damn it, she was going to make him try. She'd wake Angela, drive over to Chase's house and tell him the truth, that she loved him, that she thought there had to be a way to make things work between them, that she wanted to spend the rest of her life with him. Despite all her vows to herself that she didn't need another man in her life, could stand on her own, would be mother and father alike to her young daughter, she loved Chase Fortune, and whether he wanted to hear it or not, she was bound and determined to tell him the truth.

She'd just reached for the diaper bag when she heard a truck in the drive. Peering through the kitchen windows she recognized Chase's pickup, moonlight spangling the fenders. Her heart jolted, her pulse raced, and when she saw him stretch out of the cab, she crossed her fingers and silently promised to say what was on her mind.

Wearing jeans and a worn rawhide jacket, he walked up the path to the back door and as he stepped onto the porch, she flung open the door. "I have something I want to say to you," she said before she lost her nerve.

"Isn't that something?" he drawled. "I have something I want to say to you."

Her resolve started to crumble under the weight of his stare. His eyes were dark with the night, his jaw granite hard, his lips as thin as razor blades.

"I—"

"Marry me."

"—love you."

"Marry me." He stared at her for a second. "What did you say?"

She held her breath for a second. Was she hearing correctly? "I...I said I love you."

One side of his mouth twitched into a smile. "Well, that's handy, since I just asked you to marry me."

She laughed, trying to sort it out as his arms surrounded her. "You didn't ask, Chase Fortune, you demanded."

"I just wanted to say it fast."

"Before you chickened out?"

His chuckled was deep and low. "Because you scare the living tar out of me."

"Why's that?" She couldn't believe her ears. Her heart was pounding, the world seeming to spin more brightly than ever.

He scooped her off her feet. "Because, lady, I love you. Way too much."

Her spirit soared and as his mouth crashed down on hers, she parted her lips and opened her heart. Could it be? Did he truly love her?

"You haven't answered me." He carried her into the house and kicked the door shut with his heel. "Getting married solves all our problems, you know."

"Such as?"

"That little issue of water rights. I think if we're

careful, we can work both places off the spring runoff. We'll live in one house, keep the stock in one area and monitor what we put in troughs. Your horses will run with my cattle."

"You've got this all figured out," she teased, as he carried her up the stairs.

"It was a long plane ride from Minnesota. Gave me time to think. We'll work together and make both places profitable, but that's not what really matters."

"It's not?" Her heart was so full she was certain it would burst.

"Nope." Hauling her into the baby's room, they stared down at Angela sleeping peacefully in her crib with only a night-light and the moonlight streaming through her window giving any illumination. "It's you. And me. And Angela." His voice lowered with emotion. "We're a family, Lesley. If you just say yes."

Tears touched the corners of her eyes. "Yes, Chase," she said, overcome with a joy that started deep in her soul. "I'd love to marry you."

He gave out a whoop, and Angela started in her crib only to fall instantly asleep again. As he carried Lesley into her bedroom, she glanced out the window to the summer night. Her mind was playing tricks on her, of course, because she couldn't have seen the guardian angel she'd conjured up in December, the spirit named Sarah who had guided Chase to her disabled and frozen car.

No, she decided, kissing the man who was to be her husband, her mind was only playing tricks upon her because she was so blithely and deliriously happy.

She was soon to become Mrs. Chase Fortune.

Epilogue

Christmas bells pealed over the city, and the lights of the high-rises of Minneapolis were dazzlingly brilliant. A cold snap had blanketed the city with snow, and traffic was snarled. Chase helped Lesley and Angela out of the cab and into the Fortune Corporation headquarters where the annual Fortune Christmas party was being held.

Angela's eyes were round and bright, the ribbon in her hair sliding off a clump of her wavy dark tress.

"It's gorgeous," Lesley said as Chase guided her into the room where the party was in full swing. Guests were dressed in holiday finery. Jewels sparkled under the brilliance of thousands of tiny lights.

A lot had happened since last year, and Chase no longer felt out of place, though he still tugged at his tie, and his boots pinched a bit. He was married, the father of a beautiful little girl, and Lesley was pregnant again, barely showing, but radiant in a black velvet dress. On top of all that good fortune, his ranch, the "old Waterman place" had turned a small profit for the year because of the value of his breeding stock. He'd decided to rename the ranch the "new Fortune place."

Music and conversation buzzed around them and Kate, spying Chase and his family, waved, flagging them down as she approached. "Oh, my," she said, sighing happily. "Look at the three of you!" She hugged Lesley as if she'd been a part of the family for years. "This couldn't have turned out better if I'd planned it myself," she teased, and Chase skewered her with a look that said he wasn't buffaloed for a minute.

"You look like a million bucks, Kate."

"Do I?" She laughed deep in her throat. "Well, speaking of money, I have a deed locked in the safe downstairs. It gives you full title to the ranch. Good job."

Chase hugged her and kissed her cheek. "I think I should thank you, Kate. Not for the ranch, but for giving me my life. My family."

"Goodness." She sniffed loudly and blinked against a sudden rush of emotion. "This did turn out well, didn't it?" She glanced over at Lesley and little Angela as a crafty smile toyed at her lips. She winked at Chase and said, "Perhaps I should do this all again next year...."

*   *   *   *   *

A HOME FOR CHRISTMAS
Barbara Boswell

Prologue

A beaming Kate Fortune surveyed the festive group gathered to celebrate her eightieth birthday. A tall decorated Christmas tree stood in the center of the room, and red and white poinsettias surrounded the table showcasing her two-tiered birthday cake. Kate herself had pointed out that since her birthday was so close to the holiday, it made sense to combine the two celebrations. The Fortune canon of "target and strategize" was applicable, even for a landmark birthday and Christmas.

Kate felt a familiar burst of pride as she looked at the guests of all ages who were talking, laughing, eating and exuberantly racing around, clearly having a wonderful time. All her children, grandchildren and great grandchildren were here, along with a slew of nieces and nephews and their offspring, too. She adored them all.

The only person here who wasn't related to her was her sweet young social secretary, Kelly Sinclair. From across the room, Kate caught Kelly's eye and gave her a little wave. Kelly had done a marvelous job of coordinating this party.

Kate was well pleased at the turnout. Due to time and distance, these days it was rare to have all her loved ones under one roof, but everybody had agreed that her eightieth birthday party was not to be missed.

"Quite a gathering, Kate," observed Sterling Foster, coming to her side, his eyes sweeping over the jovial crowd. "Of course, I expected no less. It's a very fitting tribute to a very special lady."

Sterling was her second husband—her love, her best friend and coconspirator, and her lawyer. He handled all his roles with humor, intelligence and candor. He'd been instrumental in helping her with her latest plan— to bestow gifts upon additional members of the younger Fortune generation.

"Have you spoken to the boys yet?" Sterling asked.

Kate chuckled. The "boys," Chase, Ryder and Hunter, were ages 34, 32 and 29, respectively. But she understood Sterling's frame of reference. These days, she herself viewed everybody under fifty-five as boys and girls.

"I thought I'd speak to each of them separately." The trio were cousins, her late husband, Ben Fortune's, grandnephews.

She'd kept track of them since childhood; all three had grown into interesting, unique individuals. But all three were at something of a crossroads in their adult lives. They needed something, somebody, to provide the chance that would ensure their happiness and well-being. They needed their great-aunt Kate.

"I know Chase, Ryder and Hunter are going to do well with these gifts," she assured Sterling before he could voice the concern that they might not. Sterling was a dear, but he did tend to worry too much at times. "After all, I had smashing successes with my gifts to my grandchildren, didn't I?"

"I can't argue with that. You seem to possess a certain knack for arranging things, my dear," agreed Sterling. He snatched two glasses of champagne from the tray of a circulating waiter. "Shall we toast your upcoming smashing successes?"

Kate clinked her crystal goblet to his. "Definitely."

A stunned Ryder Fortune stared at the twinkling lights on the enormous Christmas tree. All around him a multitude of relatives were partying, but he stood mute with wonder as he contemplated the incredible news his great-aunt Kate had just delivered.

She was offering to *give* him a company, a design firm along the lines of the one his father used to own. His dad had intended for him, the oldest son, to join his company when he came of age, but back then Ryder had ideas of his own concerning his future.

Upon earning a degree in industrial engineering and an MBA, he had defiantly tossed aside the role of heir apparent. All of a sudden, despite—or perhaps because of—years of preparation, the business world struck him as too confining, a life sentence in a corporate straitjacket. An unbearable fate for a restless twenty-three-year-old. After all, he was a *Fortune*, born and bred—and that meant doing exciting things!

So he'd shed the shackles of his paternal legacy, broken up with his trophy fiancée—he was way too young to get married anyway!—and asked his great-aunt Kate if she had something for him to do. Something that had nothing to do with the tedious corporate grind.

Aunt Kate had challenged him at first: "Are you absolutely sure you want to give up your future with your father's company? If anyone was born to be a business mogul, it's you, Ryder.''

But Ryder had held firm, and Kate sent him to South Africa to work in the diamond mine owned by her multinational Fortune Corporation. His parents hadn't been pleased but had accepted his defection better than his fiancée Victoria, who'd staged a spectacular display of hysterics when he had ended their engagement. Ryder heard via the family grapevine, shortly after he left the country, that Victoria had married a thoracic surgeon some twenty years her senior. According to his sister, Charlotte, the mere mention of the name Ryder Fortune still made Victoria froth with fury. Ryder felt nothing at all when he heard Victoria's name.

A few years after his son's departure, James Fortune had closed the doors of his company and retired to Arizona with his wife, Sylvia. Although there was no longer a business for Ryder to inherit, at the time he didn't care.

But time had changed him, and now a mature Ryder found challenge and excitement in the prospect of running his own business. And tonight Aunt Kate had offered him his own design company.

She'd purchased the once-lucrative business for the proverbial song.

''It used to be a solid company but is currently floundering, thanks to the inept and careless decisions of its previous owner,'' Kate told Ryder, not bothering to mask her disdain. Inept and careless behavior in business offended her. ''I have faith that you can put the firm back on its feet, Ryder. Make it a player in the field again.''

Ryder had listened, too staggered by her generosity, by the thrilling vistas opening up to him, to utter a single word.

"Take the ball and run with it, Ryder," Kate said. "There is only one condition attached. You have one year to make good...."

After one year Ryder would either own the company outright or it would revert to subsidiary status within the Fortune Corporation, perhaps to be sold to the highest bidder.

One year. "I'll do it," Ryder had declared fervently. "Aunt Kate, saying thank you doesn't seem like enough for such a—"

"Don't worry about thanking me. Show me results," Kate interjected. "And, Ryder, don't spend the entire year buried in the office. To truly thrive, a successful businessman needs balance—a home, a place to unwind. Love." She gazed warmly at all her progeny who filled the enormous room. "A family."

An elated Ryder was already envisioning his triumphant entry into the business world he'd formerly rejected. He really wouldn't have time to fall in love and start a family for quite a while. After all, finding a wife meant socializing, and he was going to be way too busy for that.

Still dazed by his unexpected good fortune, he wandered out of the party room into the long corridor, preoccupied with plans. This was the happiest and most promising night of his life.

One

Whoever said "good help is hard to find" certainly knew the score, Ryder thought grimly as he unlocked the door to his office. He turned on the lights before switching on his computer and the coffeepot. A pile of mail, shoved through the slot late yesterday afternoon, lay on the floor. Ryder picked up the bundle and placed it on his desk.

Most company presidents had a staff who performed such basic tasks as opening the office and retrieving his mail. But not him. With the exception of the cantankerous receptionist who arrived far later in the morning than he did, the last member of the original office staff in place when he'd taken over had quit last week, citing his management style. They complained it was "different from" his predecessor's.

Of course it was different, Ryder fumed. His predecessor had neglected the company to the point of not even bothering to show up at the office for days on end. Now that there was a hands-on boss who expected his employees to put in a full day's work under his watchful eye, the slackers were unhappy.

Which meant that now, in the middle of January, the president of Fortune's Designs had a personal office staff consisting of one—the fiftyish receptionist, Miss Volk—who'd informed him the day they'd met that she would sue him for age discrimination should he try to fire her. Ryder hadn't. Miss Volk performed her duties competently, although her late-morning arrivals continued to test his patience.

"Are you Ryder Fortune?" A softly husky feminine voice broke into his reverie.

"No, I'm his alien clone." Ryder was sarcastic. "Of course I'm Ryder Fortune. Who else would I be? I'm here in Ryder Fortune's office at 8:00 a.m., seated at a desk with a Ryder Fortune nameplate prominently displayed."

"You could be an industrial spy, stealing corporate secrets from Ryder Fortune's company," the voice suggested. "Or a ne'er-do-well Fortune relative impersonating Ryder Fortune while gaining access to—"

"What do you know about ne'er-do-well Fortune relatives?" Ryder cut in.

He looked up from his mail to see a young woman standing a few feet in front of his desk. Her long, dark brown coat hung open, revealing a blue, ribbed sweater dress and matching tights.

"Rumor has it that Chad Fortune is slick as an oil spill. Ecologists worry about birds and small animals in the vicinity whenever he glides by. And then there is Brandon—"

"Are you some kind of reporter?" Ryder demanded suspiciously.

She was right about his cousins Chad and Brandon; the term ne'er-do-well aptly described those two. He focused his full attention on her. She did not look like a muckraking member of the tabloid press, but these days who could be sure?

She was not bad to look at, if petite slender brunettes were your type, he conceded. Of course, he had always been attracted to tall leggy women, preferably blond with big breasts. Whether natural or silicone-enhanced, he did not care.

This little girl—and he wasn't being sexist, at approximately five foot two, she really was little—had a heart-shaped face, delicate features, light blue-gray eyes and straight, dark brown hair that swung to her shoulders in a loose bob. Actually, she was a step beyond not bad to look at, she was pretty. Though she wasn't his type, not at all.

Especially if she were some nosy troublemaker out to make a buck from the Fortune name. "What do you want?" There was an accusatory note in his voice.

"Not to be here," she replied swiftly. "But like it or not, here I am. Joanna Chandler, and no, I'm not a reporter." She stepped forward and extended her hand.

Ryder rose to give it a quick shake. Her small hand was lost in his, and she quickly drew away.

He sank back in his chair. "Joanna Chandler," he repeated, stifling a groan.

Her name brought sharply to mind a post-Christmas lunch with his second cousin Michael Fortune. Michael was a hard-driving, high-ranking executive with the Fortune Corporation. His grandfather Ben had been a brother of Ryder's grandfather Zeke.

Michael was also married to this little girl's older sister, Julia. It was Michael himself who had set up their meeting, just as Ryder was taking the reins of his new trial company.

"You might want to consider interviewing my sister-in-law, Joanna Chandler, to work for you,'' Michael had said, coming straight to the point before the waiter even handed them menus. ''Joanna has recently relocated to Minneapolis to be near Julia and our children, and my wife is thrilled to have her back here.''

A job would be a further inducement for Joanna to remain permanently in the city, something Julia dearly wanted, Michael had told him. Ryder figured that whatever Julia dearly wanted, her devoted husband made sure she got. Thus, there would be a job in Minneapolis for her little sister, who had never worked in an office before. Michael had nonchalantly added that fact.

When Ryder had pressed for more information about the young woman, Michael merely remarked that Joanna's job history was ''somewhat checkered.''

Which probably meant that not only had she never worked in an office, she'd never worked at all. Ryder knew the type: a directionless, easily bored socialite. She undoubtedly partied far into the night and would show up at the office even later than Miss Volk. It was certainly no mystery why Michael had declined to give his wife's little sister a job at the Fortune Corporation headquarters. If given an alternative of passing indolent kin on to someone else, who wouldn't take it?

Ryder knew he was the alternative. *Gee, thanks for giving me the inside track on such a prize employee, cuz.*

But he kept his sarcasm from his older, richer, more powerful cousin. The brashly impulsive Ryder of five—two!—years ago would've said it. His new serious, business-minded self simply agreed to hire the little sister.

"Have her send over a résumé." Ryder had managed to keep a straight face while making the request. It would be interesting to see how the Fortune Corporation's creative marketing department—who undoubtedly would be pressed into service—rose to the challenge of making Joanna Chandler look employable.

But more than three weeks had passed since their luncheon meeting, and neither a résumé nor the applicant herself had arrived at the office. Ryder had forgotten all about her. And now, here she was.

Joanna glanced around the empty office. "Is this it?"

"Is what it?" snapped Ryder. He hated vague, time-wasting questions.

"Nobody is here but you. You're the president of the company, but you don't have an office staff?" Joanna appeared genuinely puzzled.

Unless she was being subtly sardonic? Ryder grimaced. "I have an office staff. A receptionist who sashays in between nine-thirty and ten. And you."

Her light eyes widened. Ryder noticed they were more blue than gray, though he suspected the deep blue of her dress might've heightened the color. If she wore gray, would her eyes take on a grayer, less blue hue?

He stood up and gave his head a shake to clear it of this nonsense. He couldn't believe he'd actually had such an irrelevent thought.

"Does this mean I get the job?" asked Joanna.

Was she rubbing it in? Ryder glared at her. "I guess it does, Joanne."

"That's Joanne with an *a*," she corrected patiently. "Joanna."

He heaved a sigh.

"Is something wrong?"

"What could possibly be wrong? I should be grateful that at least you know how to spell your own name."

Joanna rolled her eyes and removed her coat, turning to the tall wooden coatrack, shaped and brightly painted to look like a palm tree. Its brilliant green fronds were made to hold coats, but the papier-mâché coconuts were strictly decorative. So was the whimsical blue monkey perched atop of the tree, holding a half-peeled purple banana.

"This is—" she searched for a word to describe the coatrack tree, the monkey, the atomic-purple banana. "Amazing."

"You mean ridiculous," amended Ryder. "Garish. Tacky. At least be honest, Joanna."

"I mean amazing. Since you think it's ridiculous, tacky and garish, I guess you didn't buy it yourself?"

"Quick on the uptake, aren't you? No, I didn't buy it. This was an office-warming gift from my sister. Partying and shopping are her main occupations, too."

"Too?" Joanna echoed. "Does that mean you think my main occupations are partying and shopping, like your sister?"

"You really do have a keen grasp of the obvious. Do I dare to hope you can type ten words a minute?"

"I knew it was going to be bad, but I didn't think

it would be *this* bad.'' Joanna folded her arms in front of her chest, directing a level stare at him. ''Michael bullied you into hiring me, didn't he?''

''Nobody bullies me into anything,'' Ryder countered quickly. ''But I will admit I'm, uh, amenable to doing favors for my relatives.''

''Especially if they can buy and sell you ten times over.'' Joanna grinned. ''At least be honest, Ryder,'' she added with just the hint of a taunt.

It occurred to him that she was already calling him Ryder while Miss Volk, nearly twenty years his senior, still addressed him as Mr. Fortune. But then, Joanna Chandler was so very well connected, a point she seemed delighted to make.

''You want me to be honest? Okay, I will be. You're here, so you're hired, but you wouldn't be if your brother-in-law hadn't strongly suggested that I give you a job.''

''Michael's strong suggestions have been interpreted as threats from time to time,'' Joanna observed. ''It's not what he says but the way he says it. On paper, his words would look innocuous, but when he's speaking them…''

''Coupled with that nuclear stare of his that is intense enough to incinerate whole city blocks…''

''Not that you felt bullied or anything.''

''Of course not.'' Ryder smiled in spite of himself. ''It just seems like a very good idea to hire you.''

Joanna stared at him. His smile affected her queerly, making her pulse hammer in her ears and her skin tingle. It was sort of like being hit with a dose of particularly potent medicine. She was well versed with the effects of medication; she'd spent years in hospitals after being gravely injured in the catastrophic car accident that had killed their mother, orphaning her and Julia.

Standing here looking at Ryder Fortune, whose six-foot height, shock of jet-black hair and rugged features embodied the "tall, dark and handsome" cliché, Joanna suddenly felt as nervous and uncertain as her preaccident, teen-aged self.

She steeled herself against the sudden attack of nerves. *This just won't do.* She had to summon her postaccident strength, the Joanna who fought for control, gained it and never let go.

"Well, you've offered me a job, but I don't want to be anybody's ball and chain. Feel free to rescind your offer right now. It's okay, I promise. I'll tell Michael I didn't take the job because we're—" her eyes met his, and she quickly looked away "—we're not a good fit. Something like that."

"How do you know we're not a good fit unless we give it a try?"

Their gazes held for a long moment, and something intangible yet forceful vibrated between them. This time Ryder was the one to lower his eyes. If he didn't know better, he would think it was sexual tension causing this strange edginess churning inside him.

But it couldn't be, of course. He did know better; he knew he could *not* be attracted to Joanna Chandler. She wasn't his type—and not only physically. He wasn't interested in flighty little party girls who just wanted to have fun—a perfect description of Joanna with her "checkered" work history and influential in-laws.

He also wasn't interested in provoking "Neutron Mike" Fortune, Ryder reminded himself. Snubbing Joanna might detonate that particular fuse.

"Michael asked me for a favor, and I'm happy to oblige him," Ryder said loftily, all humor gone. "That is the sole reason why I'm turning down your offer to leave. The *only* reason." It seemed imperative that he stress that point to her. "If it wasn't for my cousin, I would jump at the chance to send you on your merry little way. Understand?"

Joanna sucked in her cheeks. "Perfectly." The self-righteous jerk! No doubt he would hold this great favor of hiring her over poor Michael's head, expecting endless recompense.

"You can take that desk." Ryder pointed to the smaller and only other desk in the office.

It was a few feet away from his own desk and stood very near the bizarre palm tree coatrack. Joanna glanced up at the blue monkey who stared back. Was it her imagination or was the creature's expression downright menacing? He looked like he wanted to belt her with the banana. *Mr. Big Shot Boss was the one who called you garish and tacky, not me,* she silently advised the monkey.

Focusing on her hostility made it easier to dismiss that strange, inexplicable flash that had passed between her and Ryder. Whatever it was, it couldn't have been sexual tension, Joanna assured herself. Ryder Fortune wasn't her type. He was too controlling, too impatient, too good-looking, too...everything!

Furthermore, on the off chance that there should ever be sexual tension between them, it would have to remain unresolved, because she was not stupid enough to fall for her boss.

True, Julia had fallen in love with Michael when he'd been her boss, and things had worked out wonderfully for the two of them. But that was different. What man wouldn't fall in love with Julia, who was perfect in every way? Perfect would *not* be an apt description of Joanna Chandler, she thought wryly. Nobody was more aware of her imperfections than Joanna herself. She wasn't about to set herself up for certain heartache by yearning for a man out of reach like Ryder Fortune.

"The last executive assistant, Saundra Something, sat there," Ryder continued, his gaze darting from the desk to Joanna. "She wasn't happy that I was in here with her, and no wonder. She couldn't take her customary two-hour lunch breaks, couldn't talk on the phone fifteen times a day, not with the mean new boss breathing down her neck."

"It is kind of unusual to share the president's office," Joanna pointed out.

She felt a pang of sympathy for Saundra Something. It couldn't have been easy with Ryder Fortune watching your every move, like a hawk eyeing a convenient chicken. Which was about to be her own fate! "Don't most top execs have their own private offices?"

"Your brother-in-law does." Ryder said it before she could. No doubt about it, she wasn't going to let him forget her brother-in-law's status. "Actually, it is

strange for the company president to share his office,"
he conceded with a scowl. "I thought so myself."

"Makes you wonder what exactly was going on
here. I could make a guess or two."

"I don't have time to waste wondering about things
like that," Ryder said grandly.

Had he intended to make her feel like a rabid gos-
sipmonger? Joanna frowned. If so, he'd succeeded
quite well.

"And I don't intend to keep this share-the-office
situation indefinitely. I'm going to set up an executive
suite with a private office for me, and one for my
assistant. But not right now. I can't waste the time or
money on interior decorating just yet. I have to get
this company back on its feet."

They lapsed into silence, a tense one that Joanna
felt compelled to break. "So I'm—um—hired to be
an executive assistant?"

"Why not? You couldn't be any worse than the last
one."

Joanna tried to look on the bright side. At least she
didn't have a renowned predecessor to live up to. On
the other hand, she was following somebody who
seemed to have soured Ryder Fortune on executive
assistants. She was going to have to prove her worth
to her new boss, and he didn't strike her as somebody
who was easily won over.

"Do you have a job description covering what an
executive assistant does?" she asked gamely. "Then
I'll know what's expected of me."

Ryder smiled—rather evilly, Joanna thought.

"I'll type up a job description for you right away.

But first, throw out that old coffee I'm reheating and make a fresh pot. That'll be one of your duties, to have fresh coffee waiting for me when I arrive every morning. Understand?"

Joanna shrugged. "Sure." He seemed to be expecting her to protest.

"I get here at eight. That means you'll have to be here earlier."

"Duh," Joanna murmured under her breath.

"What?"

"Yes, sir. I understand, and I will be here earlier than eight o'clock to have fresh coffee made," she replied in what she hoped sounded like a crisp, efficient executive assistant tone.

"I don't appreciate your sarcasm, Joanna," Ryder growled.

Joanna concluded she'd better work on her crisp, efficient executive assistant tone. "Sorry, sir." There, that was better. She sounded contrite, even humble!

Ryder sat down in his chair to type up her job description.

"Would this be a good time to ask about my salary?" Joanna ventured before he touched the keyboard.

Ryder quoted an astronomical figure. Her jaw dropped. "I'll be earning that?"

"Absolutely not. I was just making a little joke. I'm offering you—" He gave a significantly lower figure. "Plus benefits. But you'll have to be here a month before they kick in. Four full work weeks," he added. *As if she'd last that long!*

Joanna resisted the urge to point out that she didn't

appreciate sarcasm any more than he did. A good executive assistant didn't indulge in one-upmanship with the boss, did she? "I'll take it."

"Not even going to try to bargain your salary higher?" he baited her. "Why not? Aren't you interested in making more money? Of course, if you're being subsidized by your sister and brother-in-law, you wouldn't need—"

"If I wanted to be subsidized by Julia and Michael, I would have taken the faux job Mike invented for me at Fortune Corporation headquarters. I'd've moved into the ritzy apartment they offered me rent free. But I don't want to be a Fortune charity case, at least not any more than I've already been. So I'm sharing a place with friends and I'm taking this job, even though it's still Fortune largesse—kind of. But at least now that I've met you, I know you won't cut me any slack just because I'm Julia's sister. Which is good because I want to make my own way."

She glowered at him, her eyes blazing. Ryder felt chastised. Bemused, he found himself watching her as she turned to work the computerized coffee machine.

That sweater dress fit her well, and the longer he looked, the more her figure seemed to improve before his very eyes. She was quite slim, but she had a curvy little butt and very well-shaped legs. True, her breasts were small, but enormous ones would make her look ridiculously top heavy. He watched her reach for a cup on the shelf above the table. It was high, and she had to stand on her toes to get it. Those chunky-heeled shoes of hers looked like something the Wicked Witch of the West might wear, but her legs were good enough to carry them off.

Joanna turned and caught him studying her. She raised her elegant dark brows.

Two

Busted! Ryder shifted uncomfortably in his chair. Now what? An idea struck. He cleared his throat. "That—um—that coffee machine is the kind of thing I want this company to design."

"I see." Joanna was more than willing to pretend he'd been studying the coffee machine, not her. "High-tech gadgetry like the stuff specialty catalogs sell."

"We not only design household gadgets, but items for industrial and commercial businesses, as well. I'd like to see the company include state-of-the-art athletic exercise equipment, too. My own area of expertise is industrial engineering—I take inventors' ideas and turn them into practical application. We have our own in-house product designers, of course, but I also want to sign contracts with independent inventors."

His enthusiasm for expanding the company was contagious, Joanna realized. "Have you thought about a line of life-skills products?" Joanna asked eagerly. "If you're looking to discover some new inventors, there are some really creative people out there who've come up with some terrific life-skills ideas—"

"Life skills? I'm not sure I follow, Joanna."

"Life-skills products. Those are specially designed items that make everyday tasks easier for the disabled.'' This was a subject dear to her heart. From her long rehabilitative struggle, she knew firsthand the difficulty simple household tasks could present to those who were physically challenged by birth or injury. She was personally acquainted with some people determined to alter that situation with unique adaptive devices.

If she could convince Ryder to implement those designs, to tap into a very real need... The prospect was exciting. A challenge for a genuine good. ''You see, they can be something as simple as making a light switch accessible to someone in a wheelchair to—''

''I'm sure there are medical supply houses that carry that kind of stuff.'' Ryder's interest in her idea for his company was clearly flagging. ''What I'm looking for are—''

''Medical supply houses are more interested in selling large equipment,'' she cut in quickly. ''You'd be surprised how difficult it is to find simple life-skills products on the market. A few small specialty catalogs try to fill the need but—''

He wondered how she knew so much about the handicapped and hospitals but didn't pursue it.

''Joanna, Fortune's Design isn't about special-needs products for a limited market. I'm thinking big. I'm envisioning global success. A winning business operates on Darwinian principles—only the strongest, smartest and most adaptable survive in the marketplace. I intend for Fortune's Design to be among that number.''

''Is that the running-with-the-crocodiles business philosophy or something?'' Joanna grimaced.

"Are you trying to refer to the swimming-with-the-sharks metaphor?" Ryder was vaguely appalled. He'd committed passages of that invaluable business wisdom to memory, and she couldn't even keep the predators straight.

"Whatever." Joanna shrugged. "Focusing only on the strongest and smartest is—"

"The only way to succeed in business," Ryder said flatly. "And Fortune's Design has a way to go before we're there. Our sales, marketing and human resources departments aren't bad, although the employees start coming in about nine and—"

"Isn't nine o'clock pretty much the normal start of office hours?"

"Nine o'clock is practically mid-morning!" Ryder scowled his exasperation. She was looking at him like he was Simon Legree, whip in hand. He attempted to explain. "Living by the clock is the antithesis of success. When I was mining rocks in South Africa, we weren't compulsive clock-watchers, that's for sure. We were there from dawn to—"

"Rocks? You mean diamonds?" Joanna was curious.

"Yeah." Ryder actually smiled. "My great-aunt Kate sent me over there. I wanted to break out, to do something exciting, and she came through for me in a major way!" He gave a reminiscent laugh. "We had some adventures over there that played like an Oliver Stone movie with characters straight from Central Casting. We worked hard, played hard, fought hard. Had a helluva time."

"Sounds like you loved it."

"Yeah, I did," he said softly, gazing out the window at the bleak, gray Minneapolis sky. Snow was predicted again with temperatures heading for the single digits.

"Now I understand the palm tree and the monkey." Joanna spoke her thoughts aloud. "Your sister was trying to give you something of an 'Out of Africa' touch here."

"Weatherwise, scenerywise, every-which-waywise, it couldn't be more different from here."

"Do you miss it?"

He shrugged. "Sometimes."

"Then why are you here and not still over there?"

"I want to be here," Ryder replied. She looked doubtful, and he nodded his head vigorously. "I was ready to leave. I'm really glad to be here. And lucky, too."

Joanna was busy rearranging the items on the coffee table. "If you say so."

"It's true!" He seemed determined to convince her.

She sat down in her desk chair and swiveled to face him. She sensed a story coming.

Ryder launched right into it. "Last year, I uncovered a smuggling ring at one of the diamond mines. Some of the workers were using pigeons to smuggle stolen gems from high-security areas. I agreed to work undercover to catch the suspects red-handed so arrests could be made. And I did. They were caught and charged but there was some gunfire and I—"

Suddenly he stood up, removed his suit coat and pulled his shirt from his trousers. Joanna watched him, wide-eyed. When he tossed off his tie and unbuttoned

his shirt, her eyes grew even rounder. His chest re-
tained a residual tan, and that alone was striking. At
this time of year in wintry Minneapolis, most people
were pale as ghosts, herself included. She couldn't
help but notice that the muscles of his chest and arms
were strong and well-defined. Joanna swallowed hard.
Yes, very well-defined.

Ryder flung his shirt on top of his coat and tie, and
Joanna watched, fascinated, wondering what was going to go next.

It was something of a disappointment when he shed
no more clothes. Instead, he pointed to the dark pink
and purple scar on his shoulder. His very own battle
scar, she guessed.

"This is where I took the bullet," he said with a
kind of endearing boyish pride.

"Wow!" Joanna did her best to look impressed, but
she knew that in any "scar-off," she would easily
emerge the winner. After the car accident she'd had
so many surgeries that her scars had scars. Her hips,
her legs, her abdomen and chest. Even her head. She
rubbed her skull unconsciously, her fingers tracing the
unseen line where the fracture had been repaired. Of
course, she wouldn't dare whip off her clothes for a
round of I'll-show-you-mine-if-you-show-me-yours.

"It was very painful," Ryder said, moving closer
so she could examine his scar in all its glory.

"I'm sure it was." She stared at the scar, striving
to look suitably awestruck. "First getting shot and
then the physical therapy to regain and maintain range
of motion." She knew all about the rigors of physical
therapy, she'd endured a grueling regime for years and

still had exercises to keep her limber. If she didn't do them regularly, she felt stiff and sore.

"I used to call the physical therapy room the torture chamber, and I nicknamed the therapist Torquemada." Ryder named the Spanish grand inquisitor who'd known a thing or two about torture.

Joanna nodded knowingly. "Did you call the lab people 'vampires' when they came for blood samples?" She'd found that most hospital humor was essentially the same.

"Yeah." Ryder laughed. "There was one in particular I called Dracula."

There was always one of those, a lab technician who drew blood with an excess of exuberance. She winced, remembering. "Who said vampires were mythical? They're around today, except the hospital variety imbibe with long needles instead of pointy teeth."

"Too true. But when I was in the hospital, I had plenty of time to think. And all of a sudden I had this very clear comprehensive moment of insight."

"An epiphany," Joanna supplied helpfully. She'd had a few herself.

"Maybe it was. I just knew it was time to leave South Africa and come back to the States, to reconnect with my family and finally take my place in the corporate world I'd left behind all those years ago. I was prepared to be an employee in somebody else's company but Aunt Kate made me an offer I couldn't refuse—to take over this faltering design firm and turn things around. I have a year to get it back on track."

"And then what?"

"Then the company is totally mine, free and clear!"

"And if you fail, it's back to the diamond mines?"

"Oh, I have no intention of failing—which is why I'm working myself and the employees so hard." Ryder's hazel eyes glowed with messianic fervor. "We're headed in the right direction, although I can't let up the pressure. And I won't. So, do you think you're up to the job?" He wanted her to shake off her laconic air and rally to the cause, he wanted a dynamic commitment to Fortune's Design.

"What you call pressure..." Joanna smiled—laconically—and jumped up to pour him a fresh cup of the perking coffee. "Would others call it intimidation?"

Her response didn't please him. Did she have instigator potential? Having a troublemaker on the premises was one headache he could do without. Ryder frowned as he reached for his shirt and slipped it on.

"I'd like to see your résumé, if you have one, Joanna. List the places where you worked, who you worked for and what you did on the job," Ryder ordered. As CEO, he had a right to know exactly who and what had been dumped on him.

"So you can check my references? Why? We both know you're stuck with me, thanks to my brother-in-law."

Was she teasing him? Ryder studied her intently. She was smiling. She really did have an incredibly appealing smile.

She probably knew it, and played it up for all it was worth, too. His cynical streak reared its ugly head. Possibly she was stalling, trying to divert him. Well, he wasn't so easily charmed!

"You do have some typing and computer skills?" He almost held his breath.

"Suppose I say no? Am I fired?"

"Just answer the question, Joanna."

"I can type a little and I've surfed the Net."

What kind of qualifications were those? But like she said, he was stuck with her—at least for a while. Ryder tried to be gracious as he accepted his fate. "Welcome to Fortune's Design, Joanna."

"Yes, sweetie. I promise I'll be over soon." Joanna laughed softly into the phone. "No, not tonight, I'm working late. Tomorrow night for dinner? Well, I don't know."

Several feet away, seemingly engrossed in the numbers on his computer screen, Ryder was listening unabashedly to her conversation. He couldn't complain about her taking personal calls on company time because it was her lunch hour. She hadn't left the building, but had eaten a sandwich, an orange and a packaged cupcake at her desk, which had taken her all of ten minutes. She had plenty of free time left.

"What do you mean, sweetie?"

All this sugary talk was making him nauseous. Ryder frowned. *Who in the hell was "sweetie," anyway?*

"I know. I miss you, too." Joanna leaned back in her chair, absently rubbing her neck with her fingers.

Ryder watched as if mesmerized. The curve of her neck was graceful, the skin white and silky smooth. Her fingers were small and slender, and she wore a gold ring on the third finger of her right hand—the stone a square-cut, bluish violet amethyst. He'd learned a lot about gems, almost by default, during his tenure in South Africa, and he knew that particular variety of crystallized quartz from which her stone was cut, though pretty, wasn't especially valuable.

But she faithfully wore that ring every day. Obviously it held sentimental value for her. Ryder wondered who had given it to her. *Sweetie,* perhaps?

"Give the phone to Mommy now, Phoebe," Joanna instructed. "I need to talk to her."

Ryder slowly expelled a long breath as the tension drained from his body. He slumped in his chair, feeling almost limp. "Sweetie" was little Phoebe, Joanna's four-year-old niece.

"Phoebe invited me for dinner tomorrow, Jules." Joanna sounded amused as she spoke to her sister. "She said she called me at work because she wanted to talk to me. When did she learn to use the phone? What? You're kidding! Voice mail?"

Ryder smiled. Though he'd never been able to keep the names and ages of his many Fortune cousins' children straight, he did know Michael and Julia's daughters, thanks to all the photos of them adorning Joanna's desk. The oldest child, Grace, named for her late grandmother Chandler; Phoebe, four; Felicity, three; and baby Noelle, who had been born the day after Christmas.

Joanna had confided to him that her small nieces had inspired an epiphany of her own, bringing her home last Thanksgiving to stay, because her brief visits were no longer enough for her. She wanted to be near her sister and to watch the little girls grow up in person, not in the photos and homemade videos that Julia faithfully sent to her, wherever she happened to be.

And Joanna had been everywhere, it seemed.

After reading her résumé, Ryder understood why the seriously career-minded Michael would refer to her work history as "checkered." Although Joanna had held a number of jobs, they didn't conform to anyone's idea of a professional trajectory. Her education included a high school graduate equivalency degree and nothing beyond. Office work was totally unrelated to her previous positions. She'd been a nanny to different families in different cities—London, Paris, Frankfurt, Rome, Budapest.

"Budapest?" Ryder had exclaimed. "How did you end up there?"

"On a Euro-rail pass," she'd said, though her mode of transportation was not what particularly interested him.

Her restlessness did. It was greater than his own had ever been. While he had remained based in South Africa, she'd had no fixed address for years. In between her nanny jobs, she'd traveled all over Europe, camping or staying in youth hostels. When she needed more money, she would find work as a maid in a hotel or a waitress in a fast-food restaurant.

"McDonald's is worldwide and I can say 'Do you want fries with that?' in six languages." She had laughed, but Ryder had been amazed. A Fortune in-law behind the counter at McDonald's?

The past two years she'd worked as an assistant to a film location scout, traipsing all over North America finding places for movies, TV shows and commercials to be filmed. "It was the perfect job for me because I couldn't stand to be in one place for very long. I had a room in L.A. but was gone most of the time with Hal scouting for shoots."

But eventually she had decided to return home to her family in Minneapolis, just as he had. They were both close to the legendary Fortune fame and wealth, yet apart from it. Employment history aside, there were oddly similar parallels in their lives that struck him.

Ryder watched Joanna as she talked on the phone to her sister. She was animated and expressive and in constant motion, swirling around on her chair, jiggling a pen between her fingers, standing up to perch on the edge of the desk while swinging her leg back and forth. Sitting still was obviously a foreign concept to her.

She hung up the phone and slipped back into her chair, scooting it around as she rearranged her picture collection on the desktop. Watching her was never dull, and Ryder had logged a lot of time doing it during the past month she'd been working for him.

They'd had their share of ups and downs. Somewhat to his surprise, Joanna never complained about working long hours, and they often worked late into the evenings. They ate dinner in the office, trying all the take-out-and-delivery places in the vicinity. She was an entertaining conversationalist, friendly and pleasant, and all the employees liked her. Better than they liked him, Ryder noted without rancor. He didn't mind her popularity within the company.

What he did mind were some of Joanna's more maddening quirks. Though he found her hyperactivity amusing at times, other times it drove him crazy. She also tended to be absentminded, which he blamed on inattentiveness. She had to write *everything* down, and if she didn't write it down immediately, she forgot all about it. When he admonished her, she'd made a few lame jokes about her short-term memory deficit. Ryder hadn't laughed. He didn't like glib excuses.

The truth was, Joanna didn't work well under pressure, and he thrived on it. He enjoyed juggling five projects at once, but a fast pace inevitably caused her to lose focus and get things mixed up. Phone numbers, appointment times, names and addresses. He felt himself growing impatient just thinking about some of her screwups. His eyes narrowed as he watched her.

And invariably his exasperation wavered and dissolved. He couldn't seem to stay upset with Joanna. Bemused, Ryder wondered what made him willing, even eager, to excuse her for mistakes he wouldn't tolerate from any other employee. Because she was likable and cute? Or because she was the beloved little sister of Michael Fortune's wife?

Joanna looked up and caught Ryder looking at her. She paused, holding one picture frame in midair. He'd been staring at her again. She hated when he did that. It made her feel like a lab rat under the watchful eye of a scientist collecting data—or like a patient struggling to recover as therapists in every curative specialty observed and noted her every move.

''What?'' She knew she sounded defensive. She was defensive! ''Am I fidgeting too much?''

He made that observation at least once a day. Joanna knew she had to make a concentrated effort to stay still—and even that didn't always work. It was one of the more annoying aftereffects of the accident, and she was certainly aware of her defect. She did not need him to continually point it out to her.

"No wonder you're so skinny," said Ryder. "You must burn up the caloric equivalent of a three-course meal just zooming around this office."

That stung. "I am not skinny!"

She had little appetite, her sense of taste wasn't what it ought to be, another permanent result of the accident. She always had to remind herself to eat, and keeping on weight was a constant struggle.

"No," he agreed. "You're slender, but not skinny like some of those models who look like they haven't had a decent meal in years. If ever." His eyes traveled over her, perusing her carefully, lingering on her.

Joanna felt her cheeks flush. There were times when the way he looked at her thoroughly unnerved her. It wasn't a sensation she was used to, but Ryder Fortune seemed to possess an uncanny expertise in inducing it.

"I couldn't help but overhear your conversation." He shrugged, unapologetic about his eavesdropping. "Since you're going to your sister's for dinner tomorrow night, I guess I'll knock off early, too, and leave around seven."

"Leaving at seven o'clock is not early, Ryder. This is probably going to come as a shock to you, but all over America people leave their offices promptly at five."

"A shock? Not hardly. Almost everybody in this

company leaves promptly at five, even Miss Volk who doesn't get here till ten.''

"She finds it hard to get up and moving in the winter. The cold weather gives her bronchitis.'' Joanna was sympathetic. "And migraines and lumbago and—''

"Maybe she should move to a warmer climate.''

Joanna shot him a look. "Better not say that around her.''

"I know, I know. Still, I can dream, can't I?''

"Of what? A glamorous young receptionist? Let me guess—she'd be about five foot eight with a platinum blond mane and bright scarlet lipstick. Spike heels, spandex miniskirts and tight sweaters. Thirty-six, twenty-two, thirty-six. Am I on target?''

Ryder flashed a salacious grin. "I can already picture her sitting out there.'' He inclined his head toward the closed door leading to the reception area.

"I bet you would keep the office door open all the time so you could keep a close eye on her,'' Joanna said, continuing the joke. "You wouldn't mind sharing an office with *her,* would you?''

"I don't mind sharing an office with you, Joanna.'' His voice was husky.

The sound of it, along with his own admission, surprised him. "I don't mind sharing an office with you, Joanna.'' His voice echoed in his ears. Good night, he sounded as if he really meant that! He thought of the architect's drawings for the executive suites. Those plans were right in his desk drawer, and he could afford to implement them. But he kept putting off the remodeling.

Because he hated the thought of trying to work amidst the noise and dust of construction, Ryder assured himself. Who wouldn't want to postpone that ordeal? Even if it meant sharing the office with his assistant.

His eyes met Joanna's, and their gazes held for a long moment.

Joanna's breath caught in her chest as a surge of heat flooded her body. She moistened her suddenly dry lips with the tip of her tongue. There was a pleasant throb deep in her abdomen and her nipples tingled.

She blinked. If she didn't know better, she'd think she was getting aroused gazing at Ryder Fortune. And when he smiled at her, those enticing sensations rippling through her intensified.

Joanna was alarmed. *I can't be getting aroused gazing at Ryder Fortune!*

That would be both futile and foolish because Ryder was actively uninterested in becoming involved with anyone. He had made that fact clear to the women who called him, and there seemed to be plenty of them ready and eager to snare a Fortune. Joanna heard Ryder tell his would-be lovers that he was too busy establishing his business, that his personal life was currently on hold. Since she'd been working for him, she was fairly certain that he hadn't had a single date.

Two days ago had been Valentine's Day, a surefire date night, but she knew he hadn't gone out. She hadn't, either. They had worked till past 9:00 p.m., dining on take-out pizza, and Ryder hadn't even acknowledged the holiday. Neither had she.

During the past month she had heard him turn down

invitation after invitation. Though she tried not to listen, she couldn't help but overhear his personal conversations. After all, they shared this office. And there were times when she eagerly, blatantly eavesdropped. Times when listening to him brush off those overeager females made her positively gleeful.

That couldn't mean anything! It didn't mean anything! she told herself. Developing a crush on Ryder would be incredibly stupid, because on a good day she merely drove him crazy. On a bad day he wanted to dismember her. She could just tell.

Joanna suddenly felt the need for tension-reducing action. She busied herself by fiddling with the blinds, wiping down the already spotless coffee area, transferring her pens from one container to another.

"You're flitting around the office like a fly on speed," Ryder observed. "You'd better cut back on the coffee, Joanna."

Joanna suppressed a sigh. She didn't drink coffee. She wouldn't dare add caffeine to her already supercharged nervous system. "I've been here a month and you still haven't noticed that I drink tea?" Herbal tea. Decaffeinated.

Impulsively she picked up a wet, used tea bag and tossed it at him. Quick as a flash Ryder extended his arm and caught the soggy missile.

Joanna was horrified by her impulsiveness. *"You have to remember to always stop and think before you act, Joanna"*—the voices of every rehab therapist she'd ever worked with chorused in her head. Too bad she'd remembered their advice after she hadn't followed it.

"I can't believe I threw that!" She clasped her hands to her cheeks, dismayed. "I'm sorry. It was really unprofessional of me."

"I agree." Ryder's lips twitched. "But I made a fine catch." He tossed the tea bag back at her before she realized what was coming. It hit her arm, leaving a blotch on the sleeve of her blouse. "You, on the other hand, missed."

"I withdraw my apology. You're as unprofessional as I am," she scolded.

"Maybe even worse," agreed Ryder. "After all, I'm the boss. I should be above such—such—"

"Juvenile antics?" Joanna suggested.

"Kindergarten level," Ryder agreed. "Now, let's get back to work."

He leaned forward and picked up a document, his expression, his body language and tone shifting abruptly from playful to seriously business. "I need you to take this new product development plan back to marketing. Tell them I want to see more details."

Joanna thought of the groans her appearance was going to elicit from the marketing department, who'd already revised and detailed the proposal three previous times. But Ryder was a perfectionist and expected nothing less from others. Too bad she was fated to be the messenger whom marketing most wanted to shoot.

She was on her way back to her desk when she remembered that she'd forgotten to make Ryder's plane reservations for a conference in Washington, D.C., next month. She had been about to do it when little Phoebe's phone call distracted her. She would have to do it right now, Joanna reminded herself. The moment she sat back down at her desk, she would pick up the phone and—

"Joanna, dear, would you run across the street to the drugstore and pick me up some vitamin-C tablets?" Miss Volk intercepted her before she could reenter the office. "And some St. John's Wort, too. And nasal spray. I'd do it myself but it's so cold and windy out there, and every bone and joint in my body is aching."

"Of course, Miss Volk." Joanna was instantly solicitous. She knew how awful it was to ache all over. Others had helped her, and she understood the necessity of helping others in kind. "I'll get my coat and go right now."

Three

"C'mon, Ryder, come with us tonight," Charlotte Fortune half whined, half pleaded in the kid-sister tone she'd used for years to wheedle her two older brothers into doing or getting what she wanted.

Matthew, the stolid middle-born, had always been better able to hold out against her. Ryder, eight years her senior, succumbed to her wheedling more often than he cared to admit.

But this time he was determined not to give in. "Look, Charlotte, I just got back from the airport after hopscotching all over the eastern half of the country, because my idiot assistant forgot to make my plane reservations and didn't bother to tell me until the very morning I was to leave for the conference. I could only get to D.C. via—"

"All the more reason for you to kick back and relax," Charlotte interjected, clearly not interested in his airline woes. "You'll love Surf City, Ry."

"No, I won't. The name alone puts me off. I'm going to turn on CNN to see what's happening in the rest of the world and then go to bed."

"You're beginning to sound more and more like Daddy every day!" Even over the phone, Ryder could tell she was pouting. "He's in bed every night by eleven, but at least he and Mommy have a life down there in the desert. Think about that depressing fact, Ryder. Residents in a retirement community are way livelier than *you!*''

"I have a life," protested Ryder

"No, you don't. You go to work, you go home and go to bed. You're a boring workaholic, Ry, a total social recluse!" Charlotte's voice rose. "And to think that all these years I've been telling my friends how much fun you are, how adventuresome and cool!" She sounded personally betrayed.

"Char, I did the club scene in South Africa back when I was—"

"But I wasn't there to hang out with you, Ryder. For the past nine years I've only been able to see you for a few days every Christmas. Now you're finally living in town, and I want to show off my big brother to my friends. *Please* come with us tonight! I promise we'll have fun."

Guilt, flattery, cajolery. Charlotte was adept at all of them. Unfortunately, she had made some valid points. Ryder sighed. He knew he was going to acquiesce, but he attempted to set some conditions. "Okay, I'll meet you there. But I have no intentions of staying more than an—"

"Cool!" exclaimed Charlotte. "See you around eleven at Surf City. Do you need directions?"

"I'll find the place," Ryder grated through his teeth.

"Oh, and Ryder? *Please* don't dress like some stuffed-shirt executive tonight. Most people wear shorts and bathing suits to Surf City, but jeans are okay for you conservative types.''

''I am not venturing out in Minneapolis in a bathing suit on the first day of March, which has come roaring in like the proverbial lion. If that makes me stuffy and conservative, so be it, Charlotte.'' Ryder hung up.

A stuffed shirt—*him?* He trudged to his closet for his jeans and a striped rugby shirt that he hoped wouldn't embarrass his eternally cool sister and her ultrahip friends.

A combination of crusty snow and road salt crunched beneath his tires as he drove from his apartment to the club a half hour later. When he had decided it was time to return home to Minneapolis—his epiphany as Joanna had called it—he'd considered establishing closer relationships with both his brother and his sister to be a main priority. But so far his new company took so much of his time and energy that he really hadn't seen much of his siblings. Matthew, fourteen months his junior and a research pathologist at the University of Minnesota Medical Center didn't mind, but baby sister, Charlotte, made it clear that she felt slighted.

So here he was—at Surf City on Charlotte's demand.

Standing just inside the cavernous warehouse that housed the club, Ryder checked out the scene. The place was packed, loud and wild, with live music and uninhibited dancing, dim lighting, and an anything-goes atmosphere. There was a faux boardwalk setting with games and refreshment stands, there were mounds of sand and vibrating surfboards that simulated the movement of riding the waves. Ryder watched people try to stay on the boards and saw them, inevitably, get thrown off.

In jeans and dark-red-and-blue rugby shirt—not to mention wearing shoes—he was definitely one of the more overdressed patrons. Mostly everybody else wore summer attire, shorts and sandals, sundresses, even shorter shorts and, worst of all, bathing suits and bare feet.

He glanced around at the patrons, searching for a glimpse of Charlotte. His little sister and her pals liked to frequent this place? He was not pleased. It was obvious the customers could do just about anything here, though a warning was posted that having sex on the tables was prohibited by management.

Pushed deeper into the interior of the club by the burgeoning crowd, Ryder found himself perilously near several couples who seemed bent on flaunting management's lone rule. He tried not to be scandalized but...

Ryder sucked in his cheeks. He felt like a stuffed shirt, very old and very uncool.

"Joanna, come on! You gotta try surfing!" exclaimed Jenny, one of Joanna's roommates. "It's so-o-o-o much fun!"

Joanna watched the wanna-be surfers being pitched to the floor by the bouncing surfboards. Most hit the ground hard and would undoubtedly be bruised.

"Jenny, that is like getting beat up. Not my idea of fun."

Jenny didn't hear her because shouting was necessary to be heard, and Joanna didn't feel like using that much energy. She felt a little dizzy. Her ears were ringing, the drums seemed to be pounding in her head.

The consequences for succumbing to peer pressure? Jenny and their other roommate, Wendi, had been insisting that she join them for a "girls' night out" for weeks, but until tonight she'd successfully resisted. Jenny and Wendi led extremely active social lives and worried about Joanna, who did not.

Tonight she'd had no excuse. She was home before six, because Ryder hadn't been in the office. He was in Washington, D.C., attending the conference she'd forgotten to make his plane reservations for. Joanna flinched, remembering how infuriated he'd been with her when he left town two days ago. He was due back tonight, and she wondered if he would still be mad at her tomorrow.

If so, he would glower at her all day while making sarcastic remarks about her flaky absentmindedness. Joanna thought of the architect's plans for the private executive suite and wished mightily that Ryder would give the go-ahead for the project. If there were four walls between them, the tension wouldn't be so omnipresent, so unavoidable, whenever they were on the outs.

"Aren't you glad you came with us tonight, Joanna?" Jenny squealed happily.

Joanna sighed. Going out on a cold night with Jenny

and Wendi had been the last thing she'd wanted to do tonight, but she couldn't even use visiting Julia and Michael as a reason to refuse because they were out of town with the children, vacationing in the Florida Keys.

So here she was at Surf City, feeling overdressed in a short, gauzy, embroidered dress.

Joanna watched one young woman—lithe and tall and tanned, in a bright red bikini—hop onto the surfboard. A group gathered around to cheer her on. "Charlotte! Charlotte!" they chanted. She stayed on longer than most of the previous candidates, before being flung off.

Joanna grimaced as the young woman picked herself up amidst much laughter and shrieking. *"Are we having fun yet?"*

She began to wind her way through the frenetic horde the moment Jenny jumped on the surfboard to try her luck. Surf City was as overcrowded as any beach resort on a holiday weekend, and it was easy to get lost in here. Joanna intended to do just that, to lose Jenny and Wendi and escape. She was glad she'd insisted on driving her own car here, glad that Jenny and Wendi had already arranged transportation home with some other friends.

There had been a time when she would've loved this place, Joanna realized. The pulsing music and raucous crowd and over-the-top craziness would've thrilled her. She'd gone a bit wild after all those years in hospitals, feeling like she'd lost too much time and had to make up for it, but now it seemed that she had finally gotten all of that out of her system.

Joanna was both relieved and a little forlorn. It was good to know she was maturing, but she really didn't want to turn into a withdrawn hermit, either. She couldn't even argue when Jenny and Wendi—and even Julia—pointed out that her social life was non-existent.

It truly was. Sometimes Joanna wondered why that didn't bother her more. She supposed it should, yet it didn't.

For some reason she was content to spend hours working overtime for a boss who took her presence for granted. Except when she did something to try his patience—like not making plane reservations for an important conference, among other mishaps—and then he was quick to take her to task.

Of course, she didn't always screw up and he wasn't always annoyed with her. Warmth surged through her. There were times when she and Ryder Fortune got along superbly well, when they were very much in sync, talking and laughing and—

"Joanna!" A big hand fastened around her upper arm. "I thought it was you."

Because of the pressing crowd, Joanna couldn't turn around, but she didn't have to. She recognized the voice. It was downright spooky, as if her thoughts had somehow conjured up Ryder Fortune in the flesh, right in back of her.

"I was watching those nitwits on the surfboards and saw my own sister hit the floor. And then I spotted you." Ryder sounded both astonished and disapproving. "What are you doing here?"

"I could ask you the same thing. I'd've never pegged you as a Surf City regular."

"Because I'm not one." Ryder had to lower his head for her to hear him over the din. "My sister used emotional blackmail to get me here. What's your excuse?"

"Nothing dramatic like emotional blackmail. My roommates nagged me into coming. They claimed it would be fun."

"So did Charlotte. Which leads me to wonder— what exactly is 'fun' anyway?"

"Not Surf City." Joanna took a deep breath. "How was Washington?"

"Oh, the city was great, the conference was great. It was the journey to and from that was a living hell. Three takeoffs and landings in three separate cities, layovers in crowded airports... Need I go on?"

"I'm sorry, Ryder."

She sounded contrite, Ryder thought as he cast a sidelong glance down at her. She looked it, too. Oversights happen, he reasoned. It wasn't as if she'd deliberately planned not to book his flight.

"I accept your apology, Joanna. Just don't let it happen again," he felt obliged to add.

Joanna heaved an exaggerated sigh. "Ah, the trenchant qualifier," she mocked lightly, tilting her head. "A Ryder Fortune specialty."

"I was not being *trenchant.*"

"Censorious, then?"

"No." She was baiting him, and Ryder knew it. Yet he leaped like a fish lunging at a shiny lure. "You might keep in mind that I am attempting to accept your apology, Joanna. Which was barely adequate, at best. Not even approaching anything similar to heartfelt or sincere."

Despite the ear-splitting din of Surf City, Ryder was startled by his own tone of voice. He sounded trenchant. And censorious. He was taken aback. Why was he giving Joanna a hard time? Why did seeing her here in her diaphanous little dress and slim bare legs, her cheeks flushed and eyes bright, make him want to— to—*to scold her and drag her out of here?*

Joanna couldn't see Ryder's face, but she could well imagine his expression. A mixture of self-righteousness and annoyance. She'd seen it often enough directed at her. All at once a devilish impulse to drive him to sheer outrage was impossible to resist.

"You know, if you ever decide to follow in the footsteps of all those other CEOs who've written bestsellers, you'd be a natural for a how-to book, Ryder. Something along the lines of *How To Accept an Apology without Really Meaning It.* You could do an audiotape version too, demonstrating your trenchant and cen—"

"I would like to know why you are attempting to make *me* feel guilty for *your* oversight. Remember that I was the one inconvenienced by your negligence when you forgot to book my flight, Joanna."

"See, you threw my apology right back in my face, and so completely, too," Joanna said gleefully.

A trifle too gleefully, Ryder decided. He eyed her intently. "Exactly how much have you had to drink tonight, Joanna?"

"If you're implying that I'm drunk, I most certainly am not!" Joanna said indignantly.

"You didn't answer my question."

"Just one drink. A Surf City citrus slush. I have no idea what it was, but it tasted pretty good."

"Well, judging from the lack of inhibitions in this crowd, I'd say the drinks they serve here are about six hundred proof. Just one would have an effect on a little thing like you." He frowned. "And it has. You can be something of a smart aleck at times, but you've never been quite this—outspoken."

"I'm not a smart aleck," she defended herself. "Or a little thing, either."

"I said you were *something* of a smart aleck. And I'll amend little thing to—uh—person of small stature and slender frame. Is that more acceptable?"

Before Joanna could answer, a swell of people surged, nearly knocking her off her feet. She was forcefully propelled into him, and Joanna heard Ryder expel a gasp as she impacted against him. Another shove, and her knees buckled from the pressure.

His arm came around her waist to steady her. "Aside from nearly being trampled, are you all right?"

"Yes." She managed to turn her head halfway and look up at him. His light brown eyes seemed to be boring into her. And she'd thought her brother-in-law had a laser stare! Suddenly, it was imperative that she get out of here, well away from Ryder Fortune. "I—I've had enough of this place. I'm leaving."

"You took the words right out of my mouth. Let's go."

But they couldn't move. Everybody around them had begun to slow dance, though the dance floor was—actually, it was anywhere the crowd decided it to be. Right now, it was right here.

"This place is as packed as Times Square at midnight on New Year's Eve," Joanna complained, wriggling to make more room for herself.

Plastered against him as she was, she both heard and felt Ryder's sharp intake of breath. Her eyes widened, and she moved again. Was that what she thought it was?

"Don't," Ryder whispered hoarsely, his lips against her ear.

Joanna shivered at the feel of his warm breath caressing her skin. His body surrounded her completely, and there was no mistaking the hard bulge pressing insistently against her bottom.

"Everybody is dancing." Ryder's voice sounded choked, and he turned her, maneuvering her body as easily as he would a doll. He didn't remove his hands from her waist, and they naturally seemed to slide lower to her hips.

She felt small and soft, and Ryder was stunned by the effect her petite but very feminine form was having on him. The result of his sustained period of abstinence, he decided frantically. Well, he had been abstinent too long, when merely touching his executive assistant—whom he was not attracted to!—turned him on faster and harder than anytime during recent memory.

Joanna's eyes were fixed on him. The jeans and rugby shirt, sleeves rolled to his elbows, were a surprise. She stared at his bare forearms, strong and dusted with dark hair, at the virile fit of his jeans. In the office she'd seen him only in tailored business suits—except for that first memorable day when he'd stripped to show her his scar, of course. She thought of his well-muscled chest. Her memory might lag when it came to retaining sequential information, but she had perfect recall of that divinely masculine sight.

Joanna felt her face growing hot. Her head was spinning. And not from the effects of her Surf City citrus slush, she was sure of that.

Tonight Ryder looked very different from the formal, immaculately groomed executive she saw at the office every day. His hair was slightly mussed, a shadow darkened his jaw and chin. He looked…sexy. And if her body heat kept rising, she was going to melt into a puddle right here in the middle of Surf City.

"Maybe we should dance." Ryder's eyes were glazed as he stared down at her.

"To 'Surfer Girl'?"

"I know, it's surreal. But consistent with the theme of this place, hmm?"

It was surreal, all right, Joanna thought dizzily. The music, the people dressed for summer while temperatures hovered below freezing outside, the hungry glitter in Ryder Fortune's eyes...

Perhaps she was coming out of anesthesia, lying in the recovery room after yet another operation. She'd had some incredibly weird drug-induced dreams, and this one was right up there among the strangest.

Whatever, she thought, deciding to go with it. Her arms crept up around his neck. She had to extend them because he was so tall, and her sandals didn't provide even an extra inch of height. Their bodies were so close, each could feel the imprint of the other.

Sandwiched in the crowd, they swayed to the music. Joanna laid her head against his chest. Suddenly she felt too weak, too languid to hold it up. She could hear his heart pounding in her ears, and her own heartbeat took up the rhythm. Her eyes closed and she clung to him.

Ryder held her tight, resting his chin on the top of her head. She felt so good in his arms. His hands began to move slowly over her back. Joanna arched even closer.

"Ryder," she whispered urgently, her breathing as erratic as his.

He began to knead the sensitive area at the base of her spine with one hand while his other slipped around to gently cup the underside of her breast. Joanna felt sensual lightning jolt through her. She jerked backward, blindsided by her volatile response to his nearness, to his caresses.

There was a civil war going on inside her: common sense was beating a fast retreat while desire surged to win. *"You have to remember to always stop and think before you act, Joanna."*

The mantra penetrated her consciousness. Joanna remembered. She thought and did not act.

"Ryder, stop!" she whispered desperately. She was trapped in a frustrating sexual paradox, needing him to stop as much as she needed him not to.

"I can't," he fairly groaned the words. She was right, this was too much, it was too intense. And they were in public! But he couldn't let her go. "I—don't want to. Do you, Joanna? Do you really want me to let you go?"

She raised her head to look up at him at the same moment he lowered his. The noise and the other people seemed to fade into the background. She was aware only of Ryder, of his big hands holding her, his lips so tantalizingly near. Another inch and their mouths would be touching, they would be kissing....

"Hey, Ry, you're kickin' tonight!" Charlotte squealed, crashing into them.

Joanna jumped away from Ryder. If she could've, she would have run out of the place, but she was trapped by the crowd. She stared dazedly at the bikini-clad young woman—one of the ones she had watched get tossed from the surfboard—who had draped her arms around Ryder.

"This is my sister, Charlotte," Ryder said stiffly, his jaw clenched. "Unfortunately, she's the type of reckless reveler that a place like Surf City attracts."

He did not appear glad to see his sister. But Joanna felt inordinately grateful to Charlotte for literally falling upon them because she'd been on the verge of...she'd wanted to—

"Aw, Ry, you sound like a school principal or somethin'," Charlotte slurred her words and stumbled, as if unable to walk and talk simultaneously. It was obvious that she'd had one drink too many.

Very obvious. She proceeded to accidentally spill the bright pink concoction she was holding onto Ryder's shoes. "Oops!" Charlotte giggled. "Sorry about that, Ry-sie."

"You're going home right now, young lady," Ryder said sternly.

"Now you sound like Daddy. Thank God you can't ground me or cut off my allowance!" Charlotte hiccupped.

Joanna couldn't suppress her grin.

Ryder noticed. "Don't encourage her, Joanna. It's not funny." He glared from her to his sister. "Will you help me get her out of here?"

She couldn't refuse, Joanna decided. A woman in Charlotte's impaired condition really shouldn't be bouncing around in this free-for-all atmosphere. Especially not in such a brief bikini.

"Okay. Let's go." Though the other woman towered above her, Joanna slipped her arm around Charlotte's waist. Her action brought her within touching distance of Ryder once again. Their hands, their arms, brushed, and Joanna nearly succumbed to a sensual relapse.

She cast a swift, covert glance at Ryder, whose face was set in a taut mask of disapproval. There was no sign of the man who'd held her, who said he didn't want to let her go. He looked so cold, so forbidding. Clearly, he regretted their intimate little interlude. His scowl was directed at her as well as his inebriated sister.

She'd almost kissed him! Looking at him now, Joanna could hardly believe it. Her boss had nearly kissed her, and she'd wanted him to. She shivered. That Arctic stare of his cleared her head like a blast of polar air. What if they had kissed?

"I'm not leavin', it's too early," protested Charlotte.

Ryder ignored her complaints. "I assume you wore a coat. And shoes. Where are they?"

"Over there," mumbled Charlotte. "By the fruit smoothie snack bar. My flip-flops and Mommy's old fur. Somebody dumped a piña colada on it. A peach one, I think."

Ryder's expression spoke volumes. He looked the way he did when Joanna made a mistake. She felt instant sympathy for Charlotte.

"I'll go get her shoes and coat and meet you at the front door," Joanna volunteered, pointing herself in the direction of the boardwalk. How hard could it be to find a fur coat reeking of peach piña colada?

It wasn't hard at all, and she soon rejoined Ryder and Charlotte, who was singing and dancing to "California Girls," her exuberant spirits unquashed by her brother's dour demeanor. Joanna helped Charlotte into her coat, then drew her own brown wool coat around her, belting it. They inched their way toward the front door.

"Thank you for your help," Ryder said stiffly.

"No problem. What's an assistant for?"

"Assistant?" Charlotte picked up on that. "The idiot assistant?" She blinked, trying hard to focus on Joanna. "Who? You?"

"The idiot assistant," Joanna repeated. So that was the way Ryder talked about her? And he must do it often and emphatically enough for the term to have stuck in Charlotte's liquor-soaked memory. "Yes, that would be me."

She was angry. And after their near kiss tonight, she was hurt. That was the worst part.

"You work for my brother," Charlotte appeared to be concentrating very hard on putting together the facts. "And you're here with him tonight..." She flashed a triumphant smile. "No wonder Ryder doesn't mind stayin' late at work these days. You two are having an office romance!"

"No, we aren't," Joanna countered quickly. "Think about it, Charlotte. Would your brother romance an idiot?"

"Joanna, I was—" Ryder began, looking chagrined.

Joanna didn't notice. She took advantage of a sudden opening in the crowd to move ahead of the pair. She'd reached the club's front door, which led to the elevator banks of an indoor parking garage, when she nearly collided with a well-built, impossibly handsome man with a model-gorgeous woman on his arm. Both were dressed in designer-label, very skimpy beachwear that showed off their impressive bodies. The man flashed Joanna a charming smile.

"That's cousin Chad." Charlotte snickered.

Ryder didn't speak at all. He hooked his fingers around the belt of Joanna's coat and jerked her backward.

She whirled around, startled by the possessive grab. Ryder used his grip on her belt to pull her back even closer to him.

Ryder didn't glance back. He thrust through the doors, out of Surf City, half dragging the two women toward the elevators. The abrupt switch, from noisy to quiet, from packs of people to deserted corridor was jarring. Joanna gazed about, trying to establish her equilibrium.

Ryder was treating her as if she were a naive schoolgirl! Joanna was irked. "You didn't have to hustle me away from him. I—"

"I saw the look Chad was giving you," growled Ryder. "If you'd given him an ounce of encouragement, he would have dumped that siliconed swizzle stick with him and—"

"Well, I didn't give him any encouragement at all," Joanna said frostily. "Furthermore, I'm perfectly capable of making up my own mind about people."

The elevator arrived and Ryder pulled Charlotte and Joanna inside. He hit the number four on the panel as the doors closed.

"My car is on level two," said Joanna.

Ryder made no attempt to press that button, and they passed the floor before Joanna could reach it.

"You're riding with me, Joanna," he said with a dictatorial air that made her fume.

"We're not at work, Ryder. You can't tell me what to do."

"No?" The elevator doors opened on the fourth floor.

"No!"

"Just watch me." Ryder hauled Joanna out of the elevator, with Charlotte stumbling along with them.

Four

"Let me go!" Joanna tried to wrench herself free. His grip was inexorable, and she did not succeed.

"The roads are bad, and I'm not going to allow you to drive, Joanna." Ryder was adamant.

"You're not going to allow me?" Joanna repeated, momentarily diverted.

He sounded so very authoritarian. She tried to remember the last time someone hadn't *allowed* her to do something and guessed it must've been back in her teens, when her parents were still alive.

Ever since the accident Julia, her sole surviving relative, had offered only encouragement. *"You can do it, Joanna." "If that's what you want to do, go for it, Joanna."* Occasionally there was big-sisterly advice like *"Watch out for cousin Chad. Chad the Cad is heartbreak waiting to happen,"* and *"Taking a daily vitamin is an excellent idea."* Brother-in-law, Michael, supplied useful reminders about her car. *"Remember to get the oil, the antifreeze, the air in the tires checked,"* along with his own Chad Fortune warnings.

But the phrase *not allowed* had disappeared from her vocabulary. Simply hearing it was a novelty. "You sound absolutely parental," Joanna blurted out.

Ryder glowered, his nostrils actually flared. Joanna

stared at him, fascinated. She'd always thought flaring nostrils were a literary device, but Ryder made it happen in the flesh.

Ryder clenched his jaw till it ached. Parental? How on earth had she reached that conclusion? Possibly the last thing he felt toward Joanna Chandler right now was fatherly.

"You are as spacey as ever, Joanna," he said. "And you've been drinking. There is no way I'm letting you get behind the wheel of a car tonight."

"I only had one drink. You make it seem like I've been boozing it up all night!"

"I kind of was," Charlotte interjected. "Are you mad at me, Ry?"

"Yes," Ryder said grimly. "Neither you nor Joanna should've been at Surf City tonight or any other night. Haven't you ever heard of the drug that slimeballs slip into women's drinks? Well, Surf City is the type of place where that sort of thing happens. Probably on a regular basis."

"No way," argued Charlotte. "Surf City is a fun place. Y'know, you've really changed since you came back to Minneapolis, Ryder. You've totally lost your sense of adventure. These days you make *Daddy* seem zany."

Staid James Fortune was the antithesis of zany, but just in case Ryder had missed his sister's less-than-subtle accusation, she verbally bludgeoned him with it. "So that makes you like a—a Puritan or something! Strict and uptight and absolutely no fun at all!"

"If I'm a Puritan, then you're a sybaritic socialite,

Charlotte.'' Ryder was frowning as he hurried Joanna and Charlotte through the chilly parking garage. He finally halted beside his big black Range Rover. "Get into the car, both of you."

"Is he this impossible and bossy at work?" A sulky Charlotte asked Joanna. "'Cause if he is, I'd quit if I were you. I don't have a choice, I can't resign as his sister."

"I usually make it a point to stay out of sibling cross fire," Joanna said drily. "But since you asked, as a boss, your brother is—" she paused to glance up at Ryder, the beginnings of a smile curving her lips "—okay."

He arched his brows. "Thanks for the ringing endorsement, Joanna."

"Anytime, boss."

She was aware that they were flirting in a covert way. It was confusing, yet oddly exhilarating, the way their interactions tonight seemed to bounce from one extreme to another. Hot, then cold. Now a thaw was definitely in the works. She could literally feel him warming toward her, a tentative smile responding to hers.

"I guess I might've overreacted when I saw Chad look at you," Ryder admitted, a little sheepishly. "I apologize."

And watching that dog eye Joanna like a hungry wolf brought out a possessive, protective streak he'd been unaware of. Until now.

"I understand." Joanna turned to Charlotte. "My sister, Julia, mentioned that Kelly Sinclair was involved with Chad. Julia was worried about her. She said Kelly is too sweet and trusting, and Chad is a heartbreak waiting to happen. Michael says he's toxic.''

''Finally, something we can all agree on,'' Ryder said heartily. ''All right, let's go, little sister.'' He took Charlotte's elbow and steered her into the back seat.

Which left the front for Joanna. She slid into the wide bucket seat, trying to pretend she wasn't nervous.

But she was. She was very nervous indeed as she contemplated the attraction simmering between her and Ryder. She couldn't seem to stop thinking about those earlier intimate moments between them, when a very different Ryder had emerged. She wanted to spend more time with that man, who was so unlike his impatient, order-barking alter ego. She wanted to explore the enthralling feelings he evoked.

Bad idea, Joanna, she cautioned herself. No matter if Ryder had more sides than the *Three Faces of Eve,* the bottom line was that she worked for the man. As his idiot assistant. It would be truly idiotic to forget her status—and that critical evaluation of his.

A streak of anger galvanized her. ''How am I supposed to get to work tomorrow if my car is here?'' she demanded crossly as Ryder took his place behind the wheel. ''And don't even suggest that I take the bus!''

''I wouldn't dream of suggesting the bus. We'll swing by here tomorrow morning and pick up your car.'' Ryder's tone brooked no argument.

And then he calmly, audaciously covered her knee with his big hand.

"Ryder, you—can't." Joanna tried to quash the rush of edgy excitement surging through her. To take control of the situation.

"No?" His voice was seductive. "I can't do this?" His fingers began a gentle massage as he slipped his hand just underneath the skirt of her dress to caress her inner thigh. "You don't want me to?"

Pleasure shimmered through her, spreading deeper, hotter. Keeping control began to lose its appeal. When she made no protest, no reply at all, his hand moved higher.

A wave of heat sent her reeling. The intention and possession of his touch was unmistakable. *"We'll swing by here tomorrow morning and pick up your car,"* he'd said. The implication was clear. They would be together tomorrow morning because they were going to spend the night together. Tonight.

Unless she said no. Suddenly, Joanna was right back in the sensual morass that had enveloped her before Charlotte's precipitous arrival. She lifted her eyes to Ryder's face and found him watching her intensely. There was raw desire and hunger in his gaze that evoked a deeply feminine response within her.

He drove the Range Rover out of the parking garage into the blustery March wind. A few blocks farther down the road, a traffic light turned red and Ryder braked the car to a stop.

"Come home with me, Joanna," he murmured.

She turned her head to look at him, her lips parting

as she drew a short shuddering breath. He leaned in and touched his mouth to hers, gently at first, then more passionately as her mouth opened to him. Her tongue touched his, retreated, then surrendered to the bold strokes of his tongue as he pursued hers.

"*Excuse me,* I haven't felt like this much of a third wheel since—since never!" Charlotte whined petulantly from the back seat. "This is absolutely the worst. And why doesn't the damn light turn green? Is it broken or something?"

Ryder muttered an incoherent response as he lifted his mouth from Joanna's. But he couldn't make himself move away from her, couldn't bring himself to break the contact between them, despite his sister's very vocal presence. He kissed Joanna's neck, savoring the soft feel of her skin, the alluring scent of her perfume.

Joanna shivered as his lips trailed a path to the sensitive spot below her ear. And then her eyes happened to connect with Charlotte's in the rearview mirror.

Ryder's sister was staring at them, watching with unconcealed curiosity. Joanna blushed.

"Ryder," she whispered huskily. "Look."

Reluctantly he lifted his lips, following her gaze to the rearview mirror.

Charlotte gave a little wave. "Oh, yeah, I'm still here."

Ryder groaned. Joanna bashfully hid her face in the comforting warmth of his shoulder, her body trembling from the provocative little interlude.

"For a couple not having a romance, I'd say you

do a pretty good imitation of it," Charlotte observed. "Do me a favor, run this stupid light and take me home so you two can just get on with it, okay?"

"I never run traffic lights," Ryder said loftily. "But I'll be delighted to comply with the rest of your command, Char."

His hand continued to rest on Joanna's thigh, but he didn't try to kiss her again. There was no chance, because every traffic signal blazed bright green, and they had to keep moving.

"You have to remember to always stop and think before you act, Joanna." That much-repeated therapeutic advice kept echoing in her head. Taking Charlotte home and depositing her in her apartment had provided plenty of time to think.

Which was fortunate, of course, but it would've been so much easier to simply act on impulse, Joanna mused wistfully.

Should she go home with Ryder and spend the night making love with him?

She wanted to, but Joanna knew better than most that you could not always do what you want. Her mind began to drift. Or get what you want. Julia said that happiness wasn't having what you wanted, but wanting what you have.

Joanna found herself pondering this. Julia was very wise.

"You're so quiet, Joanna," Ryder said at last. Without Charlotte in the car, absolute silence reigned. "What are you thinking about?" He smiled a sexy smile. "It must be pretty intense because you've managed to sit still for nearly five full minutes."

"A record for me," Joanna conceded. "And if I tell you what I was thinking you'll be—"

"Excited?" Ryder prompted. "Even more turned on than I already am?"

"Try irritated," she interjected flatly. "You'll be exasperated."

"Never, sweetie." He was flying on a testosterone-adrenaline-fueled high. "Not with you."

"Not even if I admit that I wasn't sitting here spinning erotic fantasies about you? That my mind was off on one of those irrelevant tangents that drive you crazy? Though I prefer to call them mental detours."

"Joanna." Ryder groaned. "Everything about you drives me crazy. I—"

"Yes, I'm aware of that." *Painfully aware!* "Which is why we shouldn't, uh, act on these urges tonight. Or…or any other night."

Her mind might work circuitously, but she knew she'd made the right decision. When a man admitted upfront that a woman got on his nerves, he was definitely talking one-night stand. And Joanna didn't do one-night stands. Never.

She didn't sleep with her boss, either.

"Life is complex enough without adding impossible complications," she murmured. Somebody—Dear Abby? Oprah? Dr. Laura? she couldn't remember who—had said that once, and it stuck in her head. And proved to be an uncanny take on this particular situation.

"Going to bed with someone who drives you crazy out of it, practically guarantees disaster," she added solemnly. Dear Abby, Oprah and Dr. Laura would surely all agree on that.

"Joanna, I…hope you know that I meant that in the most complimentary way. You have to know that!"

Ryder could tell she didn't, though. Her withdrawal was tangible; she'd inched as far away from him as the seat belt would allow.

Tension, sharp and unrelieved, coursed through him. His impassioned declaration hadn't come out quite right, but did she have to misinterpret him so completely?

"Joanna, I didn't mean to imply—honey, let me start over. I want to—"

"Take me straight home, Ryder. I'll ask one of my roommates to drive me to the parking garage tomorrow morning to pick up my car."

"Baby, let me change your mind." Ryder pulled the Range Rover over to the curb, idling the engine as he tried to take her into his arms. He realized it was the act of a desperate man. Hell, he even sounded desperate!

Joanna shrank farther against the door. She knew if she let Ryder touch her again, she'd end up in bed with him. Her body was hell-bent on betraying her good sense tonight.

That couldn't be allowed to happen. Joanna silently listed the reasons why. Ryder was everything she was not: well-educated and rich, a member of the most prominent family in the state. Such inequalities might not matter in a fairy tale—she thought of her small nieces' collection of storybooks and videos, where such impossible couples abounded—and dismissed them as kid stuff. Joanna Chandler was firmly grounded in reality.

But Ryder wanted her, he was caressing her…

Trembling, she caught his wrists with her hands to fend him off. "Don't, Ryder."

Ryder stared at her, startled by the distress in her voice. She looked small and anxious. He immediately backed off.

"You don't have to look at me like I'm some sort of…of rabid gorilla," he rasped. Though, admittedly, he rather felt like one. By the expression on her face, he must've been acting like one, too.

Joanna flinched. She hadn't meant to insult him. "It's just that we have a good working relationship, Ryder," she said, trying to make amends. "And a friendship. Let's not jeopardize either by a crazy impulse brought on by a…a crazy place."

"Is that what you think? That the antics at Surf City inspired me to make a pass at you?" Ryder was outraged. He might have been behaving somewhat primitively, but how could she misread him so thoroughly? "Of course, you're an expert at misreading things," he continued. His patience, never too plentiful on the best days, was totally obliterated by the combination of exhaustion and sheer sexual frustration. "On the matter of our *good* working relationship, for example. We—"

"You're still mad about those plane reservations."

Joanna swallowed hard. She knew she wasn't misreading his expression—it was that of a disgruntled boss viewing his most unsatisfactory employee. His idiot assistant.

"Among other things," he muttered.

She was certain he was remembering everything she'd accidentally forgotten to do or had done all wrong, the various tasks she'd messed up in oh, so many ways. If she hadn't been related, she would've been out of Fortune's Design weeks ago.

"Do you want me to quit working for you?" Joanna gulped. "M-maybe we could at least salvage our friendship." His ferocious scowl made her flinch. "Or aren't we friends, either?"

"I've never felt less friendly toward anyone in my life," Ryder snapped.

A true statement, Ryder thought, because he'd never ached with urgency and unslaked desire for a *friend.* He'd never looked at a *friend* and wanted to kiss her so long and deep and slow that neither of them would be capable of arguing, let alone thinking. Conversely, a friend would never accuse him of being influenced by an obnoxious pit like Surf City!

They didn't speak again, except for her terse directions to her apartment building. The moment he pulled in front of it, she was out of the car.

"Should I come to work tomorrow?" she asked uncertainly, standing on the sidewalk.

"If you don't show up, I might have to press Miss Volk into additional service and you know how well *that* will go over!" Ryder fairly snarled at her.

Her leap from the car had fueled his aggravation. Had she expected him to pounce on her? Well, she had no worries on that score. He was not the kind of man who forced unwanted attentions on any woman!

"Okay, I'll be there," Joanna agreed, though she was dispirited. Being preferred over Miss Volk was hardly a confidence booster, not when she knew Ryder's feelings toward the intractable receptionist.

"I appreciate your cooperation."

Despite her gloom, Joanna laughed. She couldn't help herself; it just slipped out. Ryder's tone of voice reminded her of crabby old Mr. Lachlin in the rehab hospital.

She was laughing at him! Ryder was indignant. Bad enough that he'd made a complete fool of himself, she wasn't even willing to diplomatically pretend he hadn't. She felt comfortable—justified!—in laughing in his face!

He revved the engine and sped away from the curb, down the quiet street. Two blocks away a patrol car noticed the racing Range Rover and followed, sirens blaring and red-and-blue lights revolving.

Ryder received a hefty speeding ticket and a stern lecture about driving recklessly and failing to heed weather conditions, road conditions and common sense. He decided it was all Joanna Chandler's fault. The woman really did drive him crazy, and he was *not* being complimentary.

If only she were with him, he would tell her so. He visualized the scene, giving his imagination free rein....

In the scene his admonition ended with him kissing her senseless, driving her as crazy with desire as she drove him. And then he imagined taking her to his bed and making love to her until neither of them cared about anything but the sublime pleasure they found in each other.

Five

Joanna and Ryder spent the next few weeks locked in a frozen truce.

It was worse, she decided, than all-out war. At least in a war, battle lines were drawn and anger expressed. Ryder's icy politeness, his policy of speaking to her only when absolutely necessary made him unapproachable, and the distance between them grew.

Every day at the office she felt him watching her with a disparaging eye, certain that he was silently analyzing and criticizing everything she said and did. They continued to work late into the evenings, but their previous camaraderie was missing.

They didn't even order their take-out dinners from the same places anymore, though Ryder did insist on paying for her meals. Joanna was on a spicy chicken burrito kick and ordered them every night, while Ryder selected a different entrée from a plethora of international cuisines, as if to counter the constancy of her choice.

"How can you eat the same damn thing every single night?" he finally demanded, after her fifteenth straight burrito dinner was delivered to the office.

The cold anger in his tone did not invite her to share any facts about her impaired sense of taste, and his glare seemed to accuse her of consuming burritos solely to provoke him.

So Joanna merely shrugged. "I just can."

Their rift coincided with a particularly busy time. The ambitious, energetic new hires in Ryder's PR and marketing department had done a good job of spreading the word about the revamped Fortune's Design. Their efforts had brought in dozens of inquiries, many of which had turned into new contracts for the company.

Joanna knew it would've been difficult for her to keep up with the increasingly complicated and demanding workload, even in an atmosphere free of tension. But Ryder's coldness and attitude of reproach intensified the pressure.

She was positive he was waiting for her to royally screw up so he could righteously sack her. He must be hoping she would make an error of such magnitude that no one, not even his cousin Michael, could possibly fault him for getting rid of her.

As the tension between them continued to build, Joanna worried that it was only a matter of time till that monumental blunder occurred.

On the day after St. Patrick's Day, Miss Volk arrived even later than her customary 10:00 a.m. and announced to Joanna that she was quitting her job. Immediately. Forget the customary two-week notice, Miss Volk was out of there!

The reception desk was deserted, the phones went unanswered and the public ungreeted after Miss Volk left the building. The task of breaking the news of the receptionist's hasty departure to the boss fell to Joanna.

"Miss Volk's sister who lives in Pittsburgh won a hundred thousand dollars in the Pennsylvania Lottery yesterday," she began. "Miss Volk said they have the luck of the Irish without being Irish."

"Mmm." Ryder, engrossed in the thick report in front of him, did not even feign an interest in the Volk sisters.

"Both Miss Volks decided to move to Florida and buy a condo together. They've already contacted moving companies and intend to head south right away. This week, in fact. Miss Volk officially quit Fortune's Design this morning." Joanna eyed him uncertainly. "She's—uh—gone."

Ryder's head jerked up. "Miss Volk is gone?"

Joanna nodded.

"Dreams really do come true," he marveled, his expression thunderstruck.

"She says she'll sue if you try to withhold her severence pay because she didn't give advance notice," Joanna passed on Miss Volk's parting threat.

"Withhold it? I intend to give her a bonus for going!" Ryder leaned back in his chair and smiled broadly. "I feel like dancing around the desk singing 'Ding Dong the Witch is Dead.'"

"I liked Miss Volk," Joanna said tightly. His reaction felt like a vicarious slap, because she was sure he would behave exactly the same way if she were to announce that she was leaving. "I'll miss her."

"I won't, and neither will anyone else." Ryder was emphatic. "Miss Volk had a sour expression and a grievance to air for everybody who crossed her path. She's a veritable conduit of negativity.''

"Well, she loves her sister and her cat, so she can't be all bad,'' Joanna countered.

Ryder rolled his eyes heavenward. ''Didn't they say something like that about Stalin?'' He glanced at his watch and began to gather up a sheath of papers. ''I'm leaving for my meeting with Ike Olsen, our patent attorney in St. Paul.''

Joanna watched as he carefully placed the documents into his dark leather briefcase and snapped it shut.

"Since the hallowed Miss Volk is no longer with us, will you handle the reception desk and the phones for the rest of the day, Joanna?'' It was an order, not a request. ''Route all incoming calls to voice mail, with one exception. Remember that my great-aunt Kate is supposed to call sometime today, and you know I don't want her dumped into the voice mail system. Remember our policy. If her number shows up on the display, pick up the phone and tell her I'll return her call as soon as I get back.''

"I remember. I'll go out to the reception desk now,'' Joanna agreed. The assignment pleased her. She'd subbed for Miss Volk before and had never made a single mistake while doing it.

"And Joanna, while I'm gone print up my e-mail for the past two weeks.'' Ryder's voice halted her at the door. ''I've been so busy preparing my segment of the panel discussion for the Los Angeles conference at the end of the month that I haven't had a chance to respond to any messages. I plan to do it this afternoon when I get back from lunch.''

Joanna noticed that he didn't add how he'd taken care to make his own plane reservations for the L.A. conference, a snide reference he managed to mention at least once a day. The omission seemed significant, and so did his unexpected smile. Her heart turned over in her chest. For the first time since that tumultuous night at Surf City, he seemed…less than glacial toward her.

Her eyes met his, and she was the first to look away.

''I'll handle the reception desk and incoming calls and print the e-mail,'' she said quickly, though she felt a prickle of anxiety. She would be running between Miss Volk's desk in the reception area and Ryder's computer in his office. Uh-oh.

''I almost forgot—add a breakfast meeting with Hathaway on April eleven to my electronic schedule,'' Ryder tossed off the final order as he strode from the office.

Simple enough, Joanna reasoned, but she approached his computer with trepidation, feeling pressure building inside her. There was a lot at stake here. The stalemate between her and Ryder finally seemed to be coming to an end, and she didn't want to alienate him all over again by not completing the tasks he'd assigned to her.

It was a lucky break for her that Ryder was so delighted by Miss Volk's departure he'd even decided to extend his goodwill toward his *idiot assistant*. After nearly three endless weeks, he had addressed her normally again, the veiled hostility finally absent from his tone.

Joanna sat down at his desk, in his oversize leather chair still warm from his body heat. She knew that Ryder's electronic schedule and his e-mail were kept in password-protected files, with two different passwords. Something to do with security precautions, she remembered, though the long session with the electronic security expert had been taxing, and she'd had a hard time staying focused.

With a pang Joanna remembered her preaccident days and how easily she used to pick up knowledge and skills, how quickly she had been able to adapt new information to new situations. How she'd taken it all for granted. If Ryder only knew how smart she'd been back then....

Joanna shook her head. She didn't want Ryder to know anything about her past. Better that he considered her inept due to carelessness and a capricious nature. She didn't want him to know that she was truly defective.

Nobody had ever spoken the word aloud to her, but Joanna didn't let herself forget it. Everyone who'd taken care of her after the accident had urged her to face the truth about her injuries and move forward. Which she had done. She'd had to, because the truth was she would never be the same again.

No, she didn't want Ryder to know. Joanna bit down on her lower lip until it hurt more than the thought of Ryder Fortune pitying her.

The phones began to ring, and she checked the numbers displayed, looking for Kate Fortune's, to spare her a trip into the annoying labrinyth of the voice mail system.

Meanwhile, Ryder's computer seemed to have hatched a diabolical plan to keep her from gaining access to his electronic schedule file and his e-mail. "Access Denied" kept flashing on the screen as she tried first one password, then the other.

It occurred to her that she must've mixed them up, but try as she might she couldn't seem to make a correct hit. It was as if the machine itself deliberately kept scrambling them!

The phones rang nonstop. Everybody in Minneapolis—*maybe the entire world?*—had suddenly decided to call Fortune's Design. Joanna checked every number, hoping none of them belonged to Ryder's beloved great-aunt and benefactor. Because she was starting to get the numbers as mixed up as the passwords.

Perspiration beaded on her brow as she dashed back and forth from Ryder's office to the reception area, feeling trapped as a rat in a maze. The similarities worried her. Did the rats ever get out of those mazes, or did they just keep running around, accomplishing nothing?

And then, sweet miracle, she gained access to both files. Though she would've preferred to open one at a time, rather than both simultaneously, she didn't dare cross the computer that had finally deigned to grant her entry.

But something was wrong. Though she hit the essential command, the printer was not activated. The e-mail remained unprinted.

"E-mail is a mixed blessing," she quoted Ryder to

herself. He was ambivalent about it. When he'd gotten his MBA, e-mail hadn't been so pervasive, but when he'd returned from his life of adventure e-mail ruled the workplace. Perhaps as an unconscious protest, Ryder—normally a most conscientious executive—was uncharacteristically lax with his e-mail. He let it accumulate before he ever looked at it; he forgot to save messages...

Had he saved these messages? The thought struck her just as she moved to the other file, to insert Ryder's appointment with Hathaway into his schedule, but her addition didn't show up on the screen.

Annoyed, Joanna hit the commands again. If she'd mixed up the files— But how? There was the e-mail, there was the calendar.

She hit a few more keys and suddenly the monitor went blank. Bewildered, Joanna stared at it. The long scroll of e-mail messages had disappeared. Every space on the electronic calendar was empty.

The phone rang again, and Joanna glanced at the number displayed. It was Kate Fortune's. Wasn't it? She took the call.

"Can I talk to Ryan?" an aggressive male voice demanded over the line, while Joanna coped with the dawning horror that instead of being printed, two weeks' worth of e-mail had been deleted. Not only that, every scheduled appointment in Ryder's electronic calendar from January to December had been erased, as if by magic.

Black magic, Joanna thought dolefully. Accidentally practiced by her.

She tried to figure out what had happened. In her

rush to intercept Kate Fortune's call, had she mixed up the icons on the screen or the commands on the keyboards—or maybe in a spectacular goof, somehow done both—consigning the e-mail and the schedule to the trash file instead of the printer?

Even worse, her mistake had been for nothing because the caller wasn't Kate Fortune. Joanna recognized the brash insistent tone of a stockbroker on a cold call—one who hadn't even gotten Ryder's name right.

"*Ryan's* not here!" she snapped and forcefully slammed down the phone. Who had time to worry about a broker's feelings when she'd committed a drastic error? Or more.

Panic swept through her. Joanna tried to remember what she knew about computers. Wasn't there a way to get things out of the trash? She pushed the mouse around and pressed all sorts of commands on the keyboard, to no avail. It was as if the contents of those files had been totally obliterated.

What if they had been?

She raced out of the office, down to Marketing to seek help. Warren and Aaron, two nice guys she'd befriended there, agreed to try to retrieve the lost files. The three of them trooped back into Ryder's office.

The phone rang again, but Joanna was too engrossed in the current crisis to notice.

Warren did. "Let whoever it is go straight into voice-mail purgatory," he joked. "We gotta save our little Joanna's neck from the hanging noose."

It wasn't until the phone stopped in midring that Joanna noticed the display number and realized that the caller whom they'd just relegated to voice-mail purgatory was none other than the revered Kate Fortune. Whose call she'd been commanded to take.

"What a mess!" Groaning, Joanna sank onto her desk chair, clutching her head in her hands.

"Hey, we all have our bad days," Aaron offered a few consoling words. He and Warren were both hunched over Ryder's computer, rapidly hitting commands on the keyboard. "Computer foul-ups can happen to anyone."

"That's tactful of you to say, but it's not true," Joanna lamented. "Grade-school kids are savvy enough not to trash what they want to print. Gracie, my niece, is as comfortable with computers as she is with crayons."

"Strangely enough, the trash is empty," Warren murmured, frowning.

Joanna flinched. "Does that mean that I...I *permanently* deleted everything?"

"Let me try this one last-ditch thing." Warren's fingers flew across the keyboard and his frown deepened. He glanced up at her and cleared his throat. "Uh, look at it this way, Joanna. If any of those e-mail messages are of vital importance, the senders will post them again. I'll bet most were just junk, anyway," he added hopefully.

He didn't comment on the lost calendar. There was no way to downplay the seriousness of all those lost appointments.

"Why would RF want his e-mail printed, anyway?" puzzled Aaron. "Seems like a waste of ink jet and paper to me. He should read them straight from the monitor.''

"Except he can't because I sent them into oblivion.'' Joanna's breath caught in her throat. "Is everything gone forever?''

She could tell by Warren and Aaron's wrinkled foreheads and matching grimaces that the retrieval effort had failed, but she needed to hear it said. To douse that tiny flare of foolish hope that still flickered within her.

"Gone without a trace,'' confirmed Aaron. "Sorry, Joanna.''

"You said you tried all kinds of things to retrieve the files before you came to get us,'' Warren said slowly. "Somehow, some way…'' His voice trailed off, leaving the obvious unsaid.

Whatever she'd done was unable to be undone. Her vestige of hope was officially quashed. "Oh, what am I going to tell Ryder?'' Joanna cried, aghast.

"Well, you could point out there are always unexplained glitches that occur,'' suggested Aaron.

"But I *made* the unexplained glitch occur.'' Joanna choked out the words.

"There is no actual proof of that.'' Warren tried to cheer her up. "No incontrovertible evidence was left behind like DNA on a crime victim. It's within the realm of possibility that a computer virus could've been at work here.''

"That's the story to go with,'' seconded Aaron. "Warren and I will back you all the way, Joanna. I have some outdated files of my own that I could make disappear to add credibility to the virus theory.''

"The virus is Joanna Chandler. And I can't ask you guys to lie for me." Impulsively she hugged first Aaron, then Warren. "But thank you both for trying to help. I really appreciate it."

"I'll be glad to help you anytime, Joanna." Warren prolonged the hug by tightening his arms around her.

Joanna managed to gracefully extricate herself from his embrace. "I'd better get back to the reception desk. Without Miss Volk here—"

"Being Volk-less calls for a celebration!" exclaimed Aaron. "A bunch of us are going out to this hot new club tonight. Come with us, Joanna. After a day like this, you could use a night of fun."

"And Surf City is supposed to be 'Fun Taken One Step Further,'" Warren flashed a promising smile while quoting the club's latest advertising slogan.

Joanna remembered the music blasting at hearing-loss decibels, the unseasonable beachwear, the claustrophobia-inducing crowds. So that was Fun Taken One Step Further? She'd had a better time alone at home watching sitcom reruns on cable.

But tonight she would be unemployed, and sitting alone in her apartment held no appeal. Jenny and Wendi would be out; that was a given, they went out every night.

Joanna envisioned the evening that awaited her, alone in her apartment, worried sick about finding a new job so she could remain independent rather than sponge off her sister, who'd already done so very much for her.

Maybe an evening at Surf City, where it was virtually impossible to think, let alone worry, didn't sound so awful after all.

The first thing Ryder noticed when he entered the building was Joanna seated behind the reception desk…and two young hotshots from the marketing department hanging all over the desk. Vying for Joanna's attention. *All but drooling over her!*

And no wonder. She was wearing her dark strawberry-colored suit, the one with the short skirt and fitted jacket, the one that drove him crazy every time she wore it because it revealed hints of tantalizing curves while discreetly concealing them. His rational mind appreciated the garment as a masterpiece of product design—except the sight of Joanna wearing it effectively rendered him irrational.

He stopped at the desk, a fixed smile on his face. "Slow day, huh?"

The tone of his own voice startled him. He had intended to sound jovial, like one of the guys. What he'd heard was his father, in full executive mode, about to deliver an admonishment on the perils of wasting time.

Aaron apparently heard the same thing. He abruptly straightened, his expression a portrait of guilt. "Ryder, we—um—were just—er," he began.

"We heard a rumor and came seeking proof," Warren interjected with a winning schoolboy smile. "We had to see with our own eyes that it's not a mirage, that Miss Volk isn't here. And it's true, she's really gone. 'Ding Dong the Witch is Dead,' hey, Ryder?"

Ryder decided that Warren bordered on smarmy. His jokes weren't funny, either.

"I'd like you two to bring me up to speed on the Gladwin project first thing tomorrow morning," Ryder said, and felt a twinge of satisfaction at the sudden panic in their eyes. Since the Gladwin project was brand-new, very little would've been done on it, certainly nothing worth sharing with the boss at this point.

But he'd made it sound like there ought to be!

Warren and Aaron immediately announced that they were returning to their offices. But as they were leaving, Ryder saw Aaron wink at Joanna, heard him hum a verse of "Surf City" under his breath.

Joanna gave a brief nod. She appeared sorry to see the pair leave.

Ryder narrowed his dark brows, subjecting her to a piercing stare. "'Surf City'?"

She shrugged, and he noted that she diligently avoided any eye contact with him. "Good night!" he all but roared. "You're not planning to go back to that place with them, are you?"

She gaped at him, and Ryder felt a flash of pride. He'd put together the clues with astute ease.

"I...said I'd meet them there tonight." Joanna was defensive. "A group from marketing are going. It...it could be fun."

"Fun?" Ryder echoed incredulously.

He wished that his keen powers of perception had failed, because he hated what he'd just learned. Joanna was going to Surf City with two junior marketing executives who were clearly smitten with her. And if they were all over her like a rash here at work, in the anything-goes atmosphere of Surf City they would surely—

Ryder blocked that thought. "You know what that place is like, Joanna. You detested it as much as I did."

"I thought maybe I ought to give it another try." Joanna stared at the phone, as if willing it to ring. It did not. "The gang in marketing are—"

"Wild," snapped Ryder. "Not to mention partly insane. That's why they're so good at what they do. I ought to know, I'm the one who—"

"Ryder, I...I can't put this off any longer." Joanna abruptly stood up.

She caught him in midsentence, in midthought. Ryder watched her pace the small area behind the desk. She was visibly upset, almost on the verge of tears.

"Joanna, what's wrong?" he asked, his voice deep with concern.

Her hands were trembling and she flexed her fingers. Where to begin? "Your great-aunt Kate's call got routed to voice mail, Ryder. I didn't get a chance to talk personally to her."

Her distress touched him. She knew how much he cared for Aunt Kate, what he owed her, and was distraught at the thought of slighting that grand lady in any way.

"It's all right, Joanna." Ryder reached out to give her shoulder a reassuring pat, but she was moving so fast, he missed her. "Aunt Kate accepts the inevitability of voice mail. She wouldn't take offense. I'll simply call her back now. No harm done."

"Famous last words." Joanna swallowed hard.

She launched into her confession, not sparing herself by offering any excuses when she admitted that his e-mail had been erased and his electronic schedule had gone missing.

"It's no use pretending anymore, Ryder." Joanna's voice shook with emotion. "It has to be said, and I ought to be the one to say it. I'm a terrible executive assistant. The absolute worst."

She took a deep breath. She'd been mentally rehearsing her speech since Warren and Aaron had pronounced her mistakes irreversible.

"You need to have somebody with better office skills, Ryder, someone with administrative ability, and that just isn't me. The company is growing and you need somebody with a strong business background who'll be an asset, not a liability, in your office."

Ryder said nothing at all. Now that she had voiced what he often thought, he found himself unable to agree with her bald assertion.

"You've been too patient, too understanding, to fire me, so I'm firing myself. I quit, Ryder. It's only fair to you and to the company."

Ryder ran his hand through his hair, making it almost stand on end. *Joanna was quitting?* He prided himself on his perceptive skills, but he hadn't seen this coming. He felt blindsided and swiftly sought to take control of the situation.

"Joanna, don't play drama queen." He hoped she wouldn't catch the note of desperation in his voice. "I get enough of that from Charlotte, I don't need it from you."

He knew what he needed from her—and also knew

that he had a snowball's chance in hell of getting it. Ryder watched Joanna pace the reception area; his gaze, longing and hungry, following her every move.

Nothing new there. He'd had trouble keeping his eyes off her from the moment she had walked into his office on that cold January day, but he hadn't realized what was happening to him until the night of their aborted tryst at Surf City.

On second thought, his perceptive ability was a joke because he had been caught off guard by the full force of his attraction to her. Until that fateful night. Then he'd touched her, held her, kissed her, and what felt like an emotional explosion of nuclear proportions had taken place inside him. He hadn't been the same since.

Joanna turned and walked toward him, her expression of despair turning into one of annoyance. His rebuke had clearly irked her.

"I'm not being dramatic, Ryder. I'm being realistic and you know it."

Ryder watched her come closer. The short strawberry skirt accentuated the shapely length of her legs, the vee of her jacket permitted a glimpse of the creamy-white camisole underneath. He felt his heart pounding in his chest as heat streaked through him, pooling deep and low in his groin.

It was Surf City all over again.

The potent sensual memories of their encounter that night swept through him like a riptide. He could remember exactly how she had felt in his arms, the sweet taste of her mouth, her enticing feminine scent.

Ryder nearly groaned aloud. Since then, he had spent hours gazing at Joanna Chandler like a teenager fixated on his first crush. He'd watched her, inventing imaginary conversations between them, trying to find a way to break through her reserve and end the distance between them.

It was so unlike him, to lose his head over a woman. Ryder mocked his preoccupation with Joanna as juvenile and pathetic. It would've been unspeakably embarrassing…if she had bothered to notice.

But she didn't. She went about her Joanna-ish way, either unaware of the sexual tension that seemed to permeate the very air they breathed, or else blithely ignoring it. Ignoring him. Nothing he said or did shook her impenetrable air. She remained the epitome of cool—fascinating and maddening and always, always out of his reach.

"Life is complex enough without adding impossible complications." The proclamation she'd made that night she had decided they were not fated to become lovers had a nasty way of rebounding in his head. Joanna considered him to be an impossible complication, hardly a flattering view. Certainly not a romantic one.

And now she was quitting. If she left Fortune's Design, Ryder knew he would never see her again because she would make sure that he didn't. She was already planning a plunge into Minneapolis nightlife by going to Surf City with that wild bunch from the marketing department tonight!

She was irresistible, and it would be only a matter of time before some guy caught her interest. And then—

Then he would have no chance at all with her. Ever.

His every instinct rallied against that unacceptable fate. He had to do something, and fast.

"You can't quit, Joanna." Ryder's voice, stern and strident, boomed throughout the reception area.

Six

Joanna whirled around to face him. "Because you want to have the pleasure of firing me yourself?"

"If you quit, you can't collect unemployment benefits," Ryder said quickly, his mind racing.

"But if I'm fired I can," Joanna recalled that dull employee-benefit lecture, much of which she'd tuned out because she couldn't stay focused on the many arcane points. Still, she'd managed to pick up a few things.

She stared quizzically at Ryder. "Isn't it better for the company if I quit, because then you—"

"Technically, I suppose, if you're looking at the issue from that particular standpoint, it—" Ryder interrupted himself as frustration surged through him. "We are not discussing the ins and outs of unemployment compensation, Joanna! Stick to the topic at hand."

"I am!" Joanna met his glare with one of her own. "The issue at hand is me leaving Fortune's Design."

She decided that one thing she was *not* going to miss about Ryder Fortune was the way the veins in his neck bulged when he was infuriated. Like now.

"You've been wanting to get rid of me for weeks, and today I've given you more than just cause to fire me. Not even Julia herself could fault you for it. But I...I offered to quit so you wouldn't be hassled with unemployment forms," she added grandly.

"Give me a break, Joanna." Ryder hooted with laughter. "You were acting on sheer impulse. You didn't give a thought to unemployment benefits until I mentioned them."

"As always, you have to have the last word. All right, fine. Whatever. I didn't think about collecting unemployment. There, the last word is yours, Ryder."

Joanna was seething. Maybe she hadn't considered her unemployment benefits, but she had given careful thought to what she believed was her unselfish act— relieving Ryder and the company of her and her mistakes. And instead of being appreciative, he'd managed to turn her noble gesture into something stupid. Something typical of an "idiot assistant."

Well, she'd had enough. More than enough. Like Miss Volk, as of today she was history here at Fortune's Design. "I'm going to clear out my desk and get my coat and purse and go home," she declared, heading into the office they shared.

Ryder followed her, pulling the door closed behind him. And locking it.

Joanna opened the bottom drawer of her desk to retrieve her purse, but Ryder was right behind her. He swiftly extended his foot, using it to slam the drawer shut.

She straightened and jumped back, shocked. "What are you—"

"You're not going anywhere, Joanna."

Her eyes widened as she took in his unyielding stance. He'd moved to stand directly in front of her desk and was now blocking her access to it. He looked ready to tackle anybody foolish enough to attempt to get around him. Joanna was not about to try.

She was genuinely perplexed. Didn't he get it? She was ridding Fortune's Design of her maddening presence. So where was his smile of triumph? He ought to be dancing around his desk singing, instead of guarding hers like a police dog.

"I need to get my things, Ryder." She spoke slowly and clearly, the way her speech therapists talked to patients who were having difficulty with comprehension. "I'm going home now."

"It's not time to go home yet, Joanna," Ryder mimicked her delivery. "It's only two o'clock. That's too early to leave the office. Even Miss Volk managed to hang in till five o'clock."

"But...but I—"

"You have a lot of work to do this afternoon, Joanna," he said brusquely. "You have to recreate my entire electronic schedule. And since Ike Olsen and I plan to go to D.C. at the end of the month to meet with an examiner in the Patent Office, you'll need to make my travel arrangements. I'll be gone overnight so book me into a hotel the evening of the thirty-first. I want an early flight out that morning and a late-afternoon flight back to Minneapolis on April first."

Joanna stood stock-still, staring at the stripes on his tie. He couldn't have said anything to astonish her more.

After listening to his daily diatribes about making his own travel arrangements for his L.A. trip—because he didn't trust her to do it—Joanna was fully aware that his directive was far more than a routine order. It was an olive branch. A sign that he was willing to forgive and forget her previous flub.

Then again, it was possible that she'd misinterpreted him. "You...want me to make your travel arrangements to D.C.?" she asked, just to be certain.

Ryder cleared his throat. "That's what I said, yes."

"Aren't you afraid I'll forget to do it and then you'll be stuck going to D.C. via Asia or some equally arduous route?" She couldn't resist repeating one of his many taunts back to him.

"I want you to make the travel arrangements, Joanna."

Maybe it wasn't an olive branch at all; maybe it was a trap. She caught her lower lip between her teeth, biting it lightly. "But why? Especially after my computer screwup today?"

His eyes tracked her every gesture, focusing on her mouth. He drew a sharp breath. "I'm assuming that you didn't do it intentionally, Joanna."

"No, of course not, but—"

"Computer mishaps can happen to anyone. Occasionally, even me," he added magnanimously.

Aaron had offered her that same excuse, Joanna recalled. She'd found it lame then, and she wasn't buying it now. "What I caused was worse than a mishap. It was more like computer mayhem, Ryder."

"But unintentional computer mayhem," he insisted.

She folded her arms in front of her chest. Just when she'd thought he couldn't say anything to astonish her more, he did. "Ryder, did you have one of those three-martini lunches today?"

"I didn't even have one martini, and my judgment isn't impaired by alcohol, Joanna." His lips twitched as he failed to suppress a smile. "The entire incident is no big deal, but you've lost your perspective and blown it way out of proportion."

He saw her doubtful expression and pressed on. "Look, if any of those e-mail messages are of vital importance, the senders will post them again or get in touch with me by phone. Most were probably the equivalent of junk mail, anyway."

"Warren said that, too," Joanna blurted out, "but that doesn't—"

"Since you mentioned Warren," Ryder interjected, "call him now and tell him you won't be going to Surf City tonight. You can't, because you'll be working late."

Joanna noticed that his smile had been erased as completely as his e-mail. She was on shaky ground here. "If I'm working late tonight, I guess that means I still have a job?"

"I guess it does, Joanna. Now call your friends in Marketing and bail out of tonight's excursion."

She called Warren, though her conversation with him was decidedly short and stilted. How could it be anything else, with Ryder standing less than a foot away from her, obviously listening to every single word?

Joanna hung up quickly. "They're still going to-night." She felt the need to break the thick silence that had descended over the office like a layer of volcanic ash.

"I guess we can forget anything getting done in Marketing tomorrow." Ryder scowled. "After a night at Surf City, their brains will be collectively fried."

"Maybe not. You and I left there with our brains intact," she pointed out.

"I disagree," Ryder replied, and he gazed into her eyes.

Joanna blushed and looked away. He was coming dangerously close to bringing up their uncharacteristic behavior that night, breaking their unspoken pact not to allude to what had happened between them. Until now, neither one of them had.

Already off balance from his determination to absolve her of any wrongdoing today, she knew she couldn't deal with sexual innuendo, however remote. "Well, we've wasted enough time today, let's get back to work," she said, striving to sound like a driven, type-A workaholic.

"You've taken the words right out of my mouth." Ryder grinned.

A powerful surge of combined relief and happiness made her nearly giddy. Joanna smiled back at him.

"Of course, I backed up my electronic schedule on a diskette," Ryder said, retrieving it from a box on his desk. "And I also keep a handwritten calendar, as yet another backup."

"I should've known you'd have backups for your

backup.'' Joanna gazed at him admiringly. "You're thorough, Ryder. You keep track of all the details without losing sight of the big picture." She'd heard Julia describe Michael that way and decided it was applicable to Ryder, as well.

"Ah, lavish praise from my assistant." Ryder actually laughed. "Have you been reading those how-to-run-with-the-crocodiles office guides, Joanna?"

"I believe it's called *How to Swim with the Sharks.* And no, I wasn't sucking up to you, Ryder. I meant what I said."

They looked at each other. This time it was Ryder who lowered his gaze first. "Do you want to reload the schedule from the diskette to the hard drive, Joanna?"

"Are you sure you trust me near that machine?" She joined him at his desk. "It does strange things when I'm around."

"Go figure," Ryder gritted. His pulses were pounding in his head, and his entire body ached with a tension that grew more taut with every breath he took. Yes, Joanna had a definite effect on whatever she was around.

"Here, sit down." He stood up, offering her his chair.

Joanna slipped into the chair, but Ryder didn't move away. She couldn't blame him for wanting to watch what she did and how she did it, not after the electronic calamity she'd committed earlier.

But did he have to stand so close? Joanna swallowed. He was very close indeed, as he leaned over the chair. Leaned over her. When he placed his hands on both arms of the chair, she was effectively caged between Ryder and the desk. She sat ramrod straight because if she moved back even a hairbreadth, her head, her shoulders or her arms would be touching him.

Her fingers stumbled over the keys. She accidentally hit the button marked Shift, and the calendar on the monitor screen took a crazy lurch to the left.

"Oops," she mumbled.

"It's okay." Ryder bent and leaned in closer.

Now their bodies touched, and Ryder caught her subtle scent, an ethereal perfume he couldn't name but associated only with her. It seemed to make every nerve ending in his skin come alive. He turned his head slightly, his eyes tracing her profile; so close that he could see the muscles in her throat move as she gulped.

"Ryder, your schedule won't be—"

"Not to worry," he said huskily, pressing a key that righted the contents on the screen.

Joanna trembled. They were finally touching, and she wanted to be even closer to him. Their eyes met, and she knew that what she saw in his was reflected in her own. Desire. Excitement. And affection.

"I can't think." Her voice was faint, but laced with wry humor. "Not a good thing when I'm supposed to be working, Ryder."

"Don't worry, I'll coach you," he murmured, his lips against her hair.

He made his instructions simple, taking each step

so slowly and precisely that even little Felicity and Phoebe could've followed them. And while he spoke, his hand moved to her neck to sweep her hair from her nape.

His fingers kneaded the tense muscles there, his strokes gentle but firm. And intensely arousing. He extended the massage to her clavicle and her shoulders. Joanna squirmed in the chair, as wild, sweet, almost unbearably exciting sensations ricocheted through her.

"This is supposed to relax you," Ryder's low voice sounded in her ear, his breath warm against the curve of her throat. "Is it working?"

Joanna felt light-headed. She closed her eyes, concentrating hard on suppressing a moan of pure pleasure.

"It's definitely working," she breathed, "but I don't know if *relax* is exactly the right word to describe what you're doing to me."

Her words had an intense effect upon Ryder, as if she'd caressed him with her delicate, long-fingered hands now resting idly on the keyboard. Raw need surged through him.

He swiveled the chair toward him, reaching down to catch Joanna's arms and lift her to her feet.

"*This* is what you're doing to me," he growled, pulling her against him. Letting her feel the hard strength of his erection.

He slanted his mouth over hers, drinking in her small gasp, his tongue sliding over hers to rub and stroke in erotic simulation. She clung to him, holding nothing back, trapping his right thigh between hers, her hips pressed hard against him.

He slid one big hand under her skirt and cupped her intimately, shifting the hot damp silk to create friction, his fingers parting her as she shivered with uncontrolled pleasure. She groaned into his mouth and slipped her own hand between their bodies to trace the virile shape of him.

She felt him throb against her palm. He was hard, achingly hard, as ready for her as she was for him. Their kisses grew deeper and hungrier, his tongue mimicking the motions of his fingers as he caressed her.

Joanna was dizzy with passion. She wanted, she needed, she loved—

She loved him! Defying common sense and her own best advice to herself, she had fallen in love with her boss, Ryder Fortune.

Emotions that she had been suppressing broke through and overwhelmed her. She'd never felt this way before, never experienced this wanting to give to a man, to share herself with him. Now she understood why she wanted to be near him, why she'd stayed at this office with him, though he'd certainly been a bear to her at times.

But other times…she'd come to understand and admire Ryder, she enjoyed his prickly sense of humor. There were plenty of times when they were quite in sync, though even his decidedly difficult nature appealed to her.

Dealing with Ryder was challenging, and she was

a person who responded well to challenge. An easy man would not interest her.

The insight was so stunning that it smashed the sensual cocoon enveloping her. Joanna was abruptly dragged back into the unwelcome realities of time and space. She and Ryder were about to make love right here in the office, right here on his big desk, whose sleek modern design made it resemble a high-tech spaceship more than a traditional piece of office furniture.

That is, *she* was about to make love with Ryder, the first man she'd ever considered making love to. *He* was about to have sex with her. There was a huge difference between those two perceptions. Woe to the fool who didn't know it.

Joanna knew she was not a fool.

She pulled her hands away from him at the same moment she twisted her head, denying him her mouth. And before he had time to figure out what was happening, she pushed him away from her. Hard.

Ryder was left pulsing and gasping as she backed away from him, retreating to her own desk, putting it and the length of the office between them.

"Joanna." His voice was a whisky-soft rasp. His body was tense, his face flushed with desire.

"We can't do this, Ryder." She braced her hands on her desktop, using it to support herself because her knees were so rubbery she worried they might buckle at any moment. She couldn't stop shaking.

"I need you, Joanna." It was a plea.

A hard-to-resist plea. She gazed at him, needing

him, wanting him. Loving him. Emotional tears welled in her eyes, and she determinedly blinked them away.

"What's the matter, baby?" Ryder took a few tentative steps toward her, approaching her as if she were a wild animal bent on bolting.

Well, she felt wild. And panicky. And impulsive... No, she wasn't impulsive. "I remembered to stop and think before acting," Joanna said, consoling herself.

Ryder looked less than pleased, though. He heaved a sigh.

"You're right, I know you are." He took a few steps closer. "It's good that one of us stopped to think. This really isn't the place for—" He glanced around the office. "It's not the right place, but it's the right time, Joanna. Let's go to my apartment. Right now."

Joanna's jaw dropped. "Stop working in the middle of the day?" Today he kept saying things that truly amazed her.

"Yeah." Ryder took advantage of her bemusement to close the distance between them. Before she had fully registered what he had in mind, he was behind her, wrapping his arms around her waist. "We're going to quit work for the day and leave the office right now, Joanna."

Joanna let her head rest against his chest. It felt so good to be in his arms. She'd pulled away once; she didn't know if she could marshal the willpower to do it again. Or if she even wanted to.

"We're spending the rest of the day in my apartment, Joanna." His fingers splayed over her stomach, sending flames of sensual fire through her. "Consider it an executive order."

"An order from the boss?" She leaned back into him, letting the warmth of his hard frame suffuse her. "Remember that workshop the company sponsored on sexual harassment a few weeks ago?" Her voice was provocative, teasing, her slow, subtle movements against him even more so. "Your executive command could be construed as sexual harassment, Ryder."

"You think so?" He slid his hands under her jacket. "What about this?" He cupped her breasts, his hands gliding over the smooth silk of her camisole.

"Well, if I didn't want to—if I thought keeping my job depended on—" Her voice caught in her throat. It was becoming difficult to breathe, let alone think or speak, because his thumbs had begun to slowly brush over her nipples, which were already tight with arousal.

"True. If you didn't want me to touch you, and if you thought keeping your job depended on it, this would definitely be sexual harassment," Ryder concluded.

He stroked her again and again, kissing her neck, nibbling on the sensitive skin there, his lips moving in time with his caressing hands. Her hips picked up the age-old erotic rhythm, and she thrust softly against him.

"But it isn't, is it, Joanna?"

She had no idea what he was asking her about, nor did she care. Operating on pure feminine instinct, impulse and desire, Joanna turned in his arms and kissed him deeply, intimately, with all the passion and need of a woman in love.

"I want you so much, Joanna," he whispered against her lips. "Let me have you."

She inhaled sharply. "You mean, let you have sex with me?"

"You have this habit of clarifying everything!" Ryder chuckled softly, resting his forehead against hers. "You know it would be a lot more than just having sex, Joanna."

She was losing it fast. "It would?"

"It would for me," he admitted gruffly. "What about you?"

Joanna snuggled closer, unable to resist him. She'd stopped; she'd thought; she knew what she was doing. "I want you, too, Ryder, but it…it will complicate things between us."

"Things have been complicated between us since the day we met, Joanna. As for your 'life is complex enough' theory—well, this will simplify things considerably."

He kissed her, long and hard and deep.

The phone began to ring and kept on ringing, finally drawing them from the sweet world of passion to the mundane basics of life at the office.

"Nobody is at the reception desk. I should be there," Joanna said quietly, though she didn't move from his embrace. "We can't leave the office now, Ryder. It's too early, and we both have work to do."

Ryder groaned. "You're starting to sound like me."

"Your workaholic ways are contagious." Joanna

reluctantly slipped out of his arms. "I'll go back to the reception desk, and you call your great-aunt Kate, Ryder."

"Joanna, will you have dinner with me tonight?" he asked as she headed toward the door. "I don't mean a working dinner here in the office. We'll go out. And then—"

"Yes." She nodded her agreement. "To dinner and to 'and then.'"

She was halfway out the door when she turned back to him, a beatific smile on her face. "But before I do anything else, I have to make your travel arrangements to D.C., Ryder." She was thrilled she hadn't totally forgotten that crucial task, despite some very compelling distractions.

"Book yourself a round-trip flight, too, Joanna. I want you to come with me."

"To meet with a patent examiner?" Joanna was nonplussed. "I don't think I'll do you much good there, Ryder."

"You don't even have to go to the meeting. You can visit a museum or something. I want you with me, Joanna. Trust me, having you along will do me a lot of good."

Ryder was smiling as he called Kate moments later to talk about what was going on with Fortune's Design. Ryder had a detailed report to give her.

Several hours later he and Joanna were seated at a booth at La Cantina, a Mexican restaurant she had selected. Joanna had ordered her current favorite meal, spicy chicken burritos, and Ryder decided her food

quirks were charming. He could hardly believe he'd
been so curmudgeonly as to complain about the mo-
notony of her choice. If Joanna wanted to eat spicy
chicken burritos every day for the rest of their lives,
it was fine by him.

He was so glad to be with her, so madly anticipating
after dinner. Ryder felt as if he were on fire, burning
with a passionate heat that only Joanna could quench.
And she would. Tonight.

Seven

"The decor is very Ryder," Joanna remarked, taking her first look at Ryder's apartment. The combination living-dining room effectively utilized every square inch of space, and the furniture was high-tech modern.

"I'm subletting the place. It came already furnished. If you don't like it, I'll move and let you do the decorating." Ryder scooped her up in his arms. "You can make the decor very-Joanna, if you want."

She gave a nervous laugh. "Promises, promises."

He noticed the edge of anxiety in her voice. "Joanna, I'm not trying to snow you with some fast talk, I—"

"As if you could!" Joanna threaded her fingers through the hair at his nape. "Kiss me, Ryder."

She was trying to divert him, Ryder realized. And succeeding. Her lips nibbled at his, the tip of her tongue teased him. Ryder wanted to tell her that he meant what he said, that he'd never made a similar offer to another woman before.

He was slightly awed by this latest epiphany of his. He had yet to make love with Joanna, but he was already envisioning living with her. That definitely portended something big.

What was it about her that affected him so? he mused dazedly. He was sexually attracted to her, of course, but his feelings ran so much deeper. He admired her sweetness and sensitivity. She was invariably charming and fair and kind to others, and since he often wasn't, he appreciated those qualities in her all the more.

He liked her loyalty and her sense of humor. She was fun to be with, she made him laugh; not even his bad moods put her off. And she tried so hard. Even when Joanna made mistakes, she didn't give up. He respected her for that.

Ryder knew he should tell her all these things, he wanted to. But he didn't get the words out, because Joanna had pulled his head closer, deepening their kiss, and he was lost in a daze of instant passion. Striding across the room to the narrow hallway, he carried her into the apartment's only bedroom and sat her down on the edge of the king-size bed, which nearly filled the small room.

Joanna reached out to take his hand in hers, and Ryder sat down next to her. She inched even closer to him, her blue eyes wide and warm. With desire. And permission.

Ryder cupped her cheek with his palm, and she closed her eyes and leaned into his hand, letting the warmth envelope her. A soft whimper escaped from her throat when his lips brushed hers in a sweet, tentative kiss.

Joanna wanted more.

Clutching his shoulders, she climbed onto his lap,

her knees straddling his hips. He grasped her waist, steadying her as she swiftly unknotted his tie. Next, her fingers unfastened the first three buttons of his shirt and she touched her lips to the hard column of his neck.

She placed a lingering kiss there. "I want you, Ryder," she whispered against his skin.

Her urgency incited his, and he clamped one hand behind her head, tilting it to meet his mouth. There was nothing sweet or tentative in this kiss. It was hungry and demanding, and she responded in kind.

Ryder reclined back on the mattress, taking her with him, holding her on top of him, groaning as she clung to him. One kiss blended into another until both were breathing heavily, their bodies fiery with need.

He rolled Joanna onto her back and reached for the buttons of her strawberry jacket. "Ryder." She caught his hands, bringing his fingers to her mouth, kissing each one. "Could you turn out the lights?" she whispered.

He opened his eyes, realizing that the overhead track lighting was shining down brightly on them. "I must've flipped the switch on when we came into the room. I guess I did it automatically."

"Would you flip it off?" Joanna asked again, and he quickly rose to do her bidding.

The pause gave him a moment to think. "Do you have a thing against track lighting?" he asked curiously, because he knew many people did. "Or, do you have a thing about doing it in the dark?"

"Yes," Joanna replied, letting him sort it out.

The room was dark now, though a faint glow of light from the living room filtered through the half-closed door. She decided it was too dim to reveal much at all.

It wasn't only track lighting she rejected. She'd seen herself nude in brightly lit bathrooms and knew that the sight of her body was not one to be shared. Her injuries from the accident and many subsequent surgeries had resulted in a resemblance to something out of a Frankenstein horror movie. She had long, colorful tracks sewn with countless stitches, one scar meeting another, forming scar junctions.

Joanna shuddered. No, she was nothing for a lover to see.

She knew Ryder's body would be perfect and beautiful, and while she would've liked a clear view, she accepted having to settle for a kind of Braille interpretation of him. She would ''see'' him with her hands and her lips. And attempt to keep Ryder from doing the same thing with her.

That meant taking things very fast. A surge of adrenaline pumped through her and she pulled Ryder down to her, kissing him passionately. Then he took the lead, hastily tugging off his clothes and hers, dispensing with long, slow, sultry caresses. There would be plenty of time for that later, after they'd satisfied their initial, heated urgency.

Items of clothing were tossed away, landing in places all over the room. She moved her hand lower and grasped him, fast bringing him to the point where pleasure merged into pain.

"Joanna, please." The desperation in his voice was thrilling and compelling. "I...I can't wait any longer."

"I can't either, Ryder." She pressed her lips to his. "Now, please."

"I have to get something..." He managed to reach the drawer in the bedside stand and fumbled with an unopened box of condoms. "Not that I've needed these since I've lived here." He gave a self-deprecatory chuckle.

"But you're prepared." She ran her hand along his thigh.

"No Boy Scout motto jokes, please. The truth is, I've been living like a monk, Joanna. But not thinking like one. I bought this after that night at Surf City and—"

"—had unmonkish thoughts about me ever since?" she teased softly. "That's sweet, Ryder. You hid it well, though. I would've never guessed."

"I didn't intend for you to guess I was lusting after you, Joanna."

"So that's why you chewed me out at the office daily?"

"I didn't chew you—"

"You did. And when you weren't, you were freezing me out."

"You played a pretty convincing Ice Queen yourself, Joanna." He caught her hand and carried it to his lips. "I'm so glad that's all behind us, baby. Finally, we're together."

Joanna held the sheet in place with her other hand,

covering herself as she watched him sheath himself. The shadowy sight of him caused her to gape. He was so big, so strong, so gorgeous. So big.

He came back to her and kissed her lovingly. Her body instinctively arched beneath his, and Ryder moaned in pure ecstasy as he thrust into her, filling her.

Joanna clutched the headboard to keep herself from pushing him away, an urge as instinctive as every other she'd been following tonight. This was all new to her, but she was determined to come through like a champion. It was like physical therapy, she told herself, using muscles that initially resisted but following through anyway because the final reward was worth the effort.

Still, her body was screaming at her, the way it had every time her therapists in the rehab hospital tried a brand-new exercise on her broken limbs. Joanna tried to ignore it. Never mind that she'd never done this before, she would file the pain away and concentrate on pleasing him....

"Sweetheart, you're so tense." Unlike her therapists, who didn't acknowledge her pain—what would've been the point? of course it hurt—Ryder did notice. "Are you all right?"

Joanna nodded, a fine sheen of perspiration bathing her entire body. "Let's just get on with it," she said, gritting her teeth.

"Honey, I can tell it's been a while since you've—" Ryder began. A thought struck him and he instantly refuted it. No, it couldn't be. It wasn't possible. Not after the passionate way she'd kissed him and touched him, not after her eager advances.

"Joanna, exactly how long has it been for you?" he asked in a strangled tone.

She smoothed her hands over his back. The lull had given her body time to accommodate and adjust to his. Joanna felt a flash of triumph. She had won the fight against her reluctant body again, once more proving her superlative mind-over-matter ability.

"It's starting to feel good, Ryder," she said, more than a little amazed. She'd been willing to settle for the lessening of pain; she certainly hadn't expected pleasure. But pleasure was what she was definitely experiencing as she melted around his virile strength.

The hot fusion of their bodies was almost dizzyingly pleasurable. "Very good, Ryder," she whispered on a moan.

Ryder nearly gave it up then and there, but he held on. She'd been the one orchestrating things between them tonight, and it was time he took the lead. "You didn't answer my question, Joanna. How long has it been since you've made love?"

She nipped at his shoulder. Warm waves of sensual bliss were flooding her. "Not since my last lifetime, whenever that was. If ever that was," she added. She wasn't too sure about past lives.

"This is your first time?" He fairly gasped it.

"Don't be mad, Ryder. I didn't intend for you to know."

"Joanna, I'm not mad." He raised his head to look into her eyes. "But you should've told me."

"I wanted to make love with you, Ryder, not send you on a guilt trip. Which you're now about to take, anyway," she grumbled.

"I'm not feeling guilty. Okay. Yes, I am, but not about going to bed with you. Joanna, I should've taken things gentle and slow and instead, I—"

"You did exactly what I wanted, Ryder. It was wonderful." She wrapped her limbs around him and kissed him tenderly.

"You think that's it?" He was smiling as he lifted his lips from hers. "My sweet darling, we've hardly begun."

That night he showed her what she'd been wondering about, what she'd been yearning for. He taught her everything about the joys and pleasures of a man and woman making love. Joanna gave herself to him, creating and sharing bliss as they explored and finally exceeded the boundaries of their passion.

Emotion swelled within Ryder, so mingled with desire that he couldn't begin to separate them. The combination inspired a passion stronger and fiercer than he'd ever known.

Joanna was his, all his. Only his. He hadn't thought being first mattered all that much, but being Joanna's first lover meant more to him than he could ever have imagined.

Afterward, they lay together, nearly insensate with the rapture of their shattering release. Holding her tightly, Ryder buried his face in her hair, inhaling the alluring scent that was Joanna Chandler.

"Are you going to tell me how—and why—a beautiful, sensual, passionate woman like you has waited so long to—"

"I knew you'd be shocked," Joanna said lightly. "You thought because I'd traveled all over Europe on a Euro-rail pass that I'd slept my way across the continent, as well. And when you throw in my lack of education *plus* my job in the film industry—well, of course, you'd think I was something of a slut!"

"Joanna, I never thought that." Ryder was chagrined. Actually, he had thought her résumé added up to a very sexually experienced woman. But he'd never considered her a slut!

"Sure you did, but I forgive you." She kissed him playfully.

Joanna wasn't about to get into why she had remained so guarded and restrained sexually. She'd never analyzed the reason, although her feelings of inferiority about her patched-together body probably played a vital role.

She thought about those early days of posthospital freedom, when she'd partied hearty and hardy. Even then she'd set certain lines and limits for herself that she refused to cross.

"You didn't even try to answer my question, Joanna," Ryder persisted.

Joanna didn't want to delve too deeply into the whys and wherefores, especially not now. If she talked about her life-altering accident, she would have to show him her body, and that would definitely dim the afterglow.

"Let's just say I'd never let myself lose complete control before. Not until tonight," she said with a pleased little smile, nuzzling his hand that was stroking her neck.

Her answer didn't please Ryder. It occurred to him that what he wanted to hear were words he would have found sappy and unbelievable back in his cool-adventurer days. He wanted Joanna to say that she'd been saving herself for the right man, that she'd never been in love before—and that he, Ryder Fortune, was the one she'd been waiting for her entire life.

Because he was in love with her. He had never felt this way about any woman before, but he knew right then and there that she was the love of his life.

"Ryder, there's something we need to talk about, something I have to tell you." Her voice was soft, hesitant.

"You can tell me anything, sweetheart," Ryder promised fervently.

He was sure she wanted to tell him she loved him but felt shy. It was up to him to assure her that her declaration elated him. And then he would confess that he was in love with her, too.

"I can't continue as your executive assistant, Ryder. We both know that what I said in the office earlier today is true. You need somebody with business talent and skills that you can eventually promote to a higher position in the company. We both know that person is not me, Ryder."

Her words had the equivalent effect of whacking him over the head with a plank. Ryder sat up straight, reeling from the blow. "I can't believe you're saying this now, Joanna. Not after—after—"

"I didn't say I wouldn't sleep with you again, baby." She scrambled to her knees to face him, pulling the sheet around her. "I want to, I want you. But I can't be your executive assistant any longer. Ryder, let's be honest. I'm not only awful at it, but I'm potentially dangerous in the position. So far I haven't made any real costly mistakes, but I'm capable of it, and we both know that, too."

"I'm resisting the primal urge to wring your neck, because I know you're a novice at postcoital conversation," Ryder said. "Let's get one thing straight here and now, Joanna. I don't want you to leave Fortune's Design. I want you with me. I want to see you every day *and* every night."

Joanna made no reply. She was silent so long that Ryder wondered if he'd scared her. Had he come across sounding obsessive, like a crazed stalker? He decided he didn't care. What he'd said was true, and he wasn't willing to play the denial game.

"There's a way I could stay at Fortune's Design, if you'd agree to it," Joanna said at last.

Ryder realized that he would agree to anything she said. In a humbling moment of self-awareness, he knew that six months ago he would've laughed at such behavior as that of a lovelorn chump. Six months ago, he hadn't met Joanna.

"What is it?" he asked quietly.

"Since Miss Volk is gone, I could be the receptionist. That's a job I can do well, Ryder. You could hire a new executive assistant and pay me my current salary and—''

''Your current salary is less than what Miss Volk earned, Joanna.''

''Well, you always said she was highly overpaid.''

He managed to hang on to his temper. ''I'll pay you what I paid Miss Volk if you really want that job, Joanna. But I'm perfectly willing to keep you as my—''

''Keep me as your lover,'' Joanna suggested, sliding her arms around his neck and cuddling close. ''And hire me as your new receptionist.''

Ryder's new executive assistant, Madison Worth, was exactly the type of executive assistant Joanna insisted he needed, possessing superb office skills along with substantial administrative ability. Well-educated—summa cum laude in business from Dartmouth—with the talent and proficiency that guaranteed promotion to a higher position in *any* company, at twenty-three, Madison Worth was indeed an asset to Fortune's Design.

On a personal level Ryder found her brash, aggressive and supremely confident, driven and outspoken. Also, somewhat insufferable. He figured that her family—the Worths, who owned the Michigan-based conglomerate Worth Industries, Ltd.—was probably thrilled that their youngest member had chosen to seek her fortune elsewhere.

Joanna claimed that Fortune's Design was lucky to have someone like Madison Worth who was brilliant, hardworking and socially and professionally well connected.

"And she's completely loyal to you and the company, Ryder," Joanna rhapsodized. "Madison says she'll never forget that you gave her the chance to prove herself, while her own chauvinistic family tried to sideline her in favor of her selfish brother and her nasty cousin, who is also male. Madison said that the Worths don't value women at all." They'd had this conversation in June, she recalled.

Joanna got along splendidly with Madison Worth. No surprise there, she got along splendidly with everybody. Since she'd taken over the reception desk, she saw her colleagues in the company a lot more than when she'd been sequestered in Ryder's office. Her desk had become a hangout for her pals in Marketing, though they inevitably scattered if Ryder happened to come along. Her popularity spread to other departments as well. Everybody liked Joanna.

"It's a credit to Joanna's interpersonal skills that nobody in the company resents her," Madison Worth announced one day in late June.

She'd come into Ryder's office without knocking, a practice that never failed to annoy him. He suspected she'd acquired the habit in her position as the boss's daughter at Worth company headquarters, but understanding the origin of her behavior made it no less irritating.

On the first day Madison Worth had reported for work, back in March, Ryder had retrieved the architectural plans and hired a construction company to complete them. He'd added an incentive clause, a bonus if the work was finished speedily, which it was. The proximity he'd shared with Joanna would've driven both him and Madison to justifiable homicide.

And now Madison had barged into his office once again with one of her brash assertions. Ryder fumed.

"Why would anyone resent Joanna?" he demanded.

"Because of your affair, of course," Madison replied frankly in that deadpan, no-nonsense manner of hers. If she had a sense of humor, Ryder had yet to see evidence of it, though he had seen her actually laughing with Joanna and some of those social butterflies from the marketing department.

"Affairs within a company, particularly one involving the CEO are poisonous to corporate culture," Madison continued dogmatically. "Most companies strictly forbid intra-office dating, particularly any relationship that involves a superior with an underling. The potential for sex harassment charges and discrimination is rife."

"Joanna is not going to hit me with a lawsuit," Ryder said shortly.

"Not now," Madison agreed. "But what happens when you two break up? You could easily use your position as her boss to—"

"Joanna and I are not going to break up," snapped Ryder.

"Oh? When are you two getting married?"

He could've sworn he saw the young woman smirk. Ryder nearly cracked the pencil he was holding in half. The subject of marriage was a sore one with him. He wanted to get married. He wanted it completely. He would've announced his engagement to Joanna yesterday—hell, he would've announced it way back in March!—except she wouldn't go along with it.

He well remembered the first time he'd proposed to her. It had been the night she'd told him about her near-fatal accident and the severe injuries she had suffered in it. Thinking about how close he'd come to losing her still caused his hair to stand on end. He had nearly lost her before he'd ever had the chance to find her.

He tried to tell her how meaningless his life would've been without her in it. He tried every day and every night to show her how much he cared. Still, Joanna seemed to remain unconvinced.

It frustrated him endlessly.

Along with proposing to her, he had also told her he loved her that same night, the night she had finally shown him her body. It had been in their hotel room in Washington, D.C., on the trip to meet with the patent examiner. Joanna had flatly refused to share the luxurious Jacuzzi with him, without even giving a reason why. She'd also insisted on making love in the dark, despite the absence of track lighting that Ryder had agreed ruined the romantic ambience in his own bedroom.

He finally realized that she was hiding something from him. So much for his heralded insight, his terrific power of perception. Until that night he hadn't intuited that she was hiding the sight of her body.

Ryder suspected some kind of easy-to-resolve post-virginal hang-up but should have known Joanna would not be so predictable. She had finally, reluctantly allowed him to see her in full light, visibly bracing herself for...what?

He still wasn't sure what she had expected from him. Revulsion? Rejection?

The very idea incensed him. "I love you, Joanna. For crying out loud, why would you think, even for a minute, that I would be turned off by a few scars? They're barely noticeable, anyway."

"You're being tactful and that's terribly dear of you, Ryder, but you don't have to pretend with me," she'd said wearily. "I know my body looks like a map of the interstate highway system. Hardly the stuff of male fantasies."

"You are every fantasy I've ever had, Joanna. My current fantasy involves marrying you. Marry me, Joanna."

She had kissed him and told him that she loved him, too—and refused to marry him.

They'd played out similar versions of that scenario several times a week since, but Ryder was not about to give up. He was a Fortune, and inevitably he would get what he wanted. Joanna, whom he loved beyond reason, would be his wife.

But it was so damn frustrating, waiting for her to realize it.

A fact he did not care to have his efficient, officious executive assistant remind him of. No question that her "When are you two getting married?" had hit a raw nerve.

"Exactly what brings you into my office at this particular time, Madison?" he asked, not bothering to disguise his displeasure with her presence.

As ever, Madison was undaunted. She waved a large document at him.

"Here is the new-product-design plan, Ryder. I took all of the reports from each of the divisions, compiled them, tabbed them and provided an executive summary. I also figured that while I was at it, I'd do a complete time line from conception through development to market."

She laid her project down on his desk. "Now I'm going to arrange to have all of our paper files scanned into the computer system. We're way overdue on that, I think. Unless you have something else for me to do?"

"No, nothing right now, Madison." Once again, his executive assistant had impressed him. Madison Worth carried the definition of *self-starter* to new heights.

He remembered Joanna's foray into executive assistanthood. There could be no comparison between the two young women, just as there could be no comparison between Joanna and the dragonish Miss Volk. When it came to receptionists, Joanna, with her sweet friendly manner and winning smile, was beyond compare.

Just thinking about her fueled his need to see her.

"Thank you for this, Madison." He nodded at the

detailed report she'd given him. "If you'll excuse me, I have a question to ask Joanna."

Instead of leaving, Madison stood in front of his office door, eyeing him curiously. "You've certainly made no secret that you're crazy about Joanna. You're together constantly. You two practically live together. Why don't you marry her?" she asked bluntly.

Eight

Ryder was aware that only the progeny of business aristocracy, someone possessing the unfaltering confidence born of money, class and smarts would dare to ask her boss such a question. An apt description of Madison Worth.

"I don't see how my relationship with Joanna is any of your business," he said tightly.

He decided he was within his rights to fire Madison for impertinence, except it would be an ill-advised enactment of the old "cutting off his nose to spite his face" cliché.

A look of dawning comprehension was spreading across Madison's face. "Oh, I get it now. Joanna won't marry you. You've already asked her, and she said no."

"May I repeat, this is none of your damn business, Madison!"

"I don't know why she would refuse." Madison frowned, trying to puzzle it out. Being unable to comprehend anything was not acceptable to her. "Joanna is madly in love with you, she's very open about that. So why wouldn't—"

Her brows narrowed shrewdly. "Do you suppose it has anything to do with Joanna thinking that she isn't smart enough for you?"

"Not smart enough for me?" Ryder was enraged. "That does it! You're fired, Madison!"

"I am not. Calm down, Ryder. I didn't say Joanna *wasn't* smart enough for you, I said *she thinks* she isn't. She's made a lot of jokes about being your idiot former assistant, but I never thought she was serious about the idiot part. Till now."

Ryder swallowed hard, his eyes widening.

"You didn't actually call her an idiot, did you, Ryder? You wouldn't say anything so cruel, not when she'd suffered such a terrible head injury in that car accident."

Ryder stared at her. "When did Joanna's accident and injuries become common office knowledge?"

"It's not, but she's mentioned it to me a couple times. Maybe she knew *I* wouldn't call her an idiot," Madison added severely.

Ryder jumped to his feet and began to pace the office. He'd acquired the pacing habit from Joanna and found it tension reducing. Right now tension was fast building within him, and pacing wasn't helping at all. Not as he remembered...

"I think you might be on to something, Madison."

"So you did say it?" Madison glared at him. "Why, you'd fit in with the men in *my* family with your tactless, thoughtless, inexcusable male arrogance!"

"God, I'd forgotten all about what I said. I mean, it was irrelevant. I was just sounding off." Ryder groaned. "I never even knew about her accident back then. But taken in context, Joanna could think— Of course, she would think…'' His voice trailed off as he started for the door.

''If you plan to rush out there and apologize to Joanna for calling her an idiot, don't expect an instant yes to your next proposal.'' Madison's words stopped him cold.

''Why not?'' Ryder demanded impatiently. ''If I've identified and rectified the problem areas to the satisfaction of both parties, then a favorable result is to be anticipated.''

''Maybe in a business merger.'' Madison sniffed disdainfully. ''But if you ask Joanna to marry you immediately after apologizing, she'll assume you're proposing out of a sense of guilt, and refuse. What woman with any pride wouldn't? And a woman's pride is as strong and worthy and valid as a man's,'' she added, daring him to refute her declaration.

Ryder didn't. ''I know. What I don't know is how to get past her pride,'' he admitted dejectedly.

Perhaps he had been humbled or saddened enough to quell Madison's sense of outrage. Whatever, her expression visibly softened. ''I'm currently having a brainstorm, if you'd care to hear it,'' she said in her usual can-do tone.

''At this point what have I got to lose?''

''Exactly.'' Madison nodded. ''As you well know, Joanna worships her sister, Julia. She would rather be tortured than to cause her sister and brother-in-law any pain. *Or* embarrassment. I suggest you play that card. Team up with the sister. How about a party where the Fortunes announce your engagement to Joanna, you produce the ring in front of everybody and slip it on her finger? Do you think Joanna would make her beloved sister—now a Fortune herself—look foolish by publicly refuting your announcement right then and there in front of everybody? Of course not. She'd play along. So there you are, engaged. It'll be up to you to get her to the altar, of course, but you can do it. After all, you'll be operating from a position of strength.''

"The Ambush Theory!" Ryder loved the plan. "Well done, Madison. You've taken a classic business technique and applied it to life. Those classes you took at Dartmouth definitely paid off. You're a credit to your professors.''

"Tell that to my family," Madison said darkly. "They think I should be socializing like a postdeb airhead trying to trap a husband, instead of climbing the corporate ladder of success.''

"That would be a true waste of talent," Ryder said, meaning it. "With a few modifications, I think this plan will work. I want to thank you in advance, Madison.''

"I confess to a selfish motive in all this, Ryder. Since I've hitched my career wagon to your star, so to speak, I want to see you with a wife who'll make you happy and be supportive of your dedication to Fortune's Design. A wife who isn't demonic to the employees, who understands the pressures and demands of building a company. If you were to end up with a narcissistic socialite or a paranoid witch, everybody in Fortune's Design would be adversely affected, including me. Joanna fits the bill.''

"Yes, she does." Ryder smiled. "Your self-serving

interests are duly noted, Madison. And definitely appreciated.''

The few modifications in Madison's plan involved *not* directly involving Julia and Michael Fortune in the ambush engagement. From observing the sisters together, Ryder knew that Joanna's sisterly devotion was returned in full measure. Julia would never countenance ambushing Joanna with anything, no matter how well-intentioned the cause.

Guilt was a factor, too. He simply couldn't face telling Julia Fortune that he'd called her adored, brave little sister an idiot. It didn't matter that he had never meant for his words to be taken to heart; *he'd* been the idiot for ever uttering them.

Remembering how he had railed at Joanna made him cringe. If Julia and Michael knew he had wounded her so, Ryder had no doubts they would loathe him. And rightfully so. He would keep them in the dark along with Joanna, still counting on his brand-new fiancée's unwillingness to embarrass *her* Fortune relatives in front of all *their* Fortune relatives by publicly calling the engagement announcement a hoax.

Which meant he needed another Fortune ally to stage the scene. And who else would he ask but Aunt Kate? She could understand and accept that sometimes one said things in a temper, things which were not meant to be taken seriously. Or literally.

Ryder made an appointment to visit his great-aunt at her mansion one warm summer afternoon, where he confessed his thoughtless insults, his regrets and his plan.

Kate was understanding, although she did offer some advice against careless, caustic venting, which Ryder solemnly promised to heed. Sterling Foster was present at the meeting, observing and listening in silence with a poker face that revealed none of his thoughts.

"We'll have a big family picnic here on Labor Day," Kate enthused. "That will give us time to plan the party and for everybody to arrange their schedules to attend. We'll want as many here as possible to celebrate our announcement."

"*Our* announcement," Sterling repeated, speaking at last. "So you consider yourself a full-fledged co-conspirator in the lad's scheme, Kate?"

"It's all in the name of love, Sterling." Kate smiled. "Remember another bogus engagement several years ago that resulted in a wonderful marriage?"

"Aunt Kate, I can't thank you enough." Ryder breathed a heartfelt sigh of relief. "You've come through for me again and I—"

"You *are* thanking me, Ryder. By succeeding in business *and* falling in love," Kate said, patting his hand. "I believe we have another Fortune success story here, don't we, Sterling? Congratulations are definitely in order." Beaming, Kate lifted her glass of chilled Chardonnay. "To Ryder and Joanna and Fortune's Design."

"Congratulations are premature at this point, Kate," warned Sterling. "Furthermore, overconfidence can lead to carelessness. I suggest we postpone this toast until the wedding is a done deal and Fortune's Design breaks even."

"You sound like a lawyer, Sterling, not a fond great-uncle," Kate chided him.

Ryder thought Sterling sounded most of all like a dire pessimist, and he didn't dare let himself succumb to that view. Better to direct his energy to making Aunt Kate's rosy outlook for the future come true.

"Both are going to happen, Aunt Kate," he promised earnestly.

"I have no doubts, my dear. I have great faith in you."

Since the party was to be held at the Fortune estate, Kate offered Kelly's services to plan it all.

As soon as she mentioned Kelly's name, Ryder sensed something was wrong. "Aunt Kate, you didn't sound like yourself just now," Ryder said bluntly. "What's going on?"

"Oh, heavens, Ryder, I'm sorry," Kate responded. "No, I'm not sick, dear. I'm just upset about Kelly. She's pregnant. I empathize with the girl, I really do..." Her voice trailed off.

Was Chad Fortune the father of Kelly's baby, and how was she coping with the situation? Ryder wondered, as he went to meet the young woman after his visit with Kate and Sterling. Would asking her be considered an invasion of her privacy?

Although their discussion centered solely on plans for the Labor Day Ambush/Engagement Party—Kelly was enthusiastic and very helpful—Ryder decided he would be remiss if he failed to at least acknowledge her condition.

"If there is anything I can do to help you and the,

uh, the baby, please give me a call, Kelly," he murmured as he rose to leave.

Uncertain and uncomfortable, he pressed his business card into her hand. Was that too impersonal? Or too intrusive? He wished Joanna were here to lend a more empathetic touch. She dealt so well with people.

Kelly's face was a smooth mask, although she was unable to conceal the pain that flickered in her eyes. "Thank you, but I'm fine," she said quietly.

"One more thing, and if this is none of my business, please feel free to say so." Ryder paused uneasily at the door. "Is the father my cousin Chad?"

Kelly nodded her head but volunteered no further information. Ryder felt totally out of his element dealing with such a delicate matter. He understood the young woman's desire for privacy, yet was unable to simply walk away without trying to do *something*.

"Kelly, would you like me to talk to Chad about...things?" he offered. Ryder tried to envision such a conversation with his cousin and frowned. Beating Chad the Cad to a bloody pulp seemed so much more satisfying and effective.

"No!" Kelly exclaimed, as if she could read his mind. "Thank you for your concern, Ryder, but I—I'm handling this in my own way."

"I understand," said Ryder, though he wasn't sure he did. She looked so young and defenseless. He couldn't just leave her to her fate, especially when she was being so helpful in aiding him with his!

"Kelly, you don't have to face this alone, you know," he blurted. "We can rally some of the Fortune cousins to use their clout to *make* Chad do the right thing."

"Please don't!" Kelly's voice was firm and resolute. "Promise me that you won't do or say anything, especially not to Chad, Ryder."

"So I promised I wouldn't say or do anything and I left," Ryder said, recounting his conversation with Kelly later that evening to Joanna, as they walked hand in hand along a well-lit path that followed the dark, fast-flowing waters of the Mississsippi River. "I still wonder if I shouldn't get a cabal of Fortunes together and—"

"Break Chad's kneecaps? Put a financial lien on everything he owns?" Joanna shook her head. "I think you should respect Kelly's wishes, Ryder. It seems to me that what you'd consider help, she might consider interference."

She stood on tiptoe to place a quick kiss on his cheek. "But it's wonderfully sweet of you to be so concerned about Kelly and her baby, Ryder."

"Wonderfully sweet," repeated Ryder, sucking in his cheeks. "There was a time when I would've jumped off a bridge if a woman had described me that way. But not when you say it."

He put his arm around Joanna's shoulders, drawing her close. "So you'll come to Aunt Kate's Labor Day picnic with me? She's really enthused about it. And of course Michael and Julia and the children will be there, along with as many other family members who can make it."

Ryder was pleased with his cover story, that the

picnic was strictly a Kate-inspired holiday get-together for the clan. Joanna wasn't suspicious in the least.

"I'd love to go," Joanna said, slipping her arm around his waist. "I always have a good time at Kate's parties."

"Hard to believe that we never met at any of them over the years," Ryder mused aloud.

"Well, you were out of the country for nearly ten years, and for a long time I wasn't around much, either," she reminded him. "And even though we were both at Kate's eightieth birthday party, we weren't there at the same time."

"You'd left early for a date before I arrived." Ryder frowned. They'd discussed Kate's party and how they had failed to even glimpse each other there. "Well, I'm your date for Labor Day, Miss Chandler," he added possessively.

"You're my date every night, Ryder," she affirmed.

"Then let's make it official, Joanna. Let's make it every night for the rest of our lives. Marry me, Joanna."

"Ryder, things are so good between us just the way they are," she said softly. "Why can't we keep it this way? We don't have to get married to—"

"All right, never mind," Ryder said, cutting in, not caring to hear her standard rejection speech. "Forget I even mentioned it."

At least he wasn't swamped with the frustration and gloom that normally followed his rebuffed marriage proposals to Joanna. Now he had a plan to implement his dream. He silently thanked the unlikely triumvirate of Madison Worth, Aunt Kate and Kelly Sinclair. And began to think about the requisite engagement ring he would produce at the picnic.

"You've never taken off your amethyst ring, and it's the only ring you ever wear," he said in what he hoped wasn't too odd a non sequitur. He lifted her hand to look at the unimpressive gem on her right hand.

"It was my mom's ring that was given to her by her parents on her sixteenth birthday," Joanna said, gazing at the ring. "Every time I look at it, I think of her."

"It's a beautiful ring," Ryder said quietly, brushing his lips over her fingers.

His plans for the engagement ring fell into place. A simple elegant diamond, a ring that she would treasure, that she would never take off. A ring that would make her think of him and how much she loved him every time she looked at it.

"I can't believe Mommy and Daddy flew to Minneapolis just to come to Aunt Kate's Labor Day picnic." Charlotte sipped a diet soda as she talked to Ryder and Joanna on Kate Fortune's spacious, well-tended green lawn. "Do you think they're really here to spy on me?"

"Absolutely." Ryder grinned. "News of your party-girl reputation finally reached them in Arizona, and they rushed up here to cramp your style, Charlotte."

"Which they're definitely doing," grumbled Charlotte. "I missed the big summer wrap-up extravaganza at Surf City this weekend 'cause the parents are here and we have to spend quality time with them.''

"Well, we enjoyed the family dinner and the play last night, Charlotte," Ryder said rather sanctimoniously. "Didn't we, Joanna?"

Joanna nodded her head. She'd been invited to accompany James and Sylvia Rutherford Fortune with Ryder, Matthew and Charlotte everywhere they'd gone this weekend. To lunches and dinners, to the movies and the theater, shopping and the museum. She liked Ryder's parents and didn't agree with Charlotte's gripe that they were two of the most boring people on the planet. It was too bad that spoiled, immature Charlotte didn't realize how very lucky she was that her parents were alive and well.

"Your folks are great," Joanna told Ryder.

James and Sylvia had been so warm and welcoming to her, insisting that she join them, taking an interest in her, offering her advice on all manner of things. Joanna enjoyed the proxy parental attention that Charlotte and Matthew considered to be annoying interference. Ryder had claimed that not long ago, he too would've complained, but he'd mellowed these days. He appreciated that his parents cared.

Only Kate, Sterling, and Kelly knew that Ryder's parents were actually here because his engagement to Joanna was to be announced at the picnic. They'd all taken an oath of secrecy, although James and Sylvia Fortune believed the surprise announcement was to be their oldest son's romantic gesture to his bride-to-be…not a public ambush because he couldn't get her to say yes any other way.

Today the Fortune mansion was swarming with Fortunes and assorted guests enjoying the warmth of the picture-perfect sunny day on the official last weekend of summer. The estate bordered the clear waters of Lake Travis, providing swimming and boating fun for all age groups. There was a kidney-shaped pool for those who preferred water warmer than the bracing temperature of the lake, and the tennis courts were in use for a series of Fortune *vs.* Fortune matches and rematches.

Dinner—steaks, fish, as well as the traditional hot dogs and hamburgers—had already been served and consumed when Kate took center stage on the wide patio.

''Before we have dessert, there is a very important announcement to be made. Ryder…'' Kate nodded at him, and he came to stand beside his great-aunt.

They exchanged sly smiles, and Kate gave his hand an encouraging squeeze.

Brandishing a velvet ring box, Ryder proceeded to announce his engagement to Joanna Chandler.

''Joanna? Where are you, sweetheart? Come on over here and put this on your finger to make it official.'' After his momentous proclamation, Ryder scanned the multitude of Fortunes gathered before him for a glimpse of Joanna.

Joanna had moved from the patio to the grass, carrying her baby niece, Noelle, in her arms. For a few moments she stood frozen with shock as the clapping and cheers and congratulatory wishes surrounded her.

A fussy, teething Noelle gnawed her tiny fist and drooled, far more occupied with her sore gums than the commotion around her.

"Aunt Joanna, can we be flower girls in the wedding?" A thrilled young Grace rushed over with her two smaller sisters trailing faithfully in her wake. "Can we *all* be in it, even Noelle? I could carry her and the flowers."

"I think Noelle is way too young to be in a wedding, Gracie." Michael Fortune joined his daughters at Joanna's side. Baby Noelle made a leap into her father's arms, making them all laugh. Even Joanna.

She quickly sobered as Ryder's announcement replayed itself in her head. He'd just told a zillion of his relatives—including his parents!—that they were engaged. Now he wanted her to play along with the charade, to stand in the center of a circle of Fortunes while he placed a ring on her finger.

She felt like she'd been ambushed.

"Congratulations, honey." Michael hugged her. "Of course we knew you and Ryder were serious, but this surprise announcement is a nice touch. Better run up there and claim your ring. Ryder's starting to look a little nervous."

"Joanna?" Julia was beside her now, studying her younger sister with concern. "Was this surprise announcement a surprise to you, too?"

Nothing got by Julia, Joanna acknowledged, as confusion continued to surge through her. Why had Ryder done this? Didn't he realize that she loved him too much to marry him? She had tried to show him by consistently refusing his gallant, achingly tempting proposals.

How could she possibly accept, knowing full well there were all sorts of expectations and demands on a Fortune wife! Joanna pictured herself wreaking havoc on some charity ball she would be expected to chair as Mrs. Ryder Fortune—she would surely forget some crucial detail, skip an essential planning stage, delete the guest list from the organization's computer.

Joanna envisioned the inevitable chaos with a shudder. The prominent Fortune clan would be horrified by her gaffes, the charity disappointed and Ryder's standing in the business community harmed. No, she wasn't about to limit her brilliant, ambitious man's future by legally saddling him with a defective spouse. Her.

There was a place for her in his life as Ryder's girlfriend, just as there was a place in his company for her as his receptionist. Joanna accepted, even embraced her roles. After all, she had finally successfully corrected the idiot-assistant problem by becoming a good receptionist. It would be stupid beyond imagining to reverse her current excellent relationship with Ryder by turning a good girlfriend into the idiot wife.

"I never expected this, Jules," Joanna whispered. It was a relief not to have to pretend with Julia, who needed only to look at her younger sister's face to interpret her state of mind.

"You don't have to go through with it if you don't want to, Joanna." Julia took Joanna's hand and gazed into her eyes. "If you'd like, I'll say there's been a misunderstanding and we'll go home. You know that Michael and I will stand behind you, no matter what."

Joanna knew that. Julia didn't require a faux engagement to save face in front of the Fortunes. *But Ryder did!*

"Joanna, there you are!" Ryder had finally spotted Joanna, surrounded by her family, and he worked his way through the crowd of relatives to her side. "I was starting to worry that you'd had second thoughts about marrying me and hit the road," he said as the other Fortunes engaged in indulgent laughter.

It was clear that they shared a collective familial viewpoint. No woman in her right mind would have second thoughts about marrying one of them.

Joanna glanced around her, at all the smiling, expectant faces. Ryder's parents were jostling their way through the group, their faces aglow with pride and happiness. And there was Ryder…

Joanna met his eyes, which somehow were both determined and pleading at the same time. "Here's the ring, Joanna." Ryder removed it from the box and took her left hand in his.

"Joanna, honey, I meant what I said," Julia murmured in her ear.

Joanna knew. Her sister had already proven that she would stand by her through thick and thin…and dumping a Fortune in front of a bevy of other Fortunes definitely fell into the realm of "thin."

She just couldn't humiliate Ryder that way! Joanna's heart clenched. She loved him so much, she would do anything to spare him pain or sorrow or shame. Right now accepting the ring in front of the assembled Fortunes was the only option available. Later she would make Ryder see reason, she would convince him that ending their bogus engagement was in his best interest.

"I love you, Ryder," she said, her eyes shining with emotional tears. She wrapped her arms around his neck and pressed close, nuzzling his neck with her lips.

There were aahs and applause from their audience as they watched Ryder slip the simple but elegant diamond engagement ring on Joanna's finger.

"A toast to the happy couple!" Kate exclaimed exultantly, and seemingly out of nowhere an army of waiters appeared with champagne and crystal goblets. Even the fourth generation of young Fortunes were included in the toast, with ginger ale and colorful plastic cups.

Joanna and Ryder spent the rest of the day playing the part of the newly engaged couple for the other guests. It wasn't until the picnic had ended and all the Fortunes dispersed that the two of them were finally alone.

"This is the happiest day of my life, Joanna," Ryder said as he drove to his apartment.

Joanna heaved a sigh. "Ryder, let's drop the act. We're the only two here, and we both know that we're not really engaged."

"You're wearing my ring, and we announced our engagement to both our families, the Fortunes and the Chandlers," countered Ryder. "That's as real as it gets, Joanna."

Her eyes misted. "You are so manipulative, mentioning the Chandlers—" She swallowed hard. "There are only two of us left—Julia and me—and you know how much I...I—''

"Michael's daughters are half Chandler," Ryder reminded her. "I'd say the Chandlers are definitely regrouping, and our own kids will add to the number. Joanna, I know you only accepted my ring so you wouldn't embarrass Julia today but—''

"Embarrass Julia?" Joanna gawked at him. "Is that what you think?''

He nodded tersely, continuing, "But I love you, and now that we're engaged, even faux-engaged, I'm going to prove to you that marrying me is exactly what we both want and need, Joanna. Give me the chance to do that, baby.''

She sighed again, not certain where to begin. "If you think Julia would be embarrassed if I'd publicly turned you down—or even if I'd run out of the place screaming—you don't know my sister. She would back me all the way. Ryder, I wanted to save *you* from humiliation. Your whole family was there, I couldn't—I had to—I would never do anything to hurt you.''

Ryder pulled the Range Rover into the parking garage of his apartment building. Joanna's words kindled a spark of hope that he hadn't expected to feel so soon. "You took my ring so *I'd* save face?''

"Of course.'' She looked down at the diamond sparkling on her finger. "It's a beautiful ring, Ryder,'' she said softly, "but I...you—'' She shook her head and took a deep breath, trying to compose her thoughts. "Ryder, I'm not the woman you need for a wife, you need a woman who can—''

"I need you. You're the only woman I need, the only one I want. Ever, Joanna."

He braked the car to a stop and turned to her. "Joanna, I am so sorry I said things that caused you to think that I don't truly value you and adore you, because, sweetheart, I do." He tried to swallow around the lump lodged in his throat. "You're everything to me. Everything I've ever wanted and needed in a woman, in my wife."

He pulled her into his arms, holding her tight, like he never wanted to let her go. "Please make your yes a real one right now, Joanna. Let's make our bogus engagement the real thing."

Joanna clung to him, kissing him, trying to explain why she'd consistently refused his proposals, why keeping her as his girlfriend instead of making her his wife was in his best interest and in his company's best interest, too. Loving him as much as she did, she honestly had his best interest at heart, she explained fervidly.

Ryder shot down each of her assertions one by one, his counter-claims matching hers in intensity and sincerity. They entered his apartment, too involved in their discussion to more than vaguely notice that they were headed into the bedroom.

They stopped at the foot of the bed and looked at each other.

"Have I convinced you yet, Joanna?" Ryder asked hoarsely. "Because I'll stay up talking all night if I have to. Until I make you believe that you're perfect for me, because you are. Until you *know* that we belong together forever, just the way I do."

Joanna looked up at Ryder and down at the rings on her fingers. Her mother's ring and Ryder's ring. The past, the present and the future.

Did she dare risk it? Joanna wondered. Julia loved her, defects and all. Was it possible that Ryder might feel that way about her, too? He seemed utterly convinced that she was perfect for him. Should she keep trying to talk him out of loving her? He didn't look ready to agree.

"I'm tired of talking, Ryder." Decisively Joanna moved into his arms. "Show me how much you love me. All night."

Ryder gladly, passionately complied.

Epilogue

Another Christmas, another Fortune family party.

Kate surveyed her clan, many gathered around the huge Christmas tree. The young parents particularly enjoyed showing the babies and toddlers the bright strands of twinkling lights. A posse of school-age children exuberantly played some kind of running and hiding game that involved plenty of delighted shrieks. Kate savored every minute of it.

Across the room she spied her great-nephew Ryder and his fiancée Joanna holding hands and gazing out the window at the lightly falling snow. They were deep in conversation, perhaps discussing their upcoming wedding, which Kate knew was scheduled for the second of March.

Kate admired Joanna's red dress with the eye of a fashion maven. The silky material shimmered in the candlelight, and the sexy elegant style flattered her petite figure. It was the type of dress Kate would have favored herself, if she were twenty-something.

She and Sterling approached the younger couple.

"Ryder, I know we probably shouldn't be talking business in the middle of the party, but I was hoping you would look over some papers I have in the den," Kate said, her eyes twinkling. "Bring Joanna with you, of course."

The four gathered in the den, where Kate handed Ryder a pen and a document transferring complete ownership of Fortune's Design to him. "Just sign there, and Fortune's Design is yours free and clear, Ryder."

Ryder and Joanna exchanged rapt glances, then hugs. Next they hugged Kate in turn, and Joanna threw her arms around Sterling. When Ryder appeared ready to do the same, Sterling pointed to the papers. "Sign, my boy. Right there on the dotted line."

Ryder signed. He was now the bona fide owner of Fortune's Design. The company was his—and Joanna's. He felt almost dizzy with joy.

"Aunt Kate, there are no words to thank you," Ryder began.

"I never wanted words. I wanted action. I wanted results, and that's exactly what you provided, Ryder. Fortune's Design is thriving. You've taken an ailing company and turned it around in a year, showing true business acumen."

"He's shown lots more than that—Ryder has heart," Joanna piped up, gazing proudly at him. "Fortune's Design is going to carry a line of life-skills products. Ryder contacted one of my friends from the rehab center who's designed a bunch of adaptive devices to make things easier for the physically impaired. Fortune's Design will bring them to the market, even though they're not high-profit items."

"The company has a stable of high-profit items," Ryder assured Kate. "But the life-skill products will enhance the quality of life for a small, defined market and—"

"You're putting your profits to good use for a good cause," Kate interjected. "Plus you found a remarkable, lovable young woman to share your life with. I'm so very proud of you, Ryder." She hugged him again.

"This past year has been the biggest adventure of my life," Ryder declared as he and Joanna walked hand-in-hand along the corridor, back to the party.

She glanced up playfully at him. "Just think, Ryder, you didn't have to go off to the diamond mines and fight thugs for adventure, simply working in an office with me provides plenty of hair-raising thrills."

"Joanna, every day with you is an adventure, in or out of the office. And I'm not being glib, I mean that sincerely. You interest me in a way nobody else ever has. Or ever will," he added earnestly. "I love you, Joanna." He stopped to draw her close in a shadowed alcove.

They were about to kiss when a group of children ran by, shrieking.

Joanna and Ryder broke apart, laughing, mutually conceding that this was not quite the time or place for romance.

"Think we'll have our own little rug-rat zooming around with the pack one of these years?" Ryder asked, gazing down at her with love-filled eyes.

"I hope we'll have at least two little zooming rug-rats. How soon do you want to start?"

"How about on our wedding night?"

"I could be pregnant at next year's Christmas

party.'' Joanna was delighted. ''Or maybe even be here with a newborn!''

''And I'll be telling you that the past year has been the biggest adventure of my life.''

Ryder swung Joanna up in his arms and kissed her, oblivious to everything and everyone but her.

* * * * *

THE CHRISTMAS CHILD
Linda Turner

Prologue

The Fortune Corporation headquarters was decorated for Christmas and crawling with Fortunes. Just about the whole family was there to celebrate Kate's eightieth birthday, and they were doing it up in style. The food was first rate, the wine flowing and an internationally known soloist sang near the towering Christmas tree in the room. Music fit for the gods floated through the building, setting a festive mood.

Standing off to the side by himself, his hands in his pockets and a scowl on his lean, chiseled face, Hunter stared at the crowd of children, grandchildren and great-grandchildren gathered around Kate and wondered what the hell he was doing there. Oh, he was family—he carried the name—but he'd never considered himself a real Fortune, and he doubted that the family ever had, either. People didn't like to claim bastards as kin.

Not that the Fortunes had ever cut him dead—they had more class than that. But they'd been talking about him in whispers for years, and he couldn't say he blamed them. He was the black-sheep son of a black sheep, and he'd been raising eyebrows from the moment his father learned of his existence when he was twelve. It had been a shock for both of them.

Thinking back to the first time he'd laid eyes on his

old man, Hunter had to grin. He'd gone at Daniel Fortune like the wild Indian he was and punched him right in the gut. Grieving for his mother, Grace, who had just died, and seething with resentment, he'd blamed his father for his mother's death, for all the years that they'd scrimped and saved and fought just to get by on the reservation. There'd been a time when the Fortune money could have at least made life bearable for them, but that time was lost forever with his mother's death. He hadn't cared that Daniel Fortune was his father, he'd wanted nothing to do with him.

The courts, however, hadn't given him any say-so in the matter and, like it or not, he'd been placed in his father's custody. And Daniel, to his credit, had done his duty by him. A man with itchy feet, he hadn't given him a traditional home, but he'd taken Hunter with him all over the world and given him an education that he never could have gotten staying in one place.

But although Hunter had inherited his father's nomadic spirit, their relationship had never been a smooth one—too many years had passed without either knowing the other for a solid bond to develop between them. They had, however, made peace with time. He went by the Fortune name now, but he'd never really felt the family connection and didn't think he ever would. Because in his heart a part of him would always be Hunter Lone Eagle, son of his mother's people.

So why the hell was he here? He was just barely part of the clan, and even then, not an immediate relation. Kate was his great-aunt, and although he was fond of the old girl, he'd seen her little enough while he was growing up. Why was it so important to her that he be here to celebrate her birthday?

"What's going on, Kelly?" he asked Kate's social secretary, Kelly Sinclair, as she joined him on the fringes of the crowd. A pretty girl with blond hair and eyes that were the deep blue of an autumn sky, she'd always treated him like he was just as much a member of the family as old Ben Fortune himself, and he appreciated that. "Kate doesn't do anything without a reason. Why did she want me here?"

Shrugging, she said lightly, "You know Kate—she loves her secrets. And why shouldn't you be here? You're part of the family, too."

He snorted at that and would have made a comment, but then Kate started handing out gifts just as always did at her birthday parties. Amused, Hunter couldn't help but smile. Someone should have told Kate years ago that since it was *her* birthday, she was the one who was supposed to be getting presents, but she got a real kick out of surprising unsuspecting members of the family.

"Hunter? It's your turn. Kate would like to talk to you in private for a moment."

Taken aback, he blinked, sure he must have misunderstood. "My turn? What are you talking about? Kate has something for *me?*"

"I certainly do." Kate came up beside him, grinning. "In fact, I think you're the only one who could handle this particular project. I bought a construction company last year in Wyoming that needs your troubleshooting skills. It's been in the red for months now, for one reason or another, and I think you're just the man to turn it around. Get it in the black by the end of the year, and it's yours.''

Stunned, Hunter just stared at her. He didn't doubt that he could do the work. He'd worked odd jobs all over the world, everything from construction in L.A. to oil rigs in the North Sea to lumberjacking in Canada. But a *year?* He never stayed anywhere for longer than three or four months before he got the urge to see what was over the horizon. How was he going to stay in Wyoming for a whole damn year?

One

The second that Naomi Windsong opened the front door and saw the tribal policeman standing on the front porch of her small house, her heart stopped in her chest. He had bad news—she could see it in his eyes. "Did you find Laura? Is she hurt? Oh, God, what is it? Please, just tell me!"

Young, barely old enough to be let loose on the female population of the reservation, Officer Hawk looked like he would have rather been anywhere else but where he was. But he faced her bravely and said reluctantly, "No, ma'am. I'm sorry. We haven't found her yet. But there has been a break in the case. Mr. Barker's car was discovered on a deserted road in Elk Canyon. Unfortunately, there was no sign of him or Laura."

"Elk Canyon!" she exclaimed. "But isn't that a box canyon that only leads up into the mountains? Why would James leave his car there?"

"He had to know he was a marked man as soon as he kidnapped Laura from her day care," he explained. "So the first thing he'd want to do is ditch his Jeep. The cutoff to Elk Canyon's only a mile from the day care, and it's a secluded area. A smart man would have had another vehicle stashed there, driven straight to it as soon as he grabbed Laura, then make the switch before the crime was even reported. He could have left and driven right by the police station then, and no one would have looked twice at him. And with no description of the second car or its license plate number, there's no way for us to track him any further."

"So you're abandoning the search? You're just letting that monster run off with my child?"

Even to her own ears, she sounded slightly hysterical, but she couldn't help it. It had been nearly twenty-four hours since James had kidnapped Laura, twenty-four horrifying hours in which she had done nothing but sit by the phone and wait for him to call. He would call, she'd assured herself over and over again. He wasn't a deliberately cruel man—he would at least call to let her know that Laura was all right.

But although the phone had rung dozens of times as people learned of Laura's abduction and called to sympathize, none of the callers had been James. Friends, family, co-workers at the bakery where she worked. But never James.

He wouldn't hurt her, Naomi told herself for the thousandth time. Laura was his daughter. He loved her. After his divorce from his wife, he'd moved to Wyoming just to get to know her. Whatever kind of scum he was, he wouldn't hurt his own daughter.

But as much as Naomi tried to cling to that thought, fear ate away at her like a cancer. Because she knew in her heart that James hadn't taken Laura because he wanted her for himself. *She* was the one he was trying to hurt, the one he was striking out at. She'd refused to marry him—again—and he was livid. There was no telling how far he would go to get revenge.

"We're not giving up," Officer Hawk assured her grimly. "But you must know that we're searching blind now, ma'am. Mr. Barker obviously planned this right down to the last detail, and we don't even know what kind of vehicle he's driving. We're putting up posters of Laura all over the state, but unless someone spots her with him or he makes a major blunder, there's not a lot we can do. Our best hope is that he'll call—or bring Laura home after he feels you've suffered long enough. In these kinds of cases, that's usually a couple of days."

Naomi knew he was only trying to make her feel better, but she didn't have any illusions about James Barker. Unfortunately, she hadn't always been so discerning when it came to the man. She met him one night when she was living in Denver and he stopped to help her when her car broke down. He'd set out to charm her, and she'd never thought to resist. They started dating and she fell in love. It wasn't until she got pregnant that she learned he was married.

She should have recognized it—the signs were all there. In all the months they were involved, he never stayed overnight, never gave her his phone number, never took her to his place. Because introducing his mistress to his wife would have been awkward, to say the least.

Devastated, she broke off all ties with him, quit her job and moved to Wyoming and the reservation where her mother's people lived, to have her baby. That was three years ago. She'd thought he was out of her life for good—until he showed up in Wyoming a month ago after hiring a private investigator to find her. As charming as ever, he announced that he was now divorced and wanted to marry her.

When she immediately turned him down, she expected him to be furious. But he took the rejection in stride and promised he had changed and would change her low opinion of him. For her daughter's sake, she wanted to believe him, so she had given him a chance. And for a while, it did seem as if he was a new man. He visited Laura at least three times a week, and he was always nothing but charming. Then, just this past weekend, he'd proposed again, and she realized that all this time he'd been using Laura to try to get to her. Furious, she'd told him she wouldn't have him on a platter with an apple in his mouth.

This time, he hadn't handled rejection nearly as well as he had the first time. Raging at her, he'd called her all sorts of filthy names, then stormed out. Naomi thought he had left the area, then yesterday, he showed up at Laura's day care and spirited her away while the teacher was calling Naomi to see if it was all right for James to take her daughter shopping. No one had seen Laura since.

And although Officer Hawk felt like this was a typical custody squabble between two parents, Naomi knew better. In his experience, maybe a recalcitrant father could be counted on to take a child home after a couple of days, but she knew James now. He was a mean, spiteful man who was, she felt sure, somewhere close—she could feel it in her bones. It wouldn't surprise her in the least if he was hiding in plain sight, watching her suffer and loving every minute of it. It would be just like him.

And he wasn't going to get away with it. Laura was hers, she thought fiercely. *Hers!* The tribal police might not be able to do anything at this point, but by God, she could. She just needed a tracker, someone who could flush the slime out and find out where he was hiding her daughter. She didn't personally know anyone who could do that for her, but she knew someone who did.

As soon as Officer Hawk left, she quickly called Lucas Greywolf. He was the only doctor on the reservation, and his wife, Rocky, owned and operated a flying service that was well-known for its successful search-and-rescue operations. If anyone could recommend a good tracker, they could.

As she'd hoped, Lucas didn't disappoint her. He'd already heard about Laura's kidnapping, as had most of the rest of the reservation, and he immediately recommended Rocky's cousin, Hunter.

"I've seen a lot of men who can track, but never anyone quite like Hunter," he told her. "He's better than good. I don't know how he does it, but he can track an eagle across the sky. He just moved here a couple of months ago and took over Fortune Construction. Give him a call and tell him I told you to call."

Immeasurably relieved, Naomi could do nothing to stop the tears that welled in her throat and eyes. "Thank you so much," she said thickly. "You don't know how much this means to me. The police are doing everything they can, but I just can't sit on my hands and wait."

"Of course you can't! If it was one of our kids out there, God knows where, you'd better believe Rocky and I would call on whoever we had to to find them. Keep the faith, Naomi. Hunter's a good man and damn good at what he does. He won't give up until he finds her.''

Searching through the paperwork piled high on his desk, Hunter swore softly and wondered why his secretary had to choose this week out of all the weeks in the year to have her wisdom teeth out. He had a bid to send in on the shopping mall in Crow County, payroll to do and a report to fax off to Kate just to keep her apprised of the current state of affairs. She hadn't asked for any kind of monthly accounting of the business, but he felt honor-bound to let her know how things were going. Considering the trust she had placed in him by handing him the company, it was the least he could do.

He still couldn't believe she'd done it.

He would have sworn it was the last thing he wanted. And Kate, crafty old woman that she was, had known it. After the Christmas party, she'd told him he was free to turn the gift down then or at any time during the year, no hard feelings. Torn, he'd been tempted, but he hadn't wanted to disappoint her. Then, on the first day, when he'd walked into the office and seen the way the current foreman was running the place into the ground with mismanagement and workers who didn't want to work, he'd itched to get in there and change things. Right then and there, he'd been hooked.

The phone rang then, the third time in the last five minutes, and once again, he wished Isabel was there to at least handle the calls. How was a man supposed to get any work done when he was constantly being interrupted?

Snatching up the phone just as he found the figures he needed for the bid he was working on, he growled, "Fortune Construction. Hunter speaking. What can I do for you?"

"Hi. It's me," Kelly said quietly. "Kate asked me to place a call so she could see how you're doing."

Leaning back in his chair, Hunter grinned. He and his great aunt had kept in touch since the Christmas party, but he always enjoyed talking with Kelly first. They had become friends, and like the rest of his family, he was concerned about her dating his cousin, Chad. He'd tried to warn Kelly that Chad was a heartbreak waiting to happen and she was headed for trouble, but she'd refused to believe Chad would ever hurt her. For her sake, Hunter hoped she was right, but he wasn't holding his breath.

"Hey, lady. How's fortune treating you?"

"Just fine," she said, chuckling. "How about you? How's business?"

"Wild and hectic. I don't even have time for a coffee break any more."

Far from sympathetic, she laughed at his disgruntled tone. "Kate'll be pleased."

Kate was, in fact, thrilled when she came on the line a few minutes later and heard how busy he was. They discussed the situation, and by the time he hung up, they decided he needed to hire more men. God only knew when he'd find the time to do it.

Returning his attention to the bid he was working

on, he was running numbers on his calculator, figuring cost, when the outer door to his office opened. Expecting one of his foremen, he didn't even look up. "Have a seat, Fred. I've almost got the numbers on the pipe figured—"

"Excuse me, but I'm looking for Hunter Fortune. Dr. Greywolf told me I would find him here."

Startled, Hunter glanced up to find a slender, petite woman already stepping into his office. Construction wasn't the all-male domain it had once been, so it wasn't completely out of the ordinary for him to deal with a woman in his business. But he'd never dealt with one quite like the one who stood before him. He had, over the years and in all parts of the world, seen his share of beautiful women, but this one was striking. She had the coal-black hair of a Native American, flawless, honeyed skin and large, startling gray eyes that were, quite simply, beautiful. If she'd smiled, Hunter didn't doubt that she could have knocked a man out of his shoes.

Studying her, Hunter thought she might have been a woman who had once smiled easily, but not now. Her eyes were haunted and vulnerable with a pain he could only guess at, her cheeks damp from the tracks of recent tears. She appeared to be, quite literally, a damsel in distress.

Hunter's first instinct was to rush to the rescue and ask questions later. But he'd learned the hard way that that was how a foolish man got burned. Not all damsels were as helpless as they looked. The last woman he helped claimed she was trying to get away from an abusive husband. Later, when he'd given her the money for a bus ticket out of state, he discovered the whole story was a scam and she wasn't even married.

Pushing to his feet, he eyed her carefully. "I'm Hunter Fortune. How do you know Lucas?"

"He's my doctor. My daughter's doctor." With no warning, the tears that had stained her cheeks were back, welling in her eyes, and she was clenching her hands tightly together before her, as if that would help keep her from flying apart. "Please...I need your help. My daughter—"

Alarmed, Hunter started around his desk. "What about your daughter? Is she hurt? Where is she? Why didn't you take her to Lucas?"

"No, it's not that. She's not hurt—at least I don't think she is. Her father—oh, God, he took her! Kidnapped Laura. Dr. Greywolf said you're a tracker. Please, you've got to help me find her!"

She was crying then, quietly sobbing, her streaming eyes stark with despair, and Hunter felt something twist where his heart was supposed to be. "Shhh," he said quietly, urging her into a chair. "Sit down, Mrs.—"

"Ms.," she choked. "My name is Naomi Windsong."

"Okay, Ms. Windsong, why don't you start from the beginning and tell me how all this happened? Have you gone to the police?"

She nodded. "But there's nothing they can do."

Struggling for control with a strength of will that couldn't help but impress him, she pulled herself back together and told him the whole story, leaving nothing out from the moment she'd had the misfortune to meet

James Barker to the second when she realized he'd absconded with her daughter. And with every word, her voice got stronger, her anger fiercer.

"He's not going to get away with it," she finally concluded coldly. "I know he's here somewhere, and if you won't help me, then I'll turn over every rock in the county to find the snake if I have to, but he's not keeping my daughter."

She'd do it, Hunter thought, watching in amazement as she changed from a weepy, vulnerable woman to a fierce, protective mother right before his eyes. She'd fight whoever she had to, do whatever was necessary, to get her daughter back. His mother had had that same spirit. If his father had tried to take him from her before she'd died, she would have moved heaven and earth and taken on the entire Fortune clan and all their money to get him back. Naomi Windsong would do no less.

And he liked that about her. There was something about a gutsy woman that he'd always found appealing. But how could he help her? He had his hands full just trying to get Fortune Construction off the ground. There were times in the past two months when he still didn't know if Kate had blessed him or cursed him when she'd bought the failing company, changed the name and handed it over to him to run. But come hell or high water, he was going to make it work. That meant keeping his nose to the grindstone and making sure his crew did the same.

They were half finished with a fast-food restaurant on the eastern edge of the reservation, and just yesterday, he learned he'd gotten the bid for a new clinic in Cheyenne. He'd bid both projects just barely over cost because he needed the business to reestablish the company's reputation, and that meant there was no room for error. Or time to put either project on hold. Deadlines were tight, and both projects were too important to the future of the company to leave in the hands of a foreman while he took off to look for Laura Windsong.

But even as he opened his mouth to tell Naomi that he couldn't do it, he knew he couldn't let her go off by herself to look for her daughter. She was just angry enough, just desperate enough, to try it, and if she wasn't careful, she could end up in real trouble. Most of the county was still unsettled and wild, and even though her heritage appeared to be the same as his own, Naomi Windsong looked like a city girl who had never roughed it a day in her life. She'd be in over her head within the first hour. And then there was James Barker himself. Any man who would kidnap his own a child just to get back at her mother was capable of anything.

And the bastard wasn't going to get away with it. He wouldn't let him. He'd had a knack for tracking ever since he was a kid, a sixth sense that never failed him. In his travels over the years, he'd volunteered his services whenever anyone was lost. If James Barker was out there, he'd find him.

"You don't have to take off on your own," he told her grimly. "Just give me time to line someone up to take over for me here, and I'll help you find your daughter."

Two

Light-headed with relief that she'd finally found someone to *do* something, Naomi expected Hunter to talk to the police, then immediately start tracking James from the spot where he'd abandoned his car. Instead, he asked for the name and address of Laura's day care. Surprised, she frowned. "Why? The police have already talked to Laura's teacher. She couldn't tell them anything except that James had taken her."

"I realize that, but I'd like to talk to her, just the same. That was the last place Laura was seen, so that's where I start tracking. So what's the name and address?"

"Little Dear Day Care. It's at First and Main. But I still don't see why you want to waste time talking to Sarah Rivers," she said in growing frustration as she followed him out of his office. "She told the police everything she knows, and the longer you waste time talking to her, the more time James has to get away. Don't you think you should—"

Stopping in his tracks, he pivoted to face her, his brown eyes razor sharp as they locked with hers. "Let's get something straight right here, Ms. Windsong. I know you're sick with worry, and all you want to do is rush right out and find your kid. It's a natural instinct, but that's not the way I operate. I do things my way, at my own pace, or I don't do them. So if you've got a problem with that, then you'd better say so right now, and I'll give you the name of another tracker who might be able to help you.''

Her gaze clashing with his in a battle of wills, Naomi didn't doubt for a second that he meant every word. Everything about him was hard as stone—the cut of his jaw, his finely chiseled mouth, his blade of a nose. And then there were his eyes. Brutally direct and confident, they warned her that if she didn't let him run the show, she was on her own.

And for a span of ten seconds, she hated him for that. Laura was her daughter, damn him! *Hers!* And if he thought she was going to stand around like some meek little woman and hold her tongue while he dragged his feet finding her, he was in for a rude awakening. She would say whatever she liked, do whatever she had to to light a fire under him if that's what it took to get him to move. And if he didn't like it, that was just too damn bad.

But if she did, she could start looking for someone else to help her. And Lucas said he was the best.

Frustrated, resenting his dispassion when her nerves were wound tighter than a broken clock spring, she reminded herself that finding Laura was what was important here, not proving a point to Hunter Fortune. If he was as good as Lucas said he was—and she had every reason to believe that he was—then she had to trust him to know what he was doing.

Still, it wasn't easy for her to back down from a challenge, and she was less than gracious when she said grudgingly, ''I don't want another tracker. Lucas said you were the best, so do what you have to do. Just find Laura.''

''I wouldn't have agreed to look for her if I didn't think I could find her,'' he said simply, and had no idea how his quiet confidence reassured her. ''Now that we've got that settled, let's head on over to the day care. We're burning daylight.''

Sarah Rivers, Laura's day care teacher, was a middle-aged woman with a kind smile and gentle ways, but she was nobody's fool. ''Mr. Barker told me he had Naomi's permission to take Laura shopping for her birthday, but I didn't believe him for a second,'' she said tartly. ''There was just something about the way he was acting. You know…kind of jumpy? He just looked like he was up to no good. That's why I told him I had to call Naomi first. Then, when I was on the phone, he took her. I'll never forgive myself for that. I should have known better!''

''Please don't beat yourself up over this, Sarah,'' Naomi told her, giving her a hug. ''You had no way of knowing what James was capable of. As well as I know him, I never thought he would do something like this, so don't blame yourself. You're not the only one he fooled.''

''What else did you notice about him, Mrs. Rivers?'' Hunter asked. ''You said he looked like he was up to no good. What do you mean by that? How did he look?''

''Like he was going hunting or something. It was weird. He said he was going shopping, but he was wearing all this outdoor gear. You know—snow boots and a big down parka, the whole nine yards. If he was planning to walk through the mall in that getup, he was going to burn up.''

His gaze shifting to the wide windows of the day care that overlooked the school's playground, Hunter frowned thoughtfully. The calendar might say March, but winter still appeared to have a firm grip on the countryside. The snow on the ground showed no sign of melting anytime soon, and they hadn't seen the last of the winter storms. Still, the first faint hints of spring were definitely in the air, and temperatures weren't nearly as brutal as they had been in January. The only people who went around in the kind of heavy gear Sarah Rivers described were those who planned to spend an extensive amount of time outdoors.

And that wasn't something you would expect a man to do when he had a three-year-old in tow.

"What about Laura?" he asked. "How was she dressed?''

"In a pair of corduroy overalls and a turtleneck," Naomi answered for the teacher. "And tennis shoes.''

"What about a jacket? Did Barker take time to put a jacket on her before he rushed out with her?''

Startled, Sarah Rivers gasped softly. "Oh, I don't see how he could have. There wasn't time. I'd hardly left the foyer to use the phone in my office before he was racing away. Of course, he could have had something in the car or stopped and bought her something.''

Hunter didn't comment one way or the other, but he doubted that Barker stopped for anything once he got Laura in his clutches. It would have just been too risky. Considering the way he was dressed and the speed with which he had moved, it didn't sound like the abduction was a spur-of-the-moment thing but rather something he'd planned for some time, so he'd probably had a stash of clothes for the little girl in his car. The question now was where had Barker taken Laura after he'd abandoned his car. And what did he hope to gain from all this? If he was hoping to convince Naomi that they were made for each other, he couldn't have picked a worse way to do it.

There was little else that Sarah Rivers could tell them, so after thanking her for her help, they headed out to Elk Canyon and the place where Barker had abandoned his car. Hunter took one look at the snow-covered spot where the car had been nearly concealed behind a rocky outcrop and started to scowl. He didn't like it. He didn't like it at all.

"This doesn't smell right," he muttered to himself as he inspected the area. "Why would Barker drive all the way back into the canyon just to switch vehicles?"

"Maybe because it's isolated," Naomi suggested. "Only a few people live back here, so the chances of anyone seeing him had to be pretty slim."

"True," he agreed, "the cutoff for the canyon isn't that far from the day care. But once he grabbed Laura he had to know that Mrs Rivers would call the police immediately, and that in all likelihood they would cordon off all roads in the area leading out of town. Even if he did change cars, the canyon's a dead end. He had to go out the same way he came in, and once he did that, the odds were pretty good he was going to run into a roadblock once he hit the main road."

"So you're saying if he did switch cars, he should have done it closer to the day care?"

"That's what I'd have done. The closer the better. Preferably right around the corner."

"But wouldn't it be more likely that someone would see him right in town?"

"Possibly. But if I was going to kidnap a kid, I'd have taken that risk. Think about it. You snatch the kid, drive right around the corner to another car, make the switch even as the kidnapping is being reported to the police and head straight for the middle of town. Everyone is expecting you to flee the state—no one's going to think to look right in town. So you hole up somewhere and wait for things to calm down. Once the authorities figure you're long gone across country, the roadblocks come down and you drive out of town without anyone even looking twice at you."

"But James couldn't have done that since he left his car here and the dragnet would have closed around him by the time he made it back to the main road. So why did he bring Laura to Elk Canyon?"

"I don't know," he said flatly. "But I mean to find out."

The police had impounded James's car and towed it back to town after they'd searched the immediate vicinity. Even to the untrained eye, it was obvious the police had gone over the area with a fine-tooth comb. The snow-covered ground was littered with footprints, making it impossible to tell if any of them might have belonged to James Barker or his little girl.

Swearing roundly at the ignorance of men who should have known better, Hunter started at the spot where the car had been parked and slowly began working his way outward in ever-growing circles, looking for something, anything, the police might have missed. A broken branch, a mound of snow that had been inexplicably disturbed, a footprint that hadn't, miraculously, been covered up by last night's snow-fall. There had to be something—in his gut, he knew it was there. He could feel it.

An icy wind howled down through the canyon, the lonely sound echoing through the pines that stood like sentinels in the snow. Naomi shivered and dug her hands deeper into the pockets of her down jacket, but Hunter hardly noticed. Totally focused on his search, he was a hundred yards from the last footprint left by the police and making his way up the steep side of the mountain when he noticed movement out of the corner of his eye. Stopping in his tracks, he snapped his head around and searched the stand of trees off to his right.

For a second he thought he might have surprised an elk, then he saw it again, a piece of green ribbon caught on the low branch of a fir and swaying in the wind. Forest green and the exact shade of the tree it was caught on, it blended in so perfectly with the fo-liage that he never would have seen it if the wind hadn't set it gently flapping.

When he brought it to Naomi, who'd stayed by the car to make sure she didn't destroy any evidence, she took one look at it and blanched. ''Oh, God,'' she whispered, clutching it to her breast. ''It's Laura's. I tied it in her hair right before I dropped her off at day care yesterday. Where did you find it?''

''Up there,'' he said, nodding toward the trees that

had concealed him from her once he'd left the road. "The wind's always swirling in this canyon, and there's a possibility that if Barker did change cars here, the ribbon could have somehow fallen out of Laura's hair and got swept up into the trees. Or she was up in the trees for some reason and the ribbon snagged on a branch and pulled free."

"But there's no way out of the canyon up there," she said in alarm. "That only leads up into the mountains. Why would James take her up there?"

Hunter couldn't tell her that, at least not yet. But the answer was there, somewhere in that canyon. He just had to find it.

Ten minutes later he came across snowmobile tracks fifty yards from where he'd found Laura's hair ribbon. The tracks should have been buried under yesterday's snowfall, but the thick tree branches overhead had caught most of that, preserving the tracks. Studying them, Hunter knew there was no way to tell who had made them. The canyon was isolated, but it wasn't completely deserted, and anyone could have been up there recently. He didn't even know if Barker knew how to operate a snowmobile, but his gut told him he did. And his gut was very seldom wrong.

With his mouth pressed flat into a hard, grim line, he made his way back down the side of the mountain to where Naomi patiently waited for him. She took one look at his face and stiffened. "You found something."

He nodded. "Snowmobile tracks. They cut through the trees and head farther up into the mountains."

"And you think James made them?"

"If I was a betting man, I'd say, yeah. I think he's holed up somewhere in a line cabin while you worry yourself sick about your daughter. But then again," he added, "I don't know the man. Anybody who goes up into the mountains on his own in the winter damn sure better know what he's doing, or he's going to find himself in a hell of a lot of trouble. You think he's got the skills to make it up there?"

Stricken, she lifted widened eyes to the snowy mountains that seemed to tower threateningly over them. As far as the eye could see, there was nothing but snow and trees and wilderness. And somewhere up there, James could be hiding with her baby.

Horrified, she said hoarsely, "He likes to think he's a survivalist. He read all these books and stuff about living in the wild and used to think that he could do it. But he hasn't had any training—he doesn't even know how to build a fire without charcoal and lighter fluid!"

Hunter swore, his narrowed eyes, like hers, trained on the rugged terrain that rose all around them in deadly majestic splendor. "Then he's in over his head," he said coldly. "The mountains don't like amateurs."

"But why?" she cried. "Why is he doing this? Why is he putting his own daughter in danger? Doesn't he realize that they could both die up there and no one would find them until the snow melts?"

"My guess is he's not even thinking about Laura. His only concern right now is making you sweat. And he's doing a damn good job of it."

Naomi couldn't deny it. Just thinking about Laura

out there in the wilderness, possibly without even a decent jacket, was enough to make her want to run screaming into the trees to search for her. She was out there—she could feel her—so close that she could almost reach out and touch her. Did she know that she was coming for her? That she would move heaven and earth if she had to just to get her back? Was that why James was doing this? Laura was just window dressing? Was it really her he wanted to get his hands on and Laura was just the bait?

Appalled at the thought, she started to ask Hunter if he thought she might be right, when she saw him stiffen like a wolf that suddenly caught the scent of its prey. "What is it?" she asked in alarm when he stared at a particular rocky ridge high above them. "What do you see?"

"Binoculars," he retorted, never taking his eyes from the ridge. "I just caught the glint of sun off the lenses. The son of a bitch is up there now, watching us, just daring us to catch him." Glancing down at her, he said, "He really gets his kicks out of torturing you, doesn't he?"

Hugging herself, her eyes flashed with angry resentment. "It's the only thing he's really good at. All I can say is, he'd better enjoy it. Because when I get through with him after this, I'm going to make him wish he'd never been born."

And if she couldn't do it, he could, Hunter thought angrily. Any man who would put his own child in danger to torment the mother of that child deserved whatever he got. "C'mon," he growled as he turned back to his truck. "We've done all that we can do here for now."

"But you can't just leave Laura up there with that monster!" she cried, hurrying after him. "We have to do something!"

"We are. I'm going back to my place to get my snowmobile and supplies, and you're going home to pack some warm clothes for Laura just in case she needs them when I find her. I'll be by within the hour to pick them up."

Three

Naomi had a backpack packed and was waiting on her front porch when Hunter returned to her house forty minutes later with his snowmobile strapped to a trailer hitched to his truck. He took one look at the size of the pack and arched a dark brow in amusement. "I'm not taking Laura to Disneyland, Naomi. I just need a snow suit or something for her in case Barker didn't think of anyone but himself."

Lifting the backpack, Naomi shrugged into it. "I'm going with you. And since I didn't know how long we'll be gone, I thought it would be better to be prepared. Let's go."

She took a quick step toward the porch steps, but that was as far as she got before he moved to cut her off. "Hold it right there, Kemosabie," he growled. "What do you mean *you're going with me?*"

"Just what I said. Do you have a problem with that?"

"You're damn right I do! I work alone."

His tone was flat and as unyielding as stone and rubbed Naomi the wrong way. "Not this time, you don't," she retorted, bristling. "In case you've forgotten, that's *my* daughter up there in those mountains. And not you or any other man is making me stay home like the good little mother as long as she's in danger.

So you can either take me with you or I'll rent my own damn snowmobile and follow you, but either way, I'm going."

Standing toe-to-toe with him, she just dared him to argue with her, and he didn't disappoint her. "Dammit, woman, this isn't a walk in the park! You saw how rugged Elk Canyon was—the mountains are ten times more treacherous than that. There's no way in hell I'm taking a woman up there. It's too dangerous."

"Fine. Then it looks like I'll have to take myself."

Cursing, he growled, "What part of no didn't you understand? I've got enough to do up there tracking Barker without having to watch over you, too. You'll only slow me down."

"Then I suggest you quit wasting time arguing with me and get a move on," she said reasonably. "I'm just waiting for you."

Grinding his teeth on an oath, Hunter glared down at her and didn't know if he wanted to shake her or turn her over his knee. When she'd walked into his office earlier, he'd suspected she was the kind of woman a man wouldn't be able to easily dismiss from his mind, and he hadn't been wrong. The lady was trouble, and if circumstances had been different, he would have already sent her packing. All his energy was focused on getting Fortune Construction in the black by the end of the year, and nothing was interfering with that. Especially a woman. He just didn't need the hassle.

That didn't mean he would renege on his promise to find Laura, however. He didn't care how much work he had to do, there was no way in hell he was going to stand around with his hands in his pockets when a child was in trouble. He'd find her if he had to go over every damn inch of the mountains—but he didn't have to drag her mother along to do it. She really would slow him down and no doubt talk him to death, and he wasn't having it!

"Look," he said, struggling for patience, "I can understand why you want to go along. If I had a daughter lost up there somewhere in those mountains, there's no way in hell anyone could convince me to stay at home while someone else went looking for her. But I have experience in the mountains. You don't."

"That's why I came to you," she reminded him. "Lucas said you were the best."

"At tracking, maybe," he conceded. "But accidents happen. What if you get hurt and we haven't found Laura yet? Have you thought of that? I'll have to choose between getting you to medical help and finding your daughter, and you might not like the decision I make."

"That's not going to happen. I'll be careful—"

"Experienced guides have fallen off the side of a mountain being careful. If something happens to you, Laura's got no one to turn to except James. Is that what you want?"

"Of course not!"

"Then stay here and wait for me to bring her to you. I've got a cell phone—I can be in constant contact with you."

For a minute he thought he had her convinced. She hesitated, weighing his words, and he was sure she was going to give in. But then she stiffened and dug in her heels and it was all he could do not to curse. "No," she said flatly. "I'm going."

She was as stubborn as a rock. Any other time, Hunter might have laughed at the idea of this slip of a woman standing up to him, but at that particular moment, he couldn't find a damn thing funny about the situation. She was just bullheaded enough to rent a damn snowmobile and follow after him if he didn't let her go with him, and then he'd spend half his time looking over his shoulder making sure she was all right. That would cost him even more time than if he just took her with him to begin with.

"All right," he said in disgust. "Have it your way. As you pointed out, I can't stop you from doing whatever you want to do. But if you're going with me, we're going to get some things straight right here and now, or I'm not stepping off this porch with you."

More agreeable, now that she'd gotten her way, she motioned for him to continue. "Go ahead. Name your terms."

"I'm in charge."

Nodding, she said, "Fine. I already told you I don't have a problem with that. You're more experienced at this kind of thing than I am."

Stunned, Hunter didn't know how she got that one out with a straight face. She couldn't be serious. She'd been questioning his every move almost from the moment she'd met him! "I'm not just talking about the tracking," he retorted. "The minute we head up into the trees in Elk Canyon, safety is our number one priority. The snow covers up all sorts of hidden dangers, so you don't take a step without my say-so. You got that?''

"I'm not a child," she said stiffly. "You don't have to worry about me wandering off on my own."

"I won't have to worry about you at all if you do as I say," he tossed back. "The whole point is to get both you and Laura out of there in one piece. As long as you do what I say, when I say, we shouldn't have any problem. So what's it going to be? Do I have your word?"

The answer should have been easy, Naomi knew. Yes. That was all he needed to hear. But he was asking for more than a guarantee that she would follow orders, no questions asked, and they both knew it. If she was going to accompany him, he had to know that she trusted him. And that was asking more of her than he could possibly know. Because the last man she had trusted was the same man who had dragged her daughter up into the mountains without a thought to her safety. How could she trust any man after that?

But Hunter Fortune wasn't just any man, she silently acknowledged. If she knew nothing else about him, she knew that. He'd put his life on hold, just walked away from his business without a backward glance, to come to the rescue of a little girl he didn't even know, and she didn't know many people who would do that. Considering that, how could she *not* trust him?

"Yes," she said quietly. "You have my word."

She thought it would be easy. After all, how difficult could following orders be? He wouldn't ask anything unreasonable of her. He was only looking out for her safety. As long as she did what he said, when he said, she wouldn't get into any trouble. Or so she told herself, until they returned to Elk Canyon and the spot where James had left his car.

With sure, swift movements, Hunter unloaded his snowmobile from its trailer and strapped her backpack on the back along with his. Then he swung his leg over the machine as he took his position in the driver's seat and motioned her to climb on behind him. "Make sure you hang on tight at all times," he said as he pulled on gloves and goggles. "I'm not going to go very fast, but I don't want you falling off if I have to make some sharp turns."

In the process of pulling on her own gloves, Naomi went perfectly still, the thumping of her heart so loud that she'd have sworn Hunter could hear it in the sudden silence that engulfed the canyon. She'd known, of course, that they would be riding double, but she hadn't given much thought to the fact that to do that, she would have to put her arms around his waist.

She hadn't held a man in almost four years. Not since she'd made love with James and conceived Laura, only to learn later that he was a married man.

"Naomi? Is there a problem?"

Caught up in her thoughts, she blinked Hunter back into focus and found him frowning at her, his dark eyes narrowed and searching—far too sharp for comfort. Flushing, she looked quickly away. "No. I was just…thinking."

If he thought it odd that she'd picked now, of all times, to indulge in a daydream, he kept it to himself.

"If you're having second thoughts about going, it's not too late to change your mind," he said quietly. "You can take my truck and go back to your house to wait. I've got my cell phone. I'll call you the second I find Laura."

"No. It's not that. I want to go," she insisted, but still, she stood right where she was.

She wasn't, she told herself, afraid of him. Or, for that matter, afraid that he was going to take advantage of the situation. Lucas Greywolf would've never recommended him if that had been the case. It was just that she hadn't expected to get that close to him. He was an extremely good-looking man. Why, of all times, did she have to notice that *now,* when they were about to race off into the wilderness and would be alone together for God knew how long? Why, when she would have sworn that she wouldn't have uttered a word of protest if every man on the planet flew back to Mars, was she suddenly aware of just how big, how hard, this particular one was? Even with the protective clothing they both had on, there was no way she would be able to put her arms around his waist without being aware of every lean inch of him.

You can't have your cake and eat it, too, a voice snapped impatiently in her head. *If you want to be there when Laura is found, quit acting like a ninny and get on the damn snowmobile before the man thinks you're afraid to touch him because you're attracted to him.*

That got her attention. She'd never heard of anything so ridiculous in all her life. Of course she wasn't attracted to him. And to prove it, she lifted her chin, stepped determinedly up to the snowmobile and swung her leg over the seat behind him.

There should have been plenty of room for two people. The gear strapped onto the back didn't take up that much space, and she wasn't by any stretch of the imagination a large woman. She should have been able to sit well back on her portion of the seat without even touching Hunter except to hold on to him at his waist. Then she sat down, and before she realized that the space left for her was smaller than it looked, she found herself plastered to his back.

"Oh! Wait!" she began, startled.

But it was already too late. Hunter turned the key in the ignition with a flick of his wrist, and the motor roared to life. With a low growl the snowmobile lurched forward and sent Naomi's heart shooting into her throat. Gasping, she latched on to him, her fingers biting into his waist as she hung on for dear life.

She held him as if she was afraid he was going to give her cooties, Hunter thought. Wondering about the paradox that was Naomi Windsong, he revved the motor and sent the snowmobile racing into the cover of the trees. She was an unwed mother who'd had an affair with a married man, so she was hardly what he would call innocent. Yet she touched him like she'd never held a man before. Was she afraid of him?

Heading up toward the spot where he'd found Barker's tracks earlier in the day, he immediately rejected the idea. As desperate as she was to find her daughter, Hunter knew she never would have come with him—especially when she didn't have to—if she'd been afraid of him. No, it was some other emotion that had her trying to hold him at arm's length, and if he had to guess, he'd say it had something to do with Barker. Thanks to him, she probably hated all men, and Hunter couldn't say he blamed her. The jackass had gone out of his way to teach her that she couldn't trust her own instincts when it came to men, and that was a lesson a woman didn't soon forget.

Still, she was as safe with him as if she'd been in church. He knew trouble when he saw it, and though there'd been a time in his life when he'd been a sucker for a woman looking for someone to charge to her rescue, those days were long gone. He had enough headaches of his own without taking on another one. If he was racing off into the wilds with the lady, it wasn't because he was trying to make points with her. He just couldn't stand the thought of a child being in danger.

He hit a bump in the snow then, and the sudden jarring of the snowmobile sent Naomi plowing into his back, hard. And in the split second before she hastily pulled back, her breasts were nestled snug against him. It was just a quick, tantalizing brush of a soft female body against his, something he shouldn't even have noticed, considering the thick layer of clothes they each had on. But in the time it took to suck in a sharp breath, Hunter was hot and hard and he didn't even know how it happened. He just knew that they'd barely left civilization behind, and the lady was already giving him ideas, all without saying a single word. And all he could do was swear.

Four

He should have turned around right then and headed back to town. It would have been the smart thing to do. She was distracting the hell out of him, and he had a feeling the situation was only going to get worse the longer they were in each other's company. He would turn back now, take her back to her place and recommend she call Joe Little Hawk. He was a good tracker and old enough to be her father. Maybe Joe could take her with him on his snowmobile and not feel anything, but he sure couldn't. And if she gave him any trouble about backing out on her, he just might be tempted to tell her that.

But even as he started to brake, an image of a little girl flashed before his eyes. He didn't have to see a picture of her to know that Laura Windsong looked like her mother. Some things were just inevitable. She would have the same dark hair, the same wide gray eyes, the same stubborn chin. And right now, she was in more trouble than she'd ever been in in her life, and she needed him. *Him.* Not Joe Little Hawk or Michael Crow or any of the other men he'd met on the reservation who had a knack for following a trail. They were good—he didn't doubt that. But he was better. Time and again, he'd found lost souls who'd been long since given up for dead because he refused to give up. And he wasn't giving up on Laura Wind-song.

And when her mother came face-to-face with the lowlife that had stolen her heart, he was going to be there, he thought grimly. He didn't know why it was so important to him, but he knew with a certainty that went soul deep that he had to be there for her. In the meantime, there would be no going back. He would have to find a way to deal with her, and he didn't for a second fool himself into thinking it was going to be easy. Not when it was colder than hell, and the woman only had to touch him to make him sweat.

They picked up James's tracks right where Hunter had found them earlier and started up into the mountains. Naomi had thought it would be simple enough—all they had to do was follow the snowmobile tracks and they would lead them right to Laura. But she quickly learned nothing was that simple. In his rush to get away, James hadn't, unfortunately, forgotten to be cautious. Obviously expecting to be followed, he seldom traveled in a straight line. Instead, he darted in and out among the trees, winding up and around and back again, seeming, at times, to be heading in no particular direction. And every time he'd left the protection of the trees for more open ground, the previous night's snowfall had obliterated his tracks.

Holding on to Hunter as he lost the trail, then found it again, only to lose it once more, Naomi soon appreciated his skills as a tracker. There were times when the trail appeared to just give out in a smooth expanse of snow. There was nothing to show which direction

James had gone next, nothing to show that he had even been there at all. If the decision had been left up to her, she wouldn't have a clue which way to turn, but Hunter had no such problem. With a patience she couldn't help but admire, he dismounted from the snowmobile and carefully inspected the area on foot. And where she saw nothing, he found broken limbs or clumps of snow that had been carelessly knocked from low-lying branches to point the way.

Still, it was a tedious process. Hunter had warned her that finding the spot where James might have been watching them with binoculars earlier in the day wouldn't be easy, and he was right. With painstaking slowness, they kept climbing, but never seemed to get anywhere. James's tracks—when Hunter could find them—always wound higher up the mountain, with no end in sight.

And every time they lost the tracks, they lost precious time. In spite of that, Naomi hadn't been able to let go of the hope that she would hold her daughter in her arms again before nightfall. But as the sun began its downward descent and the temperature started to drop with it, Naomi had no choice but to accept the fact that that wasn't going to happen.

Exhausted, realizing for the first time the enormity of what they were up against in their search, it was all she could do not to lay her head against Hunter's back and cry. She was so tired...and not any closer to finding Laura than she had been that morning.

"It looks like we may have gotten a break," Hunter said suddenly over the low roar of the snowmobile's motor. "There's a line cabin up ahead."

Lost in her misery, Naomi hardly heard him at first. Then his words registered. "What? Where?"

"In the clearing off to the right," he said, nodding to the area fifty yards ahead of them. In the gathering shadows, the small, single-room dwelling looked deserted, but Hunter had no intention of driving right up to the front porch without checking it out first. Naomi didn't think Barker had a gun, but Hunter wasn't so sure. Any man who would kidnap his own daughter and drag her up into the mountains just to torture her mother was capable of anything.

Braking to a stop well short of the cabin, he cut the snowmobile's engine and said quietly in the sudden silence, "Stay here. I'll be right back."

He knew what he was asking of her, and for a minute he thought she was going to insist on going with him, but he only had to shoot her a narrow-eyed look to remind her that they had an agreement. She didn't like it—in fact, if looks could kill, the resentful look she shot him would have slain him on the spot—but he had to give her credit. She was a lady of her word. Her mouth compressing in a flat line, she sat back and didn't offer a single word of protest as he soundlessly slipped off into the trees that surrounded the cabin.

He was back almost immediately, his rugged face carved in shadows as he moved toward her as silently as an eagle gliding through the pines. In his hand he carried a small stuffed teddy bear that was worn and tattered and missing an ear. "Recognize this?"

Naomi took one look at it and cried out softly as she quickly dismounted the snowmobile and reached for it. "Oh, God, it's Chester—Laura's bear! She never goes anywhere without him. Where—"

"In the cabin," he said, anticipating her question. "It looks like Barker holed up here with Laura last night, then took off after he spotted us down in the canyon with binoculars this morning."

"And he made her leave Chester behind?" she said indignantly, her gray eyes snapping. "How dare he! He knows what that bear means to her. She won't even go to sleep at night without it. The one time he got misplaced, she cried for hours."

"We don't know that Barker deliberately made her leave without it," he said. "In the rush to get away, he might have just overlooked it."

"No. You don't know him. He did this on purpose to taunt me. He wants me to think she's been crying all afternoon." Her throat tightening at the thought, she could do nothing to stop the tears that suddenly flooded her eyes. "Damn him, he's not going to get away with it," she said huskily. "He couldn't have gotten that far. If we hurry—"

"We wouldn't get a quarter of a mile," he said flatly. "I know you're upset and you'd like nothing more than to get your hands around Barker's throat as soon as possible, and I don't blame you—the man's a bastard—but we're not going anywhere tonight. Look around you," he said when she started to object. "It's already dark and we've both had a long day. That adds up to an accident waiting to happen. If you want to help Laura, the best thing you can do for her right now is get a good night's sleep and start fresh in the morning."

"But—"

"This isn't open to discussion, Naomi. This is the end of the trail for tonight."

If she hadn't been teetering on the edge of exhaustion and worried to death about Laura, she might have reacted differently. As it was, all she could think of was one more man was trying to come between her and her daughter, and she'd had just about enough of it. *No one* was telling her what she could and couldn't do when it came to Laura.

"Maybe for you, but not for me," she said coolly. "As long as there's any daylight left, I intend to keep searching."

"Don't be ridiculous—"

Ignoring him, she turned on her heel and began to retrace her steps to the last spot they'd seen James's tracks. While Hunter had been in the cabin, the sun had completely disappeared behind the tallest peaks to the west, and the shadows were already darkening under the trees. If she was lucky, she might have another thirty or forty minutes before she completely lost the light. And that was thirty or more minutes that they wouldn't have to waste tomorrow looking for James's tracks.

Her head down, her eyes trained directly on the snow-covered ground at her feet, she found the trail left by James's snowmobile less than fifty feet from the cabin. They headed west, deeper into the mountains. Her jaw firm with resolve, she started to follow them.

Watching her, Hunter was half-tempted to let her go. He'd told her what could happen to her up here in

the mountains, warned her how quickly she could get
into trouble if she didn't do as he said. But did she
listen? Hell, no. Instead, she was hell-bent on going
off on her own, and it irritated him no end. Did she
think he wanted to spend one more minute than he
had to, chasing Barker all over the godforsaken mountains? He had a life to get back to and work to do,
dammit! And the sooner they found Laura, the quicker
he could get back to it.

But they weren't going to find her in the dark, and
the only thing Naomi was going to accomplish by
traipsing off by herself was to get lost. Then he'd have
to spend half the night looking for her in the dark, and
by God, he wasn't going to do it! Not after the day
he'd had. And if she didn't like it, that was just too
damn bad! Muttering curses under his breath about
stubborn, hardheaded women, he stormed after her.

"Dammit, Naomi, I'm not letting you do this!" he
growled as he caught up with her at the edge of the
clearing that surrounded the cabin. "It's too dangerous."

Up to her knees in snow, her shoulders hunched
against the wind, she never took her eyes from the
tracks that were barely visible in the gathering darkness. "You're not my keeper, Hunter. I don't need
your permission to look for my daughter."

It was the wrong thing to say to a man who had
reached the end of his patience. Swearing, he snagged
her arm and hauled her around to face him. All he
intended to do was shake some sense into her, but the
snow was deep, and he caught her unaware. Gasping,
she lost her balance and fell right into his arms.

Too late, he realized he never should have touched her. She'd spent most of the day with her arms around his waist, clinging to his back. As they'd made their way up the mountain, her breasts and thighs and hips had brushed against him with every dip and sway of the snowmobile, teasing him unmercifully. She hadn't, he knew, set out to drive him out of his mind—she'd had no choice but to hold on to him or fall off the snowmobile—but the result was the same, nevertheless. She'd lit a fire in him that had been burning low in his gut all day. And it just got hotter.

He should have released her then—he meant to. But his fingers wouldn't follow the dictates of his brain, and instead of letting her go, he drew her closer. In the dusky shadows, he saw awareness flare in her eyes, heard her soft gasp, and his gaze dropped to her mouth. He knew then he'd just lost any chance of walking away without kissing her.

It should have been simple. A first—and last—kiss just to satisfy his curiosity. There was nothing complicated about it; it didn't even require a second thought. Or so he thought until his mouth covered hers. That was when he discovered that nothing was ever going to be that simple with Naomi Windsong.

Judging by her reaction, Naomi was as surprised as he was by the sudden heat that flared between them and didn't seem to know what to do about it. She'd obviously been kissed before—she had a child, for God's sake!—but she acted as if passion was something she wasn't accustomed to dealing with. She hesitated, and he could almost feel the battle going on inside her. Then he nipped at her sensitive bottom lip, and all her defenses just seemed to give way. Bewildered, she clung to him, as soft as a kitten, and sweetly, blindly kissed him back. When he didn't want to let her go, he knew he was in trouble.

Naomi, lost in his arms, felt Laura's tattered bear crushed between them and abruptly snapped to her senses. Dear God, what was she doing? Her daughter was out there in the cold and the dark somewhere, totally dependant on a man who had ruthlessly put her in danger without a care for her safety, and what was she doing? Kissing Hunter Fortune like a woman possessed. What kind of mother was she?

Suddenly furious with herself and him, she pushed out of his arms and glared up at him in the thickening twilight, her gray eyes fierce with outrage. "I think we'd better get something straight right here, Mr. Fortune. I sought you out for one reason, and one reason only—to track down James so I could get my daughter back. That's all I'm interested in. So if you thought I insisted on coming up here with you because I might want something else from you, you can think again. I'm not looking for sex or romance or even a man, for that matter, so you just keep your hands and your mouth to yourself and we'll get along fine. Otherwise, you can take me home in the morning, and I'll find someone else to help me find Laura."

She stood toe-to-toe with him and just dared him to touch her again, kiss her again. Just because she'd once fallen for James's lies didn't mean she was still that same naive woman waiting for another man to take advantage of her. She was tougher now, stronger, and no one was ever going to hurt her again.

And something of that must have shown in her eyes, because Hunter made no move to take her back into his arms. Instead, he swore softly and said, "Look, I'm sorry. I know your only interest is finding Laura, and in spite of what just happened, mine is, too. Just for the record, I have a company to get off the ground by the end of the year, and I don't have time for anything else. Especially a woman. So you're safe with me. Okay?"

There was no doubting his sincerity. He looked her right in the eye and didn't flinch from her searching gaze. And although she had no reason to believe that he would keep his word, she did. Hugging herself, she nodded.

"Good. Now that we've got that settled, why don't we go back to the cabin and see about digging up something to eat. I don't know about you, but I'm starving."

Darkness had completely fallen, and any chance she had of following James's tracks was now gone. Shivering in the wind, she knew it was probably for the best. It had gotten dark faster than she expected it to, and the temperature was already dropping like a rock. If she'd lost her way, she could have quickly been in trouble.

Resigned to having to wait until morning to start the search again, she followed Hunter back to the cabin, where they had a cold supper. The kiss they'd shared wasn't mentioned again, but when it came time to go to bed, they laid out sleeping bags at opposite ends of the small cabin. It had been a long, tiring day, and there was no question that they were both exhausted. But when Hunter turned out the small lantern he'd brought along, it was a long time before either of them fell asleep.

Five

Every bone in Naomi's body ached the next morning when they started out again, but she climbed on the back of the snowmobile without a word of complaint. If Hunter noticed that she found a way to hold on to him without getting too close, he didn't say anything, and for that she was grateful. During the long hours of the night when she'd lain awake, trying to forget a kiss that never should have happened, she'd had plenty of time to think about yesterday and how she'd clung to him as they'd wound their way up the mountains. She'd only been hanging on to him to keep from falling off, but she could see how that might have given him the wrong impression about her. That wasn't, she promised herself, going to happen today.

So she kept her hands light on his waist and sat as far back on the seat as the gear strapped on behind her would allow. And if her palms were slightly damp in her gloves and her heart had a tendency to flutter just at the thought of touching him, no one knew that but her. Silently she prayed that they would find Laura soon.

Once it was light enough to see, they again began the tedious task of following James's tracks. No new snow had fallen during the night, but the wind was straight out of the north and blew snow right back in their faces, partially covering James's track and half blinding them at one and the same time. Swearing, Hunter was forced to slow their pace, and they seemed to crawl as they slowly wound their way deeper into the mountains. And still there was no sign of James or Laura.

Refusing to give up hope, Naomi told herself they would find them today. But as hours passed and the pace began to wear on her nerves, she couldn't help but get frustrated and discouraged. James had to know they were following him. What did he hope to accomplish by fleeing deeper into the mountains? He wasn't going to get away—there was no way out except the way they had come. And she wasn't going to give up and turn back. If she had to scour every inch of the mountains to get her daughter back, she would. Surely he had to know that.

But if he did, he showed no sign of it. His tracks continued, ever northward, quietly taunting them, leading them farther and farther away from civilization. And even as they followed, there was no way to know exactly how far ahead of them he was. It could have been minutes. But then again, it could have been hours. Her eyes steely with determination, Naomi told herself she didn't care if it was days—she wouldn't rest until she ran him to ground.

All her attention focused on the tracks in the snow up ahead, she didn't realize that they led right up to a rocky cliff until Hunter suddenly braked well short of the edge and cut the engine. "What's wrong?" she asked in surprise, her voice sounding unnaturally loud in the sudden silence. "Why are we stopping?"

"We may have reached the end of the trail," he said somberly. "Stay here while I check it out."

Confused, Naomi looked past him to the tracks in the snow that still stretched out before them. "What do you mean 'the end of the trail'?" she began. Then she saw it. The cliff edge. The snowy ground that suddenly just seemed to fall away into thin air. The way James's tracks led right up to the precipice and disappeared over the side. And her heart stopped dead in her breast.

"No," she whispered in dawning horror. "Oh, God, no! Laura!"

She didn't remember throwing herself off the snowmobile, didn't hear Hunter yell at her to stay back. Suddenly she was running in the snow, stumbling, her blood roaring in her ears, terrified of what she would see when she reached the cliff's edge.

The scene below was every bit as bad as she'd feared. The snowmobile had sailed right over the edge of the cliff to a rocky ridge forty feet below. Battered and broken and half-covered in snow, it lay on its side like a dead soldier, still and unmoving. Naomi took one look at it and could just see Laura flying over the edge of the cliff, clinging to her father as he sent them crashing to the rocks below.

Horrified, her pounding heart lodged in her throat, she didn't think—she just reacted. Tears flooding her eyes, half blinding her, all she could think of was Laura. She was down there somewhere, hurt, possibly dead. She had to get to her. A sob catching in her throat, she practically threw herself over the edge of the cliff and began making her way down the rocky escarpment to the ridge below.

Fear driving her, she didn't give a thought to her own safety. Hunter shouted at her to stop, but she couldn't have if her life had depended on it. Not when Laura was in danger. Half-blinded by tears she scrambled down the steep incline, and didn't even see the thin layer of ice coating the rocks she climbed over until it was too late. Her foot slipped, and with a startled cry she went tumbling.

Hunter couldn't catch her. Ten feet above her on the cliff face, he moved like lightning, but there was no way in hell he could reach her before she went down hard on the rocks. And it was his fault. He should have expected her to panic when she realized Barker's snowmobile had gone off the cliff, and he should have tackled her if he'd had to to keep her from going down there. But, dammit, he hadn't thought she could move so fast!

Her cry of pain went through him like a lance. Swearing, he hurried down the icy rocks to her side, cursing all the while as he came down beside her. Collapsed on her side, moaning, her cap missing and her hair tangled around her ashen face, she looked like a broken doll. She'd landed hard on her left hip and shoulder and had instinctively moved to catch herself. In the process, her hand had landed at an odd angle on the rocks, and that's when she'd cried out.

Fear making his voice rough, he reached for her. "Are you all right? Dammit, I told you to stay by the snowmobile! Here—let me see."

"No!" Whimpering, she cradled her wrist to her

breast protectively and curled in on herself, silent tears streaming down her pale face. "I'm okay. Just g-give m-me a second."

Okay, hell! Who did she think she was fooling? She was hurt, dammit, possibly seriously! He'd seen the unnatural way her wrist had bent when she'd tried to catch herself, the jarring blow that her hip and shoulder had taken when they'd connected with the rocks. If she hadn't broken something, he'd be surprised. She had to be in severe pain, and if he didn't do something damn quick, she could easily go into shock.

"You can't stay on the side of this cliff, sweetheart," he said gruffly. "I'm going to carry you back up to the snowmobile. Do you think you can hang on to me?"

"Find Laura first," she groaned. "She could be hurt—"

"After I get you back up to the snowmobile," he said firmly, and carefully picked her up before she could come up with another objection.

When she gasped and went stiff with pain in his arms, he cursed himself for hurting her further, but there was nothing he could do to make the climb up the side of the cliff any less painful for her. He found himself silently pleading with her to just pass out, but she didn't. Stubbornly clinging to consciousness, her face wet with a steady stream of tears, she clenched her jaw against the pain and didn't so much as whimper as he began the long climb up the side of the cliff.

Hunter had never seen anything like it. She'd already proven that when it came to her daughter, she would take on the devil himself to keep her safe; but he'd just thought her fierceness was nothing more than a mother's natural instinct to protect its young. He'd never suspected that beneath her soft, vulnerable beauty was one tough lady. And if there was one thing he admired in anyone, it was inner strength. She was really something.

Careful to jar her as little as possible, it seemed to take forever to make it back to the snowmobile. Hunter would have given just about anything to be able to take her to a warm cabin to check out her injuries, but that wasn't an option. Grim-faced, he carefully set her on the ground next to the snowmobile, then immediately dug in his pack for his first aid kit.

Shaking, whether from the cold or shock Hunter couldn't be sure, Naomi stuttered, "L-Laura..."

"You first," he growled. "Let me see your wrist, honey."

She wanted to argue—he could see the protest in her eyes—but she didn't have the strength. Without a word she dragged in a bracing breath and held out her wrist to him.

Hunter didn't think it was broken, but he wasn't taking any chances. He carefully splinted her wrist, then frowned at her. "How's your hip and shoulder? You think you broke anything?"

She didn't give him an immediate no as he'd expected, but instead took the time to gingerly test both joints before she shook her head. "No," she sighed in relief. "Laura—"

She was so single-minded in spite of her own pain that he had to smile. "I know, honey. I'm going. Sit tight. I'll be back as quick as I can."

The afternoon was quickly slipping away, but the light was still good as he made his way down the side of the cliff to where Barker's snowmobile lay. There was no sign of Barker or Laura, and a quick inspection of the snowy ground near the snowmobile convinced Hunter that they weren't on the machine when it went over the cliff. There were no tracks in any direction and no evidence that it had snowed since the crash.

Wondering why Barker would be stupid enough to send his only mode of transportation over the cliff, Hunter righted it and turned the key in the ignition. When the only sound was a click, he had his answer. Barker had obviously had some kind of mechanical trouble and hoped to buy some time by making them think they'd crashed. If the man knew anything about Naomi, he had to know that she wouldn't go any farther until the area was thoroughly searched and she was convinced that Laura wasn't there.

Just to be sure that Barker hadn't somehow gone over the cliff and managed to not only crawl off somewhere to nurse his injuries but cover up his tracks, he inspected the ground for a hundred yards in every direction. Only when he was convinced that the other man had never even stepped foot over the side of the cliff did he return to Naomi.

She was sitting right where he'd left her. Huddled in her coat, as pale as the snow, she struggled to stand as she saw him climb over the side of the cliff. "Laura…did you find her?"

"No," he said flatly. "She wasn't on the snowmobile when it went over the edge. Neither was

Barker. They couldn't have been. There was no sign of them and no tracks.''

He told her his theory then, and she glanced around. "Then their tracks must be up here somewhere. They couldn't have gotten far on foot. We can follow them.''

Even as she spoke, it started to snow, and Hunter knew they'd lost whatever chance they had of finding Barker for now. She was hurt and needed to rest, and he needed to find them a place to stay for the night. And judging from the darkness of the clouds gathering overhead, he didn't have a lot of time to do it. A storm was coming—he could smell it—and he didn't intend to be caught out in the open when it hit.

Quickly moving to repack the first aid kit in his pack, he said, "Not today we can't. There's a storm coming, and we've got to find a line cabin before it hits.'' With an economy of movement, he secured his pack on the snowmobile, then turned to look her over searchingly. "How's your wrist? Do you think you're going to be able to hang on to me without hurting yourself?''

"It's not my wrist I'm worried about," she said stubbornly. "It's Laura. We have to find James's tracks before they're covered by the snow—''

"No, what we've got to do is find shelter while we still can,'' he retorted. "If Barker is the survivalist you say he is, he'll be doing the same thing. After this all blows over, and he digs out, then we'll find him. For now, we're getting the heck out of Dodge, sweetheart. So how's your wrist? If you don't think you're going to be able to hold on to me, I may have to put you in front of me so I can cradle you with my body. We couldn't go very fast that way, but you wouldn't fall off, either.''

Naomi couldn't believe he was worried about such a trivial thing, when, after two days of searching, they were about to lose James's tracks. What if he hadn't found shelter? Just because he was a survivalist didn't mean he could read the weather in the sky. Right that very minute he and Laura could, for all she knew, be trudging along in the snow on foot, unaware that the mother of all storms was bearing down on them. Her baby could be caught in it, and Hunter expected her to just forget that and find shelter for herself? She didn't think so!

Suddenly furious with him, she snapped, ''I won't fall off because I'm not going anywhere. Not until I know we're going to be able to find James's tracks tomorrow. And don't glare at me like that,'' she continued, scowling at him. ''You're not going to bully me into doing what you want this time—''

''Bully you?! I never—''

''Yes, you did. You've done nothing but throw one order after another at me like some kind of drill sergeant ever since we left town yesterday morning, and frankly, I resent it. Despite what you may think of me, I do have a brain in my head—''

''I never said you didn't!''

''Not in so many words, no. But you act like I haven't got the sense to come in out of the rain, when all I'm worried about is my daughter, and I'm not taking it anymore!''

Wound up, all her worry and frustration coming to

a boil inside her, she leveled a finger at his chest and told him what she thought of him and every other man, including James, who'd tried to tell her what to do and run her life. She was tired of it and she wasn't putting up with it a second longer—not from him or anyone else.

It wasn't like her to go off on a tirade, and she knew that later she was going to be appalled. But she'd held too much back for too long, and the words just came spewing forth. To his credit, Hunter didn't say one word to stop her. But his eyes narrowed to a laser glint, and his jaw turned hard as granite. And when she poked him in the chest once too often with that accusing finger of hers, he grabbed her hand, trapping her fingers in his. But still, he let her have her say.

It was snowing hard when she finally ran out of words, but neither of them noticed. In the fading light his nearly black eyes glittered with anger. "Are you through now?"

"Yes, dammit! Let go of my hand!"

Hunter might have, if she hadn't used quite that tone with him. He considered himself a reasonable man, and he knew everybody needed to vent their frustrations once in a while. But *he* wasn't the cause of the lady's problems—he was only trying to help her. And there was only so much abuse he would take before his own patience ran thin. Naomi had just pushed him to that limit.

"The hell I will," he growled, tightening his fingers around hers when she would have pulled back. "You've had your say—now I'm going to have mine. If you want to rage at me for something I did, I'll be the first to tell you that's your right. But I'm not the one who's hurt you. All I've tried to do is keep you safe until we find Laura and get out of here, and you've given me nothing but grief for it. Well, I've got my limits, too, sweetheart, and enough is enough. You agreed to follow my orders before we ever left your house, and like it or not, I'm responsible for you as long as we're in these damn mountains. That means you do what I tell you when I tell you—"

"The hell I do!"

"And if you don't like it, that's just too damn bad. You gave me your word, and I'm holding you to it."

"You and whose army? Dammit, let me go!"

He should have. But the lady had a way of pushing his buttons and clouding his judgment, and he'd had just about enough of her temper for one day. She'd nearly gotten herself killed by not following orders, and in the process, she'd scared the hell out of him. That was going to end right here, right now. It was time she learned who was really in charge, and he was just the man to teach her. Muttering a curse, knowing he was making a mistake but unable to stop himself, he pulled her into his arms and kissed her.

Six

It happened so fast, Naomi didn't have time to think, let alone resist. One second they were glaring at each other like two fighters in a ring about to pound each other senseless, and the next she was in his arms. Gasping, her heart slamming against her ribs, she should have slugged him one. No one manhandled her without asking to get belted. At the very least she should have demanded that he release her. But although he reached for her in anger, the second his lips touched hers, it wasn't temper that drove him, but need. A quiet, desperate need that called to something deep inside her, something that she hadn't even known was there until he'd kissed her that first time and left her reeling.

She'd tried to convince herself it was just her imagination. How could it be anything else? She didn't know this man! She didn't want to want him. But he just touched her, kissed her and she melted. His arms tightened around her, his mouth moved hungrily over hers, and the rest of the world just fell away, leaving her alone with him and a need that consumed her. Moaning softly, she pressed closer.

They might have stood there for hours, lost in the taste and heat and feel of each other while the falling snow swirled around them, but Naomi made the mistake of moving to put her arms around Hunter's waist. Pain, as red-hot as a burning match, flared in her wrist, drawing a sharp, startled cry from her.

Muttering curses, Hunter abruptly drew back to scowl down at her in concern. "Dammit, I can't believe I forgot about your wrist! Are you all right? Let me see."

"No! It's fine. Really! I just moved wrong. I wasn't thinking."

Neither of them had been, but that was something he obviously didn't intend to admit. Too late, Naomi wished she hadn't, either. She couldn't deny any longer that she was physically attracted to the man, but that was all it was. Just basic, simple chemistry. It wasn't something she could control—or anything she was foolish enough to put any stock in. James had destroyed any chance she had of trusting a man years ago, and she would never again let anyone get close enough to hurt her or her daughter again.

If she couldn't seem to resist Hunter, she told herself, it was only because he was the type of man a woman naturally turned to in a time of crisis. He was a take-charge kind of guy, and for that, she thanked God. Because it would take just such a man to find Laura. But the only thing she was letting him take charge of was the search—not her. She'd do well to remember that.

Ignoring the pain that throbbed in her wrist, she frowned in confusion at the snow that had intensified to almost white-out conditions in a matter of minutes. "What happened?" she cried, stunned. "Just a second ago it was barely snowing!"

"Blizzard," Hunter said shortly. "C'mon, we've got to get out of here and find some shelter!"

They had almost waited too long. It was snowing so hard they could barely see a foot in front of them, making it impossible to get their bearings. Hunter had checked National Forest Service maps before setting out on the search and had a general idea where an old line cabin was, but when he got turned around in the snow, and the cabin wasn't where he thought it would be, he started to worry. There was no room for error in a blizzard. One miscalculation and you might not be found until spring.

Behind him on the snowmobile, Naomi held herself stiffly against him, and he knew she had to be in pain. But she didn't utter so much as a word of caution as he darted in and out among the trees, making his way farther north at a speed that was nothing short of suicidal.

With visibility worsening by the minute, he would have missed the cabin if it hadn't been for Naomi. She spotted it half-hidden among the trees just when he thought he'd missed it and would have to turn back. "There it is!" she said hoarsely in his ear. "Over to the left."

The cabin, they quickly discovered, wasn't in the best of shape. The porch roof was sagging, the front door was warped, and in the not-too-recent past, some type of animal had been nesting inside. But the roof was solid, the windows weren't broken, and the last human occupant had added to the woodpile before he left. That was good enough for Hunter. Hustling Naomi inside, he carried in their gear, then strode back outside for the wood they would need to get them through the night.

While Hunter built a fire in the fireplace, Naomi found a broom, and with her one good hand, awkwardly swept the place clean of its last animal visitor. By the time the fire caught and started to send out a blaze of warmth, the small cabin was, if not clean, at least less cluttered.

Already peeling out of his protective outer gear, Hunter looked over at Naomi and growled, "You need to get out of those wet clothes and into something dry, then we'll eat. I've got some dehydrated stew in my pack. That'll help warm you up."

Turning his back to search for it, he gave her the only privacy he could to change, and in the sudden, tense silence, the sound of a zipper being lowered seemed to set the air humming. His jaw set, Hunter tried to close out the sound, but he seemed to have radar where she was concerned and was aware of her every move. When she suddenly went still and just seemed to stand there, he scowled down at his pack and couldn't even remember what he was looking for in it.

"I thought you were going to change," he said tersely. "What are you waiting for?"

"My wrist," she said huskily. "I can't. The splint—"

Too late he realized that with her hurt wrist, she wouldn't, in all likelihood, be able to even change her socks by herself. Which meant he would have to help her, touch her. The need that had burned in his gut ever since he'd kissed her flared hotter just at the thought.

Torture. There was no other way to describe what happened next. His jaw rigid, he turned to help her and found her standing before the fire, outlined in its golden glow as darkness gathered outside. Her hair was wet and tousled from her fall and their wild ride on the snowmobile, her cheeks windburned. And still, she was beautiful.

Aching to touch her, he reminded himself that she was hurt and that was the only reason she was asking for his help. But his body, he discovered in disgust, didn't give a damn about reasons as long as he got to touch her. Already hard for her, he crossed the room and wondered how he was going to get through the next few minutes without going quietly out of his mind.

"I'll have to take the splint off," he said hoarsely. "It's probably going to hurt."

Without a word she held out her injured wrist to him.

He tried to be gentle, but there was no way he could get her out of the splint and her jacket without hurting her. She didn't so much as whimper, but she couldn't blink away the tears fast enough that sprang to her eyes, and Hunter felt like the lowest slug on the food chain. Murmuring soothingly to her, he quickly re-splinted her wrist.

Confused, she said, "But what about my sweater? I still have to take it off."

"The cuff'll stretch around the splint," he assured her. "I'll work it through, and this way your wrist will stay immobile.'' Reaching for the hem of her pullover sweater, he tried not to notice the softness of her bare skin as his fingers brushed against her midriff. But her eyes flew to his and he knew she felt it, too—the heat that always seemed to be there between them. A muscle ticking in his jaw, he rasped, ''Ready?''

She nodded, and he slowly began to work her sweater up over her head. His teeth clenched on an oath, and he tried not to touch her any more than was strictly necessary, tried not to look anywhere but at the sweater as he worked the garment off of her. But he was a man, not a monk, and somehow, over the course of the past two days, she'd managed to make him want her in a way that no woman ever had before. With a will of their own, his eyes followed the expanse of soft white skin that was slowly revealed, inch by inch, as the sweater came off.

She'd been riding behind him for days now, her breasts pressed up against his back, and he should have had some inkling of how the lady was built. But imagining and seeing were two different things. She wore a simple cotton bra that wasn't any more revealing than a bathing suit top, but his mouth went dry just at the sight of her. Lord, she was pretty! And he wanted to touch her so badly that for a second he had to curl his hands into fists just to keep from reaching for her.

Swallowing a curse, he reminded himself that she was hurt and worried to death about Laura. She trusted him to help her, and he would cut off his right arm before he betrayed that trust. So he ignored the fire burning in his belly, kept his expression neutral and, after her sweater was tossed aside, helped her out of her boots and reached for the snap of her pants.

It would have been easier if she hadn't been as aware of him as he was of her, but although she tried to pretend otherwise, her body gave her away. A slow flush stole up from her breasts to her cheeks, and when he finally got her out of her pants, she was trembling, and they both knew it wasn't from the cold. Hurriedly, he reached for the dry sweats she'd laid out to change into and began the torturous job of dressing her.

And every time his hands came into contact with her thighs, her hips or accidentally brushed the silken curve of her breast, it cost him. Sweat beaded his brow, he couldn't seem to unlock his jaw, and he'd have sworn the temperature in the cabin hovered somewhere at 110. If he'd had it to do over again, he would rather have chewed ground glass than put himself through that kind of temptation again.

"There!" he growled, when she was decently covered at last. "Sit down by the fire and warm up while I fix us something to eat. I don't know about you, but I'm starving."

Every nerve ending tingling, her blood rushing hotly through her veins, Naomi would have laughed at the very idea of eating now if she could have managed to find the breath. How could he even think about food when she could still feel his hands on her, still taste the heat of a kiss that should have long since cooled? She'd known him what? Two days? And already her body responded to his touch, regardless of how innocent it was.

Confused, she watched him heat water for the dehydrated stew that would be their supper and asked herself not for the first time if she was losing her mind. This wasn't like her. She didn't kiss men she'd only known a matter of days—she didn't even let them touch her. And, thanks to the painful lessons James had taught her, she certainly didn't trust them.

But she could trust Hunter. If she'd had any doubts before, he'd just proven that. When every other man she knew would have taken advantage of her the second he had her out of her clothes, he had barely touched her, and then only when he had to. And it wasn't for lack of interest. She'd been on the receiving end of his kiss in the snow; she'd seen the unsteadiness of his fingers as he'd started to pull her sweater up and over her head. He'd wanted her. And she'd wanted him. And that, more than anything, shook her. How had they come to this point so quickly?

It only took a few minutes for Hunter to prepare the stew, and when it was done, they sat on opposite sides of the small fireplace and ate. Forcing each bite down, Naomi had never before been quite so aware of their isolation. Outside, the storm had intensified, cutting them off from the rest of the world. The wind, howling angrily, raced around the cabin, throwing ice and snow against the windows. Icy air slipped through nooks and crevices, and despite the roaring fire, the temperature inside was anything but toasty.

"We'd both better sleep as close to the fire as we can tonight," Hunter said, shattering the silence that had thickened between them as they ate. "The wind's whistling through the logs like a sieve, and it's only going to get colder before morning."

Shivering, Naomi set her barely touched stew down and hugged herself as a cold draft whispered across the back of her neck. She didn't want to think of James out there in the cold and the snow with Laura, but she couldn't push the haunting images from her mind. "Do you think they found someplace to stay?"

She didn't have to say who—he knew. "You said yourself that James is a survivalist," he said quietly. "He would have seen the storm coming hours before it hit and found them shelter."

"But they're on foot," she said worriedly as she moved over to one of the curtainless windows and stared out at the black, snowy night. "And Laura would have slowed him down. What if they didn't have time to find a place? Or—"

"If you start playing *what if,* all you're going to do is drive yourself crazy," he warned. "If you want to help Laura, the best thing you can do for both of you is get some rest and give your body time to heal some after that fall you took today. Now that they're on foot, we'll probably find them tomorrow and Laura's going to need you to be strong. Getting out of here after this storm isn't going to be easy."

He was right, Naomi knew, but that didn't make her worry any less. With a will of their own, her eyes kept drifting to the darkened windows as the supper dishes were quickly cleaned up and their sleeping bags unrolled before the hearth. Hunter had her check the messages on her answering machine with his cell phone just in case James had done the decent thing and let her know Laura was safe. But there was nothing. As Hunter built up the fire and made sure the logs he'd brought inside earlier were within easy reach, she crawled into her sleeping bag and tried to convince herself that James wouldn't be stupid enough to let anything happen to his own daughter. But long after Hunter had slipped into his own sleeping bag and fallen asleep, she lay wide-awake, fear clutching her heart.

Miserable, she never knew when she fell asleep and began to dream. One second she was staring unblinkingly at the flames that danced over the logs in the fireplace, and the next she was fighting her way through the storm, searching, always searching, for her baby in the dark.

Mama! Where's Mama?

Muffled by the howling wind, Laura's faint cry floated out of the darkness to her, teasing and taunting and swirling around her from all directions. Glancing wildly around, Naomi stopped in her tracks, her heart pounding frantically. "Here, sweetheart!" she called desperately. "Mama's here! Where are you?"

Her only answer was the eerie moan of the wind.

Snow slapped at her, blinding her, trapping her, keeping her from her daughter. Terrified, she stumbled forward, searching, tears streaming down her cold face. "Laura? Answer me, sweetheart! Just tell mama where you are."

Mama...Mama...Mama...

Like something out of "The Twilight Zone," Laura's cry echoed back to her, slowly, slowly fading until there was nothing left but silence. Her heart stopping dead in her breast, Naomi screamed, "No! Come back! Don't leave me!"

Dead to the world, Hunter came awake with a jerk at her tortured cry. In a heartbeat he was on his knees beside her, bending over her in concern when he saw she was crying in her sleep. "Wake up, sweetheart. C'mon. Open your eyes. That's it. Tell me where it hurts. Is it your wrist again? Did you turn in your sleep and hurt it?"

Struggling up out of the depths of sleep, her eyes drenched in tears, she whimpered, "No, it's Laura. Oh God, Hunter, I think she's really in trouble!" And with no more warning than that, she threw herself into his arms.

Seven

She was soft and warm from sleep and too damn enticing to be holding in the middle of the night, when a man was at his most vulnerable. The second he instinctively caught her against him, he knew he should have released her immediately and put some distance between them. He'd been dreaming of her, of kissing her, his traitorous body aching for her in his sleep, and dammit, his heart was still pounding! He had no business touching her, not when all he could think about was pulling her down to his sleeping bag with him, but he couldn't make himself let her go. Not when she was this close.

Cursing himself even as his arms wrapped tighter around her, he huskily shushed her. "Shhh. She's fine. You just had a bad dream. Why don't you crawl back into your sleeping bag and let me fix you something hot to drink? I've got some instant hot chocolate—"

"No! Please!" she whimpered, clinging to him. "I just need to hold on to somebody for a second."

Somebody. Anybody. His jaw held back an oath as he told himself that she was just looking for reassurance and any warm body would have done. But it wasn't just anybody she was draped all over—it was him—and he could feel every soft, enticing curve of her. His blood stirred and heated, and he was helpless to stop it.

His jaw rigid, he silently ordered himself to put a stop to this now, before things got out of hand. But when he finally found the strength of will to bring his hands to her shoulders and draw her away from him, he took one look at her tear-drenched eyes, and all his fine resolves crumbled. She was hurting, and all he could think about was making her feel better.

"C'mere," he growled, and swept her onto his lap.

Naomi knew she was probably going to regret this later. But it was late and her defenses were down and she couldn't carry the burden of worrying about Laura all by herself anymore. Hunter wrapped his arms around her and made her feel safe when she'd have sworn no man could ever make her feel that way again. Then, when she was sure that was all she needed from him, he kissed her and shattered the loneliness that seemed like it had been with her forever. She could have no more resisted him than an eagle could have resisted the temptation to soar on the wind.

He wouldn't stop with just a kiss this time; she was sure of it. In spite of the fact that she had a daughter, she wasn't all that experienced and wanted to tell him. But she couldn't find the words to say that her only other experience was with James, her only other point of reference a man who put his own wants and needs first and only thought of her in passing. Because of him, she'd never been able to see what all the fuss had been about sex. It was nice, but hardly the thing that made the world go round.

Or so she thought until Hunter eased her down to

his sleeping bag and tenderly began to make love to her. Braced for quick, impatient hands, she could only shudder when he seemed perfectly content to just touch and explore and caress her. Confused, she caught at his hand and unconsciously clung to it like it was a lifeline. "Aren't you—"

"Shh," he murmured, trailing slow, warm kisses down her throat and over her breast. "Just relax and let me take care of you. That's it," he said in a low, rough voice when he beaded her nipple with his breath alone and drew a soft, startled gasp from her. "Don't think. Don't do anything but feel."

Bathed in firelight, his hands gentle and sure on her, she couldn't do anything else *but* feel. Fascination. It was there in every long, slow stroke of his hands, in the blind, hungry kisses that followed, in the husky words of praise he rasped in her ear. He drenched her in sensations, until her senses blurred and her heart thundered and she couldn't remember her own name.

And then, when she thought she couldn't possibly feel anything else, he showed her just how wrong she was. He kissed his way down her body, and she cried out as needs that were already past bearing sharpened with intensity. Tension tightened every nerve ending, and as the storm raged outside, so did the one in her blood. Hot, restless, her lungs straining, she clutched at him, drawing him back up to her, into her.

A groan was ripped from his throat, and whatever control he had left snapped. As the wind howled outside and the firelight danced on the ceiling, he set a rhythm that rivaled the wildness of the night. There was no yesterday, no tomorrow, nothing but here and now and each other. In the flickering light of the fire, his eyes met and held hers, their fingers intertwined. Intimacy took on a whole new meaning. And when they raced for the stars and shattered into a million pieces, they held each other like they would never let go.

The blizzard blew itself out during the night, and by morning the sky was crystal blue and the wind was calm. If it hadn't been for the frigid temperatures and the foot of fresh snow that covered the ground, no one would ever know the storm had happened.

Standing on the front porch of the cabin, Naomi watched Hunter carry their gear out of the cabin and couldn't help but wonder if the hours she'd spent in his arms had been nothing more than a figment of her imagination. She'd woken an hour ago to find herself back in her own sleeping bag in front of the fire and Hunter repacking the backpacks. He'd mumbled a gruff good-morning to her and asked about her wrist, but since then he'd had little time for conversation. On the few occasions when he had spoken, his shuttered expression hadn't encouraged any personal discussions. If he'd wanted to tell her how he felt about making love with her, he couldn't have picked a better way.

Hurt lodged in the region of her heart, and she told herself she had no one to blame but herself. What in the world had gotten into her? She wasn't adventuresome when it came to men—she never had been. When she'd met James, she'd been a shy, unsure virgin, and she hadn't even considered going to bed with him until she was convinced she was head-over-heels in love with him. Since she'd discovered just what kind of a lying lowlife he was, she hadn't let another man so much as touch her.

Until Hunter.

Somehow he'd slipped under her guard and gotten past her defenses, and she'd let herself forget why she couldn't trust him or any other man. Well, it wouldn't happen again. He obviously regretted the night as much as she did. If he wanted to act as if nothing happened between them, he wouldn't get an argument out of her.

"All right, that's it," he said as he stored the last of their gear on the snowmobile. "Let's go."

Without a word she climbed onto the machine behind him and tried not to notice how her heart kicked into a faster rhythm at his nearness. She was still sore from her fall yesterday, her wrist still splinted, but as he slowly took off, she was able to hold on to him without having to completely wrap her arms around him. For that, she was profoundly grateful.

With a fresh layer of snow covering everything, the mountains looked like they had been swept clean by the storm. The drifts were eight feet deep in places, and it quickly became apparent that any progress they were going to make would be slow. Not that there was much chance of them locating any tracks. What the new snow hadn't covered up, the wind had obliterated. When Hunter took them back to the spot where they'd last spied James's footprints the night before, there was nothing but unblemished snow in every direction for as far as the eye could see.

Her heart sinking, Naomi couldn't hold back the tears that flooded her eyes. She whispered thickly, "What do we do now?"

For the first time since he'd made love to her last night, Hunter touched her. Covering her good hand, which was curled around his waist, he patted her reassuringly. "Don't give up hope yet, honey. I know things don't look good right now, but if nothing else, we know the storm stopped James in his tracks just like it did us. And since we know he's on foot, that means that when he was forced to take shelter last night, he couldn't have been any farther than a day's walk from where he crashed the snowmobile. That's where his tracks will start today. We just have to find them."

He made it sound so easy. The only problem was that a day's walk from the snowmobile in every direction could cover hundreds of acres in wilderness. How could they possibly stumble across a single set of tracks in all that? It would be like looking for a needle in a haystack.

But what other choice did they have?

Since James's tracks were headed north the last time they saw them, they continued in that direction, driving back and forth across the mountain for what seemed like hours. Their eyes straining and narrowed against the reflection of the sun on the snow, they looked for anything that might indicate someone had been that way recently, but there was nothing.

Worry eating at her, Naomi told herself they hadn't come all this way only to lose Laura now. They would find her. They had to! Then she smelled smoke.

His nose lifted to the cold, crisp air, Hunter caught the scent, too. Braking to a stop, he cut the engine to the snowmobile and scanned the clear sky above the treetops off to their right. Off in the distance a thin trail of smoke climbed skyward. "Bingo," he said softly.

"Do you think it's James?" Naomi asked as he climbed off the snowmobile and unloaded their packs from the back. "What are you doing? Aren't we going to check out that fire?"

"Not on the snowmobile, we're not," he said grimly. "If that's James up there in the trees, I'd just as soon not announce our presence until we're ready to surprise him." Arching a brow at her, he drawled, "You are, I assume, coming with me?"

He couldn't have kept her away, and they both knew it. "I plan to be right behind you every step of the way." Her heart pounding at the thought of finally having her daughter safe and sound in her arms again, she quickly scrambled into her backpack. "Let's go."

On foot in the deep snow, it took them nearly thirty minutes just to climb to the ridge where they'd spotted the smoke. Impatient, frantic with worry, Naomi wanted to throw caution to the wind and go running through the trees in search of the campfire, but Hunter kept her close. His brown eyes narrowed and wary, he didn't intend to let Naomi take the lead until he knew what they were walking into.

But holding her back became impossible once they spied James frantically adding wood to a campfire in the middle of a small, sheltered clearing notched by rough, granite boulders on three sides. She took one look at the small figure lying by the fire and burst through the trees.

"Laura!"

Whirling from the fire, James glared accusingly at her. "This is all your fault! If you had stayed home and given me a chance, I would have brought her back. But, *no!* You had to come after me and force me to go higher into the mountains than I'd planned. Because of you, we got caught in that damn storm last night and nearly froze to death. It was so cold and I couldn't find any wood to build a fire until the sun came up, and now I think it's too late. Laura—"

Naomi's heart stopped dead in her chest. With a strangled cry, she rushed to her daughter's side, only to find her still and unconscious and her skin far too cold in spite of the fact that she was wrapped in James's coat and lying close to the fire.

"No!" she cried. "You bastard! What have you done to her?"

"*I* didn't do anything," he retorted without remorse. "If you want to blame someone, look in the mirror—"

Furious, Naomi didn't even bother to answer him. Dismissing him, she whipped off her own jacket and tucked it around Laura's small frame, then quickly gathered her up into her arms. "Mama's here, sweetheart," she whispered brokenly, rocking her. "Mama's here. Everything's going to be okay."

But Laura's eyelashes didn't so much as flutter, and she was as still as death in Naomi's arms. More scared than she'd ever been in her life, Naomi lifted terrified eyes to Hunter as he reached her in four long strides and knelt down beside her. "Hunter, please," she choked. "Help her."

Her cry broke his heart. Wanting to take her into his arms, knowing there was no time, he squeezed her shoulder reassuringly and quickly pulled his cell phone for his pocket. "Just hang on, honey," he said huskily as he punched in his cousin Rocky's number. "Help's on the way."

Refusing to even think about what he would do if Rocky was out, he heaved a silent sigh of relief when she came on the line herself. "Fortune Flying Service. Rocky speaking. Can I help you?"

"Rock, thank God! This is Hunter—"

"Hunter? Dammit, didn't anyone ever teach you to check in once in a while? I've been worried sick about you! Lucas said you'd gone up into the mountains with Naomi Windsong to look for her little girl, and I was afraid you got caught in that storm last night."

"I did. Listen, Rock, I need your help." Quickly and succinctly, he gave her their location and a brief rundown of Laura's condition. "How long will it take you to get here? We've got her by the fire, but I don't think there's any time to spare."

"Then I'm bringing Lucas with me. Don't worry— it won't take me long to round him up. He can be here in five minutes. While I'm waiting for him, I'll notify the police that Laura's been found and Barker is with you. Then we'll be on our way. Don't let her warm up too much, Hunter," she advised. "That's when we lose them. The body doesn't shut down until it starts to warm up, so we want to make sure she's at the hospital when that happens. Just hang on. We'll be there as quick as we can.''

Hunter didn't doubt for a minute that she knew what she was talking about. She was not only a licensed EMT, but she also owned and operated the only search-and-rescue service in that area of the state. A crackerjack pilot who didn't seem to know the meaning of the word fear, she'd started her flying service ten years ago when everyone thought Kate had died in a plane crash in South America. With the fleet of small planes and helicopters that Kate had bequeathed her, Rocky's business had quite literally taken off. Since then she'd rescued innumerable hunters and skiers from the mountains and saved countless lives. If anyone knew the dangers of frostbite and how to prevent deaths from freezing, it was Rocky.

Hanging up, he told Naomi, ''Rocky's on her way, sweetheart, and she's bringing Lucas with her. She said we need to move her back from the fire. We don't want her to get too warm.''

''But she's freezing!''

''I know, honey, but there are reasons.'' And he didn't intend to tell her what those reasons were until he absolutely had to. She was just barely holding herself together now as it was. If she had even an inkling that the real danger to Laura would be when her body temperature began to rise, he didn't even want to think what that would do to her. ''We just need to keep her comfortable until help gets here. It won't be that long—I promise.''

In actuality, it only took forty-five minutes before they heard the whopping beat of the helicopter blades,

but it seemed like a lifetime. Still refusing to take responsibility for what he'd done, James continued to
try to blame Naomi, but he was beating a dead horse.
Hunter figured that later Naomi would rip him up one
side and down the other for what he had done, but for
now, she just crooned to Laura and ignored him. Then
Rocky was setting the helicopter down in a clearing a
hundred yards away, and the only thing that mattered
was getting Laura to the hospital.

Carrying Laura, Hunter quickly turned her over to
Lucas, and then he was helping Naomi into the helicopter. Over the roar of the blades, he shouted, "I'll
see you when I get back to town!"

Startled, she grabbed for him. "No! You're coming
with us!"

He wanted to—God only knew how much—but
someone had to get their gear and the snowmobile
back to town. And there was only room in the helicopter for one more person. And as much as he wanted
to be there for Naomi when she realized just what kind
of danger Laura was in, James had a right as Laura's
father to be there instead. Even if he was the one who
had put his daughter's life in danger.

Motioning to the other man to take his place, he
stepped back. "You'll be all right," he yelled to Naomi when she tried to tell him something over the
noise of the blades. "Go on!"

Sliding the cargo door shut before she could protest
further, he signaled to Rocky that it was all clear for
takeoff. Giving him a thumb's-up, she sent the heli-

copter rising gracefully into the sky. Standing in the snow kicked up by the force of the rotating blades, Hunter watched the craft head south until it disappeared from view. He'd never felt so alone in his life.

Eight

The flight back to town would always be a blur to Naomi. Lucas Greywolf frantically worked over Laura, keeping a constant watch on her vital signs while Rocky radioed the hospital emergency room to warn them of their estimated arrival time. They were in a race against time, and no one had to tell Naomi that the situation was critical. She could see it in the grim set of Lucas's mouth, hear it in the terseness of Rocky's tone as she spoke quietly into the radio. Finally, the seriousness of his daughter's condition must have penetrated James's selfish need to cast blame. Strapped in beside her, he sat quietly, his eyes never leaving Laura's deathly pale face as Lucas started an IV.

He was obviously feeling some remorse, but Naomi felt little sympathy for him. She hoped he was suffering—it was no more than he deserved. Because of his stupid need for revenge, he'd nearly killed her baby. And nothing he could say or do could ever make up for that.

The Clear Springs hospital came into view then, and Rocky swooped down on it like an avenging angel, setting the helicopter down right in the middle of the heliport the Fortune family had donated to the hospital five years ago. The blades were still whirling overhead as doctors and nurses came running with a stretcher, and before Naomi was ready to let Laura out of her sight again, she was being whisked away into the emergency room.

James was suffering from frostbite and was led to an examining room to be treated, so within a matter of minutes, Naomi found herself completely alone in the waiting room, clutching Laura's tattered teddy bear to her breast. Too worried to sit, she paced restlessly while seconds turned into minutes, then hours, and still no one came to tell her how Laura was.

James eventually joined her, the concern that etched his face aging him decades. But she found little comfort in his company. He wasn't the one she needed or wanted at her side, and with no conscious effort her thoughts turned to Hunter and the last image she had of him as he'd been left behind in the mountains. Where was he now? Was he okay? He was, she knew, a lone wolf who didn't need anyone. She'd seen for herself just how tough and self-reliant he was, and there wasn't a doubt in her mind that he could handle just about anything life threw at him. He was the last man she should have been worried about, but she couldn't shake the image of him standing there in the snow as Rocky sent the helicopter climbing into the sky. He'd looked so alone, and everything in her had protested at the thought of leaving him.

Pacing restlessly, she tried to convince herself that she would have been just as concerned about anyone who'd been left behind in the mountains to find their way back to civilization alone. But she wasn't in the habit of lying to herself, and she knew that what she felt for Hunter was more, much more than just concern. She didn't know how it had happened so quickly, but somehow, she'd fallen in love with him.

Stunned, she stopped dead in her tracks and immediately tried to reject the idea, giving herself all the reasons why her imagination had to be working overtime. She wasn't one of those women who fell in love at the drop of a hat—she didn't trust that easily. Especially after all the trouble she'd had with James. He'd made her so gun-shy that she would have sworn it would be years before she even looked twice at another man, let alone dropped her guard long enough to fall in love with one.

But she hadn't counted on meeting anyone quite like Hunter. From the very beginning he'd treated her differently than James or any other man ever had. He was honest and straightforward and didn't play games. Even when he couldn't hide the fact that he was attracted to her, he'd fought against taking advantage of the circumstances or her. And just that easily he'd stolen her heart.

She loved him. She still didn't know how it had happened—she just knew she didn't want to lose him. And she could. Circumstances had thrown them together, but now that Laura was safe, they would each go back to their own lives. He had a construction company to get back to, one that took all his time, and he'd said himself that the last thing he wanted or needed right now was a woman. If he still meant that, there was a good possibility that she would never see him again.

She paled at the thought, but just then Lucas Greywolf came striding toward her, his rugged face set in grim lines, and a fist closed around her heart. "Laura? Is she all right? Oh God, she's not—"

"She's going to be fine, Naomi," he said gently. "I'll admit it was pretty dicey when we first started bringing her body temperature up, but she's a strong little girl. She hung tough. We've got her in pediatrics ICU right now just as a precaution, but if she continues to improve the way I expect her to, we should be able to move her to a private room by this evening. Would you like to see her?"

He didn't have to ask her twice. "Oh, yes!" Tears welling in her eyes, she started to follow him, but she'd only taken two steps when she remembered James. She turned back to the waiting room to find him standing hesitantly in the doorway. He'd heard the entire conversation with Lucas but had made no effort to intrude.

Another woman might have left him there, but in spite of all that he had done, she couldn't be vindictive just because he had. "She's your daughter, too," she told him quietly. "You have a right to see for yourself that she's all right."

More humble than she'd ever seen him, he made no attempt to hide the tears in his eyes. "Thank you. I won't stay. I just want to see her."

Nodding, she turned back to follow Lucas.

As Lucas had predicted, Laura was moved to a private room by that evening, and she was doing much better. Although she was exhausted from her ordeal, the color was back in her cheeks, and she looked like any healthy three-year-old. She probably could have gone home, but Lucas thought it was better not to take chances, and Naomi agreed with him. When she took Laura home, she wanted her to have a clean bill of health, and if a night in the hospital would assure that, then so be it.

That didn't, however, mean that she was prepared to let her baby out of her sight anytime soon. She, too, stayed the night. Afraid that Laura might have nightmares about her night in the blizzard, Naomi hovered close, but her fears proved groundless. With Chester, her dearly loved teddy bear, clutched tight in her arms, she drifted off to sleep without so much as a whimper.

Relieved, Naomi expected to sleep just as soundly. The day had been a traumatic one, a roller-coaster ride from one emotion to the next. When the nurses brought a cot into Laura's room for her, she was sure that the minute she got horizontal, she'd be out like a light. But her mind was too busy to let her rest, and hours after she'd turned out the lights and stretched out with a weary sigh, she lay awake, unable to stop herself from thinking about Hunter.

Where was he right now? she wondered. Had he made it back to the line cabin where they'd made love? Was he thinking about her and the two of them together? Or had it meant so little to him that he'd already put it from his mind?

Her heart cringing at the thought, it was a long time before she finally slept.

Lucas was back in the morning to check on Laura and pronounced her ready to go home. Laughing and crying at the same time, Naomi impulsively hugged him. ''Thank you so much! I don't know what I would have done without you and your wife yesterday. You saved her life.''

''Sometimes we get lucky,'' he said simply, patting her shoulder. ''That's what makes our job worthwhile. We've got kids of our own—we weren't going to let you lose her if there was any possible way to save her. And don't forget,'' he added, ''you had more than a little bit to do with the fact that she's here today. If you hadn't hired Hunter and gone after her, this could have turned out to be a real tragedy.''

''I know,'' she said huskily. ''It scares me just thinking about it.''

''Then don't,'' he advised. ''It's over with and she's safe. That's all that matters. Take her home and love her. She's fine.''

Taking his advice, Naomi did just that. Since she'd left her car at her house, she had to call a friend for a ride, and by noon she and Laura were walking through their front door. Within minutes, Laura was parked in front of the TV watching her favorite show, ''Barney,'' and it was almost like she'd never been gone. Almost, but not quite. It would be a long time before Naomi forgot the nightmare of the last few days.

Still, she tried. For the rest of the day, she enjoyed her daughter. She made her favorite lunch and afterward, cuddled her and Chester in her lap while she read Laura's favorite story to her. They laughed and giggled and finally Laura settled down to sleep. It was a long time before Naomi could bring herself to lay her daughter down. She loved her so much. If anything had happened to her…

Reminding herself that nothing had, she returned to

the living room and had just started to pick up the toys Laura had dragged in there to celebrate her homecoming when there was a knock at the front door. When she opened it, she wasn't surprised to find herself face-to-face with James. After he'd seen for himself that Laura was all right yesterday, he'd stepped out into the hall, where the tribal police were waiting for him. Officer Hank had warned him not to leave the area until Naomi decided if she wanted to press charges against him. She'd known then it was only a matter of time before he approached her.

"Can I come in?" he asked diffidently.

Hesitating, she almost told him no. What he'd done to her and, most especially, Laura, was unforgivable, and she had nothing to say to him. If she decided to have him arrested, she owed him nothing, least of all a warning.

But he had that look in his eye, the one that warned her he would not be easily put off, and she knew she couldn't avoid him forever. "This isn't going to help your cause," she said coolly, "but if you're determined to speak your mind, you have two minutes."

His hands balled in the pockets of his jacket, he didn't advance into the living room, but stopped just inside the foyer. "I...I just came by to...I needed to talk to you, to explain..."

"James—"

"No," he said quickly, "I have to do this. *I* did this. *I* screwed up. And I'm the one who has to make things right. Not that I ever really can. I could have killed her, dammit! Do you have any idea what that's doing to me?"

It was tearing him apart—anyone with eyes could

see that. Sinking down into the closest chair, she said honestly, "I wouldn't be able to live with myself. If you have an ounce of feeling for your daughter, I imagine you feel the same way."

His expression stark, he looked her right in the eye and said grimly, "I feel like a piece of trash, and I have no one to blame but myself. I was so obsessed with you, so determined to make you pay for refusing to marry me, that I didn't even stop to think what I was doing to Laura or you. I put her in jeopardy and scared the hell out of you, and you have every right to hate me. I wouldn't blame you if you pressed charges. Words can't make up for what I put you both through, but I can only apologize and promise you that nothing like this will ever happen again."

If she hadn't known what a miserable excuse for a human he was, she might have believed he was a changed man. But the last time she'd trusted him, it had almost cost her daughter her life. Never again. "I haven't decided what I'm going to do," she said flatly. "So if that's all you have to say—"

"Wait!" he cried when she rose to her feet. "I have something I need to give you."

Naomi looked at the cassette tape he held out to her like it was a snake coiled to strike. "What is it?"

"My taped confession. I want you to have it."

Confused, she stared up at him searchingly. "Why?"

"Because this was the only way I could think of to assure you that I'm never going to bother you or Laura again." At her skeptical look, he said, "I don't blame you for not believing me, but it's true. If you don't press charges, I'll leave the state, and I won't be back.

If you're ever afraid I'll go back on my word, all you have to do is take this tape to the police in any city in the country and I'll be picked up.''

Staring down at the tape, Naomi wondered if she was a fool to want to believe him. He deserved to be in jail for what he'd done, but he was Laura's father, dammit! She didn't want revenge, she just wanted to be left alone to raise her daughter in peace. Was that so very much to ask? Not the gullible young girl she had once been, she warned, ''If this is another one of your tricks—''

''It's not. I swear!''

He couldn't have been more sincere if he'd sworn on a stack of Bibles, but she wasn't taking any chances. Taking the tape from him, she strode over to the stereo and popped it into the cassette player. The confession he'd promised was damning. Naomi listened to every word. Afterwards, in the silence that followed, her voice was grim as she said, ''If you really intend to leave the state, I won't stop you. But just because I'm not pressing charges now doesn't mean I won't in the future. Because of you, Laura nearly died. If you ever come near either one of us again, I won't hesitate to see that you're locked up for the rest of your life if I can manage it.''

It wasn't an idle threat, and they both knew it.

''I wouldn't expect any less of you,'' he said somberly, ''but that won't be necessary. My bags are already packed and in the car. Goodbye, Naomi. Kiss Laura goodbye for me.''

And without another word, he turned and walked out of her life.

Nine

The second he got back to town, Hunter went straight to his office because he knew if he didn't, he would go looking for Naomi. And that was one thing he was determined not to do. He'd had hours to think about it, long stretches of time when silence and his own thoughts were his only companions as he was making his way out of the mountains, and he knew that somehow he had to find the strength to leave the lady alone. The days and nights they'd spent in the mountains were just moments stolen out of time, a brief encounter between two strangers that wasn't meant to last. If the intimacy they'd shared was like nothing he'd ever experienced before, his imagination was just playing tricks with his mind. The lady said herself she wasn't looking for a man, and after getting a firsthand look at Barker, he could see why. He was a bastard. After all that he had put Naomi through, the last thing she would want would be another man sniffing around her. All he could ever be was a reminder of her daughter's kidnapping, so for both their sakes, it was best if he went back to his life and let her get back to hers.

And that was all right, he thought grimly. He'd been a loner all his life—it was in his blood, a wanderlust that was as much a part of him as the color of his eyes and the stamp of his heritage on his features. If he'd grown weary of roaming the globe and had found a peace that he hadn't even known he was looking for here in Wyoming, that was nobody's business but his own. He had work to do, a business to build and less than a year to do it. He couldn't do that with a woman constantly distracting him.

But even as he tried to convince himself that things had worked out for the best, images of Naomi stirred in his mind, teasing him, haunting him. Her nervousness when she'd climbed on the snowmobile that first day and hadn't quite known where to put her hands. The stunned surprise on her face when he'd kissed her the first time. The way she'd given herself to him when they'd made love.

Irritated with himself, he slammed the papers he was sorting down on his desk before he gave in to the temptation to throw them. How was a man supposed to forget those things? he wondered furiously. How was he supposed to sleep at night, remembering what it was like to touch her? Kiss her? Lose himself in her? James might have been her first lover and the father of her child, but everything in him rebelled at the idea of Barker or any other man so much as laying a finger on her. She was his, dammit! And what was his, he kept.

The truth hit him with all the subtlety of a Mack truck, and he sat as if turned to stone, his mind reeling. He couldn't, he thought, stunned, love her. After guarding his heart well for the past twenty-nine years, he couldn't have fallen in love with her in a matter of days. It just wasn't possible. Dammit, he didn't do this kind of thing! No one got this close to him this

quickly! How had she done it? And what the hell was
he going to do about it?

Nothing, he told himself flatly. Not a damn thing.
She needed some peace, some time to recover from
the emotional rollercoaster she'd been on all week.
Laura was going to be okay—he'd called the hospital
on his cell phone and checked on her condition the
night after she'd been rescued—but neither of them
would soon forget the hell they'd been through. Only
an insensitive clod would force himself on them now.

But, God, he wanted to go to Naomi! To take her
in his arms and hold her just one more time. To kiss
her and love her before he had to let her go. He'd
never gotten the chance to tell her goodbye, and
dammit, he needed that closure. But he wasn't going
to get it. Because if he went anywhere near her, he
knew there was no way in hell he would be able to
walk away from her.

So he stayed where he was and threw himself into
catching up on paperwork. But it wasn't easy. Every
time he dropped his guard the least little bit, he found
his thoughts sliding back to Naomi. What was she doing? He knew she'd taken Laura home from the hospital, but he couldn't imagine her letting the child out
of her sight any time soon. Maybe he'd take them a
pizza after work...

Suddenly realizing that he was looking for excuses
to seek her out, he swore and pushed to his feet. In
self-defense, he drove over to the eastern edge of the
reservation to see how work was coming on the ham-
burger stand his workers were trying to finish, strapped
on a tool belt and went to work. He threw himself into
the physical labor in a desperate attempt to work the

lady out of his head, but it didn't help. By the end of the day, he'd worn himself out, but the need to see her burned in his gut like a flame that refused to go out. Frustrated, infuriated with himself, he knew he couldn't put it off any longer. If he was ever going to find any peace, he had to see her, if for no other reason than to wish her luck and tell her goodbye.

Resigned, he started to head home first to shower and change, when he realized that if he showed up on her doorstep all cleaned up and shaved, he would look like a suitor hoping to get lucky. The hell he would! Swearing, he hit the brakes and swung around right in the middle of the street, his truck tires screaming all the way. He had nothing to be ashamed of. He'd worked damn hard today, and any dirt he wore was well earned. If the lady turned up her nose at a little honest dirt, then she wasn't the woman that he thought she was and he had nothing further to say to her.

Jaw set, a scowl sitting low on his brow, he arrived at her house in a matter of minutes. Reminding himself why he was there, he strode up the steps to the porch and knocked sharply on her front door. This would, he vowed grimly, take all of two minutes.

But when she opened the door to him, the words that he had already worked out in his head just seemed to vanish on the wind. She smiled at him in delight, and he felt like the sun just broke through the evening clouds. "Hunter! I was hoping you'd let me know when you got back. Please, come in. Have you eaten? Laura and I just finished, but I can heat you a plate in the microwave if you're hungry."

The only thing he was hungry for was her, he thought, stunned by the force of his need for her. God, she was beautiful! Why was it always a surprise to him just how gorgeous she was? The first moment he'd seen her, she'd knocked him out of his shoes, and this time was no different. He took one look at her and wanted to reach for her, to enfold her in his arms and never let her go, to tell her how he'd inexplicably lost his heart to her.

But all he could think of was the hell she'd been through with Barker, and the words just wouldn't come. Instead, he said stiffly, "No, thanks. Actually, I just dropped by to check on Laura. I heard she was released this morning."

Her smile dimmed slightly at his tone, but if she wondered what his problem was, she didn't say anything. "Yes, she was. She was very lucky. She's in her room right now playing. Would you like to see her?"

He should have told her that wasn't necessary and gotten the heck out of there, but she held the door open to him, and he couldn't resist the invitation. Before he quite knew how it had happened, he was standing shoulder-to-shoulder with her in the hall outside Laura's room, watching the little girl play with that ragged teddy bear of hers. Lost in her imaginary world, she appeared healthy and whole. With time, the nightmare her father put her through would hopefully fade completely from her memory.

Barker deserved to be shot for the chances he'd taken with her, but according to the gossip going around town, Naomi had yet to press charges against him. And for the life of him, Hunter couldn't understand why. He knew she didn't still care about the jerk—she wasn't the type of woman to give herself to one man when she still had feelings for another. And even if she had some lingering fondness for Barker, that would have died the second he endangered Laura. So why hadn't she had the jackass arrested?

He told himself it was none of his business, but the minute they returned to the living room, he heard himself say, "I heard Barker's still on the loose. I thought you'd have locked him up by now?"

"I though about it," she admitted. "But he promised he'd never bother us again——"

"And you *believed* him."

"Not at first," she said, smiling at his outraged tone. "But then he gave me this." Retrieving a cassette from the stereo, she held it up. "It's a taped confession. If he ever comes near me or Laura again, he knows I'll go straight to the police with it."

"And Barker voluntarily gave that to you?"

Nodding, she told him then of her visit with James and his unexpected offer to get out of her life. "I know you probably think I'm crazy to trust him, but he's not a stupid man. He knows that even without the tape, he would be looking at serious jail time if I decided to press charges. And his freedom means much more to him than I ever did, thank God. He won't be back."

So it was over. She had Laura safely home again, and she no longer needed him. He'd known it would come to this—he just hadn't expected to feel like his heart was being ripped out by the roots. Needing some air, he headed for the door. "Good. I'm glad it worked out for you and Laura's okay. I've got a pile of paperwork waiting for me at the office, so I'd better get out of here and let you get back to whatever you were doing."

Alarmed, Naomi had the horrible feeling that he was walking out of her life for good, and she didn't know why. She just knew she had to stop him. "Wait! We never discussed what your fee was for finding Laura—"

That stopped him in his tracks. "I don't take money for helping people."

Caught up in the heat of the blistering look he shot her, she quickly apologized. "No, of course not. I didn't mean to insult you. I just…"

"What?"

Floundering under his fierce look, she struggled for words and would invariably say the wrong thing. "I just owe you so much."

"And you think that's what I want from you? Gratitude?"

He was so indignant that if the circumstances had been different, she would have been hard-pressed not to smile. But suddenly they were discussing much more than gratitude. She felt like she was standing on the edge of a cliff and a step either way could be the wrong one. What was he asking of her? Was he saying that the only thing he wanted of her was love? She desperately wanted to believe that, but what if she was wrong? What if all he wanted was friendship? Telling him she loved him would be one sure way to lose him. But then again, if he wanted her love and she just offered friendship, the result would be the same.

Torn, she hesitated, but even as she wondered if she was doing the right thing, she knew she had to tell him how she felt. Love was meant to be shared.

Taking a chance, her heart cringing at the thought that she might be wrong, she took a step toward him.

"I will always be grateful to you for finding Laura for me," she said huskily, "but what I feel for you has nothing to do with that. After I discovered what a heel James was, I thought I would never again trust another man enough to fall in love with him. I was wrong." There! She'd all but spelled out how she felt about him. And he just stood there! Suddenly afraid she'd blown it, she said hesitantly, "Hunter? I'm sorry if this isn't what you wanted to hear, but I love you. I thought you should know."

That was as far as she got.

Growling low in his throat, he reached for her then and tugged her into his arms. "I love you!" he said fiercely. "I've been in hell all day thinking I was going to have to give you up, and I didn't know how I was going to stand it. Tell me again."

Laughing, she didn't have to ask what he meant. "I love you. I think I must have from the moment I first laid eyes on you. It all happened so fast."

"Not nearly fast enough for me," he rasped, kissing her hungrily. "I want to marry you. Now. Tonight. Just as soon as we can arrange it."

It wasn't a question, but a need, one that echoed in the very depths of her being. She knew others would say they hadn't known each other very long—they should take the time to get to know each other better before they even considered getting married. But her heart had recognized his, instantly, and love had nothing to do with time. "Yes!" she cried happily. "Yes! Yes! Yes!"

Epilogue

His year was up and he'd passed the test.

Standing in the large room at the Fortune corporate headquarters for another Christmas party, Hunter had to admit that for the first time he felt less like a black sheep and more like a part of the family. Success—and more important, marriage—had a heck of a lot to do with that. And neither could have happened if Kate hadn't taken Fate into her own hands and pulled a few strings in his life.

With Naomi at his side and Laura in his arms, clutching the dearly loved Chester, he watched various family members congratulate Kate on her eighty-first birthday and couldn't help but grin. She was something else. This time last year when she'd announced the gifts she was giving to him and Chase and Ryder and the conditions that went with them, he'd wondered if the old girl was getting senile. He couldn't have spoken for his cousins at the time, but the last thing he'd wanted or needed was the responsibility of a construction company that was struggling just to keep its head above water.

How could she have known that instead of hating it, he'd love it? She'd saddled him with ties, knowing full well that he was a man who never stayed anywhere for more than three or four months at a time, and dared him to like it. More than once in those first few months, he'd wanted the chuck the whole damn thing. But he couldn't resist the challenge, couldn't let down Kate when she believed in him. She'd seen something in him that he hadn't known was there, and thanks to her generosity, he now not only owned Fortune Construction lock, stock and barrel, but he had everything a man could want right within reach.

Gazing down at Naomi, there wasn't a doubt in his mind that he was the luckiest man on earth. Dressed in a long, green silk dress, she stole his breath every time he looked at her. God, she was beautiful! The day he'd married her, two months to the day she'd told him she loved him, he'd thought it wasn't possible to love her any more than he already did, but he'd been wrong. The day she'd told him she was carrying his child, love couldn't begin to describe the emotions swelling his heart. She'd changed his life forever.

Another child to love, he thought, nuzzling Laura's neck and making her giggle. In another five months, he would have another daughter to love. *He* was now Laura's Papa—his adoption of her was finalized just last month—and he knew he had his own special spot in her heart. A soft, sweet little arm circled his neck, wrapping him around her little finger, and he wondered how he could have ever thought he wanted to go through life alone.

At his side, Naomi nudged him gently and whispered, "What's going on? It looks like Kelly's about to make an announcement of some kind." Hunter turned to see Kate's very pregnant secretary step to the front of the room and nervously clear her throat.

With his cousin, Mac, at her side, she faced the entire Fortune clan.

"Please excuse me for interrupting," she said huskily, "but I have something to tell you all. We want everyone to know. Mac and I are getting married."

A shocked silence fell over the room. It was Kate, not surprisingly, who recovered first. Stepping forward, she embraced Kelly lovingly. "Married? Why, that's wonderful! You've always been like a member of the family—now this makes it official. Congratulations, you two. This calls for some champagne!"

"Aren't Chad and Mac brothers? Or do I have it confused?" Naomi whispered to Hunter as the various family members pushed forward to congratulate the couple.

"No, you've got it right," he said grimly.

Hunter knew how hard this announcement must have been for Kelly to make. He remembered just how difficult it had been for her earlier in the year to tell the family about her pregnancy. She hadn't known what kind of reaction the news was going to generate, but she should have known that the Fortunes took care of their own. And her baby was a Fortune in spite of the fact that his biological daddy hadn't shown the least inclination to give him—or her—his name.

Irritation momentarily flared in Hunter's dark brown eyes. He would have liked just five minutes alone with his cousin Chad to knock some sense into him. But it wouldn't have done any good. Chad enjoyed his bad boy image too much.

Halfway across the room, Kate gave herself a pat on the back for a job well done. She freely acknowledged that she hadn't been quite sure of her three great-nephews when she'd decided to work a little magic in their lives, and there'd been times over the course of the past twelve months when she wouldn't have been surprised if the lot of them had told her just what she could do with her so-called gifts. There was no doubt about it—she'd handed them trouble—but they'd all three risen to the occasion, and she was proud of them. They'd matured and grown and, in the process, also found love. And life didn't offer a greater reward than that.

Now, she thought with a twinkle in her eye, if she could just do something about the great-nieces....

* * * * *

Want to know what happens after Kelly marries Mac? Look for their story in

The Honor Bound Groom

by Jennifer Greene

Over the next six months, their story will be just one of the exciting love stories from Silhouette Desire as part of Fortune's Children: The Brides miniseries.

And now for a sneak peek of
The Honor Bound Groom,
please turn the page.

The wedding was a mistake. Getting married had seemed an outstanding idea to Kelly Sinclair two weeks ago, last week and even when she'd woken up this morning. But that was then and this was now. At this precise moment, Kelly realized—with a flash of brilliant clarity—that she'd have to be bonkers to go through with this.

The creamy gardenias clutched in her hands started trembling and wouldn't quit. Anxiety sloshed in her stomach in sick, dread-filled waves. Maybe most brides suffered some nerves on their wedding day, but the average, normal bride wasn't seven months pregnant. She not only felt scared; she felt ugly, fat and scared—a lethal combination. To add insult to injury, her pregnant condition made a swift escape more than challenging. Her fastest speed was a waddle. A duck could probably beat her in a sprint.

Abruptly she heard the first strings of the "Wedding March." Adrenaline bolted through her bloodstream, and a lump bigger than the Rock of Gibralter clogged her throat. She couldn't go through with this. She just couldn't.

If Kate, the eighty-one-year-old matriarch of the Fortune Cosmetics empire, noticed the bride's crepe-white pallor or the frantic alarm in her eyes, she never let on. "Kelly…I'm so honored that you're letting me be the one to give you away. I'm sorry your mom isn't still alive to be part of this—she'd be so proud. But I want you to know, I couldn't care more for you if you were my own daughter."

Well, spit. Her conscience was already suffering from muck-deep guilt, and Kate's words only made her feel worse. She *had* to tell Kate that her mind was made up; the wedding was off—there was no way she could possibly go through with it. But somehow she couldn't get the words said.

"There now." Kate also heard the music, and firmly, securely tucked Kelly's arm in hers. "Here we go…just take a deep breath, and don't worry about a thing. Everything's going to work out."

In those teensy milliseconds, Kate had propelled her to the middle of those open doors, in full view of the guests. In one sweeping glance, Kelly saw the guests all rising in traditional respect for the bride and thought, They aren't gonna like it when I cut out and run.

The minister smiled reassuringly at her from the front of the room. His smile was going to disappear fast when the bride hiked up her skirts and took a fast powder, she predicted.

But then a strange thing happened.

It wasn't as if the minister or Kate's grip or the whole sea of faces instantly disappeared…but her gaze suddenly locked on the groom.

Mac.

His shoulders looked beam-broad in the black tux, his height towering, his thick hair darker than charcoal and shot with silver. Black suited him. His angular face was set with strong bones and an elegant mouth and a no-nonsense square chin. Nobody messed with Mac. The lean, mean build had nothing to do with it. She'd never heard him raise his voice, never seen him angry, but he had a way of silencing a whole room when he walked in. Those shrewd, deep-set green eyes and mouth reflected an uncompromising nature, a man who loved a challenge and never backed down from a fight. Mac was a hunk, yet he was also one intimidatingly scary dude—at least for a woman who was uncomfortable around powerful men.

His eyes met hers with the directness of a sharp, clear laser beam. He didn't smile—yet the look of his immediately affected the panicked beat of her pulse.

A year before, Kelly had been wildly, blindingly, exuberantly in love. The father of her baby had been an incredibly exciting man. A man she'd believed in, heart and soul. A man she would have done anything for, anytime, anywhere, no questions asked.

Mac wasn't the man she'd been in love with.

He wasn't the father of her baby.

He was just the groom.

SILHOUETTE® Desire®

Do you want…

Dangerously handsome heroes

Evocative, everlasting love stories

Sizzling and tantalizing sensuality

Incredibly sexy miniseries like **MAN OF THE MONTH**

Red-hot romance

Enticing entertainment that can't be beat!

You'll find all of this, and much *more* each and every month in **SILHOUETTE DESIRE**. Don't miss these unforgettable love stories by some of romance's hottest authors. Silhouette Desire—where your fantasies will always come true….

DES-GEN

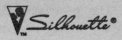

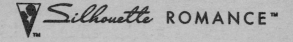
Silhouette ROMANCE™

What's a single dad to do when he needs a wife by next Thursday?

Who's a confirmed bachelor to call when he finds a baby on his doorstep?

How does a plain Jane in love with her gorgeous boss get him to notice her?

From classic love stories to romantic comedies to emotional heart tuggers, **Silhouette Romance** offers six irresistible novels every month by some of your favorite authors! Such as...beloved bestsellers **Diana Palmer, Annette Broadrick, Suzanne Carey, Elizabeth August** and **Marie Ferrarella**, to name just a few—and some sure to become favorites!

Fabulous Fathers...Bundles of Joy...Miniseries... Months of blushing brides and convenient weddings... Holiday celebrations... You'll find all this and much more in **Silhouette Romance**—always emotional, always enjoyable, always about love!

WAYS TO *UNEXPECTEDLY* MEET MR. RIGHT:

♡ Go out with the sexy-sounding stranger your daughter secretly set you up with through a personal ad.

♡ RSVP yes to a wedding invitation—soon it might be your turn to say "I do!"

♡ Receive a marriage proposal by mail—from a man you've never met....

These are just a few of the unexpected ways that written communication leads to love in Silhouette Yours Truly.

Each month, look for two fast-paced, fun and flirtatious Yours Truly novels (with entertaining treats and sneak previews in the back pages) by some of your favorite authors—and some who are sure to become favorites.

YOURS TRULY™:
Love—when you least expect it!

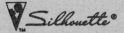

Silhouette®